American Spanking Story

Shadow Lane Volume 13

by

Eve Howard

CCB Publishing
British Columbia, Canada

American Spanking Story Shadow Lane Volume 13

Copyright ©2024 by Eve Howard
ISBN-13   978-1-77143-599-4
First Edition

Library and Archives Canada Cataloguing in Publication
Howard, Eve, 1953-, author
American spanking story shadow lane volume 13 / by Eve Howard. -- First edition.
Issued in print and electronic formats.
ISBN 978-1-77143-599-4 (softcover).--ISBN 978-1-77143-600-7 (pdf)
Additional cataloguing data available from Library and Archives Canada

Cover artwork by Butch Simms
Cover model: Violet October

Publisher: CCB Publishing
               British Columbia, Canada
               www.ccbpublishing.com

To Danny and Dana, forever my friends

"Love and work are the
cornerstones of our humanness."
- Sigmund Freud

Contents

Glossary of Terms and Names

Anal
Most frequently used in this book, to describe an erotic orientation. An anal bottom might enjoy exposure, anal spanking, butt plugs, possibly enemas, embarrassing clinical examinations and related forms of discipline. An anally oriented top would be the administrator of such stimulation to a willing submissive.

B&D
Bondage and Discipline. Most players practice it for fun or foreplay with their partners. A "B&D club" is a salon where such amusements may be enjoyed with trained professionals for a fee.

BDSM
Bondage, Discipline, Sado-Masochism, Dominance and Submission all fall under these umbrella initials.

Bettie Page
The most famous and beloved pin-up girl of the 1950's, who was photographed and performed in numerous bondage shoots for the legendary magazines and films of Irving and Paula Klaw.

Birch Rod
A bunch of twigs, trimmed and bound together at one end to form a handle, used as an instrument of correction.

Booful
The nickname of a character named Candy Floss from an adult cartoon strip called Wicked Wanda, that ran in Penthouse Magazine from 1973-1980. Candy Floss was Wanda's naughty blonde companion, who was occasionally spanked by her mistress.

Bondager
Someone who plays with bondage, by tying others, or by

being bound. What players do and don't do in bondage is often a highly specific choice. Some submissives enjoy corporal punishment while they are bound, others merely crave tickling or teasing, kissing or caressing, while the decadent may long to surrender to full penetration. Wriggling in a hogtie while plugged may prove orgasmic. Absolute purists may simply seek to remain beautifully bound, either nude or in stunning fetish attire, for long periods of time or to test their skill at getting free, a la bondage princess Bettie Page, aka The Escape Artist.

Bottom, Bottoming

A bottom is a submissive player; bottoming means submitting to discipline, punishment or other forms of stimulation, such as tickling, teasing, bondage, etc.

Caning

The preferred mode of corporal punishment in classic British discipline scenarios. "Six of the best" is considered the standard amount, especially for a beginner. Even moderate caning can leave behind marks that range from faint pink to deep weals. Approach this implement with caution and respect.

Catfishing

Practiced by a person pretending to be someone else, often of the opposite sex, to obtain thrills or monetary gains.

Cinch

Short for waist cinch, a braless, open bottomed corset that laces up the back and usually hooks down the front, often with garters attached, and designed to reduce or enhance a dainty waist and produce an hour-glass figure effect.

Club

A house or salon where clients may engage tops, subs or switches for consensual play sessions. Or, a membership organization that hosts parties, conventions or other events for the BDSM community, either in a nonprofit or a commercial manner, or a permanent hall for events, with a set entrance fee.

Dom
Short for dominant or dominatrix; interchangeable with "top" as a noun or verb.

Dungeon
Any playroom dedicated to the practice of the B&D arts. A professional dungeon would employ a Mistress or Mistresses as well as Submissive and Switchable players. A private dungeon refers to a play space within any residence, set aside for fetish activities. A typical dungeon room would be equipped with a leather covered bondage bench, a whipping post, a spanking bench and a variety of restraints, with accessible implements of corporal punishment.

FemDom
Refers to a scene or entertainment that is female dominant in theme, featuring a mistress or dominatrix, a teacher, aunt, mom, nurse or any other female authority figure dispensing corporal punishment, orchestrating bondage training or administering any type of discipline to a consenting submissive.

Fetish Pumps
Extremely high heeled ladies' dress shoes, often 1950's retro-styled.

Foundations
Corsetry, girdles, and all structured undergarments molded to enhance the female figure.

Ink
Tattoo.

Las Palmas
A real street in Hollywood, where in the mythical B&D club, The Keep is located.

Marchesa Gown
A fashion house known for lavish, dainty and exquisite couture.

Mistress
Elegant dispenser of corporal punishment and other forms of discipline to clients, lovers or mates.

Never on Sunday
Jules Dassin's 1960 film about Ilya (Melina Mercouri), a carefree Greek prostitute, beloved in her neighborhood, who captures the interest of an American intellectual who attempts to educate and reform her.

Playing
Engaging in fetish recreation either professionally, just for fun or as foreplay.

Pre-Code
Sound films produced in Hollywood between 1929-1934, prior to the introduction of the Production Code in June of 1934, that essentially censored sophisticated sexuality out of American movies, ushering in a period of blandness only relieved by noirs.

Pro
Someone who receives allowance for playing with a client.

Raise the Red Lantern (1991)
A Chinese film picturing the life of a concubine in 1920's China. Sensuous foot massages were one of the luxuries permitted to favorites of the lord.

Role Play
Assuming different personas while playing. Example: master and maid, nurse and patient, teacher and student, etc.

Safe Word
Any agreed upon word, such as the classic "mercy" or a color code, such as "red" to signal that a pause is desired

in play, either because of excessive pain or discomfort.

A Scene
What goes on during a play session. A scene can be elaborate or simple, depending on the tastes, imagination and desires of the participants.

The Scene
The totality of the spanking fetish subculture, including its entertainment, literature, social organs and all the activities that comprise this amusement, which is a fixation that can remain mental or express itself through role play, foreplay, therapy, exhibitionism, affection or any number of creative endeavors aimed at diverting or mating enthusiasts.

Service Slave
A submissive who is willing to perform menial tasks and chores and/or offer sexual servitude on command.

Service Top
A friend in the scene who furnishes discipline or other forms of esoteric stimulation to a bottom.

Session
When a client books time with a dominant, submissive or switchable player, that play period is called a session. A session may or may not include overtly sexual stimulation and may or may not conclude with a sex act or orgasm. Sessions may also be traded for considerations other than financial or bestowed as favors upon the deserving.

Slave
A humble submissive or masochistic player whose greatest joy is in being of use to a mistress or master.

Spankee
One who receives this form of corporal punishment.

Spanking Enthusiast
This applies to anyone who is into recreational spanking

on any level. This includes fantasizing about spanking, hunting for spankings in books and movies, writing spanking erotica, playing spanking games with friends, lovers, partners and all available, obtaining spanking pen pals, placing and answering personal ads, corresponding with spanking friends in other countries, dating or mating with fellow enthusiasts, hosting or attending social scene events, creating spanking entertainment or performing in same.

Story of O
Pauline Réage's 1954 novel of classic female submission in an exclusive club called Roissy, where every member has the right to sexual servitude from every girl in residence. The French author penned the fantasy to please her lover.

St. Andrew's Cross
A wall mounted X frame, sometimes designed to rotate 360 degrees, fitted with cuffs to restrain a captive for exhibition, discipline or teasing.

Sub
A submissive. "Sub to" means submit to.

Switch
A player who enjoys either the dominant or submissive role.

Teasing
Lightly caressing and/or tickling, a (usually bound) submissive, to gently arouse them.

Top
A mistress, master, disciplinarian or other player, who administers erotic stimulation, punishment or training to a consenting submissive.

Toys
Implements of corporal punishment, nipple clamps, cock rings, items of restraint, butt plugs, dildoes, vibrators, and

other paraphernalia used as accessories to play.

Vargas Girl

Alberto Vargas (1896-1982), arguably the king of 20th century pin-up girl art, painted glamorous and provocative posters for the Ziegfeld Follies, pre-code Hollywood and magazines like Esquire and Playboy.

Video

In terms of this book, specifically, a well-produced spanking or bondage scene that has been filmed for commercial release.

Persons of the Drama

Hope Spencer Lawrence
Assistant manager and top girl at The Venus Club.

Carola Campi
Glamour photographer, fetish model, magazine editor, dominant switch, B&D Club manager; sister of Cassandra.

Cassandra Campi
Manager of The Venus Club, mother of Amanda Sands, versatile player.

Victor Kesselring
A notoriously unpleasant European master; classic sadomasochist.

Cameron Hayes
A sex researcher with a grant from Johns Hopkins to mine the B&D scene for data. Top.

Colby Hodge
Harvard sophomore, boyfriend of Amanda Sands, athletic top.

David Lawrence
Hope's husband, English teacher at Braemar Prep, top.

Ambrose Bartlett
Owner of Bartlett's department store, husband of Pamela, best client of The Venus Club, top.

Brooke Neuman
Hope's best friend from their Hollywood club days, now a film editor in Boston, submissive.

Marion Craig
Savvy Boston attorney, decadent submissive player, bisexual thrill seeker.

Naomi Norling
Workaholic statistician from Boston, craves extreme play sans romance, submissive.

Anthony Newton
Musical composer, patron of The Venus Club, partner of Susan Ross. Top.

Susan Ross
Anthony's young mistress, graphic artist, illustrator, sister of Laura Sands. Confident, managing submissive.

Hugo Sands
Publisher of The New Rod Quarterly, owner of Sands Antiques shop, father of Amanda, married to Laura, top.

Laura Sands
Graphic artist and illustrator, Hugo's wife, Susan's sister, submissive switch.

Michael Flagg
Former detective, owner of the tavern, husband of Marguerite, top.

Marguerite Alexander
Author of sublime spanking fiction, co-owner of the book shop, wife of Michael, sensual, powerful switch.

Sloan Taylor
Co-owner of the book shop, handsome top, married to Paula, often drafted to model in photos, always sartorially correct.

Diana Currie
Interior decorator, Susan's best friend, wife to Plastridge Currie, bondage and spanking submissive.

Plastridge Currie
Diana's indulgent husband, owner of an ad agency, bondager extraordinaire.

Carl-Adam Johanson
Researcher at MIT, amiable switch, side squeeze of Diana Currie.

Josette
The Newtons' new chef, recent graduate of The Culinary Institute, beginner submissive.

Dennis Cowper
Anthony's amiable Man Friday, British switch with a shoe and foot fetish.

Rusty Cabot
Real Estate developer with a twenty-year crush on Carola, top.

Jesse Pomander
AKA, model Wilhelmina Willoughby, twenty-two-year-old staff submissive and general assistant at The Venus Club.

Dru Baxter
Engaging Random Point switch, at Art school in Boston, but homing back to The Cape to help out at The Venus Club whenever needed.

Polyxena Guzman
Glamorous Dutch dominatrix, current owner of the Random Point gym, switchable.

Raphael Price
Owner of the Random Point art galleries, handsome, switchable lover of Polyxena.

Felix Pildash
British historical novelist renting the Random Point lighthouse and frequenting the Venus Club to play, switchable.

William Random
Architect and real estate developer, designer of The Venus Club, husband of Damaris, dominant.

Damaris Random
Fashion designer, wife of William Random, partner of Pamela Bartlett, submissive.

Pascal Robbins
Photographer husband of Phoebe, shoots for Carola and Hugo, not in the scene, but knows how to play.

Phoebe Robbins
Actress and protégée of Anthony Newton, wife of Pascal Robbins.

Baldwin Rosemead
Phoebe's sometimes theatrical co-star, a stout, married man.

Wally Pell
William's construction site manager, built on monumental proportions, attractive and not in the scene.

Danny Yu
Cassandra's ex, Amanda's step father, lovable yoga master and secret bondage enthusiast.

Juni Park
A Korean American bondage model visiting Random Point to film with Hugo and Carola.

Belinda Cowper
Blonde British nanny (to Marguerite and Michael's two-year-old), sister of Dennis.

Chapter One

Morning at Carola's

On a balmy morning in early September, beautiful, serene Hope Spencer Lawrence, drove into Boston to spend her last day before turning thirty, with a couple of savvy girlfriends in the scene. And if she happened to stay out quite late, she had packed a valise and would spend the night in the city, as her husband had been informed.

She had dressed with her usual attention to detail and knew her cream suit, white blouse and two-toned spectator pumps would win the approval of her meticulous friends.

She was a slim, untroubled goddess of love, with a cheerful nature and an instinct for collecting friends who enjoyed her. And she was glamorously employed as assistant manager and top girl, of Random Point's exquisite new spanking salon, The Venus Club.

Hope easily found Carola Campi's triple-decker in Brookline. It was a wooden structure, well painted and maintained. The second story bay window had a discreet sign proclaiming it to be the Campi Photographic Studio. Hope parked her late model sedan, took her white and cream envelope purse, walked up three wooden steps and rang the musical chime. A moment later the door was opened by a charming young brunette with straight hair to her waist, in a black jumper, white blouse, black stockings and high heeled maryjanes.

"Lydia!" Hope said with delight at the sight of her new friend, adding, "how cute are you today!" in appreciation of the young lady's winsome outfit. They had met for the first time during the summer, when Lydia had visited Random Point to session at the new club.

Lydia was Carola's lead girl and often manned the desk in an office off the foyer. The house had been built in the nineteen fifties as three separate apartments, but Carola had occupied them all for over fifteen years and had arranged the floors to her particular needs.

"I'll run upstairs and let her know you're here," said Lydia, "why don't you wait in the dining room? I've started some coffee and we have croissants. Go right down this hall." Then the lovely girl disappeared up the dark wooden staircase.

Hope went into the dining room, which was painted palm green, with street side windows shaded by wooden blinds. The large wooden table matched the dark wainscoting that was surmounted on one wall by a gilt-edged mirror as wide as the table. Hope was admiring herself in this handsome looking glass when an extremely slender and attractive dark-haired woman in a full skirted shirtwaist dress walked into the mirror image behind her.

"Hello!" cried Hope, hugging Carola. "I love your dress! And is that a French roll?" Hope asked, admiring Carola's immaculate, shining jet black hair, swept back and rolled on her neck.

"Yes, thank you. And am I really seeing you in a suit?" Carola regarded Hope approvingly. "You look like a whole other person," the older woman observed. Then both of them turned towards the mirror to look at themselves side by side. "I like your hair pulled back," said Carola, her arm around Hope's small waist.

"I'm turning thirty tomorrow," Hope confided.

"Really?" Carola knew exactly how old Hope was because she had asked her sister, Hope's boss. "You could pass for 23," said Carola.

"How old are you?" Hope asked.

"I just turned forty," said Carola, raising her sculpted

brows ironically.

"You certainly don't look it either," said Hope. "But you know that."

"Oh, forty is nothing is B&D years," smiled Carola.

Lydia brought in a tray with coffee cups on saucers, spoons, milk and sugars and set it on the table. Then she left for a moment.

"Will you give me a tour of the house?" Hope asked.

"Right after we have a snack," promised Carola. Now Lydia came back with the coffee pot and poured for everyone before exiting again. Hope and Carola pulled back two heavy wooden chairs and sat down.

"Magnificent table," said Hope, admiring the turned wooden legs and glossy surface.

"Most of my things came from Hugo's shop," Carola disclosed. "When I first moved here, he helped me furnish the whole house in return for letting him shoot photosets for the magazine."

"I knew that you and Cassandra were his first models," Hope said with the reverence such a distinction merited. Now Lydia returned with a tray of croissants, butter and jam, though none of them touched the butter or jam.

"I'm going to take mine back to the office so I can cover the desk," said Lydia, putting her coffee and croissant on one of the trays and exiting with a smile.

"She's everything, isn't she?" asked Carola, when her shapely assistant had gone. "She manages my website too."

"Isn't she still in school?"

"She's in grad school at B.U. for English literature. She works on her thesis here between sessions."

"Sweet!"

Now they both nibbled on croissants and drank the excellent coffee Lydia had brewed.

"I have someone coming in about twenty minutes who may be an old friend of yours," said Carola, when they had finished their refreshments and were standing up to tour the house.

"Really? Who?"

"I'm not going to tell you, in case I'm mistaken. But if it is someone you remember fondly from your old Hollywood days, might you be interested in sessioning here today?"

"Well, I won't say I couldn't use some extra birthday money," Hope grinned. "What are your rates?"

"It's five for the hour. Normally I do a fifty-fifty split with my girls, but in this case, I'd just keep a hundred for the rental of the dungeon, since you're not on staff," explained Carola crisply, so there would be no misunderstanding.

"Okay, I'll let you know," said Hope. "I want to see who it is before I agree."

"Fair enough," laughed Carola, leading Hope through the first-floor rooms, which included a pantry, kitchen and bathroom. They stopped briefly in the nicely decorated office where Lydia was working at a computer. The room contained large wooden desks, rolling chairs, floor to ceiling shelves filled with art and photography books, and dozens of framed covers from pinup magazines that Carola had photographed or modeled for covered the walls.

Hope could have stood looking at the beautiful covers for an hour, but Carola pulled her quickly along, into the next room, the well-furnished front parlor, with a bay window on the street, and then across the hall into the downstairs dungeon, which she opened with a key. This room was painted pearl gray and contained a long, broad, upholstered bench sturdy enough for two people to play on, recline on, or be tied to, a double tiered spanking bench with a kneeling step, and a broad-seated, straight-backed chair, all covered in black leather. Dove gray velvet curtains covered the windows, but were looped back with heavy tassels at that moment, to let in the light and green tones of the back garden. Against the back wall was a massive ebony armoire, filled with ropes, harnesses and shelves of toys. In one corner stood a black whipping post. The other walls had large, black framed mirrors. All implements and objects were discreetly stowed out of sight.

"I keep it as minimally dungeon like as possible," explained Carola. "Of course, I have my fetish photography to explain the presence of all these things. But still..."

"Mr. Newton wanted the Random Point club to be the same way. It's just somehow nicer," Hope agreed. But immediately noticed the tiny frown that creased Carola's smooth brow when she heard the name Newton. Now they went upstairs to the second story.

Carola showed Hope her art and photography studio, the second-floor dungeon, which contained an X-frame of black leather and brass studs, the large wardrobe, prop and dressing room, lined with looking glasses, and a green and violet bedroom, with a velvet slipper chair. "This must be where the cross dressers take their naps in hogties?" Hope asked, nodding towards the lavishly brocaded bedclothes. Carola grinned and replied, "Yes, when they get tired of trying on clothes and having their pictures taken."

"I call this my cozy sleeper lounge," said Carola, leading Hope into a mocha-colored room with a brown wooden platform bed covered with a European style white cotton duvet. "It's right next to the bathroom and kitchenette," said Carola, taking Hope through each room. "I keep it ready for clients and friends who need to spend the night in Boston."

"Beauty!" said Hope, with appreciation. "Do you have any partners in the club?"

"No, it's just me," answered Carola, straightening a velvet curtain at the window.

"What's your nut?"

"Thirty-five hundred a month, forty-five if you count

utilities."

"And you have to come up with that all by yourself every month?"

Carola nodded gloomily.

"But you have such a small staff, how in the world do you do it?"

"Well, I make some money off the bondage videos and the website," said Carola. "And I have a handful of luxury class bondagers, over-nighters, and vacationers who take me along to tie them. I'm going to Berlin next month for a week with one of my regulars. That'll cover the rent for two months."

"Do you have slaves clean the place?"

"Oh no, I stopped doing that years ago. I don't have time to supervise free labor."

"Do you have a boyfriend?" Hope asked.

Carola smiled. "I have many boyfriends. They're all at Harvard or MIT."

"Seriously?"

Carola shrugged, "Somehow they find me. Usually for a spanking. I hold onto the cute ones. I like having sex with much younger men. Don't you?"

"I don't know," said Hope. "I may not have ever had sex with someone who is younger than me. But I recall that teenaged sex in general, was very hot."

Now they ran upstairs to Carola's private apartment. This consisted of two bedrooms, a bath, kitchen, sitting room and study. The study, with its bay window, was where the women stopped to look out the window down at the street.

"Want to smoke a joint?" Carola asked, not waiting for an answer, but lighting one.

"Thanks!" said Hope, who took her first hit as a taxi drove up and dislodged her prospective client. She saw a tall man in a suit, with short, neatly trimmed gray hair, exit the cab and walk quickly towards the front steps. But she couldn't get a good look at that angle and didn't recognize him.

"He's here, we'd better smoke fast," said Carola. Each of them took one more hit and then ran downstairs, with care, on their four-inch heels.

Hope stopped short behind Carola in the front parlor, where there stood a man she did know very well. Her heart dropped into her stomach for a moment as she said, "Oh my!"

"Well," said the man, looking Hope up and down with a smile, "if it isn't the Lorelei of Las Palmas!" He had a sort of English accent, though he was Swiss, with a lean frame and lined, though not unattractive face. The last time she had seen Victor had been six years before, when he had been in his forties. He was a hard, demanding session, the kind who gave her a pain in the stomach to contemplate. She had seen him once every three weeks for a whole year, except for his several vacations abroad, and they had been her very worst sessions.

But he had given her a charming compliment and that went a long way with Hope. She smiled at Victor and considered hugging him, but changed her mind. She tried to think of a friendly way to decline a session, if he asked. There was nothing about him that she enjoyed and the special services he required had never been to her taste, and less than ever now that she had an agreeable husband who still aroused her. But how to say no without offending Victor and making him cross with Carola?

"I heard you'd gotten married and become respectable. Are you working here now?" Victor asked.

"Just visiting. I'm working at a new club on the Cape," said Hope, instantly regretting the admission, as the last client Cassandra would wish to entertain would be this old-guard sadist.

"My sister's new place in Random Point," said Carola.

"The Venus Club."

"A B&D club in Random Point? Does Hugo own it?" asked Victor with great interest.

Carola exchanged a quick look with Hope, then she said decisively, "My sister Cassandra owns it." Hope smiled at Carola with approval, for it was an unwritten rule of the Venus Club that its patron, Anthony Newton, remain anonymous.

"Is it nice?" Victor asked. "Is there an ad for it online?"

"There's a video online that I did to promo the club," Hope replied. "It's in Hugo's members site. You can see all the rooms."

"What about staff?" Victor asked.

"At this point, it's me, Mistress, Carola's staff every couple of weeks, and a few local part timers," replied Hope.

"Marguerite?" Victor asked, "And Laura?"

"You know them?" Hope was surprised.

"Oh, I've been to Random Point several times," said Victor. "And I played with Laura at Isabel Bruno's dungeon in June."

"Laura played with you?" Hope couldn't envision Laura kneeling to Victor. Laura was not a trained submissive. She was only moderately submissive even to Hugo.

"She did. Twice. Ask her about it sometime," said Victor, adding, "how about sessioning with me now?" he asked.

"I'll let you two talk," said Carola, excusing herself and disappearing from the room, but not before adding on the way out, "If you decide to play, my darling, I can easily corset you."

"I don't know, Victor," said Hope weakly, walking to the window and looking out on the sun-dappled street. "I just got back into sessions and I'm not used to your level of severity. The suspension bondage, the breast whipping, that's just not me. It never was. Not to mention other

8

things that wouldn't be appropriate for me to do anymore."

"Because you're married?" he asked carelessly.

"Yes," Hope replied, semi-truthfully. She had never cared to service her tops and now that she had the best possible excuse not to, she hastened to employ it. She knew very well that there was nothing more deadly to a session than evoking the name of another man, but she wanted to kill Victor's interest in one. However, instead of repulsing Victor, her reluctance seemed to inflame him. "And another thing," she added, "I'm supposed to do a shoot the day after tomorrow. I can't be marked."

"Oh, a few little cane marks will be gone in forty-eight hours," he brushed off this protest.

"Honestly, I'm just here for the day to visit some friends and do some shopping. Tomorrow is my thirtieth birthday and I'm giving myself a little treat," she again attempted to shut down the session.

"What's an hour out of the whole day?" Victor persisted. "You can't tease me like this. You know you were always my favorite. I saw you more than any other sub in Hollywood."

Hope sighed and said, "I'll go put on a corset. Meet you in the downstairs dungeon in ten minutes." Then she went in search of Carola.

Carola was waiting in the wardrobe room for Hope, armed with a pink satin corset trimmed with rosettes, a pink bra and G-string to match, along with beige seamed stockings. She also produced the joint they hadn't finished.

"Why did I say yes?" Hope mused, carefully removing her suit and blouse and folding them over the back of a chair. "I hate him!"

"Here, smoke. What size shoe?" Carola asked.

"Seven," Hope said, inhaling deeply and exchanging her white lace bra for the pale pink push up one Carola handed her. Carola took in every aspect of Hope's extremely well-proportioned body as she undressed and redressed Hope in the Victorian foundation garment.

"He always wants a blow job and he always leaves me in tears," Hope cried with frustration. "Why did I agree?"

"Because you're my new best friend?" Carola suggested, hugging Hope with uncharacteristic warmth. Then she handed Hope a pair of black patent leather fetish pumps and left her alone to finish dressing.

Chapter Two

Cameron Hayes

An hour and ten minutes later, with her long, blonde hair disheveled and the lipstick worn away from her beautiful mouth, Hope stumbled out of the downstairs dungeon with a hand pressed to her cane striped bottom, feeling for possible welts. Her lovely face wore an ironic half smile as she dutifully escorted Victor out to the hall. In doing so, she passed by the door to the front parlor, in which a young man sat waiting. Although she passed to and from quickly on her way back upstairs to change back into her street clothes, Hope was fairly certain the waiting client got a glimpse of her tightly corseted body and cane striped bottom. Even in ordinary street clothes, such as the smart suit she had come in, Hope's lithe figure made an immediate impression, but in a glove tight lacing corset, her delicate proportions were of pin-up perfection.

Hope successfully concealed her pique from Carola as she hurriedly powdered her face, redid her lipstick, brushed her hair and dressed. She was mostly displeased with herself, for allowing herself to be tempted by four hundred dollars to do such a degrading session with such a horrible man. But she was slightly peeved at Carola as well. Carola knew exactly how horrid Victor was to submissive girls. Yet she had suggested Hope play with him as though it were the slightest inconvenience. Now Hope regarded her striped bottom in a mirror with a frown of real frustration. There were six red welts crossing each cheek, already puffy and raised. Carola came into her with an ice pack and pressed it to Hope's bottom, saying, "This should bring the marks down by half."

"Well, he was as awful as I remembered him being," confided Hope. "But I didn't let him get away with it this time, anyway, not all of it."

"I'm delighted to hear it!" Carola said, with some surprise.

"I don't know what I'm going to do about these marks. I didn't tell David I was going to be playing today."

"Is he jealous?"

"Hell yes, he's jealous! He's only grudgingly letting me work at Cassandra's club because I whined so piteously about how hard my old job was. But he thinks I'm mainly giving spankings to guys, not getting them. I'm going to have to spend the night in town to give the marks more time to fade before I see him."

"You can stay here if you like," said Carola.

"Thanks, but I think I'll stay at Hugo's apartment. I have a standing invite to do that. No offence, but I don't want to chance coming back here later and getting roped into another session."

"No doubt you're right," said Carola. "No one who sees you here is going to want to leave without playing with you." The slim mistress handed Hope her four hundred dollar bills.

"Make sure you stop in the parlor on the way out. The client in there saw you pass the door just now and he'd like a word with you."

"The cute man with the trim beard?" Hope asked. For even though she had only glanced into the parlor, she had taken careful note of the client.

"He is cute, isn't he?" Carola grinned. "I haven't interviewed him yet, it's his first time here. But I hope he's submissive."

"Why? Don't you sub to cute tops?" Hope asked.

"Yes, but he'll ask for Lydia if he's a top."

"Don't be so sure," said Hope, glancing admiringly at

Carola's tiny waist. Carola smiled.

"Oh, I'm not saying he won't get around to me eventually," the brunette conceded.

Hope lifted the icepack and examined her bottom in a mirror. "Looks a lot better, but the welts are still there," she sighed, and quickly donned her street clothes.

"Keep icing it later tonight," Carola advised.

"I will. Bye honey," said Hope, hugging her new friend and running downstairs. When she stopped in the parlor the client sprang to his feet and extended his hand to shake hers.

"Hello," he said. "I hope you're not on your way out."

"Hello. Actually, I am."

"But, you do work here regularly?"

"No, I'm visiting from out of town," Hope said, pulling her small hand from his large one without haste, as his attractive blue eyes held hers for a moment.

"May I introduce myself?" he asked, in a manner she was wholly unaccustomed to. Gentlemen who visited B&D salons generally used nick names, or first names only when conversing with the staff. This tall, slim young man actually produced a card, which Hope took and glanced at.

"What's AHSS of John Hopkins University?" she asked, looking up at him, adding, "Mr. Cameron Hayes?"

"It stands for Aspects of Human Sexuality Study. It's a five-year survey being conducted internationally by researchers like myself; and a massive report will be published by the university at its conclusion. You can look it up online to verify the project is legit," recited the young man by rote. "And here's the fun part, we're paying people for interviews," he added, with an ingenuous smile.

"Oh, so you're not really here as a client?" Hope looked at him uncertainly.

"If you like, but for your time, rather than your services. I have a budget of up to a hundred dollars an hour for my interview subjects. And I've been lucky enough to draw the field of professional B&D entertainment as my assignment."

Hope looked at him with interest, appreciating how quickly he had gotten to the point.

"Why do you say lucky?" she smiled. "Is it because you yourself are a fetishist?"

"Clever spot, but it's also a plummy assignment, because producers, performers and club workers are a lot more fun to interview than isolated textbook deviants."

"Well, it's nice you're not trying to prove that we're all twisted," said Hope in a friendly tone. "I don't mind being interviewed today, the rate of compensation is fair, but I'm running a bit late. Could you come with me and interview me on the way to a few errands?"

"I could easily record our interview on the way," said Cameron, excited at the opportunity to capture this beauty's experiences for the study. "Oh, and I will be emailing you a follow-up questionnaire, to fill in some of the blanks. Do you enjoy writing?"

"I love writing," said Hope.

They exited the house and Hope led him to her car. He got in the front seat beside her, set his phone to record, and they headed off to Back Bay.

"We're going to a corset shop," she told him. "The patron of the club where I work has arranged to have a birthday present waiting for me there."

"Oh, it's your birthday!" Cameron smiled.

"I'm turning thirty tomorrow," she gaily replied.

"I turned thirty this year too," he disclosed.

"Is this your full-time job, or are you working on a thesis?" she asked.

"It's my job, medical research. I joined the staff of this study a few months ago."

"And it's a five-year gig? Congratulations!"

"Thank you. The pay is decent and I get to travel on an

expense account. I'm spending the winter between Boston and New York, then off to the west coast."

"You should have worked it the other way around and spent the winter in California, silly," she smiled. "In any case, I can give you lots of contacts for when you to go to L.A."

"I'd be very grateful for that."

"Where did you go to school?" Hope asked.

"NYU and Columbia," he replied. "What about you?"

"Regrettably, I've only done one year of college at U.C.L.A.," Hope admitted with embarrassment.

"Why only one?"

"Because I discovered the B&D scene in Hollywood the year I started college and it distracted me away from my studies. I partied, played, modeled and clubbed and was generally too naughty to be a serious student."

"How long have you been married?"

"Almost six years."

"And how long have you been working at clubs?"

"Five years in Hollywood. Then I took six years off. But now I'm back."

"May I ask what your home life was like?"

"Oh, very nice!" Hope said. "My parents are darling, laid-back bohemians. He's a letter carrier and she's a beauty who still does nude figure modeling for art classes and works at a food co-op. They were both indulgent and very kind. I'm their only child. And no, I was not subjected to corporal punishment of any kind as a child. But I had friends who were, and stories of their punishments always fascinated me. And I devoured any books, movies or TV shows that had spanking scenes or bondage scenes."

"So, you'd say that exterior cultural influences determined your sexuality?"

"Well, I can't be one hundred percent certain that I wasn't stroked or patted on my bottom while still an infant in such a way that turned it into my primary erogenous zone. I believe such things can happen, through no one's specific fault or determination."

"That's an interesting angle," said Cameron.

"I know. When does a fetish fixation actually take hold? Some people can trace the exact moment."

"The people who can trace the exact moment, have you met many of them?"

"Oh yes!"

"Boy, I really hit the jackpot with you," said Cameron, with excitement. "We'll have to have more than one interview, I can see that. But tell me more about the ones who can remember."

"I will, but now I have to find a parking place," she said, as they had reached the corset shop on the corner of Boylston and Exeter Streets. "Come in with me," she said when they had parked a block away.

The small shop was furnished with glass cases full of lingerie, mannequin torsos clad in elaborate brocade and satin foundations and mirrors. A thin, attractive, gray-haired woman in a smartly belted gray dress came out from behind the back counter to greet them. Hope told her she was here to pick up an outfit that had been ordered by Mr. Newton. The stylish older lady beamed at the name of her favorite customer and went into the back of the store to fetch Hope's present. This she brought out on a hanger instead of in a box, for it was an elegant, lavishly trimmed ecru velvet corset gown, with a low-cut halter style top and an underskirt frilled with rows of white lawn, slashed to the knee in front to reveal legs that would be booted in the accompanying high heeled lacing Victorian style boots in bone leather.

"If you would step in back and try it on, we can see if it needs any alterations," said the clerk, whom Hope also judged to be the owner of the shop. "But it was made to order with your measurements," the shop keeper added.

"Isn't it stunning?" Hope asked Cameron, who nodded

and politely inquired of the clerk how much it cost as Hope took the gown and boots back to the fitting room.

"Fifteen hundred dollars for the gown, and seven hundred for the boots," the corsetiere replied. Hope heard these figures before she disappeared into the fitting room and felt immensely appreciated by Mr. Newton. A few moments later she emerged glamorously clad in the torso hugging gown and turned her back to the lady of the shop for a final tightening of her corset strings, which were part of the dress. Cameron asked if he could take her picture in the gown. Hope assented and struck several poses for him around the shop, including one with its smiling owner.

"If he likes the picture, Hugo Sands may give you a plug for the shop in his magazine," Hope suggested.

"That would be so kind of him!" said the lady, resolving to look up Hugo Sands and find out what magazine the beautiful blonde girl was referring to. She had charged many corsets and corset dresses to Mr. Newton's account in recent months, but always assumed they were for actresses in his Broadway shows. The owner of the shop had no idea that all the foundations and retro gowns had been ordered for B&D club girls to pose and play in.

They all decided that the gown needed no alterations. It was taken off, zipped into a hanging bag, another shopping bag was produced for the boots, and Hope led Cameron out of the shop.

"That's quite a present," said Cameron, as they deposited the treasures in the trunk of Hope's car.

"I have some very generous friends. Look, I'm starving, shall we find a cafe and have some lunch while we continue the interview?"

"Yes! There's a good little Greek place right down the street," Cameron suggested. They decided not to give up the parking place, but to walk to the cafe. Hope felt happy and relaxed now, as though the painful, embarrassing and awkward session with Victor had happened a year instead of an hour before. She ordered a lamb sandwich, roasted potatoes and a glass of white wine. He did the same and while they waited for their food, he tapped the record button to continue the interview.

"When you walked past the parlor, you were still in just your corset and I couldn't help but notice that your bottom was marked," said Cameron. "Is that typical?"

"No. That client happened to be a mean top. He's never happy unless he leaves the submissive marked. It's really jammed me up. I should never have taken that session. I know that client of old. But I let myself be flattered into accepting it. And I momentarily forgot how much I disliked his sessions. Now here I am, all marked up, and I never even mentioned to my husband that I was going to be playing in Boston. He could potentially be very peeved and he isn't easily soothed."

"Does that mean he'll beat you too?"

Hope laughed. Then frowned. "We don't say beat. But you're very intuitive. My husband is a top and his fetish is spanking. And once in a while, he does try to dominate me with the threat of one. But this would be more likely to cause him to sulk and rail against the profession I've chosen to reenter."

"He doesn't he want you to do sessions?"

"What normal husband would? He's not only jealous of other men playing with me, but afraid they'll hurt me."

"Does he have a point?"

"He needn't be jealous," she smiled; "I'm madly in love with him. I just like to play for fun and for the allowance. As for the danger factor, he has a point, but this is usually as bad as it gets," she gestured to the area of her bruised bottom, "and that seldom happens. Most tops aren't mean."

The food arrived and they paused to eat and drink. But towards the end of the meal, Cameron renewed his chain of questioning again.

"How would you describe your personality?" asked Cameron.

Hope thought for a moment, then grinned and said, "Sunnily narcissistic. I take full advantage of my privileges, but try to be helpful to my friends when I can."

"Like Emma?" Cameron asked, somehow knowing she would know who Emma was, even though she only did a year of college. The way she spoke, carried and conducted herself, bespoke a high degree of literacy.

"Not exactly," Hope grinned; "when I meddle and manipulate, things actually happen the way I plan them to."

"So, when did you read Jane Austen?" he asked.

"My husband is an English teacher. I always read the books he assigns to his classes, write all the papers, take the exams."

"What grades do you get?" Cameron said, greatly envying her husband.

"All A's!" she replied.

He handed her his phone and said, "Please enter your contact info and I'll send you the questionnaire I'd like you to fill out."

Hope did as he asked. Cameron pulled an unsealed envelope from his jacket pocket and handed it to her. She opened it and saw a crisp one-hundred-dollar bill, adorned with a golden feather. Then he handed her his tablet and had her sign a receipt for the payment.

"You ought to go back to Carola's and interview her," said Hope. "In fact, if it's in the budget, put her on retainer and use the club as your own personal laboratory this winter."

"That's not a bad idea," said Cameron, remembering how beautiful he had found the mistress of the club, not to mention the charming receptionist with the long, black hair.

"You know, you could probably get to interview some of the clients without even paying them. I mean ones who are dying to talk about their fetish to someone. Carola can sift them out for you. They would probably be mainly submissives and cross dressers. They might even let you sit in on a session once in a while. Some of them are terribly exhibitionistic."

"Even though I'm a male?" Cameron said with surprise.

"Sometimes they have female alter egos. Or, they like the added humiliation," Hope disclosed. "Some are bi or just plain exhibitionist sluts."

"One hour with you has yielded me more useable information than days with a civilian. Thank you!" said Cameron. "May I come out and see you and your mistress at the Cape Cod club as well?"

"Yes, so long as you can guarantee all of us relative anonymity when you write up your study. Random Point is actually stuffed with fetishists. There's an entire scene's worth of players there."

"Wonderful!" said Cameron, paying the tab. "And don't worry, no one ever sees scientific studies but other researchers, doctors and students."

"Can I drop you somewhere?" Hope asked as they emerged on the street again.

"No, thank you, I'm staying with a friend a few blocks from here and I can just walk."

Hope put his number and email address in her phone, shook hands with him warmly and walked back to her car.

Chapter Three

Marion Craig

As Hope still had a few hours to fill before meeting her friend Marion, she drove to a gym she knew on Mass. Ave. that shared membership privileges with her gym in Random Point. Taking the gym bag she always kept packed in the trunk and a fresh change of lingerie from her overnight valise, Hope went into the small facility, which featured an outdoor swimming pool and spa. She debated swimming, which would mean having to wash her hair, but realized that she had plenty of time and was craving the deep relaxation only swimming could bring, after the driving, and beating, she had taken that day.

She sat on a bench in her swimsuit, warming herself in the sun and texted Amanda Sands, another scene girlfriend in the city. Amanda was currently starting her sophomore term at Harvard and Hope hated to distract her in any way, but needed to get the key to Hugo's apartment in Back Bay from Amanda, his daughter. Amanda answered Hope's text immediately, explaining that she was going to be chained up in the library all night, but that she would send Colby to meet Hope at the apartment with the key whenever she wished. How lovely it was, thought Hope, being so well connected. Boston was taking very good care of her that day. Except for the hard caning.

Hope smiled at the thought of Colby Hodge. Amanda's tall, handsome, hunky boyfriend was always so obedient to that young lady. He wasn't submissive. But he was smart. And being Amanda's boyfriend had already given him access to sexual adventures beyond the ordinary, even for a good looking, blond and blue jock.

The pool was nicely heated, and the steam room, Jacuzzi and sauna pleasantly empty. Her full cut one piece completely hid the cane marks she now bore, but she was also careful when changing into her street clothes again, never to lower her towel and reveal those welts, as there were other women in the locker room. Relaxed and refreshed, she spent a long time in front of the mirror, with a hair dryer and brush, restoring her long, wavy light blonde hair to artless perfection. The last thing she did before leaving the locker room was to slip her high-heeled pumps back on.

Marion Craig, a smart, slim brunette in her early thirties, was pacing up and down in heels as high as Hope's, before the tony Newberry Street gastropub, a cell phone to her ear, when Hope arrived. Marion had fine, slightly wavy, chin length brown hair, parted on the side, that nicely framed her pretty face. Her eyes were dark and her mouth wide and humorous. She was tall, leggy, lean and angular. Her black suit was well tailored and her shoes extremely sexy.

"Have you been here before?" Marion asked, ushering her through the door, they were immediately greeted by a discreet maître d'.

"No, but I'm not very hungry. I had a late lunch."

"That's good. They basically have a tasting menu with tiny, bite-sized appetizers."

"Perfect!"

"And this is on me," said Marion as they were seated at a window table, as befit their beauty, fine clothes and the twenty Marion slipped into their host's hand. The brunette was a successful attorney, who had recently discovered that she could live out her most perverse fantasies safely, discreetly and luxuriously, with Hope and her friends in Random Point, any time she chose to visit that tiny village on the Cape.

When Hope consulted the menu, she was very grateful that Marion had offered to treat, as she was not used to such prices. Marion also ordered them a bottle of white wine. Then they settled down to talk.

"What have you been doing today?"

"I visited Carola Campi's club in Brookline," said Hope.

"I've heard about that," said Marion with great interest, "What's it like?"

"Oh, very nice! Painted in rich, dark colors, with cream crown molding. The furniture is just what's needed, no more. The decor is very minimalistic, no knickknacks or clutter. Though she has a magnificent wardrobe and prop room. But the best part is that the walls are all hung with mirrors or framed photos that Carola took."

"What kind?"

"Oh, she's been a glamor photographer and a bondage rigger for twenty years. She's got every magazine cover she ever photographed, dozens of models in fetish clothes and poses, lots of regular cheesecake."

"Lots of photos of girls? Erotic ones?"

"Yes, you should go visit," said Hope.

"I would love to do that," said Marion, who liked girls as much as she liked men.

"You know, you could moonlight there once in a while," said Hope. For Marion had agreed to come out to her club in Random Point once every couple of weeks to session and or play there.

"Oh, I don't think so," said Marion, "it's too close to home."

"I guess you have your career to consider."

"Did you meet anyone there?" Marion asked, intuitively.

"I was persuaded to stay and do a session," Hope confided. Then she remembered something. "Say, can I ask you something?"

"Sure."

"I know you played with David at Amanda's birthday party," Hope began. Marion blushed. And she wasn't the sort of woman who normally did that.

"Yes. He's delightful. I'm madly in love with him."

"Yes, you seemed to be madly in love with all the local tops that night. But tell me, do you consider yourself a man's woman or a woman's woman?"

"Oh, a woman's woman, no question," Marion answered without hesitation.

"So, if I asked to keep a secret from David, any secret that I may tell you at any time, could I trust you to keep it?"

Marion didn't betray relief at Hope's refraining from questioning her minutely on exactly what had gone on between herself and Hope's husband when the door to the so-called School Room shut behind them, but she felt it.

"You can trust me with any secret," swore Marion. "As long as you tell me it's a secret. For example, do you not want David to know that we met for lunch today?"

"Oh, I do want him to know that," said Hope, with a laugh. "I just don't want him to know the real reason why I'm staying in town overnight rather than going home."

"And what is that?"

"That I played at Carola's dungeon and now I have fresh cane marks. I'm hoping they'll fade overnight and that I can put off actually being alone with David until at least tomorrow night."

"I won't say anything to him. Not that I ever talk to him. I just played with him that night. But we haven't emailed or anything since."

"Swell!" said Hope, anachronistically.

The wine arrived and the first round of tiny food stuffs on enormous plates.

"Tell me about the session," said Marion. "A bad man marked you?"

"This European master I used to session with at The

Keep happened into Carola's while I was there and insisted on playing with me. I didn't want to say no because it was dead in there and she needed the energy and allowance. I like her."

"What do you mean European Master?" asked Marion, nibbling at a tiny architectural pyramid of pate with the edge of a cracker. She drank her first glass of wine quickly.

"Terse and harsh, wants tears and head. If you haven't met the type, consider yourself lucky."

"I like that kind of top!" Marion said seriously.

"Really? Do you always blow someone after they punish you?"

"Depends on if they're manly men," Marion smiled.

"David is a manly man. Did you give him head?" Hope demanded. Marion fell back against the leather booth in surprise.

"Uh, um, let me think. I played with so many handsome men that night," said Marion thoughtfully, "And I gave more than one of them head. Why? Would it bother you?"

"Not if it's just what you normally do," said Hope. "Any way, it's good to have the ledger tipping in my favor. I'll take that as a yes and file it away."

"Really, I don't think I did David," said Marion. "Or maybe it was Hugo I didn't do," she mused. "Honestly, I can't remember properly at all right at this moment, but it's been a long day."

Hope said, "In any case, there's a twist to today's story. Before we started our session, this Euro master happened to mention that he knew Laura, did you meet her at the party?"

"Hugo's wife," said Marion. "Yes. The graphic artist."

"That's right. Victor, the master, said he'd actually sessioned with Laura Sands this summer, which blew my mind because she doesn't play hard. I had a minute after

Carola laced me into a corset, so I called Laura and asked how she'd handled Victor. Laura told me that the first time she played with him, a few years ago, he had made her cry. But this last time, in June, he let her thrash *him,* at Isabel's dungeon, and he took it happily. That's when I realized I might have to renegotiate the session. Well, he started in right away, just like the old Victor. Hard spanking, nipple twisting, having to keep my tongue stuck out the whole time, strapping on the bottoms of my feet, rough digital penetration, and finally, the severe caning."

"That sounds delicious to me," said Marion.

"It's nice you're a debased masochist. You'll go far," said Hope; "However, to me, it was awful and I knew I couldn't take a dozen cane strokes. Or the customary butt plugging and nasty, uncut cock down my throat that always came after the caning. I said mercy at six."

"Did that end the session?"

"No. I got up and looked at him and said it wasn't right how he was treating me after not seeing me in so long and I wanted satisfaction. I said I wanted to make him whimper and force a dildo down *his* throat, things like that. He didn't even blink. He just got down on his knees to me and lowered his eyes. I'm usually a mild-mannered top, but I took that cane and broke it on him. I slapped his face so hard my hands hurt. I made him kiss my bottom but told him not to dare try and rim me."

"Why not?" Marion cried, becoming more interested in her bold new friend by the moment. Hope just shuddered. "Oh, you do have an exciting life," said Marion, adding sincerely, "I envy you!"

"Just tell me the day you plan to come out to Random Point to work at the house and I'll have Carola let Victor know. He's already interested in the club and Cassandra doesn't have any local girls as mentally deranged as you to give him."

"I can come soon," said Marion, picking up the heavy

check.

Hope followed Marion's luxury sedan in her own car to Marion's sleek, modern condo in Cambridge and spent the next few hours there. She showed Marion the glamorous outfit Anthony Newton had bought her for her birthday and modeled it for Marion. Marion sat with a glass of white wine and a joint watching with pleasure. Marion especially enjoyed inspecting Hope's cane striped bottom.

"See how bad it is?" Hope cried with frustration. "This makes it impossible for me to not tell David I sessioned in Boston today. And that will make him incredibly grouchy. Never mention what I told you to him."

"I won't."

"Thanks. I'm trusting you."

"Do you like girls?" Marion asked, as Hope exchanged the exquisite gown for her evening outfit, a short-sleeved shirt, cargo shorts, urban walkers and crew socks.

Hope looked at her hostess with a smile and said, "Yes, but just as friends."

"So, you're not bi?" Marion asked, unable to conceal her disappointment. "I thought you said you're a woman's woman."

"No, that's what you said. I love my girlfriends but don't have sex with them."

"How can you play in B&D and not be bi?" Marion wondered. "Don't you have to do doubles with other women?"

"Yes. That's fun," Hope explained, "But if I wasn't getting paid to do it, I wouldn't seek it out."

"That's too bad. You're so beautiful. I would be your slave in a second," said Marion. Hope smiled and said, "Thank you."

"Do you have male slaves?"

Hope shook her head and said, "Not anymore. I used to, back at the club in Hollywood. To tell the truth, the

Random Point club isn't geared towards that angle, it's more about the boy spanks girl, girl spanks boy mystique. We also plan to cater to couples."

"I like that idea," said Marion. "Where would you put them?"

"In the loft. It has the connecting spa and it's detached from the house," said Hope.

"Have you had any honeymooners yet?"

"We have several couples coming in on consecutive weekends in October. And of course, we're going to have a Halloween party. You have to come."

"I will!"

"Who did you like playing with most at the party?" Hope asked, referencing the Venus Club's inauguration night the previous month.

"How can I pick one? It was the literal realization of my favorite fantasy, to play with that many hot men in a single night. But let me think back. I played with Colby Hodge, Hugo Sands, your husband, Ambrose Bartlett and William Random, in that order. Of course, it was a thrill to go sub to the editor of the New Rod Quarterly, that was on my bucket list. Ambrose Bartlett was divine. He was the most ruthless. That really turned me on. William Random was also really sexy, he seemed to like my head best of anyone. But how can I lie, my favorite is Colby. My original crush. He was the first male from your group I met and played with and at nineteen, you can imagine his level of virility. Unfortunately, I fucked that up over the summer, getting too obsessed with him. His girlfriend noticed and put a stop to it by ordering him to bring me into the scene so other men could make use of me."

"Yes, Amanda is very clever and managing for her age," Hope agreed. "She has genuine problem-solving skills."

"Have you played with Colby?" Marion asked.

"No. It never even occurred to me," said Hope. "Though of course I think he's a darling boy."

Chapter Four

Colby Hodge

Hope broke away from Marion at around eight, feeling pleasantly tired after her eventful day. She stopped at a deli and pastry bar to pick up some milk and a loaf of crusty bread for the following morning. She texted Colby, requesting that he meet her at Hugo's apartment, then drove directly to Boylston Street, where she parked. He was waiting for her in front of the eight-story brownstone, a tall, broad-shouldered, clean cut, blond boy, in a white T shirt, khaki shorts and cross trainers.

"Hi honey," said Hope, hugging him. "Thanks so much for bringing me the key."

"Hi Hope," he smiled at her engagingly. He was good looking and confident, but not forward.

"Come up for a while?" she asked immediately, as he handed her the key. "I've never stayed over and you can show me where everything is."

"Sure thing," he said casually, well aware that she was unable to hear the violent thumping of his heart. He took the valise and small bag of grocery items that she carried out of her hands.

They went into the cool tiled foyer of the Beaux Arts building and took the elevator to an upper floor. Presently he led her into Hugo's charming condo, a well-furnished and smartly decorated three-bedroom flat, amply stocked with weed, wine and chocolates. He showed her around the kitchen and she put away her milk and breakfast items. Meanwhile, he placed her suitcase in the master bedroom.

"What have you been doing all day?" he asked, when they finally came to rest in the sitting room. She handed him a bottle of beer from a microbrewery, that she'd found a cache of in the refrigerator. "Thanks!" He accepted it enthusiastically.

"I think I've been being decadent," Hope admitted, curling up in a leather chair.

"Aren't you having one?"

"Oh no. I've just been with your other girlfriend and she had some unbelievably strong bud."

"My other girlfriend?" Colby asked surprised.

"Marion."

"Oh!" he grinned. "She's not, though."

"I know. She told me all about it."

"What did she say?" he asked, more curious than worried.

"Just that she came on so strong that you wound up cutting her off," said Hope. "But how did you wind up getting so intimate with her so fast?"

"Oh, you don't know that story?" he chuckled.

"No, tell me!" Hope encouraged him, for she had done more than enough talking about herself that day and was in the mood to hear someone else's stories.

"I'd much rather hear about how decadent you were," he grinned, for he loved the sound of her voice and how she spoke, so casually, yet charmingly, about the scene that fascinated him so.

"I'll show you if you like," she said, getting up and unzipping her cargo shorts before waiting for a reply. He was shocked and intrigued at this move, especially as she quickly followed up by lowering her shorts and not lowering her panties, but pulling aside the seat of white cotton bikinis to reveal the lower portion of her perfect, creamy, heart shaped bottom, striped with six pink cane welts. "I wound up doing a session at Carola's, with a sadistic bastard I used to see in Hollywood and he left me with these. Aren't they dreadful?"

"Awful!" he agreed, coming closer to examine her beautiful bottom. "Though, I like marks," he admitted.

"Really? Would you like to put an ice pack on my bottom and soothe me a while?"

"Yes!"

"Go and look in the freezer, I'm sure there are some," said Hope, not bothering to pull up her shorts. A few minutes later, she had sat him in the middle of a sofa, disposed herself across his lap and was instructing him on applying the ice pack. "I think this will help," said Hope. "I can't let David find out I was moonlighting today at Carola's."

"Those marks won't fade for three to five days," he said knowledgeably. For he and Amanda had done some experimenting with the cane over the summer, at her request, and he had noticed even the much less severe stripes he had left on Amanda's bottom lasting for several days.

"I know. Tomorrow is my birthday it will be ruined if he's angry at me all day."

"I'll bet Hugo has some cream. I could massage you with it," Colby suggested, when Hope claimed her bottom felt quite numb with cold. She agreed and went to look in the bedroom. She came back with a jar of cocoa butter and happily slid back across his lap. Then he even more happily began to knead her firm cheeks.

"You were going to tell me the story of you and Marion," Hope reminded him. "In fact, I'm eager to hear about all your adventures this summer. You must have had some in Europe with Amanda."

Colby smiled, thinking Hope very nice, in addition to being one of the most exquisite beings he had ever met.

"Well, you remember that when Hugo and Laura went on their honeymoon, he left Amanda and me in charge of answering the emails for the magazine?" Colby said, rubbing her very slowly, from the tops of her thighs to the small of her back, with the fragrant cream. "I answered the female queries and Amanda answered the male ones. We thought it would be more fun that way. It was, until I figured out that many of the letters from females were really from catfishing males. Anyway, even so, you wouldn't believe how many spank-starved women write to Hugo on a monthly basis. They don't even know there's a scene out there full of men to spank them."

"And Marion was one of them?" Hope said helpfully.

"Yes, and not only that, she was in Boston. So, when I took that temp job in the law firm, we were working within five blocks of each other, five days a week."

"And therefore, inevitable that you relieve her spanklessness."

"Exactly. But she really is a crazy bitch. Did you notice that?"

"She seems a bit high strung," Hope said tactfully.

"She wanted me to treat her like a whore."

"And what exactly did she mean by that?"

"I wasn't sure myself but I thought it was kind of a dangerous thing to ask an almost total stranger to do. Don't you?"

"Yes."

Colby laughed and said, "I shouldn't admit this, but I totally pimped her to a super shy friend of mine, who, incidentally, really needed to spank a lady and was happy to pay for it, and I also kept the money."

Hope laughed, "I'd heard you're an economics major!"

"It was part of her fantasy."

"Come to think of it, I remember once, when I first came out to Random Point and I let myself be tempted into doing a session with Anthony Newton for a whole lot of allowance, David found out and made part of the punishment taking the money away from me. At least part of the money. I thought that was kind of hot."

"So did Marion. I used the money to buy Amanda some boots."

"Good man!" Hope said approvingly. "Tell me more of your adventures." She unconsciously wriggled across his lap and then consciously noticed that a rather large erection had sprung up under her tummy.

"I don't know where to begin. It's been the best summer of my life because of Amanda, of course."

"She's very kind to you?"

"She's more than kind. Which is funny because she was crazy hard to get."

Colby told Hope of how Amanda had arranged for them to play doctor and nurse to Pamela in Anthony Newton's customized exam room, on which occasion he had, with the complete assent of Pamela, subjected the slim brunette to an enema induced orgasm. He went on to describe a double date which Amanda had organized, with Pamela and Dru Baxter, that had included a Moliere play and had culminated right here, in Hugo's apartment one evening in June. In the course of that evening, Amanda herself had suggested the boys blindfold them before strapping them while face down on the large master bedroom bed. This was so that they could pretend later not to know who was strapping, and later, fucking who.

"So, you got to make love to Pamela while Dru took Amanda?"

Colby said, "Yes!"

"And you didn't mind giving Amanda up to him?" Hope asked, looking back at him over her shoulder.

"Well, I had Pamela," Colby replied, smiling at the memory.

"And Dru is a very nice and modest young man," said Hope. "But are you equally cool about all of her other admirers?"

"No," Colby admitted. "A couple of them get under my skin."

"And who might they be?"

"The geriatric roué who own the department store."

"Ambrose Bartlett isn't old, he's barely forty-two," said Hope.

"Right. That's my parents' age. But I had a change of heart about him when he bankrolled Amanda's entire European vacation. The economics student in me recognized the value of this connection."

Hope chuckled and wanted to say, "You do have the soul of a pimp, don't you?" but realized she was still over his lap and her bottom was still sore from Victor's caning. Instead she asked, "Who's the other geezer you're suspicious of?"

"Good word to describe the feeling that oily photographer arouses."

"Pascal Robbins?" she laughed again. "He's not unctuous."

"Another ancient who keeps thinking up ways to get Amanda's clothes off."

"He's a very good photographer."

"I know," Colby sighed. "Every one of my rivals is good looking and fascinating."

"Who else is on that short list?"

"The only one that isn't decrepit with age, the gallery owner, Raphael Price. He came by on her birthday and the second I saw them standing together I knew he'd closed the deal some time over the summer, probably while I was in Boston working at the law firm."

"You don't mind massaging me?" Hope asked, looking at him again. He laughed. "It feels nice!" she encouraged him. "You have such big hands and such beefy thighs. I can see what Amanda sees in you. Big something else too," she added, as his desire for her was impossible to ignore. "Tell me, did your adventures continue in Europe?"

"I scored four major spanking bonuses in Europe," Colby replied at once, as though he'd been reviewing them often in his mind. "But wait, let me think if Amanda would mind my telling you," he said, pausing to mentally review them all, then deciding it would be acceptable to share all of his erotic mementos of the trip with her.

He told her of how they had gotten away with both playing and having sex in a first-class train carriage between Venice and Paris, exactly as illustrated in Milo Manara's The Art of Spanking. Colby then described how Amanda had brought him to meet Susan Ross and Diana Currie in an elegant Parisian hotel and when they got there, Diana was already in bondage, curled up on the bed like a present for him to unwrap. Susan and Amanda then went out shopping together, leaving him to entertain Diana, a beautiful little bisexual spanking and bondage enthusiast. Amanda allowed it all.

Next, he, Amanda, Diana and Amanda's ex-boyfriend from freshman year, Ronnie Van Horn, took the train to Amsterdam and thence to The Hague, where they all spent the afternoon playing in the legendary Club Doma, another milestone in Colby's budding scene life. Finally, he briefly told of the most unexpected and piquant encounter of all, between himself and an adorable spanking-deprived English wife, in Hammerfest, Norway, while Amanda apparently caned the husband in the woods.

"Your girlfriend is very good to you," said Hope.

"I know."

"What did you do to deserve this special treatment?"

"I let her boss me around and frankly, she needs my help in Economics. She wound up with a B+ last semester because I tutored her."

"I like your modesty," said Hope, wriggling a bit on the iron bar that had sprung up under her. "And I like you. So, what are we going to do about this?" she teasingly bounced a bit.

"What...can we do?" he asked tentatively.

35

"Anything we want, if you have a condom," she said, springing off his lap and pulling her shorts back up. Then she took him by the hand and led him back to the master bedroom.

An hour later, they were lying naked in bed together, in the soft light of two small bed lamps, their fair heads propped up on large white pillows, with the counterpane and sheet pulled up to their waists.

"This is such a cozy lair. I love it here. Do you and Amanda use this place often?"

"We usually spend Saturday night and play house here until Sunday afternoon. Big advantage over the dorm, we can play here without anyone knowing what's going on."

"I'm getting hungry," said Hope.

"Me too!" Colby agreed without hesitation.

"The restaurant Marion took me to served food in bites. I think I had five."

"There's an Italian place on the next block that stays open till eleven and does thin crust pizza," said Colby. "Call an order in and I'll run and pick it up."

"Okay, good!" said Hope, searching out the bistro on her phone. "I don't want to keep you out too late though."

"It's okay, Amanda is studying all night."

"Yes, she says that, but she'll be looking you up later tonight, believe me."

"You're probably right," he agreed, jumping out of bed to quickly dress.

"I think this has been the best possible way for me to spend the night before my 30th birthday," she confessed with a sleepy smile. Colby grinned at her.

"Have you figured out how you're going to explain those marks to your husband?" he asked, after they had divided (three quarters for Colby, one for Hope) and eaten their pizza and each drank a glass of Hugo's red wine.

"Not yet, but thank you for reminding me of David. I haven't even let him know I'm staying overnight yet!" Hope recalled, with a thrill of anxiety. She immediately grabbed her phone up, flinched when she saw it was already eleven thirty and hurriedly texted her husband that she would not drive home that night. She was relieved when he didn't text or call her back immediately. That meant he was happily ensconced somewhere, either with the theatre club, of which he was the director, or at Michael Flagg's tavern.

Hope and Colby stood hugging each other in the foyer for several minutes before his departure, sometime around one a.m. She looked up at him and invited him to kiss her one last time. "You'd better shower and change your clothes before you go to Amanda," advised Hope, running her hand through his short, straight blond hair and caressing his smooth face. "Or she'll smell my perfume on you and know what you've been up to."

"She'll know just by looking at me. She knows everything," Colby said philosophically. "But she did send me to you," he shrugged.

"Well, then tell her it was an ego thing for me, since I'm turning thirty tomorrow, to score a Harvard boy."

"Yeah, she's really gonna believe you need an ego thing," he laughed, taking her around her small waist and lifting her up off her feet.

"Put me down," she protested. "I love you too."

Chapter Five

Return to Random Point

As it happened, Hope's husband, David Lawrence, was at that moment, very pleasantly engaged with Cassandra Campi, the mistress of the club where Hope was top girl. The first time David had come to the club, it was indignantly, seeking to spank Cassandra, for luring his wife back into pro B&D. After Cassandra good naturedly submitted to the outrageous demand, both were more than a little aroused and neither fought the impulse to kiss and make up, in bed.

That night, sensing that Hope would linger too late with her friends in Boston to drive back to the Cape, David had considered himself a free agent and ended that long, tiring, first week of term day, not at Michael's bar, but at Cassandra's posh club. He wanted to have a drink with her, to talk to her about Hope and how his wife was comporting herself at the club, well knowing that he'd get nothing out of Cassandra not completely in Hope's interest, but eager to hear Cassandra speak on the subject of his wife.

He would ask about all the customers she'd had that week so far, for after all, he was also in the scene and it was of interest to him, who was patronizing the club where Hope now spent most of her time every day. Again, he would get nothing out of Cassandra that would compromise anyone, but he would grill her. At last, gauging her mood from her tone and body language, he would introduce the notion of sessioning with her, as before, and taking all of the liberties he had taken the first time.

He did expect her to be demure, for he had spanked her very hard the first time, and she was demure, citing exactly that very hard spanking as a positive discouragement to a return engagement. He replied that he needn't spank her at all this time. She blushed and smiled and shook her head, protesting that he must be teasing her, yet knowing that he was as serious as he could be. In the end, she drew him by the hand into her bedroom and there he stayed with her until dawn, when he got up, dressed, and went home to prepare for the day.

If it wasn't for the fact that David Lawrence was Hope's husband, this was just the sort of adventure Cassandra would have shared with her assistant. As she showered and dressed in a cotton sundress and mocs, Cassandra reflected that she'd become the Never On Sunday live wire of Random Point.

David had a busy day before him and an even busier evening, and was also mindful that he hadn't yet got a birthday present for Hope. When he got back to the cottage to shower and dress for class he noticed Hope's text from the previous night and then another, asking him if he wished her to bring back anything special from Boston. As this last had only been sent moments before, he requested a corned beef sandwich from the deli at Coolidge Corners. She texted back immediately that she would bring it to Braemar on the way home and they could have lunch together in the park down the road from the school. This contented David, for he didn't teach a class until two, leaving enough time to take her into Woodbridge and buy her a present. The arrangement gladdened Hope as well, for she could now enjoy her husband's company midday, instead of waiting until he was exhausted at the end of the night, with no danger of him glimpsing her bruised bottom during their luncheon date.

Hope had formed an excellent plan for diverting David's attention away from the evidence of her Boston escapade, which had to do with getting to work early and spending the entire day and most of the night there. It being her birthday, she determined to generously allow everyone to give her birthday spankings, preferably with wooden implements, especially switches and canes, in the hopes that fresh marks would soon conceal or blend with the old ones, so as to be indistinguishable as to origin when her husband finally saw her at the very end of the night. She remembered him telling her that he was staying late at Braemar to conduct a casting call for the drama club's production of Hamlet that he was directing. This meant she might not see him until perhaps midnight, which left oceans of time to enact her plan.

They met, as planned, in the little park nearest Braemar, which abutted the woods and bordered the village brook and walking path. David was waiting at the little stone bench where they planned to lunch, a lithe, handsome, clean shaven man, just turned forty, in a light weight suit, white shirt and foulard tie, his short, dark hair neat and trim, his regular features lit up with a smile that came from his heart at the sight of Hope emerging from her car in a cherry red dress with a swing skirt and three-inch stack heeled pumps. Her smoothly wavy flaxen hair was down around her shoulders and her color was high as she gathered up her lunch sack and hurried up the path to meet him.

"Nice of you to bring this!" he said, kissing her lightly on the cheek and relieving her of the package. "Your car must smell like a deli now."

"Yes, I've been starving for the last two hours smelling it," she agreed. "Look, I even got you a celery," she said, pulling out two bottles of the amber pop whose name she deliberately mispronounced.

"You're so thoughtful," he said. "By the way, Happy Birthday."

"Thank you," she smiled.

"Did you have fun?" he asked, unwrapping his corned beef on a Kaiser roll and falling to immediately.

"Yes, I had the best time!" she said sincerely. "Carola was so gracious and her club is really charming."

"How does it compare to The Venus Club?" he asked.

"Well, everything is on a more compact, less luxurious scale, of course, but it's very tasteful and immaculate, with everything necessary and nothing more. The heart of the house is Carola's photography studio on the second floor. Really interesting lady."

"Did you have lunch with her?"

"She gave me tea and croissants."

"How'd you spend the rest of the day?"

"What didn't I do?" she laughed. Then she told him about going to the corset shop in Back Bay where Anthony had arranged for her to pick up the beautiful Victorian gown. Nor did she omit describing her escort, the young man, Cameron Hayes, who was conducting a study for Johns Hopkins and paid her a hundred dollars to interview her on alt sex workers. She described going for the swim and spa at the gym on Mass Ave. Then she told David about the expensive restaurant Marion Craig had taken her to, with the miniature appetizers and costly wines, and their subsequent long and intimate visit at Marion's condo, where more stimulants were consumed and confidences exchanged. "But I couldn't quite worm out of her whether she did or did not give you a blow job when you played during Amanda's party," Hope concluded, contentedly pausing now and then in her speech to nibble on her sandwich.

"She certainly did not!" David said with conviction.

"She said she thought not," Hope replied; "In any case, she pleaded a foggy memory of that night based on the sheer number of men she bottomed to."

"She's nice," said David, "but too bony and brittle. It was like playing with a paper bag full of wire coat hangers. So why didn't you stay over her place last night?"

"Oh, I'd already talked to her for hours," said Hope. "And I was dying to see Hugo's place. That was as good as staying at a five-star inn."

"What do you think of Marion, really?" he asked. "Could she ever be a close friend?"

"I like her, but she was making amorous advances to me and it was awkward."

David laughed to think of this and said, "You're the only girl in the scene who isn't bi."

They finished their sandwiches and went back to her car. "Let's go into Woodbridge so I can get you a birthday present," he suggested.

Hope thought this was brilliant and happily let him drive her to Bartlett's Department store, where she immediately led him to the jewelry department and unhesitatingly selected a set of drop pearl earrings and a single pearl pendant on a black velvet ribbon. It was an extravagant set, but Hope was slipping the allowance she'd begun earning at the club into their joint account, so she didn't feel guilty.

Chapter Six

The Venus Club

The Venus Club was a sprawling, gleaming and modestly luxurious, two-story Cape Cod compound, built by a paranoid millionaire in the 1950's and accordingly fitted out with subterranean living quarters, fortified to bunker standards, the lower floor accessible via multiple stair cases and two elevators. The house itself contained many spacious and inviting rooms, including a lounge with piano bar and billiards table; a sitting room and neighboring library, each with a fireplace; two large and handsomely furnished salons; an exam room, a school room, one general playroom; two guest bedrooms with baths plus a master suite; a gleamingly well equipped kitchen, pantry and dining room; a creatively stylish office and numerous bathrooms off numerous halls, the entire house tastefully yet minimalistic furnished, with richly colored paper and paint or paneling on the walls; heavy, shiny planked wooden floors and plantation shutters throughout, except for in the two large salons, which were both elegantly curtained. The halls served as galleries for beautifully framed art and every room was hung with gilt edged or carved wooden framed mirrors.

The basement level had been entirely finished, with beautiful tile flooring, a large kitchen, many bathrooms and a quantity of spacious living, sleeping and playing rooms, suitable for guests, sessions or filming.

A screened-in porch ran the length of the east wall of the house, beside which lay the driveway and opposite to which, stood the second building, with a capacious garage in front and a lodge-like suite with loft in the rear, joined to a complete spa.

Behind the house, stood a thick wood full of pitch pine trees, with one of the Random Point streams winding through it.

Hope arrived at the house at around three, having gone home, changed and played with her cats. She parked in the garage and was just taking the outfit Anthony had bought her across the driveway and when Michael Flagg arrived in his pick-up, with a case of champagne from his tavern. He was, as ever, the tallest, fairest, most Celtic godlike creature Hope had ever known and his masculine magnificence never failed to crinkle her eyes with a smile.

"Hi Hope! Happy Birthday!" Michael said, stooping to kiss her cheek before proceeding with the case to the porch door that led to the kitchen. "This is for your guests," he said, gesturing to the bottles.

"Guests?" she asked, opening the screen door to the porch for him and then the kitchen door.

"I heard lots of people are coming," he disclosed, over one broad shoulder; "What with the offer."

"What offer?" Hope asked Cassandra, who was standing in the kitchen, charmingly dressed in a pale blue sundress with a crisscross back and neat little flats. Cassandra was spritely, she moved with athletic grace and radiated calm. She hugged and kissed Hope happy birthday and explained, "The fifteen minutes for a hundred-dollar session offer we're running all day."

"Oh, really?" Hope replied, with interest.

"So, everyone can get a chance to spank you for your birthday," said Michael informatively, pulling out a kitchen chair and pulling Hope across his monumental lap without further preamble. Hope made no protest but was secretly glad she had chosen to wear capris into the club, for Michael Flagg had an extremely large and hard hand. "I know you won't mind if I take advantage of the offer right now. I have to get back to the tavern right away and won't be able to get back here until much later tonight," he explained, then cheerfully began to dole out thirty solid swats, each of which rang out resoundingly through the large kitchen.

"And we have visiting talent today too," said Cassandra.

"Really?" Hope said between "Ows" and leg kicks, lifting her head, "Anyone I know?"

"A character from your past; she's getting ready in Skylight One," said Cassandra, alluding to the first guest bedroom. All of the rooms in the house had descriptive names. The mistress of the house disappeared with Hope's lavish birthday costume to let Michael finish the birthday spanking, and reappeared the moment he had gone, for Cassandra was eager for a few moments of conversation alone with her assistant before a great parade of friends and clients began arriving. She found Hope rubbing her bottom through her capris with a grin on her flushed face.

"He's so cute," Hope said. "I hope you didn't really charge him for that tiny spanking."

"It's okay, people want to spoil you for your birthday. Go with it," Cassandra reassured her, brushing Hope's long blonde hair back behind one of her pink ears. "Before people come, tell me what you did to make my termagant of a sister adore you so? She sent me the most effusive text this morning, praising your many virtues and asking to borrow you again, whenever possible, and there was something about you bringing her luck."

"Really? I wonder what she meant by that," Hope mused.

"Have you checked your phone today?" Cassandra suggested.

"No, I've been having lunch with David. And best luck, he has to work until really late. So, when I see him, way later tonight, I can pretend I got these dreadful cane stripes today instead of at Carola's club yesterday, where he doesn't even know I was playing." Hope turned, lowered her capris and allowed Cassandra to examine the residual damage from her interlude with Victor.

"I didn't know you were going to play there," said Cassandra, tentatively touching one of the still slightly raised pink weals with her fingertip.

"An old client from The Keep happened to show up and he flattered me into agreeing to let him top me," Hope said, pulling her pants back up and glancing at her phone for the first time that day. The first message was from Colby Hodge and it made her blush. She immediately deleted it. Then there was a text from the young man who had interviewed her the previous day, Cameron Hayes.

"Oh!" cried Hope, "listen to this, this adorable boy I met at Carola's yesterday, he's a sex researcher, he's coming here today to check out the Venus Club! He's happy to pay any girl who works in B&D a hundie to interview her. Think of how many people he could talk to while he's here. Smart boy to pick today of all days to come out."

"Should we make him do some sessions as well?" Cassandra suggested.

"Try and stop him, I'm thinking. He's playing coy for the moment, but I sense he's a spanking man. Oh, I got a text from your sister," Hope said, and paused to read it before looking up with a grin to report, "I can see why Carola is pleased with me now. That fellow I just mentioned, Cameron, has put her on payroll as a research assistant for the entire winter for five hundred a week. I suggested to him he should use her as a resource! Yay, yay, yay for me!" Hope crowed with gratification.

"Really? You just handed my sister an extra two grand a month for the entire season? How did you do that?"

"I don't know. But I know I was feeling sympathetic towards her after she told me what a huge nut she has to make all by herself every month; so, the minute Cameron told me about the budget for his project, it seemed quite natural to push him into her lap."

"You did very well indeed," said Cassandra, elated on Carola's behalf.

"Would you like to see the outfit?" Hope asked, leading the way back to the guest bedrooms. The visiting talent was taking a shower in the room the girls were accustomed to use as a dressing room. Hope assumed she would be staying there overnight as well. She followed Cassandra into the other guest bedroom, the one Cassandra's daughter was to occupy on her holidays from the university. They removed the corset dress from the hanging bag and lay it out on the bed.

"It's magnificent. Let's get lots of photos. Do you want to put it on right away or wait until the sun goes down?" Cassandra asked.

"I'll wait a while, I think. Do I have any appointments?" Hope asked, opening one of the wardrobes and taking out a white sundress to slip into for the next few hours.

Cassandra took out her notepad and consulted it.

"You have your Cameron at four and Ambrose Bartlett at six. Everything else is amorphous at the moment."

Just then the bell rang and Cassandra left Hope to answer it. Hope opened the connecting door into Skylight and saw a tall, slim, young twenty something brunette emerge from the bathroom, wrapped in a white towel. When the girl shook back her smooth, straight, long, dark hair, Hope recognized her friend at once with joyful disbelief.

"You? Here?" Hope hugged the young lady, whose name was Brooke Neuman and Brooke kissed Hope's cheek. They stood back and looked at each other.

"Yes! I've just relocated to Boston," said Brooke, "for a sweet little job restoring vintage film footage at the Boston Historical society."

"Oh, how wonderful!" Hope cried, for though she hadn't

had this dear friend close at hand since she left Hollywood, six years before, they had been faithfully corresponding. "And you're going to visit our club to session?"

"I do think I will," said Brooke, looking around her at the well-appointed room with approval.

"Oh, you'll just love the Mistress," said Hope. "She's my best friend now."

"I thought she was charming when I met her just now," said Brooke, herself a slender, polished beauty.

"Put on something comfortable and we'll go for a little walk in the woods before people start arriving."

"I'm booked at five with an Ambrose Bartlett," said Brooke.

"Of course you are. I'll roll us a joint," said Hope.

Brooke opened her suitcase on the bed and shook out a short, open collared cream knit halter dress and smoothed it out on the counterpane. She was small busted and could forego a bra without discomfort. When she dropped the towel, it was to slip into a tiny pair of cream string bikinis. The dress went on over her smooth, lean torso next and she finished her outfit by slipping her pretty feet into a pair of tan huaraches.

"You're looking great," said Hope, caressing Brooke's smooth hair admiringly.

"So are you! I can't believe you're thirty! Can you believe I'm 24?" They looked in the mirror together and smiled at each other, well pleased. Looking into mirrors with her friends was what Hope did. Hope finished prepping the joint and took Brooke out one of the back doors, through the back garden and into the woods. It was a perfectly balmy day, one final breath of summer in September and the girls remarked on the beauty of the weather and the woods.

"You actually get to work here?" Brooke laughed, as they both remembered the much humbler club in which they'd met.

"Isn't it marvelous? You can actually bring a client out here and give him a switching in the woods. And we have a beautiful loft with a St. Andrew's Cross and a full spa."

"It's B&D heaven."

"Wait until you see all the rooms. There's a schoolroom, parlors, a sexy exam room, a library, a whipping room, and I don't know how many other choice spots, and downstairs, the entire basement is finished for shooting. There's I don't know how many bathrooms, and we have a regular cleaning crew, twice a week. And all the bills are paid by the owner. We don't have to make any nut at all. Just keep the session fees to pay ourselves. This house, all the new furniture, the utilities, the computers, security, water, heat, everything is bought and paid for, so no stress on us."

"Who in the world is this beneficent owner?"

"I can't tell you but you'll find out in due course. Suffice to say, he's a patron of the scene and has been taking care of B&D girls for years in a number of ways. This place is a local's club for our patron and his friends, and a players' club for spanking people. But there aren't any walk-ins. You need to apply for membership and it costs a mint. Or you need a referral. It's only been advertised on The New Rod Quarterly website. So, it's pretty exclusive."

"Sounds like a Castle Roissy."

"But it isn't. Men can't ride roughshod over girls here. The owner is very anxious that abuse not be a part of The Venus Club. It's really mostly for spanking people anyway."

"Tell me about this Ambrose Bartlett."

"Well, he's got a big back story," said Hope, passing Brooke the joint. "And it starts with David."

"Ah! My favorite former English teacher! I still have a gigantic crush on him, of course. I hope I'll get to see him while I'm here."

"He'll be by at the end of the night to pick me up. He'll be so happy to see you."

"Tell me about Mr. Bartlett."

"Okay, when we first moved out here, David had a tiny affair with Paula Rohan, the guidance counselor at Braemar. I found out about it, of course. Luckily, with the help of Hugo Sands, you'll meet him later, we were able to hook this spank-starved Paula up with the very Ambrose Bartlett you're going to see today. He owns the luxury department store in Woodbridge, Bartlett's. He's a huge spanking fan and he loves playing with new girls, especially skinny ones. He has a waist fetish."

Brooke's hands unconsciously went to her small waist.

"Yes, he'll adore you," said Hope, smiling. "But to continue, Ambrose and Paula fell in love and got married. But things weren't fine between them. Pre-bridal stress reduced her down to a size four for the honeymoon. But pretty soon she was back up to her normal size six, and then perhaps an eight."

"Pretty lady?" Brooke asked.

"Stunning. Just juicy. But Ambrose has this thing for skinny bitches. Then one night she baked him a Christmas torte that anyone would die for and he made a crack about her weight. It was over in a minute. She stone cold left him the next day. It was really kind of awesome of her, because Ambrose is pretty hot."

"What happened to the lady?"

"Oh, she's happily married to the half owner of the bookstore where I used to work, Sloan Taylor. You'll meet him later. In the scene, very handsome."

"Is Mr. Bartlett single again?"

"Oh no! He subsequently married a beautiful fashion designer who had a lot of degrees but worked in his store at the time she first crossed his path. She's since become the co-owner of a really cool design house, Damaris. Have you seen their clothes?"

"I love Damaris clothes!" Brooke said enthusiastically.

"So do I! We'll go to the shop tomorrow. Everyone will make a fuss over you. They'll probably ask you to model. Anyway, Ambrose's Bartlett's wife Pamela, looks something like you, but with a long bob. She's in the scene too. They've been married less than a year. She's interesting and very well read. You'll like her. And here's the twist, she used to date Sloan, who is now married to Ambrose's ex-wife. In essence, they traded partners."

"If Mr. Bartlett has a lovely wife, why does he need to do a session with me today?" Brooke asked.

"Oh, he's doing a session with me too. He's our best client. Unfortunately, he's always a bastard the first time. Really a hard spanker, I mean."

"If it's really hard I'll charge him more," said Brooke without concern.

"Good, that'll excite him even more."

"The rates are already high at this house, aren't they?"

"Five an hour. You get to keep three, plus tipping is normal here, not like in Hollywood."

"I'll tell him I need a grand for the hour if it's going to be hard," decided Brooke.

"I see you've developed into a hard-headed business woman!" said Hope admiringly.

"Well, it's to discourage very hard sessions," Brooke explained.

"Oh, Brooke, I'm so glad you're going to be in Boston now. I've missed you so much and we can have such fun!" cried Hope, putting her arm around Brooke's waist and squeezing it. "And did I mention that Mistress' sister also runs a club in Boston? You can go and moonlight there whenever you like. She's a sleek, elegant mistress with a photography studio and video business on the side. She'll love having you visit her house. She has taste. I'm sure she'll ask to photograph you straight away. Her magazines and clips are slanted towards leather, latex, boots and rope bondage, very smart and editorial."

"That would be minimally scandalous, so I'd be thrilled. My new job doesn't pay particularly well and I need extra sources of income," Brooke admitted, adding, "I think I'll stay overnight. Cassandra invited me too. And then tomorrow, will you take me around and show me everything?" Brooke asked.

"I would love that more than anything," replied Hope. "We'll go for a bike ride, I'll show you our house, we'll visit the bookstore where I worked for six years, Damaris' shop and Bartlett's! Oh, I can't believe my friend is really here!"

"Hadn't we better start back? I should get ready for my session."

"Me too. An interesting young man I met in Boston yesterday, is coming in to see me again today. In fact, I'll introduce you straight off. He's a Boston based sex researcher and very attractive. I hope he's not getting a crush on me. If he is, your being here is handy. I'll divert him to you."

"Is he cute?"

"Very."

Chapter Seven

Hope and Cameron

The girls gained the house in a few minutes and began to prepare for their sessions, changing into high heels. Hope gave Brooke a quick tour of the house, informing her that Mr. Bartlett would choose the room he wished to play in and declaring that she would entertain her client, Cameron Hayes, in the schoolroom.

They came to the lounge, a posh paneled room, with its timbered roof and planked wooden floor, and there found Cassandra showing Cameron the group portrait of The Venus Club ladies, which now hung over the hearth mantelpiece. She had just been pointing out which of them would be stopping by that day, which did occasional sessions, which had sessioned in the past, which had modeled or edited scene related material, which were simply local players. Cassandra paused when the girls entered to introduce Cameron to Brooke. Brooke and Cameron shook hands and murmured a greeting, taking each other in from head to foot, in a glance, before turning back to Hope and Cassandra.

"Cameron just made us all an interesting proposal," said Cassandra, motioning for them to sit in the comfortable leather chairs ranged around that portion of the large room. "Tell them," said Cassandra, encouraging the young man, who sat on the edge of his chair and looked once more at Brooke before beginning.

"Well, as I explained to Hope yesterday, I'm documenting a large study on pro B&D and related entertainment, and collecting material in the form of questionnaires, audio and video interviews. I've already amassed dozens. But I need help transcribing the interviews into text files. That's one job. I was thinking that if you and Hope had time and the inclination," Cameron nodded towards Cassandra, "You could take on the transcriptions piecemeal and I would pay you so much for each finished interview. I'm not sure how much yet, you would need to tell me how much time the jobs take you."

"We definitely have the time," said Hope. "Sometimes we only get one client a day here, sometimes none."

"I agree," said Cassandra. "We have the time and we are both good typists. I'd be interested in working on the project."

"Wonderful!" said Cameron. "You really relieve my mind of a lot of anxiety. I have these jobs piling up and I don't want to trust the material to a vanilla assistant. This will come much easier to you."

"I can type too," said Brooke helpfully. "And I'm looking for extra sources of income."

"I have something else in mind for you," said Cameron, smiling at her. "Cassandra told me you're a videographer and film editor. I'd like to assign you some of the video interviews, of the people who don't mind their faces showing, models and producers, for example. And then, as a secondary assignment, if I like your techniques, you can help me edit a documentary style film with extracts from the interviews. This will be a project that will take some years and would be an excellent professional portfolio piece for you."

"In that case, I hope you do like my techniques," said Brooke, hardly believing such a plum could fall into her lap.

"And I hope you like mine, I've booked a mini session with you," he smiled again.

Brooke blushed.

The moment Hope closed the door behind them in the school room, Cameron took her hand and kissed it, thanking her for the introduction to Brooke.

"Ever since I met you yesterday, everything has fallen into place for me," he said confidentially, rubbing her smooth hand against his own cheek for a moment before relinquishing it reverently.

"How so?" she asked, slatting the wooden venetian blinds to let the perfect amount of golden afternoon light into the wood paneled room.

"I've got my research team, my Boston base of operations, instant access to multiple players and performers, writers and producers, and now I've even got my video editor. Knowing you is a golden key to the heart of the scene. And on top of that, now I'm going to get to play with you.

"But Cameron, are you sure all this money you plan to pay out will be sanctioned? What if you're audited, will you be able to justify it all?"

"How sweet of you to be concerned and conscientious," he smiled. "Yes, I've been approved for a research staff, videographer and hundreds of interview fees."

Hope felt comforted and showed him around the play room, equipped with student desks, black boards, a long cloakroom behind a paneled wall, and the trompe l'oeil window (looking down on a street in Edwardian London) that Laura Sands had painted. The illusion was irresistible. Hope told Cameron he could meet and interview the artist later that evening.

"Would she be up a for video interview?" Cameron asked.

"I think she would. Her photo is already on the back of her graphic novels, she has a website with her pictures," said Hope.

"Then I'll have Brooke do the interview," Cameron said decisively, eager to put Brooke to work.

"Well," Hope grinned, "I can see where your head suddenly is. What else can I do to help you with Brooke?" She sat on the edge of the teacher's desk and looked at him with interest.

"Really? You'd help me? Advise me?"

"I'm in the best possible position to do so, I know her well," said Hope with amusement. "And I know that at the moment, she's completely single."

"Well, tell me this, if you were me, and were going to do a session with Brooke, what sort of session would you do?"

"Well, given the nature of the club, spanking, or something related to it," Hope replied. "Come to that, you never did tell me what you yourself are into.

"Didn't I?"

"I don't think so."

"Spanking and anything related to it!" he declared cleverly, leaving her to wonder whether it was true or he was merely trying to strategize regarding his Brooke campaign.

"In that case, I would advise that you give her a little taste and no more, not even lifting her skirt. In my opinion, this would differentiate you from everyone else she's going to play with today and strike her as interesting."

Cameron nodded, while looking at Hope thoughtfully. "It's very sensible advice," he said, "and I may gain an advantage by following it. But how should I console myself for the loss of her bare charms? Let me answer that question for you. I will require my present hostess to strip completely nude for her birthday spanking." He paused to look at the large, round, brass clock on the wall to see how much time they had left of the mini session. "At once, I think," he added, noting that twelve minutes remained.

"You're bad," Hope cried, undoing the buttons on her cropped shirt and removing it to reveal a white push up bra delicately embroidered with butterflies.

"I may never have another opportunity to spank you at these rates," Cameron replied cheerily, and looking around for a place to sit, found a very broad, straight backed wooden chair against a wall and brought it forward. Now Hope unzipped and stepped out of her capris and turned to let him see the sheer back of her white bikini panties. "I see you still have those marks," he observed.

"It's okay though. They don't hurt." Now she undid her bra and let it fall. Next came her panties.

"Wow," he said. "You're something else. There's a bit of Bardot to you. Or maybe it's Claudia Schiffer."

"Can't it be Tuesday Weld?" said Hope.

"Of The Many Loves of Dobie Gillis?" Cameron replied.

"Do you love retro pop as much as I do?"

"If it's good, I do," he replied. "And yes, I'm getting the strongest possible Tuesday Weld vibe. Come over here, Miss Venus Club," said Cameron. Hope came to him, let him put an arm around her waist and look at her. He pulled her down across his lap gently.

"So, you think I should only spank Brooke over her clothes," Cameron reviewed her advice, while smoothing the satiny skin of her round bottom under his palm. "But how hard?"

"Show me now how hard you normally like to spank and I'll tell you if it's a good level for her."

"Do you know her that well?"

"Yes, of course I do."

Cameron began spanking Hope's curvy bottom and she said right away, "Yes, that's fine. You can spank her like that all day!"

"Really? I thought it was a bit hard."

"But, it's going to be over her clothes."

"Oh, that's right. I'll bet she's beautiful."

"Certainly she's beautiful. Flawless," Hope agreed. "I

hope you two hit it off."

"How can I make her like me?" he asked.

"Just be a darling, of course."

"And what does that mean?" he laughed, pausing halfway through the thirty smacks.

"Oh, good humored, amiable, helpful, respectful, encouraging."

"What about sex? What's she into? Do you know?"

"She's into bedroom discipline, why else would she be a club girl?"

Cameron finished spanking Hope and let her up. He took her back on his lap the right way up and hugged her.

"Thank you for letting me cuddle you," he said. "I'm so turned on."

"I get that," she said, feeling his erection under her as she sat on his lap. She rubbed her cheek against his and they exchanged one kiss on the lips before she jumped up. "You're mildly dangerous, aren't you?" she asked. "I'm starting to get a little turned on myself!"

"Why don't we extend for fifteen minutes, go into the cloak room and I'll ravish you?" Cameron suggested.

"Oh, you know about extending, do you?" she grinned.

"Show me the cloak room, anyway," he said.

"All right," she said, opening the door to the narrow connecting room, with its row of brass hooks on one side, a mirror at the end and a spanking bench set before it.

"I love this," he said, going over to the bench and patting the seat while beckoning her. "Come over here," he said. "Just bend over here and I'll get behind you. It'll all be over in five minutes," he assured her, pulling out a wrapped condom to show her he was responsibly prepared.

"Cameron, stop! I told you yesterday I'm married," she cried, though still smiling.

"Oh, come on, are you telling me you never favor clients with the ultimate thrill? Never, ever?"

Eve Howard

"No, of course I don't," she replied. "Not even close."

"Not even close?"

"Maybe once in a while, back in the old days, with a super favorite, who was also cute..." she let her recollection trail off, with a naughtier smile. "But I wasn't married then."

"Do you permit digital penetration? Toy penetration? A Hitachi wand?" he pressed her teasingly.

"That would be telling," she replied, putting the bench between them, though unable to resist looking at herself in the mirror. He looked at her too.

"Wouldn't you like to watch yourself in the mirror, getting fucked by me? You're so beautiful with your hair streaming down your back," he said, seductively, suddenly at her side and pulling her against him, grabbing a handful of her long, blonde hair in his hand, rather expertly and slightly pulling her head back before kissing her on the mouth. She turned her head to look at the image they made together, he in his light gray suit, white shirt and no tie, with his arm around her waist, drawing her slender nude body against his clothed one. "And after all, it is your thirtieth birthday. You're going to remember it. You're going to want to have fucked more than one man on this particular birthday. Aren't you? Don't I know you that well already?"

She looked up at him gravely, speechless at how well he knew her already.

"Lock the door," she breathed.

Before escorting him back to the lounge, Hope gave Cameron one more word of advice regarding Brooke, which was to, "Let her chase you a bit before closing the deal."

"Can I trust you not to give my game away?" he asked Hope lightly.

"You can," she replied firmly, adding, "And we won't let

her know how bad we've just been either."

"You're so flushed," Cameron said, touching her radiant face. "Anyone you meet right now is going to know you just had an orgasm."

"Do you think so?" Hope stepped up to the mirror at the end of the cloakroom and looked at her face.

"I think you're right," she agreed, allowing him to put his arms around her from behind and nuzzle her throat and her ear.

"Thank you for letting me seduce you," he murmured. "This will make it so much easier to behave with all due propriety when I play with Brooke."

Hope laughed and said, "Thank you! That justifies my narcissistic sluttiness admirably!"

"Seriously," he turned her to face him and lifted her chin, "you're a goddess and I'll never forget this favor as long as I live."

"From this day forward, we'll be best friends," said Hope with conviction.

Chapter Eight

Ambrose Bartlett

After a shower, Hope called upon Cassandra to help her into her champagne corset gown and smoke a pipe to prepare her for her birthday session with Ambrose Bartlett.

"I'm sure he's brought you fabulous presents," said Cassandra, tightening Hope's corset strings and tying them into a neat bow at the back of the glove tight gown. "He arrived with ever so many boxes."

"Should I wear my hair up or down?" Hope asked, regarding her magnificently cinched waist in the mirror with satisfaction. Mr. Bartlett would be enchanted.

"Let me do a loose French braid for you," offered Cassandra, "it'll only take a minute."

Cassandra conducted Hope to Mr. Bartlett in the dark blue salon. He had dismissed Brooke some minutes before and was checking his hair and tie in the mirror when they entered. Elegantly suited and immaculately groomed, he was a handsome man in his prime, with a serious, focused demeanor. He gazed with admiration at Hope in her glamorous ball gown, kissed and wished her a happy birthday, then turned his attention to Cassandra, who had begun to slip quietly out of the room, saying, "Just a minute, young lady. I didn't tell you to go." Cassandra came back and stood before him as he looked at her critically up and down, shaking his head in exasperation.

"Is that how a mistress dresses on an important night at her club?" he asked over folded arms. Cassandra was still in the cotton sundress and pretty little round-toed flats she had worn all afternoon.

"Do you think I should change?" she asked deferentially, but with a twinkle of mischief in her own dark eyes.

"Certainly you will change," he declared, going to the pile of flat store boxes he had brought with him from his department store that afternoon. He selected the slimmest one and handed it to Cassandra, saying, "Open it!" She pulled on the ribbon and lifted the lid. "I'd anticipated something like this so I brought you a few trifles to wear for me today," he explained as she took out a tissue wrapped garment and undoing the golden paper seal that held it together, disclosed a sheer black nylon halter gown of mid-calf length. "These came into Lingerie today and I immediately thought of you," Ambrose said, handing Cassandra the filmy garment.

"It's very revealing, isn't it?" she grinned, holding the delicate nightie up.

"Total Vargas girl," he agreed. "But that's not the whole ensemble." He now placed the two remaining boxes side by side on a table and opened them. "I brought some cute shoes for each of you." The boxes contained two pair of ballerina slippers, one in bone and one in black, each with 8" heels.

"Fetish ballet shoes!" Hope cried. She pulled out the bone shoes and sat down on one of the grand burgundy sofas to lace them up.

"Me too?" Cassandra asked doubtfully.

"Of course, you too. Can't you see they're a size 6?" replied Ambrose.

"These can't have come from Bartlett's," Hope observed.

"I special ordered them from England," said Ambrose. "Now put them on," he told Cassandra.

"Am I joining you, then?" Cassandra asked.

"You're joining us," Ambrose confirmed.

"I haven't had shoes like these on in years," Hope said,

"I wonder if I can still walk in them?" She held onto the arm of the sofa to get up on her legs and not letting go of the sofa, began to gingerly walk around it. Cassandra gazed at her in fascination. Hope straightened and began to walk with more confidence, the knack of balancing on eight-inch platform shoes coming back to her.

"Cassandra, what are you still doing in that dress?" Ambrose demanded. "Take it off and everything else you have on and put on the sheer gown for me." He sat on a high backed, wide seated, brass riveted, armless burgundy velvet chair close by them, loosening his tie, taking it off and unbuttoning the top of his shirt. "I'm just going to sit here and watch the transformation."

Hope was still experimentally walking back and forth across one of the beautifully figured Persian carpets that covered part of the planked wooden floor, as Cassandra unfastened her summer dress and let it drop to the floor. Her small, round, shapely breasts were unrestrained and stood upright, with rose nipples at full attention, but the dominant's eyes dwelt with keener interest on her exquisitely sculpted torso, with its concave abdomen and gently flaring hips.

"My panties too?" Cassandra asked, feeling her face grow warm.

"Silly, of course," said Ambrose. "Unless you think white panties go with a sheer black nightie."

Cassandra stepped out of her bikinis and now nude, picked up her garments, folded them and placed them on an end table nearby. Now she slipped off the little shoes and stowed them out of sight. She was nude, with a small, brown triangular Venus mound on display fore, and a firm, rounded, oval bottom aft. All of her movements were unhurried, thoughtful and graceful and her many attractive features brought a smile to Bartlett's normally critical face. This wasn't the first time he'd studied Cassandra's fair form. They'd played several times, with

Hope as second girl, simple spanking games, and he had already seen her bare bottom. And at the gym, where they both worked out regularly, he had taken many a yoga class with Cassandra, affording him whole hours together to observe her supple femininity. He found her genuinely lovely and had decided to turn her into one of his toys.

Cassandra slipped the sheer black gown on and became glamorously transformed into a sylph more provocative than when fully nude.

"Now let Hope help you on with the shoes," Ambrose said, approving the effect. The girls sat together on the long, broad sofa and Cassandra placed her small feet on Hope's gowned lap to have her fetish ballerina shoes laced and bucked on. Once securely shod, Cassandra watched how Hope got to her feet and imitated her technique. Her highly tuned balancing skills came into play at once and served her well in staying upright.

"Now the two of you must go for a walk around the room," said Ambrose, sitting back in his chair to watch. Hope and Cassandra took each other about the waist and began to promenade up and down the room in their 8" fetish pumps, the blonde in the luscious corset gown, the brunette in the sheer black sheath, both bottoms lifted high and projecting, both waists delicate.

Ambrose sighed, content with his club. It wasn't precisely his club. Anthony Newton's money had furnished the house and everything in it, but most of what was in it, had come from Bartlett's store and Ambrose himself, in some measure to kick back a generous portion, but mainly for his own pleasure, was the club's best customer.

Presently he stopped them and bending them over the backs of two chairs, side by side, he pulled up their skirts and spanked them. But his mood that afternoon was much more playful than severe, and he only left their bottoms pink and rosy after belaboring them with his hand for a few minutes. Then he pulled Hope to her feet, set her dress to rights, kissed her, pulled an envelope out of the inner pocket of his jacket and dismissed her.

Cassandra turned her head, but didn't get up. "You're sending her out?" she asked.

"Yes," said Ambrose. "You don't object to letting Hope get back to her birthday, do you? I'm sure she wants to show off her shoes to whoever stops by in the next hour or so."

Cassandra heard Hope totter from the room and the door softly close behind her. The next thing she heard was Mr. Barlett's zipper coming down. She turned to look at him and saw him getting out a condom. She looked at his zipper and a large, pink cock emerged and merrily wagged its head at her.

"What?" she cried. "Really? With me?"

"Where do you keep the lube?" he asked, stuffing his penis back into his pants. "Is there some in the closest bathroom?"

"The big cabinet by the door. Middle drawer," she replied, unconsciously swaying her bottom while watching him go to the oversized armoire that contained toys and other supplies.

He came back to her and turned her head to see herself in a long gold framed mirror opposite them. "See how well that gown and those shoes suit you?" he asked. "You should never dress casually for work," he admonished her, slapping her smartly again. "You're the mistress of an elegant house, you should be concerned with your image at all times."

"Like my sister?"

"Exactly so," he agreed, deftly dividing her labia and applying a few drops of clear lubricant to the entire area with a light, neat touch. "Oh," he said with surprise, digitally penetrating her for the first time, "did you know you were already wet?"

"How could I not be?" she replied. "You dressed me up

so beautifully." They both turned to look at the effect she made in the mirror. Then he got behind her again.

"Tell me something, Cassandra," said Ambrose, caressing her waist. "What makes you come?"

"Why do you want to know that, Mr. Bartlett?"

"I want to be closer to you," he said honestly.

"Then let's go to the bondage bed. You lie on your back and let me get on top. And while I'm there, you might finger my bottom," she replied, with equal honesty. "That will work."

Chapter Nine

N. Norling

As the evening came on, everyone in the house gathered in the richly paneled dining room, where Hope, still arrayed in her gorgeous gown, but now on three-inch heeled gold slippers, was presiding over an impromptu supper, provided by Anthony Newton, who had bid his secretary to order cold and warm dishes sent over from the Inn and cakes delivered from each of the bakeries in the village. Cassandra, now smartly clad in a black zip front leather dress and black boots, was pouring champagne and other libations for the guests ranged around the table, and filling their plates from the sideboard, when the bell summoned her to the front door.

There on the porch in the gathering dusk, stood a tall, slender girl of perhaps twenty-three to twenty-nine years of age, her fine, straight, light red hair pulled back in a black velvet clasp, her body snugly clad in a smoke blue suit with a short pencil skirt and fitted jacket, her long, slim legs graced by high vamp, 5-inch stack heeled pumps. She was very pale and her features fine. Her only make-up was a touch of rose lipstick and her only jewelry, a small pair of gold earrings and a golden neck chain. She carried a large black leather envelope purse and had the air of a professional as she put out her hand to shake Cassandra's and introduced herself with a confident, "Hello. I'm N. Norling. Are you Cassandra? I texted you yesterday for an appointment."

"Oh!" Cassandra cried, clasping her hand with a smile. "N. Norling is a lovely young lady! Come in. Right this way," said Cassandra, leading her guest directly into the dusky rose sitting room, off the foyer. Closing the door behind her, Cassandra gestured to one of the high-backed wing chairs that flanked the fireplace and asked her to be seated. N. Norling took in the charming room from polished planked floor to cream crown molding in a glance and smiled faintly with approval, saying, "I knew this place would be a dream."

"Thank you," said Cassandra, perching on the edge of the other chair and regarding her guest with increasing appreciation of her many attractions. "But, am I to understand that you are visiting us today as a client?"

"Does that surprise you?" the girl asked, leaning her purse against the leg of her chair and relaxing back into it.

"Well, it's not as though I've never heard of a lady booking a session, but it's a rare enough event to be remarkable. Unless..."

"Yes, unless what?" N. Norling asked.

"Unless you're seeking a female play partner, in which case, it does make a trifle more sense," Cassandra replied with a smile.

"Oh no, I want a male top, please," N. Norling replied.

"May I ask why you think you need to book a session to get that?" asked Cassandra, smiling indulgently at her guest.

N. Norling sighed and said, "Let me give you a little background about me."

"Please do!"

"My name is Naomi. I'm 29 years old and I work at the Pru, as a statistical analyst. I went to Cal Tech and then MIT. I've been at my present job for four years and head a department. I've always been focused and not frivolous. I make real money and have a lot of responsibility. My time is largely taken up by work and whatever bits of exercise I can fit in each day. I've never had time for relationships and the few boyfriends and lovers I've had have been, to a certain extent, unfulfilling. But as far back as I can remember, I've been into spanking. Starting in high school, I discovered The New Rod Quarterly and the world of spanking videos. In high school, I didn't have crushes on movie stars, I had crushes on spanking video tops. But the few dates I've had off personal ads and meet ups at support groups, have left me cold. None of the guys I've met seem to get me, and most of them want me to also spank them. That won't work for me. So here I am, with plenty of money to spend and lots of frustration to lose. What can you do for me?"

"Well, you picked an excellent day to stop in, Naomi," said Cassandra. "We're having a birthday celebration for my assistant manager, and the house is full of good looking male tops. They are friends of the house and locals. Any or all of them would be charmed beyond measure to entertain you. And if you really feel you have to pay someone, you can pay the dungeon rental fee."

"Well," she hesitated, then went on firmly, "are they really cute, the men who are here right now?"

"Oh yes, extremely cute! You mentioned you've been reading the New Rod for years; the editor, Hugo Sands, is here."

"Really? I'm about to meet Hugo Sands?" cried Naomi, her whole face lighting up. "And you think he would play with me?"

"Oh, honey," Cassandra grinned, "try and stop him, after hearing what you've come for."

"Is he as attractive as his photos?"

"I think he is," said Cassandra. "But may I ask what kind of session you had in mind? I mean, the tone of it."

"Oh yes, thank you for asking. Apart from playing with Hugo Sands, which I would love, love, love to do, I think, no, I know, I would prefer a very strict disciplinarian who will make it very real. I think I'd like to cry, at least once. I'm told it's cathartic and I've been harboring so much stress since taking my first SAT, I feel that I need to completely let go. I might not like it. But I want to find out if it's satisfying. And then, secondarily, I think I would like to experience an orgasm in a dungeon."

"We have playrooms, rather than dungeons."

"I gathered that from the video I saw on the New Rod website, the one with your assistant walking through all the rooms in different outfits. She's stunning. I couldn't take my eyes off her and I'm not even bi," said Naomi. "Yes, I loved that the rooms are rooms instead of black painted cells. It really made me feel this place is different."

"The strictest top I know is here right now, Mr. Bartlett. Are you sure you don't need some folding money? He'd happily pay a grand to be your first real top."

Naomi smiled and said, "You're not a very good businesswoman, are you? I'd ask five times that for someone like me."

"You're very astute, N. Norling," Cassandra readily agreed, "I'm a terrible businesswoman and I believe five K was exactly what Mr. Bartlett paid in the past to one Harvard girl who let him spank her to tears and give her an orgasm. Shall we ask Mr. Bartlett for that?"

"Let me meet him and I'll let you know," said Naomi.

"In that case, let me introduce you to everyone," said Cassandra, opening the door and allowing Naomi to precede her out.

"Everyone," said Cassandra, leading Naomi to the table, "this is Naomi, from Boston. She'll be joining us this evening."

Naomi took in the scene before her with surprise, not expecting to be led into a room full of attractive and handsomely dressed people of both sexes, some seated at a long table, others standing at a long sideboard loaded with platters and dishes of savories and trays of miniature cakes. The group of pretty people smiled with interest at her, pausing in their conversation as she smiled back and looked from one face to another, coming to rest at a tall, interesting looking sandy haired man in his late forties, standing at a bar at the far end of the room and pouring himself a glass of white wine.

"Isn't that Hugo Sands?" she asked Cassandra, who followed Naomi's gaze to Hugo.

"Yes, of course, I'll take you to him right away," said Cassandra, lightly taking Naomi by her slender hand and leading the newcomer to her former lover. Hugo smiled at Naomi and shook her little hand.

"Hello, are you joining Cassandra's staff?" he asked, directly.

"Is that really the only reason a girl would find her way here?" Naomi marveled. "No, not at all."

"She came to book a spanking session with a male top," Cassandra explained, smiling at the absurdity of the idea.

"Seriously?" Hugo laughed. "Just look around the room and pick any fellow out. They'll spank you for free."

"You included?" Naomi asked, her hazel eyes sparkling with excitement. Her normally pale face was tinged with pink as she gazed at her idol.

"Of course, me included. Need you ask?"

"I've been following your magazine for years. I have all the back issues as well. They got me through high school, college and grad school," she confided.

"Really?" He had heard this kind of thing before, so he was gratified but not surprised. Charmed by the lovely girl before him, he asked, "What name do you subscribe under?"

"N. Norling. Did you think I was a man all these years?"

"Yes! One of those customers who buy everything but never write anything. Generally, when a lady finds me, she writes me almost immediately," said Hugo.

"I am backward that way. It's just that I've been focused on having a career and didn't dare let myself get sidetracked by... well, that much fun," she admitted.

"Well, I'm glad you finally decided to emerge from your cocoon," Hugo said. "You look like a shy girl. Are you?"

"I'm extremely shy, normally. I'm actually horrible at dating. But here I feel as though I'm among friends."

"Do you want to go play now?" he asked.

She nodded eagerly.

"Come on then," he said, taking her hand and leading her out of the room, with many curious gazes following them.

"How old are you?" he asked, leading her across the corridor and into the paneled school room.

"Twenty-nine," she replied, her eyes immediately arrested by Laura's Trompe l'oeil window on an Edwardian street.

"What a perfect illusion," Naomi exclaimed, going closer to the mural.

"My wife painted that."

"I should have known her style," said Naomi, for she had been following Hugo closely enough for years to know that he was married to the co-illustrator of her favorite graphic novels. "I have all of their books," she said.

"I know you do," he smiled. "You've bought everything in my catalog. You have no idea how many times I've put together an order and thought, Good old N. Norling! He really likes my stuff." Hugo said, closing and locking the door.

He let her wander around the room, looking at the classic decor touches, including an old fashioned blackboard, a large teacher's desk podium and large sized retro wooden seat and desk sets.

"I'm glad you realize that you ought to be spanked," he said, finally pulling a large straight backed wooden chair away from the wall and setting it at the front of the room.

"I do?" she asked.

"You know it was imprudent to waste eleven years of

your life not being in the scene, once you knew that it existed. So, come over here," he motioned to the chair, sat down and waited for her. She did not hesitate.

After the first spanking of her life, Naomi Norling was hungry and allowed Hugo to escort her back to the dining room, lead her to the sideboard, then leave her there. She was slowly and thoughtfully selecting roasted chicken and green salad when a good-looking man of about forty in a finely tailored suit stepped up to the sideboard and introduced himself as Ambrose Bartlett.

"Oh!" Naomi said, looking up and smiling, "the strict one!"

"Who said that?" he asked.

"The Mistress," Naomi replied.

"They tell me you're here to play, not work, is that true?" he asked, taking in her slender, somewhat angular body with appreciation.

"Yes. I've never played before a half hour ago."

"And, what do you think?"

"I think I shouldn't have put this off for so long," she admitted.

"Listen, are you going to be in town tomorrow? I really want to play with you."

"I do have the day off tomorrow. I could stay over if I found a room in the village."

"Cassandra has a beautiful loft suite that she rents for overnights. Why don't you just stay here? I'd be happy to cover your expenses. Then we could play tomorrow. I'd play with you tonight, but I've already been here for hours and my wife is about to come by and I'll be leaving shortly."

"Did Cassandra tell you what I'm looking for?" Naomi asked straightforwardly.

"As a matter of fact, she did," Ambrose said. "Why do you think I'm so eager to make a date? I always make girls cry and forced orgasms is a specialty."

"Hugo did just make me cry. It was a shock, the way a spanking really feels. I cried in ten swats. Over my clothes," she confided.

"I'm glad you already got that out of your system," said Ambrose. "The other thing you're into is actually more interesting to me."

"I can probably stay around until about four or five tomorrow afternoon," said Naomi.

"I'll see you back here at two," he said.

"That would be perfect," she agreed. Then they stood looking at each other wordlessly, smiling.

"Do you come here often?" she asked.

"It's my home away from home," he admitted. "I delayed a long while before coming out in the scene," he said, "and I've been making up for that over the last few years."

"I delayed coming out until tonight!" she replied, amazed to meet another like herself.

"You look very professional, by the way," he commented. "Are you under a lot of stress in your job?"

"Yes!"

"I can see that in your shoulders. You should go take a yoga class at the gym tomorrow morning. It will relax you for later."

"Good idea," she agreed, smiling.

Ambrose wanted to ask Naomi if she was anal, but was distracted from this important query by the entrance of his wife, Pamela and her partner in their design business, Damaris. Pamela was a sleek, leggy twenty-nine-year-old beauty, with a Louise Brooks bob. Damaris Random was petite, voluptuous and strikingly attractive. The designers had just come from their studio and bore a large ribbon wrapped box for Hope.

"Who is everybody here?" Naomi asked Ambrose as she noticed him merely smile and wave at his wife without leaving her side.

"Hope, the ravishing blonde in the fancy gown, is the assistant manager of the club. It's her birthday and my wife Pamela, the tall brunette and her partner Damaris, the short brunette, are giving her a birthday outfit," said Ambrose.

"And that other skinny brunette?" Naomi asked softly, regarding Brooke Neuman, who was seated at the table beside Cameron Hayes.

"She's a film editor from Boston who may be moonlighting here and at Cassandra's sister's club in the city."

"I heard there's a club in Boston. It sounds intriguing."

"It isn't as big or posh, but it's been around a long time. I'm going to visit soon, myself."

"Who is the fellow she's talking to?"

"He's a sex researcher whose been busily recruiting research assistants from Cassandra and her sister's staff."

"What is he researching?"

"BDSM workers and entertainers."

"So, he's really legit?"

"Either that or he's come up with a very roundabout way to spread pelf around in the scene," said Ambrose.

"Who's the other pretty blonde sitting across from the birthday blonde?" Naomi asked.

"That's my ex-wife Paula. She's currently married to the fellow sitting across the table from her, Sloan Taylor. And the redhead sitting next to him is his partner in the village bookshop."

"And everyone here is in the scene?"

"Yes. The redhead is Marguerite Alexander, she writes as Alma. You've probably read her stories in Hugo's magazine."

"I have! She's wonderful. Will you introduce me?"

Hope had sprung up from her seat and was expressing

her rapturous approval of the selection of tweed separates that Damaris and Pamela had brought her from their smart little shop. This left the seat beside Marguerite Alexander empty and Ambrose presently deposited Naomi there before joining the trio examining Hope's presents.

"It's a classic hacking jacket," said Pamela, holding up the garment she had tailor made to Hope's exact measurements. "And you've got riding pants, a coordinating skirt and cropped vest."

"And two white shirts," said Damaris, bringing out the beautifully tailored pieces from the deep box.

Off to the side, and momentarily abandoned by Brooke, who had gone to assemble a small dessert plate, Cameron Hayes was at leisure to inspect the newcomer as Naomi engaged the gratified Marguerite with her heartfelt praise of the writer's novels.

Cameron overheard Naomi confess that she had literally learned how to orgasm through reading Marguerite's books.

Cameron was eager to engage the red-haired girl in conversation as soon as possible, not only because she was so attractive and composed, but because he now knew for a fact, that she had actually walked into the club as a client. The psychological make-ups of clients were an important part of the study he was engaged in, and the rarest of all clients were female. But the young lady somehow eluded him throughout most of the evening. After spending some time at the table with Marguerite Alexander, Cameron saw Hope and Pamela lead Naomi from the room, for a stroll around the house and grounds that seemed to him, to last a very long time.

When he wandered into the lounge to wait for the girls to reemerge, he noticed Ambrose Bartlett behind the bar, pouring something amber colored over ice. Cameron sat at the bar and said, "Got another one of those?"

"Sure," said Ambrose, prepping a Scotch.

"Was that your wife who went off with Hope and the auburn-haired girl just now?"

"Yes, wife is Pamela," Ambrose returned with a smile. "And the auburn-haired girl is Naomi."

"I guess you've made good progress then?" Cameron observed.

"I thought she was a pro when she first walked in and was happy to book a session with her, but she's a play-starved thrill seeker from the business world, here to collect some experiences with us. She's Boston based, like you, so you'll have no end of chances to court her," said the department store owner helpfully.

Ambrose had no desire to keep any one girl exclusively to himself. He was too thinly spread as it was, and wasn't yet done collecting pets. And then, he was growing fonder of his own wife all the time. Pamela's recent independent successes with her clothing line had given her a confidence and dash she had never had before. He congratulated himself on the aplomb he had displayed in not meddling with her harmless love affair with Dru Baxter. Dru had gone happily back to college the previous week and Pamela glowed with her own daring and sophistication.

Scene couples from the village came and went in the lounge over the next hour, and everyone Cameron was introduced to by Cassandra, was disposed to chat agreeably with him for as long as he wished, about the chain of events which had caused he or she to come out in the scene and begin seeking interactions with their own kind. Naomi finally reappeared and made for the bar. Cameron slipped behind it, in order to serve her.

"What can I get you?" he asked.

"Just a club soda," she replied, looking just a trifle like a business girl who had been up since six, done a full day's work, had the most eventful evening of her life, cried real tears from a spanking and was quite ready to go to bed.

"I've been wanting to meet you all night," he said.

"Hello," she said, putting out her slender hand to shake his. He pressed her hand lightly then handed her a glass of sparkling water. She sipped and looked at him over the rim.

"You're the sex researcher from Boston, right?" she asked.

"I am. You're from Boston too, I hear."

"Yes. But I don't want to be researched."

"Oh, that makes me sad. You look so interesting."

"You look interesting too. Maybe you should call me sometime. But not to ask me sex research questions."

"Give me your number," he said, handing her his phone. Naomi put her number into it. "If I call you, will you go out with me?"

"You mean have a play date?"

"Any kind of date," he said helpfully. "Though of course, a play date would be outstanding."

"I'll see if I have time later in the week," she promised.

"Thank you!"

"Maybe we could meet at that dungeon I've been hearing about in Brookline, the one the sister of the mistress here owns."

"Perfect, I'm there quite often."

"Oh?"

"Carola, the mistress of the house, is helping me collect data."

"Is she training you how to spank girls?"

"I already know that," he replied.

"Good."

Chapter Ten

Players, Not Sweethearts

Early on the following Wednesday evening, Naomi betook herself to Carola Campi's club in Brookline, to meet Cameron Hayes. She was admitted by Lydia, the curvy graduate student with hair to her waist, dressed in a short leather jumper with a pleated skirt, stack-heeled oxfords and white anklets. Lydia led Naomi directly into the front parlor, where her new playmate was on his feet, waiting for her.

"Hello," he said, taking her small hand in his large, cool hand and holding it for just a moment. "Thank you for coming."

"Didn't you think I would?" asked the slender statistician, pausing to look at him intently.

"Let's sit here and talk for a moment," he said, leading her to the long, upholstered window seat under the bay window that looked out on the street. "May I ask you a few questions before we go in a dungeon?"

"Of course," she said, sitting down beside him, and smoothing the pencil skirt of her beautifully tailored light brown wool suit, with its nipped waist and narrow lapels. A white blouse with short collar points and sexy brown stiletto heeled booties completed the young businesswoman's outfit to crisp perfection and Cameron was charmed by the obvious care she had taken in presenting herself to him that night. Around her slender throat she wore a pink pearl on a gold chain and there were pink pearl studs in her delicate ear lobes. Her skin was creamy white and her shoulder length light auburn hair was straight, shiny and parted on the side, sometimes falling forward, over her brow, in the style of Veronica Lake. Altogether, Naomi looked twice as provocative as the other night in Random Point.

"You look just lovely, by the way," he began, pressing her hand lightly again. She smiled but didn't thank him. Her mind was racing ahead of this interview, to the terrible and delicious moment when he would take her by the arm and turn her over his knee. "But do you consent to me raising that smart skirt tonight? Or would you be more comfortable if it were to be over your clothes the first time?"

"What would you propose?" she asked.

"I would propose starting over your clothes but peeling away the layers in stages."

"Is that how it's normally done?"

"That's how I normally do it."

"What other questions did you have?" she asked.

"Fast and stingy, or slow and thuddy?"

"I don't know. I've only played twice in my life, and both times occurred the other night. I have no idea of what I like."

"Well, what happened the other night?"

"Do you really want to know how two other men... handled me?"

"Why not?"

"It wouldn't make you jealous or turn you off to hear that sort of thing?"

"Certainly not. It's kind of what I do for a living."

"Well, Hugo Sands, the editor, spanked me over my clothes, hard and fast, with no warm up. It was a very short spanking and I was crying on the sixth swat. There were ten all together."

"Oh!"

"Don't look worried. It was my first spanking. I didn't know what to expect. I wasn't prepared for it being so hard or hurting so much. But I had always wanted to cry from a spanking. And afterwards, he hugged me. I knew he'd be a hard spanker. I've been reading his magazine since high school. Anyway, I was bound to cry. It was my first spanking. I was emotionally moved by it."

"I see. What about the second one?"

"That happened the next day. Mr. Bartlett, the department store owner, came back to the club in the early afternoon and we went into the medical examining room. I had always wanted to orgasm from a spanking. I had told Cassandra that. She set me up with Mr. Bartlett because, well, I guess she knew he had the skills to make that happen; and he likes skinny girls. She suggested that I charge him money to spank me, but I make good money so I'm not interested in that."

"She tried to turn you out?" Cameron chuckled.

"Yes. But it wasn't in a mercenary way. She was just bemused that any young lady would pay a man to spank her. The opposite way seemed to make more sense to her."

"She's only basing that on the fact that women usually have no trouble finding men to play with them, whereas men have a lot of trouble doing the same thing."

"I get that. Men can be very dorky."

"Yes. That's true. I hear a lot of women complaining that men are like kids nowadays. So, they don't look up to them anymore."

"I'm not close to any men, so I couldn't comment on that."

"That may be about to change," thought Cameron, taking her by the hand and leading her across the hall into the cocoa toned, snugly shuttered and dark wood paneled playroom Carola designated as Dungeon #1. They entered the room two strangers and left it, an hour later, as lovers.

Meanwhile, upstairs, on the second floor, Carola Campi was pacing her photo studio in a state of disgruntled anxiety. She had known Cameron Hayes just one week, had seen him just three times, when he'd come to the house to interview models and professional girls. She'd been put on his payroll with a handsome monthly stipend, for allowing her club to serve as his laboratory for the season; and she'd given him a few lessons in bondage and related BDSM arts. Their relationship had so far been strictly professional, and Carola was displeased by that. And now, before she had even had a chance to seduce him, as she was entirely partial to younger men - he was about ten years her junior - a willowy redhead had appeared to beguile him away from her. Carola knew the minute she looked out the window and saw slender, faultlessly tailored Naomi, emerge from her sleek sedan, that she had a dangerous rival. She knew even before that, when her sister Cassandra had sent her a text about the interesting young lady who had showed up as a client the other night and was determined to make Carola's club her go-to rental play space in Boston.

For the first half hour of the session, Carola heard the usual smacking noises through the floorboards. She identified hand, leather paddle, wooden paddle, leather strap, and even birch. This went on with brief intervals of silence in between implements. But for the second half hour, Carola heard nothing at all. And yet, they didn't emerge. Therefore, Carola knew that the play date had already morphed into a hook up. This knowledge caused stab after painful stab of jealousy to shoot through her flat stomach, as the hour dragged on. Finally, their time in the dungeon was up. Cameron had pre-paid her for an hour's time and she now went downstairs and lightly knocked on the door then disappeared into the office to tell Lydia that she had a session at ten and could go to dinner now for the next few hours.

Cameron escorted Naomi out to her car and watching out the window, in spite of her resolve not to be so obvious, Carola saw him kiss the redhead on the mouth before putting her into her car and watching her drive away.

"This is bad," Carola thought, "very bad. They'll be married before I have a chance to get him upstairs!"

But when Cameron came back to collect his computer before going home, she simply smiled at him and asked him how it had gone, with the mildest of academic interest.

"It went well," he replied, with a similarly mild smile. "What a case history she'll be when I finally get her talking."

"Right, I didn't hear you doing much talking," Carola grinned, content to be his buddy for the moment. There was no hurry to have him that minute. Much, much better to wait until he visibly hungered for her too. And that would happen. It had happened many times before.

Cameron had the grace to flush a bit at her allusion, but didn't comment further. They said good night and he promised to return in a day or two to continue with the interviews.

Over the next ten days, Cameron and Naomi met two more times at Carola's club, the second time playing in Dungeon 2, upstairs, the room with the St. Andrews Cross on the wall and the high bondage bed, and the third time, returning to the first-floor playroom. Each time, Cameron punished her thoroughly first, then made extremely creative love to her, safely and with some of the sexy toys he'd purchased for this use at the hippest shop he could find in the Combat Zone. He didn't hesitate to submit her to a butt plug, a Hitachi wand, double penetration masturbation and spread and plugged bondage plus spanking, to force her to climax, each and every time, so far. As they got to know each other better and became more at ease with each other's bodies, the need for these accessories would gradually decrease, but for now, he felt it necessary to wow her each time she presented herself to him.

Naomi insisted on paying for the dungeon rentals after their first meeting. For, during their after-play conversation, she had extracted exact details from her new friend about his financial position, and had learnt that he was on a tight budget. Cameron thought that sweet but also felt it was high time to move out of the dungeon and into the realm of dating. They found it easy to talk to each other, even easier to make love to each other and the chemical attraction between them was growing stronger every day.

Therefore, at the conclusion of their third play date, as Naomi was buttoning up her blouse and casting a rueful grin back at her slim, rosy bottom, glowing through a pair of sheer bikini panties she had just pulled back on, Cameron began to talk to her about taking their sexual friendship to the next level. But the moment he did so, she started to shake her head, her straight, shiny hair falling across her cheek, then flipping back. He loved her hair and pushed it back behind her small ear caressingly.

"Why, no?" he asked; "Don't you like me?"

"I don't have time to date," she replied firmly. "My job is incredibly demanding. I work late every night and I'm up early. After I go to the gym, I'm exhausted. I just want to go to sleep. I'm not fit for any relationship."

"Well, why not work a little less?"

"I can't. I'm a department head."

"Delegate responsibilities."

"I'm the only one I trust to do certain things."

"I see," he replied, displeased at the turn of the conversation. He thought it would be simple to transform their play relationship into a real one and never dreamed she'd fight the idea. "Okay. I understand," he said.

"I'm sorry, Cameron. I'd understand if you didn't want

to see me anymore. I don't want you to feel used by me," she said softly.

"I could hardly feel that. We've both had fun. The most fun two people in the scene can have. No one has used anyone. We've served each other, that's all. And I'm happy to continue in this way," he said, suppressing his desire to take her back over his knee, and giving her a gentle kiss instead.

It happened that as they were leaving the club, one of the girls he had met on his visit to Random Point several weeks before, and had given a large amount of work to do, was at that moment entering. Brooke Neuman, the young film cutter, was dropping off for Cameron, several expertly conducted, shot and edited video interviews, that she had prepared for his study. He had set her up with the interview candidates, placed her in one of Carola's dungeons or parlors, and she had done the rest, based on a list of questions he had supplied her with.

"Hello!" cried Brooke, meeting them in the hall. "I have the first two interviews!" Dressed in skinny black jeans, thigh boots and a cropped black leather jacket over a white open collared shirt, she was dynamically beautiful. Brooke blushed under Cameron's admiring gaze and pulled a few DVDs in plain black cases out of her shoulder purse.

"You work fast!" he said appreciatively. "Oh, Brooke, do you remember Naomi? She was at the Venus Club a few weeks ago."

"Yes, of course," said Brooke, warmly smiling at Naomi. Naomi smiled back, though with less warmth and said, "Hi."

"Do you want to wait a minute and I'll write you a check?" he asked.

"Look at them first and make sure they're okay," suggested Brooke. "You can mail me the check tomorrow."

She had the air of a young woman with many more stops to make that evening and Cameron didn't try to detain her. But the faint redolence of her light floral perfume hung in the hall for moments after her departure.

Cameron walked a thoughtful Naomi out to her car on the quiet street, through which the first cool breeze of September whipped. Suddenly she turned to him and said, "All right. We can have a date."

Chapter Eleven

Brooke Neuman

Between her absorbing work at the Historical Society, adjusting to life in a new city and the freelance video interviews she had been working on for Cameron, Brooke hadn't had time to reflect on the absence of a romance or relationship in her life. But now, as she walked up to Mass. Ave to catch the tram, Brooke did begin to ponder on her single state, suddenly realizing that she was achingly in need of a love affair.

Brooke was now beginning her professional career. She was in a marvelous city, with a rare opportunity at the Historical Society, that would assure her a respectable career for the rest of her life. But the documentary film that Cameron was putting together, was even more pertinent, for she herself wanted to shoot independent films. The experience she'd get with Cameron, would get her in the game immediately.

After dropping off her first projects to Cameron, and seeing him for just a moment, in the hallway, with the very attractive Naomi at his side, Brooke began to consider her new boss. She had pretended to be in a hurry to leave, because of the presence of Naomi, but would have liked to have stayed and chatted with Cameron. On the tram, Brooke mused upon whether he would watch her videos right away or merely toss them on a pile.

She stopped at a small market and bought some fruit, bread and cheese. Her apartment was a second-floor railroad flat in a curved Beaux Arts building within sight of Fenway Park. It had, as yet, but a few sticks of furniture, which gave her a great deal of space in which to pace restlessly back and forth across the creaky dark wood floors. At least her bedroom was properly set up, with a pleasant queen-sized sleigh bed, a few wooden chests, a cheval mirror and a leather upholstered trunk bench.

Brooke finally began unpacking her clothes and putting them away. When she came to her collection of fine lingerie, including Loire silks from Paris and costly custom corsetry, all gifts from her wealthy former patron, Carter Webster, Brooke remembered that she was lonely.

She picked up her phone and texted Cameron, "Are you presently engaged?" He texted back immediately, "No, I was just heading home." For he had parted from Naomi and had been walking towards the tram stop to return to his flat in Myrtle Street on Beacon Hill. Now he leaned against a lamp post to continue their message exchange, which rapidly proceeded to Brooke inviting him over to share her bread and cheese and asking him to bring a bottle of Shiraz.

Thirty minutes later he was knocking at her door, bearing two bottles of wine. She led him into the dining room, in which there was a solid round wooden table and four chairs. Brooke asked him if he would help her uncrate her favorite posters and hang them, as her most important possessions had just arrived from New York, where she had most recently resided for several years. He readily agreed and also opened the first bottle of wine.

They sat and nibbled on the crusty French bread, mild cheese, apples and walnuts Brooke had brought home. They talked and drank wine, making each other laugh and smile. He pried about her past in a clinical manner that she found impossible to resist. As a sexual researcher, he was interested in her level of experience without judgment or jealousy. Though, with his growing personal admiration for the beautiful Brooke, he was eager to learn of her tastes in detail in order to more successfully seduce her.

He had taken Hope's advice and only given her the smallest of spankings during their fifteen-minute session at The Venus Club, treating it as a formality he was undergoing for the sake of wooing her as a research assistant. He was instantly hungry for her, but she didn't have to know that. He had found sex much more exciting when the girl thought it was all her idea. He wanted Brooke to seduce him. And it seemed as though they were on that exact road, for it was she who had invited him over. He supposed he had Naomi to thank for that, just as he had Brooke to thank for Naomi's finally agreeing to see him outside of the club.

Come to that, he wondered if he shouldn't confess to Brooke, how far things had already gone with the enigmatic statistician who was so wild behind dungeon doors. Or was he getting ahead of himself? He suddenly noticed that the first bottle of wine was almost gone and that Brooke seemed to be insisting that he hadn't really seen a movie until he'd seen a pre-code one.

"You don't know much about early twentieth century culture, do you?" she accused him. "I can teach you things about sex you never even thought of, just by showing you an early Lubitsch film."

"I want to learn," he asserted, smiling at her.

"You do?"

"Of course! Be my muse."

"You seem to have a knack for saying the right thing," ventured Brooke.

"I just listen first," he admitted.

"Is that how you broke down Hope's resistance?"

"Who said I did that?"

"I'm just fishing."

"Don't be naughty."

"She used to never have sex with clients," said Brooke; "back in Hollywood. But that was six years ago. Six years

89

is a long time with one man, even as fine a one as Mr. Lawrence."

"He used to be your teacher, didn't he?"

"Yes, my high school English teacher." Brooke sighed.

"Are you still in love with him?"

"Of course," Brooke admitted, handing him the second bottle to open.

"Did you two play that night?"

"In Random Point? Oh no, it was too late and I don't know, it seemed too abrupt to start playing out of the blue." Brooke looked at him and noticed that he had barely drank one glass of wine. She saw him studying her face and said, "Are you thinking about how easy it would be to take advantage of me now?"

"Stop reading my mind," he returned.

"Are you seeing that girl, the one who was with you tonight at Carola's?" she asked.

"We've played, but we haven't gone out yet."

"Are you going to start dating her now?"

"I was going to," he admitted.

"So, you like her a lot?"

"I do like her," Cameron replied. "So, I should probably leave now."

"You think it would upset her if you...saw me too, once in a while?" Brooke ventured.

"Would that arrangement work for you?"

"It might," she said lightly.

"I don't want you to think I'm not dying to take you right this second, but I don't want you to feel that I'm just using you for casual sex."

"So, don't be casual about it. Give it all you've got in you. Make it real, make it matter," said Brooke, fixing him with an intense gaze. "After all, you're a sex researcher. Own it. Perfect it. Widen your experience as well as your second-hand research, I say."

"You sound like you're making up my mind for me," he

smiled, taking her hand and kissing it on the back.

"I like what you just said about taking me right this second," Brooke encouraged him, her eyes going to the table.

They rose at the same moment and silently began to clear away the plates and utensils.

The next morning, they woke up together, had coffee together for the first time, and felt comfortable with each other. They'd had sex in the kitchen. Then went to bed and had sex again. It was all very normal. Which puzzled Brooke. She had thought him to be in the scene. But that he gave her no spanking foreplay perplexed her. She thought back to the fifteen-minute session at the Venus Club. He had hardly spanked her then. Not by her standards. Now she began to wonder whether he wasn't an ordinary vanilla. She asked him this over coffee and toast.

"No, I'm just playing it cool," he smiled. "Didn't want to come on all pervy the first time we were together."

"Why not?" Brooke asked, looking cute in white babydoll pajamas, her long black hair loose.

"I don't know, I thought it would seem predatory," he explained.

"But I was the one who asked you over," she protested.

"Am I being overly civilized?" he asked.

"Over civilized like a fox," she accused him. "You just want me to chase you for that spanking, don't you?"

"Yes," he confessed. "You're one step ahead of me."

"Why do you want me to chase you?" she asked.

"I just find that sexual response is better when the object is fully invested in the outcome."

"You're too smart by half," she credited him.

"Well, let me go back to my place and review your videos," he said, getting up to leave. She had to quickly dress for work herself and saw him to the door without detaining him.

"Thank you for keeping me company last night," she said, "I was feeling blue all alone in this small city and I reached out to you. You were there for me and I won't forget it."

"Believe me, it was my pleasure. Call me anytime," he said, hugging her warmly. "I'll be in touch."

Chapter Twelve

The Player as Artist

Cameron went home to shower and change his clothes, then proceeded, with Brooke's edits, to Carola's club, where she had set him up a comfortable work station in her office. When he got there, Carola was in a session, but Lydia, her usual assistant, was at her own computer, answering queries and captioning a photo story for one of Carola's damsel in distress bondage magazines. Cameron set up one of Brooke's DVDs in a player and he and Lydia reviewed it together, agreeing that the interview had been well conducted, filmed and edited by Brooke. Lydia was in a black velvet dress with white collar, black stockings and stack heeled maryjanes. Her long, shiny brown hair was straight almost to her small waist and she had the face of a Pre-Raphaelite muse. Cameron asked her if she wanted to be part of his transcription team, turning the videos Brooke was editing into transcripts, for one would be needed for each film. Lydia told him she was a good typist and currently completing a master's degree in English at Boston University. She asked him how much the job paid and he told her to do one and tell him what she thought fair.

At this point, Carola came down, bid her client goodbye in the hall and looked in on them. Carola was pleased at Cameron adding Lydia to his ongoing budget, for she was very fond of her pet and this was further proof of her new benefactor's good sense. She looked at some of the video Lydia was going to transcribe and told Cameron that she might be able to take similar videos of selected male clients, and thus furnish him with a different demographic.

"Some of them are exhibitionists and are dying to talk about themselves and their fantasies," she explained. "I have quite a few clients who would jump at the chance to be in a fetish survey, especially when they imagine sexy female graduate students, in white coats, skirts and pumps, studying their case histories."

"I won't charge you much per subject," she said. "I already have a studio set up and I shoot quickie videos there all the time."

"Whatever you think is fair after you've done one."

"It won't need editing. I often shoot with one camera," she said confidently.

"Smart!"

Carola smiled, happy to have gotten her way so easily, feeling even more elated at this new source of added income. She asked him what his plans were for the afternoon. He said he was going to interview a lady who described herself as a thrill seeker and was contemplating coming to work for Carola.

"Oh, you mean Marion Craig. Yes, I'd have her working in my dungeon tonight if she wasn't so paranoid about being spotted and outted. She's sexually frustrated and has little free time. She needs an outlet. You should let me conduct the interview and you can film us together. Then, if it goes off the rails, I can use the second part as a video. But she can only be filmed without her face showing."

"What do you mean goes off the rails?"

"She's such a little slut, that girl."

"Carola, you talk like that?" Cameron smiled.

"You'll see."

Cameron did see exactly what Carola meant when Marion arrived, slim and sleek in a curve hugging black suit and shiny black pumps, her dark hair worn in a long, wavy bob, parted on one side and brushed back from her brow. Her skin was pale, and her features fine. Marion's large, dark eyes were full of mischief that day, especially when she saw how attractive the academic who had contacted her about the interview really was.

Marion had no objection to Carola conducting the interview or Cameron working the camera. They went up to the studio and were set up in minutes, due to Carola's efficiency and experience. Having just done a role play session where she had acted the part of a teacher, Carola was suitably attired in a gray pencil skirt, a white open collared shirt and a pair of stack-heeled gray and white oxfords with five-inch heels. Her long, black hair was pulled back in a black velvet clasp. The women sat, Carola in a leather chair, and Marion on a leather sofa, at interview distance from each other. Cameron supplied Carola with a list of questions and they began. He had learned, earlier in the week, how to operate Carola's cameras and tripods, and they had agreed to set this shoot up in a way that would protect Marion's anonymity.

For the first fifteen minutes, Marion behaved with propriety. But she became increasingly impatient to start having fun and began to answer some of the questions put to her recklessly or provocatively. Marion liked women and Carola was the most beautiful and elegant player she had yet come across in Boston. Carola radiated power and poise and Marion wanted to submit to her. Confident that she could get Marion to sign a model's release later, or at the very least, sell Marion the footage for her private use, Carola discarded her questions, took Marion by the hair and forced her to her knees at her feet. Then she looked down into Marion's upturned face and told her how tightly she intended to tie her and how shockingly she intended to tease her and then how severely she intended to spank her, to teach her not to be such a little slut.

Marion melted into a pool of acquiescence as Cameron

found himself transformed from documentary film maker to professional fetishographer. Constantly adjusting his cameras, he proceeded to capture Carola stripping Marion, hogtieing her on the sofa, tickle torturing her, and finally, dragging Marion over her skirted lap for a protracted spanking.

Marion was allowed to take the video home and watch it for a few days before deciding whether she would allow Carola to release it. Cameron was authorized to, at the minimum, keep the written transcript for the study. And Carola had broken in her new girl. She even made sure that Marion got a session before sending her home, as a spanking switch happened to visit late that afternoon and was easily intrigued by the idea of topping a pretty, slender brunette in a business suit.

Before he left Carola's club, Lydia handed him the transcript she had taken from the tape he had left with her earlier in the day. She told him she thought the job was worth $100, as it had taken her a total of three hours, but if he planned to give her regular transcription work, she would pro-rate it to $75 a job. He wrote her a check for $75 dollars and left the club with a sense of accomplishment.

Cameron knew that Brooke got off work at five p.m. and looked up the address of the Boston Historical Society Film Restoration Annex, a three-story brownstone in the neighborhood of the Museum of Fine Arts. He was on the pavement outside the front entrance of the building in time to catch her coming out. It was still sunny and balmy on that early September evening and Brooke's delighted demeanor at the sight of him matched the weather's soft embrace.

"You came to meet me?" she cried, giving him both her hands for a moment.

"I thought you might like to get a bite with me. And

then let me show you where I live," he suggested.

"Sounds good! Where shall we go?"

"Have you ever been to The Charles Street Steak House?"

"No, but I love the name."

"It's right in my neighborhood. We'll catch the train, shall we?"

They went down in the subway, quickly caught a train to the Boston Common, got out and walked the few blocks up to cobbled Charles Street, where Cameron conducted her to an unpretentious grill featuring a limited menu consisting of steaks, baked potatoes and green salads. Within ten minutes they were seated at a table in the window with their savories before them and Cameron pouring them red wine from a half bottle he'd ordered.

"Did you get a chance to review my video?" she asked.

"Yes, and I already have a transcript of it. Lydia at Carola's club prepared it for me."

"So, satisfactory?"

"Extremely professional. You do nice, clean work. Mistress saw it too and suddenly got very competitive."

"Carola? What do you mean?

"She not only assured me that she too was capable of filming interviews, but that she could also provide me with subjects, and even interact with them on camera."

"How, interact?"

"As a visible interviewer, and more." Cameron chuckled at the memory of the show Carola and Marion had put on today. "And whatever I can't use for the study, she'll market under her own imprint. Clever, she is."

"I was thinking of going to work at her dungeon part time, but if you're satisfied with my work, I'd rather use my energies on your project, especially if some of it could go into my portfolio. I think it would be a better career move and a better use of my time, don't you?"

"Absolutely!"

"You really can give me regular work like this?"

"All you can handle. But you never told me how much you're charging me for the filming and editing."

"Why don't we say two bills a job complete?"

"Sounds fair to me."

"If some jobs are longer than others, I'll amend that," she added.

"I agree."

"How many case histories do you plan to document?"

"Five hundred."

"In that case, recruiting Carola isn't a bad idea."

After they finished their meal, Cameron led Brooke two blocks up and across Beacon Hill to the hundred and ten-year-old walk-up on Myrtle Street, in which he occupied the top floor back apartment. The tiny one bedroom had been recently remodeled with wooden floors, fresh paint, tiling and appliances. Brooke was not surprised to observe how ergonomically furnished and well equipped the space was. The main room was arranged as a sort of office/den, with a long wooden computer table, two media storage chests on wheels, two rolling desk chairs, a large TV monitor mounted on the opposite wall, a gray tweed sofa and two matching armless chairs.

Brooke asked him if he wanted to smoke a bowl. He assented and showed her how the kitchen window led out to a roof where they could sit and watch the Citgo Sign change colors as the sun went down.

"What are you doing this weekend?" he asked.

"I thought I'd go back to Random Point and hang out with Hope at the club. She said an old client of ours from the Hollywood days was coming out to the Cape specially to see us. And we're each getting a grand."

"I thought you said you weren't going to do sessions now," he protested mildly.

"I'm not going to seek them out, but this is special, and

of course, The Venus Club is going to be my happy place, from now on," she confided. "It's a lot different from Carola's, isn't it?"

"Yes, I see that. It's where the best of the best belongs," he replied.

"You agree then, it feels safer and more discreet, doesn't it?"

"No question. And then, that formidable former detective has the house next door."

"Exactly. Whereas, at Carola's, you could get walk ins. It's sketchier."

They smoked for a minute without talking.

Then Cameron said, "I'm going to encourage my friend Naomi to start moonlighting at Carola's."

"Really?"

"She has so much catching up to do."

"You haven't actually seen her outside of at Carola's yet, have you?" Brooke asked.

"No. But I left it up to her to pick a day or evening she had free. Now I hope she doesn't."

Brooke didn't speak for a moment. Then she said, "That's good to know."

"I'd better come to Random Point with you," he said decisively.

"Oh?"

"I still have so many people to interview there," he disclosed. "And someone should at least try to prevent you from seducing Hope's husband."

"I agree. Someone should try."

Chapter Thirteen

Mrs. Newton

Anthony and Susan were married in the middle of September, in the Greenwich Village townhouse, by a Justice of the Peace, with only a small group in attendance, composed of Hugo and Laura Sands, Diana and Plastridge Currie and Sherman and Patricia Cooper (nee Fairservice). They immediately adjourned to their favorite neighborhood bistro and feasted for several hours. As Anthony was involved with the final preparations for launching a new play, no honeymoon had as yet been scheduled. Susan had kept the original wedding dress Anthony had bought for her several years before, when they had been going to piggyback their own wedding onto Damaris and William's, in Las Vegas. Susan had backed out at that time, having witnessed an unpleasant breakup between Marguerite and her then husband, Malcolm, that same day. But she had hung onto the Valentino dress. The dress was exquisite and Susan was in full late-twenties bloom, golden haired and pink cheeked with embarrassment at being the center of attention.

The first thing next day, Anthony had to go to the theatre. And the little cook, Josette arrived. For she would be able to complete her final course requirements by commuting to the Culinary Institute twice a week and would be able to qualify for her diploma in a few months, while simultaneously beginning her tenure as the Newton's resident chef.

Susan descended to the kitchen of the compact and well-ordered house, dressed for work, in a short, gray tweed suit, white blouse and black knee boots, her long hair loose but ready to be crowned with the black wool beret she had brought down with her along with her large, envelope purse. Small, neat Josette was standing in the middle of the gleaming red and blue tiled kitchen, receiving instructions from Dennis, on how the appliances worked and where supplies were stored.

A modest Englishman of thirty, Dennis was slim, clean shaven, short haired, handsome, and soft spoken. He wore black trousers, and a gray vest over his white shirt with the sleeves rolled. Dennis had never worn a uniform, but received a nice clothing allowance on top of his generous salary, with which to dress sharply, and did.

He seemed a little flustered that morning at the sudden responsibility of initiating Josette into the household, and was additionally uncertain as to the attitude he should take towards her. He'd come to know and like Josette over the summer, when she had her fellow student chef had worked in the kitchen of Anthony's house in Random Point. But now there was no male co-worker for Josette in the house besides himself, and he was most definitely in domestic authority over her.

Not that Josette would need any watching, chiding or corrections, she was a well-trained cook and had put out ambrosia for them all for several months running. But Mr. Newton had hinted to Dennis that Josette was "subbed out" and in need of a "toppy" love interest as soon as possible, and then he had raised his eyebrows meaningfully at Dennis. And he had added that nothing would make him, Anthony happier, than to see Dennis properly settled with a nice young lady who would value his many fine qualities and never let him down.

Anthony had also discussed with Susan, the possibility of Josette and Dennis becoming a couple, and she had thought the idea sound. For while it was true that in the past, Dennis had displayed many submissive tendencies himself, his innate bossiness had been asserting itself in recent years and he had, in several ways, demonstrated dominant capabilities. At any rate, Anthony and Susan had agreed that Dennis could always keep a mistress on the side for purposes of foot worship., etc., without impinging upon or damaging this prospective primary relationship with a submissive girl of his own.

Susan thought of these things as she regarded her new cook over a cup of coffee, that first morning of her married life.

"Let's sit down," said Susan, motioning Josette to a seat across the long wooden table from her. Dennis disappeared into the pantry to take an inventory of the stores, but still remained within earshot of his mistress and new co-worker.

Susan made Josette pour herself a cup of coffee and then smiled at the tiny brunette, with her short, shiny, straight black hair and large dark eyes, set in a charming little face with a rosebud mouth.

"Is that what you'll be wearing every day?" Susan asked, regarding Josette's typical black pants, white chef's tunic and little black shoes.

"Is it all right?" Josette asked, her hand going nervously to her collar.

"Is that what you want to wear?" Susan asked.

"Do I have a choice?" Josette asked timidly. She had only encountered Susan a few times, over the summer, as Susan had only come out to the Cape on weekends, until the very last few weeks of the season, and their interactions had been minimal. Now, instead of being Josette's boss's vacationing girlfriend, she was the mistress of the house, and about to leave for her own job. Susan thus suddenly seemed a much more important personage than Josette had formerly considered her.

"Oh certainly, why not?" Susan asked. "What would you like to wear? You don't have to wear a uniform at all, you know."

"Then, I'd prefer pants and a shirt, with a cute apron over them," Josette replied. "This jacket is too hot most of the time and white gets dirty so fast. It's not practical."

"You will have all the cute aprons you like," Susan smiled. "Now, let me tell you just a few things about your master," Susan began. She knew, straight from Anthony's lips, that Josette was a romantic child who wished to consider her new boss more in the role of master than employer and was not opposed to this arrangement. "He's busy and his time is very valuable. Try to stay out of his way, unless he sends for you. He likes you very much, because you are quiet and competent. Cultivate these traits and you'll have this job for as long as you wish. Am I right, Dennis?" Susan addressed her last remark to Dennis as he reentered the kitchen.

"To be sure," Dennis agreed, then began to make up that day's shopping list.

"All right, young lady, bring him up his coffee, you know how he likes it, and he'll let you know if he wants any breakfast," said Susan, rising to leave. "Normally Dennis would go up, as you know, but I believe he wants to give you some instructions about dinner."

Dennis followed her out of the kitchen and stopped her in the foyer, handing her an umbrella from the stand by the door. "It's going to rain," he said.

"Oh, thank you," she smiled, adding, "How do you think it's going with Little?" she nodded back in the direction of the kitchen, inwardly delighted to finally be taller than someone in the house.

"It's going well," he said, and they both paused to watch Josette start up the stairs with the coffee tray.

When she was out of earshot, Susan said, "She's adorable, isn't she? Like a little doll. Take her shopping later and buy her some cute aprons. Lots of them. Anthony will like that."

But when she brought her eyes back to Dennis' face, she saw that he wasn't looking after Josette anymore, but fondly gazing at her. It was the first genuinely affectionate glance he had given her since their trouble the previous year, after which relations had greatly cooled between mistress and man.

"Why are you smiling at me like that?" she asked.

"I'm just glad you're finally married, and behaving so confidently with the girl. It reminds me of when you first began living here and constantly bossed me around in front of your girlfriends."

"Whatever the reason, it's nice to see you smile. Now you have someone of your own to boss around," said Susan.

Anthony Newton came down to the kitchen a few minutes later, grabbed his second cup of coffee, sat at the long wooden table and reached for a tablet to read the headlines, smiling at Josette, and ordering scrambled eggs and toast to be prepared, just as he liked them. Josette tremblingly set to work, thrilling in every fiber to be near him like this again.

"Are you happy to be here?" he asked, only half paying attention to her murmur of assent, as he scanned the New York Times. "I want Dennis to take you shopping for the kitchen today, Josette. I expect you'll want equipment."

"I can probably do better from professional suppliers online," Josette suggested.

"That's fine. My secretary Paige will be in at ten and she'll set you up with any passwords you might need. Let Dennis take you out shopping anyway. He'll show you all our local markets and shops."

"I can't wait," smiled Josette.

"Did you see Susan before she went out?"

"Yes, she was very nice to me."

"I'm happy to hear that. She's your mistress now and

you won't find a better friend once she knows you," said Anthony, looking up to survey his newest employee from the shiny crown of her short black hair to the tiny, even shinier black shoes on her feet. "My, but you're a small girl, aren't you?" he observed with amusement. "Susan must feel tall beside you."

Josette blushed, pleased to be admired for her petiteness.

"Do you want a little welcome to Greenwich Village spanking?" he took her by surprise by asking, pushing back his chair and motioning to her. Josette glanced at the stove, relieved she hadn't started to melt the butter yet and nodded shyly but eagerly.

"Just a quickie," he promised, pulling her across his lap and locking her little waist under one hand before dispensing six medium swats to her still trousered bottom. Then he let her up and was not surprised to see her face pink with warmth. "Okay, you can get on with the eggs now," he told her, going back to his headlines with a satisfied sigh.

When she brought him the dish of perfectly scrambled eggs and buttered toast, he caught her tiny hand and placed a small kiss on the back of it. "You're a good girl," he said. "I'm glad I hired you. But you need to get more spanking in your life. Remember we discussed the New York club scene and you going out in it?"

"Yes," she replied, once more completely taken aback at his expressing a personal interest in her that seemed both friendly and nurturing.

"Don't just dream of having adventures. Have them now, while you're young and fearless."

"I'll ...try," she replied, in some confusion.

"You don't have to try hard, just put yourself places where scene people collect. They'll do the rest, believe me. But don't go by yourself, take Dennis along as an escort and bodyguard. He's happy to do it, we discussed it."

"Really? That's very nice of him."

"He's in the scene too. And he's trustworthy."

Now he paused to address the eggs and smiled up at her in approval.

Chapter Fourteen

Weekend on the Cape

After spending the afternoon in Random Point, Brooke doing her big double session at the club with Hope and Cameron conducting interviews in the apartment above Marguerite and Sloan's bookshop, the new couple rendezvoused at Hope and David's house, Cobweb Cottage, over-looking a cove a mile out of the village. As the sun began to go down on another balmy, mild day, David and Cameron basted the chickens turning on a rotisserie grill in the small garden behind their house, while Hope and Brooke set the table in the screened in back porch and prepped a salad and side dishes in the small cottage kitchen.

Brooke was in a dusky rose halter dress with a fitted torso and pleated skirt, her graceful feet in green platform espadrilles, her long, straight, dark hair unbound. Hope wore a cranberry sundress, with wide black patent leather belt and black pumps. Her hair was up in a long ponytail. They'd spent a delightful afternoon playing together at The Venus Club with their former client and now continued to bask in each other's company.

"So," began Hope, "are you and Cameron a couple?"

"Oh, I don't think you could say that yet," Brooke said, arranging radish rosettes and carrot sticks on a plate beside greens. "We've spent two nights together. But I'm really not sure he's one of us. And then there's that other girl."

"What other girl?"

"The redhead, who was at your party."

"Oh, the girl who came looking for a session."

"Yes, Naomi. He's been playing with her at Carola's dungeon."

"So have a lot of people."

"Really? Who?"

"I know Mr. Bartlett saw her in town this week," said Hope. "And Carola told my mistress that she was going to hand her over to every likely top she came across from now on."

"That's good to know," said Brooke, thoughtfully.

"But why don't you think Cameron is one of us? I played with him on my birthday and I thought he was one of us."

"He hasn't given me a proper spanking yet."

"No?"

"I wonder whether he's a vanilla, just using the scene for sex, having discovered through his research that submissive girls are easy," Brooke mused.

"Cameron's not a user."

"How do you know?"

"Just a vibe," Hope said. "Anyway, look at the work he's brought us. He's nothing if not benign."

"Oh, I don't question his value as a supplier of freelance, but he may well be opportunistically skimming sex off the top from his grateful corps of assistants."

"You may be onto something at that," said Hope, unable to discount this astute assessment of their new man. She would never admit that her own breeched virtue had proven the accuracy of Brooke's analysis, for this fact would never be revealed and therefore, was of no moment. "But don't hold that against the lad," said Hope; "after all, he's healthy and normal and perforce thinks about sex every waking moment because of his job. Can you really blame him if he closes the deal once in a while?"

"I can't blame him for anything but forgetting the foreplay," said Brooke.

Outside, David was telling Cameron how happy he was about the academic work the researcher had farmed out to Hope and Cassandra. "Those girls should have something to think about besides waiting for someone to come do a session. They're both better than that," said David, noting with approval that the fowl were browned to a turn. "And giving work to Our Miss Brooke," David continued, "is a good way to keep her out of dungeons too."

"You don't approve of clubs?" Cameron asked. "You should let me interview you for the study."

"Send me the questions, I'll write in my answers. Save you time."

"Great."

"I like clubs just fine, but I don't like Hope working at one. I tried to stop her, but couldn't."

"As clubs go, it's a honey of a one," said Cameron.

"Oh, I know," David sighed. "That's what I'm up against. And now she's best friends with the mistress. It's hopeless. I'll never get her out of there."

"Is it causing discord between you?" Cameron ventured.

"Not really," David conceded, then, hardly knowing why, he added, "I've been consoling myself now and then with Cassandra. Don't say anything. You're the only one I've told. It's not anything I'd mention in an interview, but off the record, the scene has a way of smiling on well-connected tops."

Cameron nodded gravely, remembering his thirty minutes in heaven with this man's wife on her birthday.

"Are you and Brooke officially seeing each other?" David changed the subject abruptly, seeing the girls through the kitchen window getting ready to start bringing out plates.

"I'm not sure."

"I wouldn't let that one slip through your fingers," said David.

"I think she likes me," Cameron admitted, "but not as much as her old school teacher."

David laughed.

"Seriously. She's still crushing on you hard. Don't be surprised if she makes a move any day now."

"What kind of a move?" David asked.

"She wants to consummate."

"Oh!" David said, neither surprised or delighted, though he did like Brooke very much and found her more beautiful than ever. "Why do they always have to go there? I don't want to get overextended and have my life turn into a French farce. I'm already pushing it. You'd better rein your girlfriend in," David suggested.

"Order her not to run after you, you mean?"

"I would."

"You don't think she'd resent that, on such short acquaintance?"

"I think you should show her you care," David said.

"I do care, but I don't necessarily want to inhibit her natural impulses. After all, she's only in her 20's. She has the right to have all the fun she wants."

"Are you saying you wouldn't care if she did, say, have an affair with me, while she was seeing you?"

"I guess I'm not the jealous type," Cameron shrugged. "Though I do want to spend as much time with her as I can, now that I'm getting to know her better."

"Well, Hope is the jealous type and she would flip if she thought I was making love to Brooke. So, do me a big favor, and discourage these impulses in her as far as you can."

At that moment, Hope and Brooke began to bring out dishes for the table. And in a few minutes, they were all companionably eating and drinking wine.

Brooke had never felt so contented. She felt sophisticated to be sitting here, in this very adult manner, with three of her favorite people, the crisp evening air, the savory aromas of the cooking, the velvety darkening sky, all contributing to her sense of ease and satisfaction. With her former lover, the very important Hollywood writer, she always felt somewhat awkward when out with his friends. They didn't take her seriously or even notice how mature and intelligent she was. And she thought them crude and shallow. But here she was among true peers, lovely people who were sincerely fond of her, who knew her to the core and cherished her for her many endearing traits and useful accomplishments. Of course, she was especially enjoying this new intimacy with her adored Mr. Lawrence, but to dine together in this fashion, with her dearest friend Hope by her side and her handsome new boyfriend across the table, seemed in and of itself the most rarified form of social intercourse. She was not thinking of seducing Mr. Lawrence at all at that moment, but simply enjoying her honored position, in this, her dear circle of friends.

A few hours later, Cameron and Brooke returned to The Venus Club, where they had arranged to occupy the split-level loft suite for the weekend. They went straight upstairs to the bedroom and Brooke took a sheer white nightie from the closet and retired into the adjoining bathroom to change and brush her teeth.

The upstairs room was rustic, with a pitched roof and skylights, through which a velvety, starry sky was now visible. Cameron paced between the kneeling bench and double wide play bed, simple sturdy platforms, each well padded, leather upholstered and trimmed with brass studs. He noticed a large wooden chest on the floor and opened it to find an array of paddles and straps of leather and wood, along with switches, crops, floggers, canes and a variety of flexible leather restraints, such as cuffs, collars and anklets, all fitted with rings for linking them together with boat hooks, the simplest method of bondage.

He dropped the lid of the trunk when Brooke emerged in the diaphanous gown, running a brush through her long, straight, shiny, dark hair. He hadn't seen her in a nightgown before and was enchanted. She smiled shyly at him.

"Shall I brush your hair?" he asked.

"All right," she agreed. They sat down on the bondage bed and she turned her back to him.

He began to brush her hair slowly and carefully. Then he said, "I feel like I should try to prevent you from trying to seduce David Lawrence," he confessed.

"Really?" she replied, with a little smile, that he saw in the mirror opposite them. "How would you do that?"

"Spank you," he said, putting down the brush and pulling her over his lap.

Cameron spanked her soundly, but she didn't kick or cry. She was eager to surrender and her squirming and grinding on his lap confirmed to him that he was finally on the right track with Brooke. When he let her up, she climbed back across his lap the right way up and wound her arms around his neck.

"It's good you finally did that," she confided, "I don't date vanilla men."

"You'll refrain from seducing David Lawrence?" Cameron asked.

"Did you refrain from seducing Hope Lawrence?" Brooke demanded.

"No," he replied candidly.

"Then you have your answer," Brooke declared serenely.

Chapter Fifteen

The Further Uses of Carola's Club

A few days later, in the early afternoon, when Cameron and Lydia were working in the office and Carola returning phone calls and scheduling models upstairs in her art studio, a beautiful young lady arrived with a tinkle of the front doorbell. Carola emerged at the top of the stairs to see Lydia admit a small, sleek, well dressed brunette, whom the mistress of the house recognized.

Diana Currie looked up and smiled as Carola came down to her, in her usual 5-inch pumps and full skirted dress. "Hello, Mistress, do you remember me? We played at the Venus Club party in Random Point a few weeks ago," said the petite visitor, whose dark eyes were sparking with excitement at the errand she had come upon.

"Of course I remember you, darling," said Carola, taking her hands and pressing her cheek to Diana's. "I tied you up and teased your adorableness while your handsome master watched."

"He's my husband," Diana confided, "and I'm being very naughty today, visiting here without him. He thinks I'm shopping. So, don't give me away at any future point, will you?"

"Never! But how naughty? Am I tying you up today?"

"No mistress, not today. Though your techniques are extremely delightful."

They walked into the downstairs sitting room and each took a comfortable, well upholstered chair.

"Then, you're meeting someone?" Carola asked with a

grin.

At that moment, the bell rang again. This time, Carola went to answer it and opened the door to a young, blond, giant of a boy, into whose arms Diana rushed as soon as he hove into her view.

"This is Carl-Adam," said Diana to Carola, "my college sweetheart. We haven't seen each other for two years."

The young man looked from Diana to Carola and back again, his attractive face flushed with pleasure at meeting his former lover and this new, provocatively dominant looking beauty, in an exclusive BDSM salon.

"He's all done with grad school and now he's got a job here in Boston," Diana explained proudly, holding hands with the gentle and adoring young player, who had been her emotional slave/dedicated disciplinarian during her senior year. For his part, he could only drink in Diana's beauty in her 27th year with awe. She was certainly another man's wife and resided most of the time in another city, and was the mother of a two-year-old as well. But clearly nothing had changed between them, as the light in their eyes confirmed. And then they were off to the first-floor dungeon, from which the familiar sounds of a spanking soon began to issue.

Carola was stunned at her sudden good fortune, which again seemed to emanate from her sister's circle of Random Point friends and contacts. This 6'4" Viking god in just his middle twenties, now lived in Boston, was in the scene, and the little Diana would be flying back to her own large New York bear mate in a day or two. She hadn't missed the flicker of appreciative interest in Carl-Adam's eyes as he took her in. Carola knew a latent submissive male when she saw one, and perhaps this lad wasn't even so latent at that.

Meanwhile, at the same time, in Cambridge, David Lawrence sat in a cozy gastropub, a street or two away from Harvard Square, awaiting his luncheon guests. He was in casual tweeds, a handsome, still youthful man, whose long fingers often played fitfully with any object that came to hand, replacing a smoking habit from years past. Now it was a tablet stylus. However, he did not have long to wait before seeing Amanda Sands enter the pub and make her way towards his booth in the back. Now a sophomore at Harvard, with a year of modeling and a Summer trip to Europe behind her, the willowy blonde moved with an assurance that only added to her full complement of physical charms. She was dressed charmingly in a white polo sweater, short gray tweed skirt and over-the-knee boots. She first hugged, then slid into the booth opposite him, smiling with delight.

"Thank you for inviting me to lunch, Mr. Lawrence," she said.

"Thank you for coming, Amanda. Another friend of mine will be joining us. Someone I've been meaning to introduce you to."

And as soon as he'd said this, a small girl, with long, straight nut-brown hair and blue eyes, was at the booth. This young lady also was dressed in a classic preppie sweater and skirt outfit, hers in camel wool and argyle vest, over a white shirt, with stack heeled oxford booties.

"Gigi!" David cried, getting to his feet to embrace the small girl, whom he hadn't seen since her graduation from Braemar Academy two years before. "Gigi, this is Amanda Sands. Hugo's daughter," he informed his former student. The girls shook hands, exchanging solemn, friendly, wondering looks.

"Hugo has a daughter?" Gigi said, sitting down beside Amanda in the booth opposite David. "You've been a well-kept secret!"

"Amanda, Gigi was one of my students at Braemar," David explained. "And she's in your class at Harvard now. I'm surprised you haven't met before."

"I think I've seen you around, but we're not in the same classes, are we?" Amanda said.

"I'm concentrating on social sciences," said Gigi.

"Liberal arts," Amanda said.

"Well, that explains it," said Gigi. "But...you're Hugo's daughter?"

"Tell Amanda how you know Hugo," David suggested, as the waitress brought them waters and menus.

"Well," Gigi admitted, "my boyfriend Dru and I used to read his magazine. And one night we actually crashed one of his play parties that was being held at Anthony Newton's mansion."

"So then, you're in the scene?" Amanda asked, even more delighted to meet this adorable new friend. Gigi nodded. "Did you say your boyfriend was named Dru? Dru Baxter?"

"Yes, why? Do you know him?" Gigi's face grew warm, for though she hadn't seen Dru since senior year of high school and fancied herself still peeved at him over the quarrel that had broken up their years' long affair, the sudden recollection of him gave her a sort of thrill in the pit of her stomach.

"Yes, in fact, we've played," Amanda admitted. Though that was all she intended to admit.

"Remember I wrote you about the new club that just opened up in Random Point?" David asked Gigi, "Amanda's mother is the Mistress. And Dru spent a few weeks helping to get it organized. Hope is working there too, as the assistant manager."

"Is your mother a dominatrix then?" Gigi asked Amanda with fascination.

"Oh, no, far from it. She's a honey lamb," Amanda replied, "but naturally, she knows how to spank. Her sister, my aunt Carola, operates another club, here in Boston, and you could certainly call *her* a dominatrix."

"I'm stunned. All of this actually happening in Random

Point and I'm finally of age..." Gigi mused.

"Anyway, you girls should become great friends, don't you think?" David suggested.

"I certainly do!" said Amanda to Gigi with a smile. "Are you seeing anyone?"

"No," said Gigi wistfully, "that's why I've been plaguing Mr. Lawrence with love letters lately."

David smiled gently at her, saying, "And that's why I'm trying to distract you now."

"I've been trying to seduce Mr. Lawrence into playing with me," said Gigi. "And he's been resisting and resisting."

"Mr. Lawrence, you played with me last year, for my own good. Why not Gigi?" Amanda pointed out.

"Honestly, I came into Boston today to finally do just that," he said.

"Really?" Gigi jumped up and down, clapping her hands.

"I thought we could go visit Carola's club later," he suggested. "I haven't been there before."

"I've only just seen the place once, for a minute," said Amanda, adding, "My boyfriend doesn't trust me not to do something crazy there."

"Crazy like what?" Gigi asked.

"Like sessioning for allowance."

"Is that an option?" Gigi asked.

"You can talk to the mistress about that," said David, knowing from her tone of interest that she would anyway.

The waitress came back and they placed their orders.

Later that afternoon, David escorted Gigi to Carola's club. The mistress set them in her second-floor dungeon, and after they had played, made herself available to Gigi to answer questions about working at the club part time. The University girl was a tiny beauty, who looked as much as a schoolgirl as it was possible to look at nineteen, particularly dressed as she was that day. Carola looked at Gigi and saw a great increase of business that fall. Gigi looked at Carola and fell instantly in love. And David knew he had done well that day.

The very next afternoon, Carola's prediction about Carl-Adam came true, when he arrived at the club alone, and asked if she would favor him with a corporal punishment session. Carola was free to play and took him to her playroom on the first floor, where she made him remove every strap and paddle from a leather trunk and choose an array for their hour together. Carl-Adam chose both leather and wood and Carola wore out her arm on his muscular buttocks and hockey corded thighs. He was handsome and trim waisted, tall and immaculately metrosexual, with broad shoulders and mild eyes, and feathery soft, short blond hair. She was so attracted to him that she soothed him with affectionate caresses after his punishment and even led him back to the bondage bed, placed him on his back, and looking into his eyes, unzipped her cotton shirt waist, stepped out of it and her crinoline slip and approached the bench to mount him. Carl-Adam was ready for her, in a style to do honor to her beauty and power. As with little Gigi, whom she had also just met, Carola's playful relationship with the Viking was destined to continue for the rest of their lives.

The interesting connections had not yet concluded for the day at Carola's club, for just as Carl-Adam was taking his leave, Naomi Norling was arriving for an appointment Carola had arranged between the thrill-seeking statistician and one of Carola's dominant male clients, who was awaiting the redhead in the front parlor. But as they passed each other in the hall, Naomi and Carl-Adam exchanged looks and smiles.

Carl-Adam waited until Carola had led Naomi and her client up to the second floor before taking his leave.

"Is that girl a top?" Carl-Adam asked.

"No, an inexperienced submissive. Come back and spank her next week," Carola suggested, for Carl-Adam was big enough to share.

Chapter Sixteen

Shopping in New York

On the way to Columbus Circle, where Dennis was dropping Anthony Newton off that morning, his employer brought up the subject of Josette again, urging Dennis to take her out on a nice shopping trip that afternoon and expressing his wish that Dennis should find the time to escort her to a B&D club as soon as that coming weekend.

"She needs to start enjoying the scene more," said Anthony. "But I don't want her running around in the city at night without a guardian. Can I count on you, Dennis?"

"Of course," Dennis said at once, then added helpfully, "I expect she'll need some proper shoes and boots to go clubbing in?"

Anthony grinned at the back of his chauffeur's head.

"I'm sure she will. I fully authorize a shoe shopping trip to accompany the pots, pans and aprons."

Well pleased with permission to spoil Josette in his favorite way, and at his boss's expense, Dennis sped home through secret short cuts to collect the small cook and take her out.

They visited a cookware shop, where Josette deliberated long and hard about every purchase, until Dennis began to grow impatient and hurried her along with, "At this rate, we won't be home in time for you to organize Mr. Newton's tea." Josette looked worriedly at her watch, then nodded in agreement and wound up her shopping in that store by choosing six aprons in rich colors.

"Mr. Newton asked me to take you shoe shopping as

well, to equip you for the club scene," Dennis explained, watching her lovely little face eagerly for her reaction to this extra bonus.

"He's so thoughtful," Josette cried. "It's true, I haven't any heels at all."

"Or boots?"

"No boots either, except my booties that I wear to work and hike in."

They proceeded directly to a shop in the Village that Dennis particularly liked. It was the type of shop where the clerks would answer questions, but didn't hover or wait. Dennis himself was at liberty to kneel at Josette's tiny feet and help her on and off with every pair of shoes and boots she expressed an interest in. As her size was unusually small, several of the numbers that attracted her had to be specially ordered, which Dennis took the liberty of doing, for Anthony had an account at the shop and was personally known to the owner. Even so, at the end of one of the pleasantest hours of the young Englishman's life, Josette had acquired two pairs of boots, one knee length, one thigh high, a pair of 5-inch stack-heeled closed toe pumps, stiletto booties, patent leather maryjanes, and a pair of Victorian side button heels in cream leather, all of the same heel height. While helping her on and off with the various shoes, Dennis was privileged to exchange her white cotton socks for little peds, and then place her inexpressibly dainty white feet in and out of the shoes she tried on, watching her walk across the floor and back in each pair and discussing the fit of each with her in turn. All the while, she had no notion of why he was so willing to assist her in this procedure, and she couldn't help giggle, being madly ticklish, every time his fingers chanced to brush the bottom of her feet.

When they left the shop together to hurry to the grocery to buy the food for their employer's late afternoon repast, they felt much closer to each other than they had before entering it. Josette's task that day could not have been simpler. Susan was dining with friends after work and Anthony had requested a steak and fries for his early dinner before leaving for the theater. On Dennis' insistence, she had also prepared Anthony's meal for Dennis and herself. "Mr. Newton doesn't stint," he told her. "You'll find that you were very lucky to have gained this position." And he proved it as soon as she was finished cleaning up after dinner, by telling her that he had been instructed to drive her home.

Josette was delighted not to have to go down in the subway and her little face glowed with pleasure at the special treatment. She felt lucky indeed. Most young cooks work in high pressure environments among every type of co-worker, including crude and abrasive ones. She had fallen on velvet instead, with a soft spoken, respectful supervisor, a kindly young mistress and a splendid master at the head of a well-ordered house; only three people to please, and those all easy going and already well disposed towards her.

They went out to the street, got in the Bentley, she on the front seat beside him, and he drove across the street and parked on the other side. "We're here," he said.

"What do you mean? I live down on 10th Ave., in Hell's Kitchen," she said.

"Do you? Come with me," he told her authoritatively. He buzzed them into a slim, three-story gray stone building, with a smart foyer and set of gold doored elevators. He led her into one and pressed the button for three. Up they noiselessly rode, as she looked at him in mystification. On the third floor, they stepped into a gray carpeted hall with a door on either side. He opened the one on the right with a key and motioned for her to follow him into a beautifully decorated little studio apartment, just the right size for a small, single girl.

"Mr. Newton got this place for you. I live downstairs on

the second floor," Dennis explained.

"Truly? For me?" Her face with pink with pleasure and excitement as she flew about the spacious room, which smartly combined a kitchenette, a well-furnished and appointed sitting room, and a demi bedroom with a wood platform bed and armoire. There was an elegantly renovated bathroom, the floors were of polished wood, and there were several large closets. The windows looked out on a tiny backyard garden and an ivy-covered wall. "I can't believe it," she breathed. It had been a terrifically exciting day, starting work, getting the affectionate spanking from Mr. Newton, Susan and Dennis being so nice, the dinner they had just eaten being so choice. She suddenly felt as though she could fall asleep as soon as she sat on the bed.

"I'll have to go home and get some things," she said, reluctantly.

"I'll take you right now," he told her, knowing it was too soon in their friendship to ask to be allowed to stay and tuck her in.

Chapter Seventeen

Cameron's Highly Nuanced Demographic

"I hate using overused words," Naomi Norland said to Cameron Hayes across a table in a bistro in Back Bay towards the end of September. This was the long postponed first date they had agreed upon and which he had been anticipating with some reluctance. After a fierce first ten days, when they had met at Carola's and played intimately three times, Cameron had simultaneously drifted into a far more serious relationship with Brooke Neuman, and had been trying to think of a diplomatic way in which to discontinue playing with the much more perversely demanding Naomi. It wasn't that he balked at her preference for intense role playing, while submitting to severe discipline and humiliating toy insertion, but doubted he could sustain that level of seriousness as a top. He was himself, of a more amiable and casual nature than that which she seemed to crave submitting to and found behaving like a master to be work. However, he had nothing to fear, as she quickly disclosed, continuing, "But there is truly no better word than 'amazing' to describe the way in which my life has been transformed since that party in Random Point three weeks ago."

"Say on," he encouraged her, pointing to a bottle of wine on the menu their waitress proffered.

"I've been going to Carola's and sessioning with strangers!"

"No!" Cameron grinned back, feeling the stress leave his neck and shoulders as he relaxed.

"And I've got a new best friend. Did you meet that girl Marion Craig? She's a subbed-out attorney; skinny, good looking brunette, about thirty?"

"Yes, Carola interviewed her for me and I filmed them."

"She's even worse than I am. Much worse. She wants to be on her knees giving head to her tops. And she's ravenously bi. But I'm not, as you know. Initially I almost had to fight her off. Now she's settled down and we're just a tag team. We've even doubled together! We're taking a trip to Manhattan next week and we're going clubbing there."

"So, you've gone from having no social or sex life whatever to a booming double one?"

"Exactly so!" she cried.

"Well, it's certainly been improving, young lady," Cameron remarked, noting the beautiful color in her face and the sparkle in her eyes. "You've come to life."

"I know. At first, I resisted the lure of this life, but Carola explained to me that I am now a spanking debutante, with all the rights and privileges that implies."

"And what does that mean?" He laughed, but was fascinated by this new angle on the lifestyle and psyche of the professional player.

"Once people pay you to give you orgasms, it changes everything. As you know, I don't need the money. But it puts one space of removal between me and the men in the scene who want me. I can play, sans the emotional responsibility of a romance. I give my all and my client tops are pleased, and at the end of an hour, we part, owing each other nothing. It's the opposite of a stressful dating situation. Of course, my regular work has suffered. I've stopped putting in twelve-hour days. I go home at five, like everyone else, so I can go out to Carola's and play until ten."

Chapter Eighteen

An Upsetting Visit

Meanwhile, Carola, the enabler, was having a better day than she could have imagined if she'd tried. Anthony and Susan Newton had arrived at eleven a.m., by appointment, to be photographed. Recently wed, Susan had requested the composer's approval to commemorate their eight-year relationship with a graphic novel she planned to work on that Autumn, featuring themselves as characters. Carola's job was to supply the photos upon which Susan planned to base her drawings. They had planned for three hours of shooting, including poses with Anthony carrying Susan over his shoulder, untying her from a St. Andrew's Cross, and many positions of punishment, with Susan in varying states of dress, lingerie and nudity. Anthony had brought several flawlessly tailored suits and some casual clothes as well. Carola's girl Lydia, who was extremely experienced in dressing long hair, would be on hand to arrange Susan's long, wheat gold hair according to her costumes, as well as helping organize Susan's wardrobe.

Giving up three hours of his life for the project seemed a pleasant indulgence to Anthony, who was taking advantage of a few days of his theatre being dark due to repairs, by planning a visit to Random Point. This stop in Boston, at Carola's house, felt a more than suitable post wedding visit. His own club, in Random Point, the Venus Club, was run by Carola's sister Cassandra, one of Anthony's favorite ladies. Carola wasn't a favorite of his, as yet, but she was improving all the time. He liked her look today, in her black capris, mock turtle top and flats, with her hair in a long ponytail. Carola was always retro, today she was channeling Audrey Hepburn, circa 1957.

There were no other scheduled appointments that afternoon, but at one p.m. Carola heard the front doorbell tinkle and sent Lydia down from the studio to see who it was. They had been posing a shot with Susan in a dressing gown at a vanity table. This would lead into a scene where Anthony spanked her, while seated on a nearby velvet covered pouf. Lydia was only gone a moment, when she came coming running back upstairs with a card, which she handed to Carola.

"He says the house has been sold and he's here to inspect the property," Lydia reported breathlessly. Carola's heart jumped as she looked down at the card, which read: Russell Cabot, Metropolitan Property Management, with a website and email address.

"Would you excuse me a minute?" Carola asked Anthony and when he nodded, ran downstairs.

"That doesn't sound good," Susan observed as Lydia picked up a tortoise shell hair comb to try in Susan's hair.

"I know," Anthony agreed.

Carola found Russell Cabot waiting in the hall, a tall, lean, clean cut, craggy faced, forty something man in khaki pants, work boots and a short sleeved white shirt. He had a small cloth case slung over one shoulder, and a black tablet in his hand. He smiled and extended a large, well-manicured, hand to shake hers, saying, "Miss Campi? Rusty from Metro Property. Did the young lady tell you why I'm here?"

"Yes, but, why didn't you let me know about this before? Did you plan to conduct your inspection now?"

"Is this not a good time?"

"No, it isn't," Carola carefully controlled her voice, trying not to betray her anger and anxiety at this untimely intrusion. "I'm in my studio doing a photo shoot and can't leave my clients right now. Can't we make an appointment for another day?"

"Certainly. What day would be convenient?"

"Well, how long will this inspection take? And for that matter, what's the upshot going to be for me? Are they planning to tear the building down?"

"That depends," he said.

"On what?"

"The results of my inspection."

"In what sense? Will I be required to leave?" Carola felt her eyes welling. She had been in the location over sixteen years, gradually taking over the entire three-story house. Would it be possible to find such another perfect site in the city?

"If the structure proves sound and the property well maintained, the owner may decide to leave everything as is," said Russell Cabot reassuringly. "It costs a lot to build a condo complex. And all the other small house holders on this end of the block would also have to sell. I wouldn't worry about that yet."

"Well, how long will this inspection take?"

"About three hours," he replied.

"All right. Tomorrow morning, then?"

"Sounds good. Ten?"

Carola nodded and opened the door for him. He smiled and departed. She watched him climb into a new Ford pickup truck parked at the curb and zoom away.

"What will a three-hour inspection entail, I wonder," Carola murmured to Anthony and Susan when she reported the development.

"Oh, he'll definitely be looking in closets," Anthony predicted.

"If he figures out that it's a club and tells the owner, that might be the end," Carola said.

Susan said, "Pretend all the gear is for your glamour photography."

"And don't worry," said Anthony. "If you have to leave, we'll help you get resettled somewhere nice."

"You will?" Carola looked astonished.

"Of course," he assured her serenely. "The scene needs you."

The next morning, when Rusty arrived promptly at ten, Carola was dressed to dazzle and intimidate in full Betty Page armor, from her jet-black hair arranged in an elegant French roll, to her wasp-waisted, crinoline petticoated, cleavage enhancing halter dress, to her stacked 5-inch patent leather pumps. She gave him some very good coffee in her first-floor dining room and proposed they begin at the top of the house and work their way down.

"Oh, will you be with me?" he asked, smiling.

"Of course," she replied, again, feeling her temper rise. Did he think she was going allow him to trample through her house unescorted? But she merely said, "I have all the keys. There are so many," she shook a heavy key ring. She thought it a well to begin with her living quarters, the most unsensational apartment in the building, descend to the second floor, which housed her studio, wardrobe rooms and just one playroom, and finish on the first floor, which included her business office with all the magazine covers on the walls to prove her legitimacy as a model and photographer, and the other dungeon. Three apartments, various sleeping and living rooms, but only two dungeons. She just might manage to slip those by this dreadful man, palming them off as prop rooms, as Susan Newton had suggested, if he were so infernally nosy as to poke into the closets.

As Carola preceded him up the two flights of stairs to her third-floor apartment, she noted that he hung back behind her far enough to get a good look at her legs in seamed hose.

"Are those real stockings or pantyhose?" he asked casually.

She turned to look at him for a moment, then said, "What do you think?"

"I think I'd like to find out," he replied.

She ignored this and continued upstairs, letting them into her flat. She led him through her study, with its bay window on the street, two bedrooms, a living room, bathroom and kitchen. All the rooms were handsomely furnished and meticulously maintained, with sunlight streaming in through the slatted blinds. As Anthony had predicted, the property management man looked in every closet. Up here, he only found color coordinated dress racks, dozens of built in shoe boxes and a kitchen squared away to naval neatness.

Rusty made some notes in on his tablet and asked her if she had a ladder, so he could get up into the attic. She told him there was a ladder in the hall utility closet and he went to fetch it. While he was clattering around in the attic, Carola slipped into her bedroom, checked her coiffure in the mirror and made sure her stocking seams and heel squares were perfectly straight. So, he was flirting with her already. You don't flirt with a woman you're about to evict.

Rusty returned, put the ladder back in the hall closet and told Carola they could proceed downstairs. Now Carola unlocked the apartment, dominated by her photographic studio and wardrobe room. This flat also contained a bedroom and a sleeper lounge, kitchenette and bath. And one dungeon. But it was an unmistakable one, with an X frame on one wall, a long, high, wooden, leather upholstered bondage bed down the middle, a large gilt mirror opposite it, an armoire (containing toys) and a large walk in closet full of harnesses, latex and rubber suits, man sized corsets; and on shelves, neatly coiled rope in black and white, blindfolds, gags, collars and cuffs.

When Russ saw the X Frame, he paused and turned to her.

"That's an interesting decor piece," he observed. "What do you do with it?"

"Photograph models posing against it," she replied coolly.

"Oh!" he exclaimed. Then he opened the equipment closet. Carola looked at him over folded arms. "More things for models to ...pose with?" he asked.

"My models are edgy," she replied.

"Interesting," he said.

"Isn't it?" she replied.

Now they returned to the first floor, where Carola conducted him through the kitchen, pantry, bath, dining room, front parlor, and the other play space, which was notable for its bondage bed, spanking bench and whipping post. He made some notes.

She ended the tour by leading him into her office, adjacent to the front hall, where she and her assistants worked on magazines, bookings and the club's website. She had just offered him a seat near her desk when the phone rang and she chatted with a model for a few minutes about an upcoming shoot. This allowed Rusty ample time to examine the many magazines covers that lined the walls, most of which featured Carola herself as cover girl, in latex, leather, corsetry, club wear and various other classic fetish costumes. There were also covers featuring a collection of her own favorite models, photographed by herself.

Carola concluded her call and offered to show him the backyard and cellar access so he might conclude his inspection. This was done within fifteen minutes and Russ prepared to leave, all smiles and gratitude for her helpfulness and full of compliments on the order and cleanliness of her entire building.

"And do you know what you plan to recommend to the owner?" Carola asked.

"Yes, I'm going to suggest he put in a new air conditioner," Russ smiled.

"Oh! That would be nice," she agreed. "But do you think they'll keep the property as is?"

"I can't think why they wouldn't," he serenely said.

"Okay. Great. I'll wish you a good day then," she said, extending her hand to shake his. He held her slender hand for a moment in his.

"Thank you for being so gracious," he said. "And if anything ever goes wrong, from a leak to a mouse, don't hesitate to call me first. Every landlord should be so lucky as to get a tenant like you."

Chapter Nineteen

Why Do They Always Want to Sodomize the Mistress?

The next day, Carola packed her BMW sedan with wardrobe for Susan and drove out to Random Point to continue shooting photos for Susan's new graphic novel. There were many locations on Anthony's estate and in Cassandra's club that might serve, as well as interior shots of Hugo Sands' Antiques and Marguerite Flagg's bookshop, each of which would provide important settings for graphic scenes.

She was staying with Cassandra at The Venus Club, and after her photo shoots that day and the next, her sister had booked her several sessions with locals. Between the sessions and the generous allowance Anthony was providing her with for giving so much time to Susan's project, this week would be her most profitable of the year, not even counting the additional stipend from her resident sex researcher.

Therefore, late that golden September afternoon, as she sat across from her sister, in a wooden booth in Michael's Tavern, Carola felt completely relaxed. Somehow, some way, Cassandra's magical ability to conjure cash out of thin air, had finally begun to radiate in her direction; and she knew she'd easily make her nut at on the 1st of the month. Anthony Newton getting fully on board as an affectionate patron came as a sudden shock. She'd been firmly convinced that he could barely tolerate her, but here he had promised to see her through if the building got sold out from under her and then awarded her this multi-thousand-dollar photography gig, not to mention allowing her the privilege of creating the first and doubtless only, portfolio of fetish art he would ever appear in, and with his new bride. This plum might not surface for twenty years, but when it did, everyone would know Carola Campi, not as a mistress, but as a high fashion fetish photographer.

Then the sight of someone made Carola sit up straight and stare across the room to the bar, where the man from Metropolitan Property Management, with whom she had spent three hours the previous day, was ordering a beer.

"Sandy, that lean man at the bar talking to Michael, have you seen him before?" Carola asked.

Cassandra followed her sister's gaze and nodded, "Yes, that's Rusty Cabot, a big real estate developer who's just bought a half dozen houses between here and Woodbridge. William got a huge contract to do most of the remodeling. He's been one of Hugo's subscribers since he was in college."

"He's in the scene?" Carola felt her face grow warm.

"Yes, he's already been to the club twice and he had me book a dinner date with Polyxena for him just last week."

"Really? Would be it too much to hope he's submissive?" Carola asked.

"Yes. He's a top. And he's into sodomy."

"And Polyxena saw him? I thought she was a mistress."

"She's a switch who only plays with hand-picked clients. I guess she liked the look of this one and he was willing to meet her steep allowance requirements."

"Why do they always need to sodomize the mistress?" Carola mused, finally allowing herself to meet Russell's eyes as he turned with his mug of ale to survey the room.

"Why, do you know him from your club?" Cassandra asked.

"Yes, but not as a client. Apparently, he just bought my house and he was looking the place over yesterday. But he never said he was in the scene. Played completely dumb when we went through the dungeons."

"He has the first New Rod Quarterly, with you on the cover," said Cassandra.

"He's coming over."

"Hello," said Rusty, stopping at their booth. "How nice to see you again so soon," he smiled down at Carola.

"Join us," said Cassandra, moving over to allow him to slide into the circular booth beside her. "This is my sister," Cassandra said to Cabot.

"He knows that," said Carola coolly. When Hugo had begun publishing the New Rod, Carola and Cassandra had been his two original models and copy editors, and their sisterhood had been established in the captions and blurbs.

"Don't be mad," said Rusty to Carola.

"Excuse me a moment, would you? I just saw Hugo come in and I must confer with him," said Cassandra, jumping up and going towards the bar, leaving Rusty and Carola alone.

Carola looked at him from under her long lashes, rolling the stem of her martini glass between her manicured fingers.

"What's your game?" she asked.

"Nothing," he said.

"You spent three hours with me yesterday, within squeezing distance, going over every inch of my establishment, without admitting you're in the scene, and because of your subterfuge, scaring the hell out of me that you're going to sell my club house out from under me. I feel as though I've been taken advantage of. If you wanted three hours of my time, why didn't you pay for them?"

"Oh? You feel like I got a free session?" He smiled lazily at her, not taking her pique in the least bit seriously.

Carola shrugged.

"I'll pay for three hours of your time any day," he said cheerfully, and double for the omission yesterday. As a matter of fact, I've wanted to engage you for years."

"Then why wait so long?" she cried; "I was a lot cuter twenty years ago!"

"I think you've improved," he told her. "And why I waited so long to do any sessions with anyone is that I was married and content with my wife, but she's no longer with us - due to a driver texting, and therefore, I'm now free to play."

"Oh no, when did this happen?" Carola asked, looking at him intently.

"Almost two years ago."

"And, how long were you together, if I may ask?"

"Since college."

"What college?"

"UCLA. She was in the film school, I was in business economics. She got a job as a script supervisor, I went into real estate."

"Did you play?" Carola asked.

"Yes! She loved spanking. And she partook of the fantasy enthusiastically. She had cheer leader outfits, schoolgirl uniforms. She wasn't sleek or glamorous, more cute and perky. Picture Celeste Holm in Champagne for Caesar. We'd go to parties all around the country, play with other couples. Once we went to England to play spanking in a castle. We went to Club Doma in The Hague on Halloween," he concluded, realizing she was staring at him as he reminisced, noticing that his eyes were glistening. She covered his large hand with her small one momentarily.

"I'm so terribly sorry," she said. "What happened to the murderer?"

"He's doing five years in a Utah prison, nice Mormon boy, and after that, he plans to join Doctors without Borders as a medical assistant. I'm good with that."

"Well, this revelation causes me to consider you in a much different light," Carola admitted. "But, I've heard about your sessions and I don't know if I want to commit to going that far that fast."

"I own all your movies."

"All of them?" Carola blinked in surprise.

"All the spanking ones, some of the classic bondage ones."

"So, you used to enjoy your wife dressing up in fetish gear?"

"I loved it," he smiled.

"I probably have more outfits than all the mistresses in Boston put together."

"I know. When we toured your photo studio the other day I felt as though I'd entered the inner sanctum."

"What a cad you are not to have said something," Carola observed.

"I'm sorry. Let me make it up to you."

She only smiled, yet felt relieved that he didn't suggest she punish him for his deception. She had begun to make plans for this faithful husband and they didn't include her becoming his dominant. It was delightful to spank a nineteen-year-old Harvard boy now and then, but in spite of her naturally domineering personality, physically disciplining men didn't particularly arouse her. Whereas playing the submissive, often did.

"Where are you staying?" she asked.

"Oh, I kept one of the houses I bought, for myself. The remodel is complete. It's just lacking furniture. Would you like to see it?" he asked eagerly.

"I would."

"Let me take you to dinner later and you can come by," he suggested.

"All right, pick me up at The Venus Club at seven," said Carola, "I'm staying with my sister for a few days."

They were at The Venus Club, getting Carola settled in one of the bedrooms, by five. Cassandra had booked Carola a session that evening at nine-thirty with Ambrose Bartlett, during which Carola planned to eagerly submit to pretty much everything Russell, the real estate developer, wanted. The difference was that Mr. Bartlett owned a department store. This was to be her first big session with him and both Cassandra and Hope had assured her that his generosity was legendary. Moreover, Carola found Mr. Bartlett very attractive. She knew he was a big fan of small waists and her own tiny one had been her calling card as a fetish model for years. It was always more satisfying to play with someone who genuinely admired one.

Carola found Hope in the office, answering client queries, and immediately grilled her about Rusty Cabot.

"I saw him once and Alison saw him once," Hope replied.

"Who's Alison?"

"Scene girl from the village who moonlights here. Our go-to girl for anal enthusiasts. She'll do enemas, plugs..."

"Sodomy?"

"I think she stops just short of sex with the clients. You saw her boyfriend the first time you were out, Freddie Johanson, a big, husky switch."

"Oh, yes, I liked him! But tell me about your session with Mr. Cabot. What did he require and what did he get?"

"He spanked me," Hope said helpfully, "and there were some intimate caresses. But I opted out of everything else. I have a very nice husband for that."

"What was he like to play with?" Carola posed the most important question.

"Oh, classic spanker, real gentleman. Nice firm, muscular thighs, knows how to hold a girl, starts medium, gets somewhat harder, but nothing I'd call severe; took his time in getting me bare, didn't ask for full nudity, didn't ask me to touch him or spread or anything untoward, did ask permission before he touched me, and only used two fingers, and didn't go back there, because I said, not this time, please. Let's see... he didn't talk much once we started, just seemed to enjoy playing with me. He had a good rhythm, alternating between slow, thuddy swats and quick, stinging volleys. He only used his hand, by the way. And he tipped me a hundred dollars."

"Why was Cassandra saying he insists on sodomy then?" Carola wondered aloud.

"He said he preferred a complete experience if possible and when we told Polyxena about him being in the scene - she'd already been ogling him at her gym, where he'd started to work out, she was 100% down with granting him total access."

"Do you know what he paid her?"

"Five grand."

"Show me Alison," said Carola, pulling Hope into the lounge, where a large, framed photo hung, showing all the female members of the Venus Club, dressed in black or white, taken the week the club opened. Hope pointed to the slender brunette, Alison Albrecht.

"She looks like a dressed down version of me," Carola observed, "and Polyxena is a voluptuous version of you. It seems Mr. Cabot's tastes are all encompassing."

"Is he interested in you?" Hope asked.

"He's taking me to dinner at seven and I'm going to see his house."

"But you will back in time for Mr. Bartlett?"

"I wouldn't miss Mr. Bartlett for anything. He's bringing me a Marchesa dress."

Russell arrived at seven to pick Carola up. She answered the front door, carrying an envelope purse and dressed in a beige halter dress and strappy high heeled sandals. Her hair was black silk, parted on the side and pearls were at her throat and in her ears.

Her date was driving a luxury sedan, which he handed her into gently. It was the first time he had touched her and she made a mental note of the event.

They dined in the village, at The Ball and Feather, in the formal dining room, telling each other their life stories. Since she refused dessert, they were able to leave for his new house, which he had promised to show her, within the hour.

Carola got a pleasant surprise when he parked in front of a large, French country style house, with hipped roofs and shutters, set in the same cul-de-sac as William Random's house.

"The first photoshoot I ever did for Hugo Sands was in that house," Carola told Russell, looking at William's own splendid red brick house.

"I have that magazine," said Russell.

She looked at him thoughtfully, then said, "Well, let's see yours."

He let her into the high-ceilinged front foyer of the newly refurbished house, with its richly painted walls, cream crown molding and freshly laid expensive dark wood floors. A wide, winding wooden staircase with a polished wood banister led up to the second floor, whose gallery of windows flooded the foyer with the glow of late summer twilight.

"Should I take off my heels?" she asked, regarding the new floor.

"Oh no," he protested, with a smile. Then he took her all around the large house, pointedly asking her opinions on what he should do with the rooms. They finished the tour in the back yard, where a separate pool house with a glass domed roof proved an unexpected attraction.

"Is it going to be heated year-round?" Carola asked, as they walked around the inside of the pool house, which was beautifully tiled and featured a pristine blue pool.

"Certainly, when I'm in residence. I'll probably spend

the weekdays in Boston and the weekends here when it's finished being decorated," he replied.

"Maybe I'll come swim someday," she suggested.

"Come swim every day," he countered.

"Well, I'd better be getting back," she said, adding frankly, "I have a nine-thirty at the club."

"So, you *are* doing sessions while you're here," he said eagerly.

"I'm mainly here to do some photography for a client," she replied evasively.

"Look, can't you fit in a session with me while you're here as well?" he asked.

"Are you saying that now that we've spent some time together, you still want one of those go-all-the-way sessions with me?"

"Of course, I do! But, that's not a deal breaker. Hell, I've been fantasizing about you for twenty years, just let me spank you!"

"So, the idea of playing with me still turns you on?"

"Yes! I'm crazy about it."

"You think I'm nice?"

"Very nice!"

"And are you very nice?"

"I hope so!"

"Not a secret sadist?"

"Oh no, not even close."

"Are you all intact? That is, functional?" she asked seriously.

"If you're asking what I think you're asking, see for yourself," he said, taking her hand and pressing it to the front of his trousers, where she immediately felt the answer to her question. "I can't not be hard around you," he admitted.

"Very well then. Listen carefully. You can have everything you ever wanted in a session, all in one night, with me, on our wedding night."

He looked at her with curiosity.

"Did I hear you correctly, Carola?"

"Please, call me Carol," she said, with a smile. "And yes, you did. Ben Franklin said, 'If you'd know a woman, go and see her on a Saturday.' You did just that. You looked in every corner of my house and saw what kind of woman I am. You've followed me for twenty years and know I haven't changed very much. You've had your fling with the fancy sessions. It's time to settle down with your ideal. And it's time I got to live that 1950's domestic goddess fantasy I've been reenacting for so many years, in a charming setting with a respectable, good-looking, age-appropriate man, who definitely isn't a secret sadist. All I ask is to be able to keep my photography and video business going in the Boston house and enjoy unlimited personal freedom."

"How long does it take to get a marriage license in this state?" Russell replied, only taking her hands in his and kissing each one, then releasing them.

Chapter Twenty

Town and Country Mistress

Carola returned to Boston in a daze, certain that the entire course of her life was about to change, yet still unable to believe that all she had to do was ask. It was Cassandra and Anthony Newton all over again. Her sister had gone to the patron, asked for the B&D club and he had created one for her. Cassandra had set the example and Carola, had taken it one step further. Because she really did want to be Carol again.

She went downstairs at ten and found Lydia and Cameron in the office, reviewing some written interviews she'd been transcribing for him. Cameron smiled up at her, as he always did. Lydia jumped to her feet to give a full report of the day's schedule, which included sessions for each of them, around noon. She also handed her mistress a small box which had come by special delivery for her that morning.

"You want me to open that for you?" Cameron asked helpfully. She smiled and nodded. He was such a nice young man. She sighed. "If I'm not mistaken, that box contains a ring," she said. The packing box disclosed a jeweler's box and it did contain a diamond ring, along with earrings and a necklace. Lydia gasped and wondered aloud if they were real.

"Of course they are," Carola replied. "They're an engagement present from my fiancé, Mr. Cabot. He was here the other day, looking over the house. Remember him?"

"Yes, but, you're fiancé?" Lydia cried.

"I know, it's unexpected," Carola admitted.

"This reminds me of every film noir with Joan Bennett," Lydia mused.

Carola assured her favorite, "There's nothing suspicious about Rusty. He's been a fan since my first magazine shoot."

"He's been stalking you for twenty years?" Lydia continued to tease, seeing the lovely blush come into the ivory complexion of her mistress. "Then pretended to be a handyman to spend the whole day with you. And now you're getting married?"

"I found out in Random Point that he's very substantial. He owns multiple properties there, including a gorgeous house, badly in need of a mistress. Yes, he pretended to be small, to see how I am to ordinary people. I was charming. It was a very nice test. Because I passed it brilliantly."

"Hoorah for mistress!" Lydia cried, embracing her boss. "But are we all ceasing sessions?"

"No, you and Tai and whoever else wants to, can session out of my house, but I'm going to concentrate on photography and videos from now on. The handyman owns this building. And so, I'm done paying rent on it."

"What else?" Lydia demanded; "Tell us all about him!"

"I just know he's ...a find," said Carola with a smile.

"I liked his look," said Lydia. "Oh, you two will make a beautiful couple!"

"And here's the best part, my new house is right up the street from William Random's house, with that path through the woods to the beach, remember we shot there?" Carola reminded Lydia.

"Oh, how divine!" cried Lydia.

"Anyway, who am I playing with this afternoon?" Carola asked.

"Karen," Lydia replied, using the code name of Carola's most refined cross dresser.

"Good! Prep wardrobe and the sleeper lounge for me. And who do you have?"

"My Korean tickler."

"You might as well take dungeon two then."

Lydia saved and closed her files and ran off to ready the play rooms.

"Come upstairs with me, I want to talk to you about something important," said Carola, leading Cameron up to her private apartment on the third floor. She brought him into her handsomely furnished study, with the bay window over the street. She perched on the edge of her writing desk, swinging her slim, hosed legs before her and drawing his attention to her elegant, high vamp, high heeled pumps.

"My entire life is about to change," she confided, "and there's one thing I never got around to doing." As she was looking him in a way he'd never seen, or noticed, before, he only smiled and waited to hear her further thoughts, but as he looked into her large, dark, expressive eyes, he suddenly understood her meaning.

"Do I understand correctly, that mistress is putting me in charge of her bachelorette party?"

"If by party, you mean locking the door and pulling the blinds, yes," replied Carola.

A few hours later, after her session with her most generous and loyal client, a refined cross dresser, and received a handsome wedding present from him, the soon to be married dominatrix began to plan her honeymoon wardrobe. But as she was deciding between a cotton dress or capri outfit for the plane, she stopped short and found herself staring into space and wondering if this was all real and more importantly, correct. She recalled Lydia's comment about film noirs. She was about to marry a man she'd met the previous week. It was time to do her due diligence.

She knew that Rusty was also at home, in his Back-Bay condo, organizing himself for the trip and called to ask if she might visit for a short chat. He welcomed her enthusiastically and she left the house, still in her charming session outfit, a full skirted cherry red shirt waist with a broad black patent leather belt encircling her tiny waist and matching spectator pumps.

His building was on Marlborough Street, a late Victorian brownstone, now divided into two condos, tiny but completely refurbished and gleaming. He owned both apartments, but only occupied one, renting the other. She walked one flight up and found him in a small but charming living space, well-furnished and perfectly suited to a comfortable bachelor. He was in khaki pants and a white shirt, his regular outfit, and greeted her with a radiant smile.

"I didn't expect you to visit, but I'm very happy to see you. Can I get you something?" he asked, after their somewhat awkward hug.

"Could I trouble you to make some coffee?" she asked, eager to see his kitchen, which was more of a galley, well organized and stocked. She leaned against a counter and watched him grind the beans, murmuring, "I see you've brought some civilized ways back with you from the Golden West."

"It's a medium roast, is that okay?"

"Perfect."

"This place is small, but I needed a base of operations in the city and this is as close to the center as anyone can get, so I grabbed the building last year," he explained.

"It's delightful. Just another wonderful surprise. Which brings me to my visit."

"Yes?" he was barely paying attention to her words, so taken was he with the glamor girl standing in his own kitchen, within reach, and almost his to completely possess. And all he had to do was marry her. And yet here she was, looking tentative, which made his heart contract with anxiety that she might be planning to back out.

"I was packing for Vegas and I suddenly realized, he really knows nothing about me. Am I being fair? So I came over to give you the opportunity to, ask me anything you wish, and then, to possibly reconsider your rash acceptance of my immodest and desperate proposal."

"Why desperate?" he asked with fascination.

"Because the truth is, I'm tired of working so hard just to make my overhead on the building. It's why I'm always broke. And you should know that. All things being equal, I might have eventually had sex with you and let you sodomize me anyway, because I like your look and at the very least, you were going to get me a new air conditioner. But you're being well off was a big factor in my decision to demand a real commitment. Especially after you told me about your excellent marriage, which speaks to your character. But I'll be honest, most of my relationships have been with younger men and have been completely frivolous. I've never even dated a mature grown-up before, no less been anyone's wife. I think I could easily love you, but I'm not in love with you yet. I just wanted to be up front about all of this and give you a chance to hit the cancel button."

He remembered she took milk in her coffee and set two glass mugs by the pot while it brewed.

"Thank you for being so conscientious," he told her, amused and pleased by her well-meaning candor. "But I wouldn't let you out of this engagement for money."

"Why?" she asked.

"I told you the other night over dinner. I've been following you for twenty years. I love the idea of liberating you from sessions so you can focus on your creative work. I'll be a proper husband to you in that respect. If I can be your top, that's everything to me."

"I should have asked you before, but do you get high?"

"Be yourself, Carol, I'm from California," said Rusty, laying his hand on a pipe and a jar in a twinkling. She smiled and they smoked while drinking coffee.

Walking around the small apartment she seemed to be thinking of a new plan. Suddenly she turned to him and said, "I've come to a decision, Russell."

"Yes?"

"I don't want to go to Vegas at all. I want to go right to the house in Random Point and start getting it organized."

"You do?" he asked, astonished.

"Yes, it turns me on so much to think about decorating it and playing house there and having William and Damaris for our best friends and my sister and Hugo in the village. I want it so much!"

"Okay," he said affably. "But what about getting married?"

"We'll just apply for a license here in the proper manner, get our blood tests, and if it's in the budget, have a little party at The Copley Plaza, with a dozen guests and the honeymoon suite."

"Why not?" he agreed at once. "We can always have a proper honeymoon a little later, after we get settled."

They put down their coffee cups and embraced. He was much taller than she, but her 5-inch heels allowed her to look straight into his eyes. He kissed her and she wrapped her arms around his narrow waist and rested her face against his chest, breathing him in and allowing herself to surrender to the sensation of security without restrictions.

She looked at him again and said, "You said you and your first wife played and went to parties. How did you handle sex with other people?"

"It was an open marriage to the extent of playing in the scene. And once in a while, that did involve sex. In any case, we weren't really jealous of each other in that way. We always told each other what we did. But we had an unusually close bond, we "got" each other, and it was different than a conventional relationship. I can't answer for myself with you. I might get jealous."

Carola walked into the small, well squared away bedroom with the large, walnut bed with its pearl gray comforter and snowy white linen. He followed her. She was looking about the room with a practiced eye for furniture suited to playing. There was a tall, broad seated, straight backed leather chair with a large hassock. Before the bed was a long, leather upholstered storage bench. She nodded with approval and said, "Are you thinking what I'm thinking?"

"Over the knee spanking on the chair, followed by sex from behind with you on all fours on the bench?"

Carola grinned and said, "It seems we also "get" each other!"

Chapter Twenty-One

October

By Halloween, many strange and wonderful changes had taken place in Random Point. Polyxena Guzman was courted and won by Raphael Price, who was certain he had finally found the perfect mistress to introduce him to the world of esoteric erotica. She gave up the lighthouse and moved into Raphael's splendid house near the shore. Her affair with Ambrose Bartlett thus concluded, for with the unattached younger man, she knew she could have everything she wanted in a lover without sharing him with a wife.

With Anthony Newton's blessing, Cassandra invited Carol to become her partner in running The Venus Club. For Carol would bring twenty years' experience as a dominant switch and a large following to the new club. Finding that she loved her new home on the cul-de-sac of Shadow Lane very much, also, her new husband, and especially admiring the lavishly appointed Venus Club, Carol determined to give up the Boston house entirely and transport all of her furniture and accoutrements, including her photography studio and extensive wardrobe room, to the empty basement level of Cassandra's house, effectively furnishing the entire floor with one stroke. This greatly enhanced the bondage and discipline capabilities of the club, adding another St. Andrew's Wheel, multiple whipping posts and spanking benches, wardrobes, mirrors, etc., equally usable for sessions, overnighters and filming.

Dru Baxter and Carl Adam Johanson were recruited to

set the rooms up after the furniture came in a truck from Boston. The Brookline club was closed and Rusty regained the property for his own use, which he promptly sold for a great profit.

Brooke and Cameron were now a couple, but Brooke had accepted Hope's invitation to come and session at the Venus club several times a month to enhance her income. Cameron also visited the club to conduct interviews.

Anthony Newton's new show was put on hold for the entire winter season, as the theatre in which the show had been mounted, was undergoing a major refurbishing. Thus, for the first time in their lives together, Anthony and Susan were able to reside together in his Random Point mansion for many months together, enjoying the Venus Club and all of their closest scene friends on a daily basis.

At the same time, Dennis and Josette, who naturally accompanied their master and mistress to the Cape, slowly, softly and gently, began to think about conducting a romance of their own. Josette was very young and wholly ignorant as to the ways of running a large household, but Dennis was full of common sense advice and demonstrations, for which she was very grateful. She was, in fact, enchanted with her new life. Not only was she employed in the field she had trained for, but her working conditions were superb, her environment luxurious, and her employer charming and easy to please. Intent on showing his bride all the respect he felt she deserved, Anthony had determined not to carry on any intimacy with Josette, even as adorably spankable as she was, for the last thing he wanted to do was create a rivalry or any sort of tension between Susan and their young chef. This was one of the reasons he was so interested in promoting the love affair between Josette and Dennis.

Dru Baxter, the college boy who had been a part of the Random Point scene since before he should have been, was so much in love with the Venus club, its mistress,

Cassandra and his occasional lover Pamela Bartlett, that he decided to switch to a Boston college in his junior year, in order to be in easy driving distance of the Cape. He loved being useful to Cassandra and now, to the glamorous and much stricter Carola, who became a daily visitor to The Venus Club.

Diana Currie had resided in Random Point for several weeks while decorating Carol and Russell's new home. She had stayed in Susan Ross's triple decker Victorian across from the cemetery. The cemetery house had only one perpetual occupant, Carmen, the barmaid at Michael Flagg's tavern. Susan had struck a deal advantageous to Carmen, offering to let her stay in her big house, rent free, simply to serve as caretaker of it. The house contained various parlors and dining areas, four fine bedrooms, a studio for Susan and Laura to draw in and a large play room equipped with bondage furniture and chests full of toys and costumes. Diana not only enjoyed the house for its own sake, but her bisexual libido melted for the hot tomboy Carmen, with her blonde pixie cut and strong, toned, shapely body. Carmen had begun to visit The Venus Club on a weekly basis to play with clients as a submissive switch. Carmen was becoming a sexual sophisticate and relishing the transformation.

Anthony Newton was delighted to see his club operating so efficiently on so many levels, as a play space for clients, as well as their local clique, as a superb party space, as a B&B for scene couples and overnighters, as a shooting and photo studio and simply a social club for his favorite girls and most intimate friends.

As soon as they had resettled for the season in Random Point, Anthony and Susan began to visit Cassandra's house on an almost daily basis. They loved walking and playing in the woods and along the brook behind the house, sitting and chatting with Cassandra and Hope and friends who happened in, and Susan was still planning and laying out a new graphic novel, in which Anthony was a character, along with herself. This called for many specific photo sessions, so that she could capture action sequences on film and later draw from. The visiting girls and mistresses coming to the club on a weekly basis continued to provide fresh models for Susan to draw from and Anthony hadn't the slightest objection to pose for her spanking different young ladies, or tying them to bondage furniture or carrying them over his shoulder. In fact, he thought it the most original and endearing honeymoon present any bride could give her husband. Susan had never been happier. For she had never realized, until she was his wife, how much she had longed for that honor and respect. Susan was also amused and touched by the care Anthony was taking to make sure their adorable new live in cook didn't annoy or threaten her in any way. He'd only given Josette once small, welcome spanking, when she'd joined their household, then, rather formally ceded Josette's supervision to Dennis, whom everyone agreed, was in need of a girlfriend.

Little did Anthony suspect just how much Susan was enjoying having her own chef, and a sweet little submissive she herself could chat freely to and even draw. Everything about her new position contented and thrilled Josette to the point of robbing her of speech around her employers. She didn't dare to do anything to jeopardize her pampered position, with its big salary, fine accommodations, the charming Dennis to guide her and a couple like Anthony and Susan to work for. They were as affable to her as though she had been a family member and not an employee. But Dennis explained to her that that was because she was a part of their scene, which was a kind of family.

"If Mr. Newton hadn't played with you at The Venus Club party that night," said the young English man who had been with his master more than ten years, "he would never have thought of hiring you full time." Dennis spoke with confidence because Anthony had confided as much to him. He hastened to add, "It's not because he intends to exploit your leanings, you've probably realized that by now. But it adds a level of comfort and ease that he and Susan can be as much themselves around you as me."

"Does that mean you're in the scene as well?" Josette had asked hopefully.

"Well, I am English," Dennis replied gravely.

The adventures of the youngest players in the Boston to Random Point spanking scene were becoming tangled up and intertwined with the advent of the Venus Club. Amanda and Colby found their way to Random Point every other weekend. Now in the second year of their love affair, they were fiercely attached to each other and tried to have sex wherever and whenever they could. They made a point of playing in every room of the club, which had gained even greater dimension with the addition of Carola's furnishings and equipment.

When the St. Andrews Cross arrived from Boston, Colby, Dru and Carl Adam installed in the largest basement playroom, while Amanda, Hope and Gigi, formerly Dru's high school girlfriend, currently a sophomore at Harvard, looked on.

"It should be tested," said Hope.

"You test it," Amanda told Colby, who stared at her. "Why not?" she challenged him. He shrugged and said, "Okay." They strapped him in and Amanda kept him spinning around a long time, in spite of his repeatedly petitioning to be taken down.

"Good installation," she declared, asking her friends to give her a three-minute head start before freeing him.

Relations between Gigi and Dru were slightly chilly, due to their somewhat acrimonious break up, but neither of them could keep away from the club once it existed, so each decided to proceed with cautious civility. One of the biggest draws of the club for Gigi was the possibility that she could arrange another play date between herself and her high school idol, David Lawrence. David had made no secret of Gigi's ongoing infatuation with him to Hope and of course, that wise young lady understood the depth and power of such an obsession and had no animosity towards the university girl on this head. Not a year had gone by in David's fifteen years teaching high school English without multiple girls becoming obsessed with him, to the extent of stalking him. Instead of resenting the unsolicited admiration her husband received from these girls, Hope considered it a priceless counterbalance to the continual attention that she garnered from men. Therefore, she had smiled benevolently upon Gigi when she began to visit the club and gave her to understand that playing with his former student in the club was something David might do without offence to herself.

Dru wasn't upset by Gigi's sudden appearances at the club. He was more disappointed in himself than her for the way their relationship had ended. He knew he had bungled the power exchange and she had not yet forgiven him. Meanwhile, the ravishing Pamela still made shameless use of Dru, as a stud, whenever she felt the need of such release. Then, there was the exquisite joy of being around and being useful to the sisters, Cassandra and Carola, two very different goddesses, equally fascinating and exciting. Carola had just gotten married, but Cassandra was still unattached. Dru had the patience to wait for his moment with her, just as he had done with Marguerite Alexander, when he was still in high school and she was not yet wed to anyone.

Meanwhile, Dru had become friends with both Amanda Sands and Colby Hodge, after their one-night hook up with Pamela in Boston. And Colby entered the Venus Club with a different degree of excitement since his splendid night with Hope in Back Bay. Other electrified Hope Lawrence fans included Cameron, who, even though he was now officially Brooke's boyfriend, could not forget his enchanted interlude with Hope in the cloakroom beside the school room.

As for Carl Adam, he was both amazed and confused by the recent addition of the club to Random Point. For not only had it reintroduced Diana Currie into his love life, but Naomi had come directly to him from it. He'd begun to date the enigmatic statistician, functioning as her top and not revealing to her any part of his submissive nature. And he was of course, also playing the dominant with his old college lover, Diana, now married but apparently free to sojourn with her friends in Random Point whenever she had a mind to. But he also had the urge to serve a mistress, and had adored Carola since becoming one of her clients in Boston.

The photographer Pascal Robbins was also drawn to the club. He was already recruiting models for himself from the girls and women who traveled out from Boston to do sessions and film with Hugo or Carola, and he was conducting shoots in the club and in the woods behind it, gladly paying Cassandra rental fees and paying the girls' allowance. But while he was ostensibly going in and out of the club for these shoots, he was now and then running into the two most exciting girls he'd had to do with in recent years, Amanda Sands, the university girl and Susan Ross, the graphic artist who had recently become Mrs. Anthony Newton. Both of these intoxicating blondes he had made love to only once, but he was interested in return engagements, if they could ever be discreetly achieved. He knew they both loved their own specific partners, but he also knew he'd given satisfaction, thus he dreamed. Meanwhile, the club was a treasure trove of magnetic women coming and going, most of them enjoyed posing for cameras and few had any inhibitions whatever.

Chapter Twenty-Two

Girl Friday

One afternoon Anthony Newton and Hugo Sands were sitting in the lounge drinking the Irish coffees Hope had just brought them, with a chilly autumn rain softly falling outside the windows when the doorbell chimed and Hope ran off to answer it.

"Cassandra and Hope stay busy, don't they?" Anthony observed.

"This place is a hotbed of activity," Hugo agreed.

"I think they need a live-in maid, assistant, or general dogs body to help out," Anthony declared.

"Really?"

"Of course, they can't be fetching and carrying and cleaning up after every guest and employee all day long, they'll get too exhausted to play," Anthony said.

"I see your point."

"Don't you know a simple scene girl who might need a gig? We're not talking major housework, Cassandra has a cleaning crew for that, but someone to answer the door and the phone, clear off dishes, serve drinks, clean up dungeons. She can have one of the downstairs bedrooms."

"I do know a girl named Jesse who might suit perfectly," Hugo realized. "She's 22, has A.N. Rocquelaire type fantasies and she just got laid off from her job."

"What was her job?"

"Hotel desk clerk. In Dallas. We'd have to fly her out. And once she was out, we'd have to keep her, so think about that. She is dying to get out of Texas though."

"Go on," said Anthony.

"Well, she just started getting my magazine a few months ago and she writes to me constantly. Here's Jesse," said Hugo, taking out his phone and showing Anthony a photo of a pale, slight, beautiful little blonde in a sundress.

"She's adorable," Anthony enthused. "Is she a model at all?"

"Not yet, but give her a minute after she gets here and I'm sure we'll all be getting her in front of our cameras."

"I'll say. With those looks, she'll be booking sessions right and left as well," Anthony agreed, adding, "But tell her not to expect The Story of O. She's being hired to be useful to Cassandra and Hope. If she's a competent assistant and fancies working in a dungeon, great, but naked floor scrubbing would work Susan's last nerve."

"Let me run it by Cassandra," said Hugo, going in search of the mistress of the house, who was in the back yard supervising the installation of an herb garden that Anthony had ordered for her use. "Take a look at this girl," he said, showing her Jesse's photo. "Might you like to adopt this waif as a live in Girl Friday? Anthony thinks you and Hope need an assistant to pick up after guests and girls and he's willing to fly this one out and underwrite her relocation and pay her a generous salary. She could live downstairs. What do you think?"

"Scene girl?"

"Ardently submissive. She's lucky to be falling into our combined hands at this point. You can let Carol train her and that should satisfy her urge to serve for the moment. Then you can reserve her for ball busting masters. That should be enough abuse for a hungry neophyte."

Cassandra looked at the photo of the pretty young girl. "She's tiny, isn't she?"

"Barely a hundred pounds, I'd guess. Baby Venus. And by the way, she's a very nice young lady. Self-deprecating and unabashedly wayward. A little goth. She might stubbornly cling to black nail polish."

"Carol won't stand for that," Cassandra said.

"I'll instruct her that all preppie all the time is the only thing that'll make her new mistress happy," Hugo said.

"I'll bet she has a huge crush on you," Cassandra guessed shrewdly.

"Well, she just recently found the magazine, so I'm a bit of a revelation to her. She'll get over that when she sees how many local tops there are for her to sub to."

"Amanda and Colby will eat her up, I think," Cassandra grinned, "and she'll give Dru something new to think about. I love the idea!"

When Jessica Pomander debarked from the train at the Random Point station on the penultimate day of October, it was once again gray and lightly misting with rain. She was dressed in black leggings and high shaft boots, a cream cowl neck sweater and a leather trench coat. She wheeled a black leather suitcase and wore a small black leather backpack. Her straight pale blonde hair touched her slender shoulders and her lips were dark red, with a flawless crimson manicure to match. Carol met her on the platform, smart as a page out of a 1950's Vogue, in a fitted light brown woolen dress and pumps, the keys to her new luxury sedan in one perfectly manicured hand. Jessica approached the older woman shyly and seemed relieved when Carol spoke first, "Jesse, is it?" Jesse nodded and said, "Carola?"

"Yes, but how did you know?" Carol began to lead her towards the small parking lot beside the station, scrutinizing everything the girl had on as well as her every gesture.

"I recognize you from the magazines," said Jesse. "Your photosets are so beautiful!"

"Oh!" said Carol, with surprise. "You're a student of fetish?"

"Of course!" replied Jesse, most respectfully.

They reached the shiny car and Carol put Jesse's luggage in the trunk. "I'm in charge of you, young lady," Carol told her, before taking Jesse for her first tour of Random Point, during which the veteran player described the life and routines upon which she was about to embark.

"You live here?" Jesse wondered, completely star struck by her new mentor.

"I do," Carol replied, "though I was based in Boston until about a month ago. I had a B&D club there since you were in kindergarten. But now I'm co-mistressing at The Venus Club, here in Random Point, with my sister Cassandra. Have you ever worked in a dungeon?"

"No, but I've been to a couple, just to play."

"I'm happy to hear you're not a complete novice."

"Oh, I'm a complete novice. I know zero about anything," Jesse disclosed confidently. Carol noticed that her new assistant was smiling. She looked sharply at Jesse. Girls didn't normally please her so much so quickly. This one seemed to have a knack of saying just the right thing at the right moment and leaving it at that.

"See that Antiques Shop on the corner, Jesse? That's Hugo Sands' shop. The offices where he puts together his magazines are behind the shop. You can pay him a visit later."

"Thank you!" Jesse murmured, smiling goofily.

"That really makes you happy, I can tell," Carol observed, with approval. "Be very grateful to Mr. Sands. Your current good fortune is wholly a result of his suggesting you to the generous patron of our club. Now you are ostensibly being hired on as a sort of personal assistant to the club, to help keep everything neat and orderly and manage the traffic, but obviously, you are suited for a wide variety of uses, my dear. See that bookstore on the corner? That's Marguerite Alexander's shop. She writes for Hugo under the penname Alma. I'm sure you've read her stories."

"I have, I have!" Jesse cried. "I adore her. She's my idol."

"Well, you'll meet her soon," Carol promised.

"I can't believe it," Jesse murmured quietly.

"I like what you're wearing," said Carol, "that is proper attire for a young lady, in my view. But while you're on duty, you're to avail yourself of the extensive wardrobe we keep on the premises for video and photos shoots and sessions. You'll find a complete selection of leather, latex and PVC dresses and cat suits that are appropriate for club wear day or evening, in your size, but during the day, I think I'd rather see you in cotton and wool, skirts and blouses, perfect little dresses and jumpers, anything dainty and classic that emphasizes your femininity."

"I love the way you dress your models for photo shoots," said Jesse helpfully.

"Looking at you now, I see you're even smaller than I thought. Luckily, a pair of dressmakers are friends of the house, they will help you build a wardrobe. Now, the house is divided into two levels. You could consider the upper level my sister's domain and the lower one, my own. I've furnished it entirely with good pieces from my former club, including top grade dungeon furniture. There are many rooms downstairs and they are available for shoots and sessions. The rooms that ring the periphery of the lower level all have high windows, so it's by no means claustrophobic. You will have one of these rooms, with a private bathroom. The only other person who lives in the house is Cassandra, on the upper level, in a master suite. There's a full kitchen downstairs, so you can cook your own food if you wish, but I'm sure Cassandra will invite you to eat with her more often than not."

"And I don't pay rent?" Jesse asked.

"Your accommodations are part of your employment

package. You'll receive a nice salary, probably twice what you were making at your last job. And if you decide to do sessions and or video or photography gigs, you'll make lots of cash right away. We'll take out all the appropriate taxes, so you won't get into trouble later. With no rent, you should be able to start saving money, which I advise you to do. Look over there, see that dress shop?"

"Damaris?"

"Yes, that shop is co-owned by two lovely scene ladies. They are the ones who can fit you perfectly. One of the owners, not Damaris, but the other one, Pamela Bartlett, is married to the owner of Bartlett's Department store in Woodbridge, the next village over. Why am I mentioning Mr. Bartlett? Because he's the best customer of the Venus Club. It's his hang out, he plays with all the girls and brings us clothes as presents. Just letting you know, it's something you might look forward to. He can't resist a skinny girl. But he is a very hard player, at least the first time."

"I want to play hard!" Jesse said with conviction.

"Great. We'll be using you a lot for that sort of thing then. My sister is very compassionate and doesn't encourage severity. That's why you're going to be my Girl Friday. She already has her own Girl Friday, Hope Spencer Lawrence."

"I have her videos," said Jesse. "She's so beautiful. I can't believe I'll be working with her!"

"Oh, you'll be working with her alright. Two beautiful blondes fit into just about every scene any client ever imagined."

"What is Cassandra like? I want to please her and not get on her nerves so she'll let me stay in her house."

"It's good you think like that. Just be helpful and don't tire them out with questions. They will reveal every truth to you in time, but you're coming at a pretty hectic moment. Tomorrow is Halloween, the night of Hugo's annual party and it's happening at the club. You'll be plenty busy tomorrow just trying to remember everyone's name and where things go."

"Copy that," Jesse replied softly.

"By the way, have you got a boyfriend?"

"No. I was married briefly, but got divorced almost immediately. No one right now," Jesse replied cheerfully.

"In the case of guests and visiting boyfriends, no overnighters for now."

"I'm not looking for a boyfriend," said Jesse.

"You're a lot more interested in playing with Hugo Sands right now, aren't you?" Carol grinned. Jesse nodded vigorously.

"Jesse, check out that Tavern, it's Michael Flagg's place. He's Marguerite Alexander's husband. They have a beautiful house right next door to The Venus Club. He's a tall, handsome hunk, you'll enjoy being over his lap. But the nicest thing about him is that he's a former detective and about the best trouble shooter a dungeon can have. I call it a dungeon, but your new home is gleaming and shiny, with crown molding and more bathrooms than you can count. Do you like to read?"

"I love to read!" cried Jesse.

"One of the rooms is a library and there's a huge piano lounge with a wet bar and billiards. Mr. Bartlett furnished most of the upper floor from his department store. Our patron paid, of course. Mr. Bartlett is blowing through his profits though, with all the sessions."

"What will be the hardest part of my job?" Jesse asked candidly.

"Pleasing me," Carol replied.

"What do I have to do to please you, Mistress?"

"Just be perfect."

The denizens, friends and patrons of the Venus Club, had all agreed to share joint custody of Jessica until she seemed comfortable in her new home, job and village. Thus, when Carol arrived at the house with its new resident in tow, she enlisted Dru Baxter, who had been visiting with Hope and Cassandra, and was waiting to meet them in the lounge, to settle Jesse in her new quarters and familiarize her with the rest of the house.

Now nineteen, the handsome blond boy stood a foot taller than the petite newcomer and came as a surprise to Jesse. The last thing she'd expected was to have a hot young man put at her disposal and a wide smile spread across her beguiling face.

Dru led her down a paneled corridor lined with framed Ray Caesar prints to an elevator that took them to the lower level. Her little suite was at the rear of the house, with two high windows facing the back garden and woods behind it. There was a sage green bedroom and connecting bath and large walk-in closet. It was furnished with the smart bedclothes, linen, lilac velvet chairs, dainty desk and polished chests of drawers that had filled Carol's overnight sleeper room in Brookline. Jesse had never spent the night in such an elegant room, no less lived in one. She was enchanted as she admired the many shelves and slots built into the closet, the shiny nickel fittings of the burgundy tiled bathroom, the planked wooden floor.

"Do you work here?" Jesse asked Dru.

"Oh no, I'm just a friend of the club."

"You seem way too young to be a customer," Jesse observed.

"I kind of bluffed my way into the scene here when I was still in high school. I worked at the bookstore part time and my boss, Marguerite Alexander, encouraged me to have fun with the scene. Hope worked there at the time – she's the assistant manager of this club – and she was happy to scene-flirt with me too. So, I'm lucky enough to know the right people, otherwise, I'd never be here. While I am here, I try to be helpful," Dru concluded. "Do you want me to help you unpack?"

"Yes, so I can bombard you with questions."

"Okay," he grinned, opening her suitcase on the bed and immediately beginning to transfer garments to the dressers.

"Do you know Hugo Sands?"

"Of course. The first party my girlfriend Gigi and I ever snuck into was one of his Halloween parties, three years ago. Hope's husband, Mr. Lawrence, was our English teacher. This club didn't exist, the party was at Mr. Newton's house on the Cliff. We were way too young to be at a scene party. I paid a penalty. So did Gigi. We're all lucky no one ever found out about that night. We were incorrigible."

"How old are you?"

"Nineteen. How old are you?"

"Twenty-two."

"Older women drive me distracted, I'm just warning you," said Dru.

"God, you're so cute I may have to fuck you before you even give me the tour," Jesse said.

Dru's head whipped around and he stared at her.

"Yes, I said that," she confirmed.

"You're naughty, aren't you?" he rejoined at this unexpected turn, feeling in his pocket for a condom.

Fifteen minutes later, Jesse ran a brush through her pale blonde hair and grinned into the mirror, where she saw Dru zipping up his jeans.

"Do you always make up your mind so quickly?" he asked, admiring the rosy glow that suffused her flawless face.

"No, but mistress threw down the gauntlet, telling me I had to have overnight guests approved. Is she going to try to run my sex life?" Jesse wondered, pulling her boots back on her tiny, white socked feet.

"I don't think so," Dru replied, looking at the paperbacks she had packed with interest. "Robert Heinlein fan, huh? Me too. The thing is, Cassandra lives here alone at the moment, even bringing you in is a big innovation, so it wouldn't be correct to introduce a stranger. She doesn't know you or your taste in men. She's a refined lady and this is an expensive house. Even the clients have to pay a big membership fee to visit, no walk-ins allowed, and they have to have references. Scene locals excepted."

"I'll bet she'd let me keep you with me overnight," Jesse said.

Dru grinned, "Yes, I'm sure she would! Do you want me to stay with you tonight?"

"Yes!"

Dru began conducting Jesse through the house, showing her the various play spaces and other rooms, as well as the detached loft with spa, then they went out into the back garden and a little way into the woods, along the brook path.

"I'd expect to be some sort of indentured sex slave in exchange for all this luxury," Jesse ventured.

"You'd think so, at the very least, but no. The patron of the house suggested bringing a girl in to help Cassandra and Hope keep everything squared away. Hugo suggested you, I guess you'd been writing to him?"

"Constantly."

"But when everyone saw how camera ready you are, the plan expanded to include sessions and shoots. If you care for the work, you'll be kept busy."

"You know all these things?"

"I'm such a groupie of these women," Dru admitted. "They're all so used to me by now, they talk about everything in front of me."

"Okay, so I get management doesn't plan to use me as a sex toy, but what do the clients expect?"

"Well, it's primarily a spanking club, so even though

you're coming in a submissive, don't be surprised if you find a hairbrush in your own hand sooner than later. Most clients are switches, I'm told."

"Are you a switch?"

"That would be telling."

"You are!"

"Maybe I am, but with a tiny girl like you'd, I'd top."

Jesse blushed with pleasure.

"Oooooh, what goes on in this neat room?" she asked, as they entered the examining room.

"Look in that cupboard," Dru told her, for it contained a stack of new, cellophane wrapped anal plugs and enema equipment. "Can't you see yourself on that examining table or kneeling on that spanking bench?" he asked.

"Yes! Yes! Yes!" she cried, kneeling on the spanking bench and twerking her bottom at Dru, who came up beside her, took her by the waist and administered a dozen resounding smacks to her small, jutting backside in the soft jersey leggings. "Ooooh," she said again and wiggled. He let her go and they resumed their tour.

"Are you still in school?" Jesse asked Dru as he conducted her to meet her new best friends.

"Yes, I just transferred to the college of arts and sciences at B.U. I'm in my sophomore year. I'll have to go back to Boston on Monday."

"But you come to Random Point frequently?" Jesse asked hopefully.

"I can't seem to stay away."

Chapter Twenty-Three

The Cliff House and Environs

Cassandra was in her office with Hope when Dru brought Jesse in.

"We've been invited to Mr. Newton's house for lunch," said Cassandra, smiling softly at Jesse and taking her by the hand.

"Lucky girl!" said Hope, giving lunch at Mr. Newton's a thumbs up. "He has the best cook."

Mr. Newton's chauffeured Bentley was waiting at the curb outside the house. "Hi Dennis," said Cassandra to the young Englishman behind the wheel. "This is my new assistant, Jesse Pomander. Jesse, this is Dennis Cowper."

Dennis smiled over his shoulder at Jesse. He was very good looking and she smiled back at him. Then she looked at Cassandra, admiring her lithe figure, long brown hair and sweet face.

"Who is this Mr. Newton that he loves us all so much?" Jesse asked.

"He's a patron of the scene who showers us with love," said Cassandra.

"Is he friends with Hugo?"

"Best friends. Hugo introduced Mr. Newton to his wife, Susan Ross, the illustrator. You may have seen her graphic novels. She works with her sister, Laura. Laura is Hugo's wife."

"Do you know Hugo well?"

"I do. He's the father of my daughter, Amanda."

"Oh!" Jesse cried. "Really? I remember a photoset in the magazine last year, with a beautiful blonde girl named

Amanda. That's his real daughter?"

"Yes, she was my well-kept secret until the day she started college. I had left Hugo while I was pregnant with her and never told him."

"Oh my god, why not?"

"I didn't think he wanted a family."

"Did he not?"

"We'll never know. I only sent Amanda to meet him when she had a Harvard dorm room key in her pocket. Naturally he was very impressed, not to say bowled over. Especially when he found out she's in the scene. You will like her. I know you'll become friends. She has a delightful boyfriend too. You'll like Colby."

"What is Mr. Newton like?"

"He's charming. Truly amiable."

"Where have I heard that phrase before?" Jesse wondered.

"Jane Austen. That summed up the ideal gentleman for her."

"I should read more Jane Austen!"

"Of course, you should."

"Does Mr. Newton read Jane Austen?"

"I'm sure he does. He's a great artist in his own right as well."

"What kind of one?"

"He's a musical composer."

"OMG, he's not The Anthony Newton?"

"Yes. You know his plays?"

"I do know them!"

"Obviously, we don't spread his name around to the slightest degree. Discretion matters. But he's our patron."

When they arrived at the Cliff House, Anthony and Susan were in the dining room, but he was on his feet, as if ready to depart. Jesse was dazzled by the elegance of his person, this attractive celebrity, whose albums her mother had played constantly when she was a toddler. Anthony explained that he had to rush over to Braemar, where ground was being broken for the new theatre he was endowing at that school. But he warmly shook her hand in way of welcome to Random Point and told her Susan would take her shopping after lunch for some club wear.

"Come with me," said Anthony to Cassandra. "I want you to see the site of the theatre. Susan and Dennis will escort the little one to Bartlett's after she's had some lunch."

Anthony drove them over to the prep school in a roomy SUV. "I wanted to have you alone so I could ask you what you think of your new employee," he said to Cassandra. "Can you see her living with you long term?"

Cassandra laughed, "Well, I've only known her twenty minutes, but so far I'm finding her adorable. She's already having an affair with Dru!"

"Really?"

"Yes, she asked me if he could stay over with her tonight and keep her company in her room."

"That's great! He needs a baby to look after. And she needs a decent young boyfriend. It'll keep her grounded. And I love the idea of you having a man on the premises at night, whenever possible."

"Honestly, if she could charm my sister, she has great people skills."

"I think she does. She managed to stammer out two words to me just now: thank you and I love your music. What a little beauty. I can't imagine Susan not turning her into a character in the graphic novel she's working on."

"I'm very happy to have a pretty little girl living with me again. It wasn't easy parting with Amanda. And even though Carola is determined to play Wicked Wanda to Jesse's Booful, I'll have her after Carol goes home every night."

Susan encouraged Jesse to fill a plate from a sideboard loaded with seductive salads and dainty sandwiches, puff pastries, fruit and chocolate. The ponytailed blonde sat beside Jesse and asked her questions while the novice explored with wonder the most exquisite chicken salad she'd ever tasted and sprinkled salt on the reddest beefsteak tomato she'd ever seen. She was very hungry and seemed to behold a feast worthy of Hogwarts.

"I love your books so much," Jesse told Susan. "They are so exciting, exactly what I like!"

"Your adventures at The Venus Club could inspire a whole new graphic novel," Susan told her cheerfully.

"Why is Mr. Newton so kind to us all? Is he a player?"

"Well, so long as you realize, you must never "out" a celebrity to a vanilla of any sort, especially anyone involved with the media, of course, he's a player. He's a straight top with a classic spanking fetish."

"How nice!" Jesse breathed.

"Dennis, who will drive us over to Woodbridge later, is a player too, with a partiality for beautiful footwear on elegant feet. He'll be taking us shopping later and will personally assist you in lacing boots, etc. He's good people, another big brother in the local scene for you."

"Wonderful!" said Jesse. Then finishing her meal, she gave a satisfied sigh.

"You've been going nonstop all day, haven't you?" Susan asked, noticing Jesse's slender shoulders droop a bit.

"Yes, I've been up since five am," Jesse replied.

Susan took Jesse upstairs to one of the guest rooms and bade her rest for an hour before they went shopping. She fell asleep the instant her head touched the pillow and awoke twenty minutes later, refreshed and amazed at the excess of luxury into which she had fallen, through no merit of her own beyond writing charming letters to Hugo Sands and being beautiful. The French doors of the bedroom gave onto a balcony that overlooked the cove below, with its lapping waves and wheeling gulls. The rain had ceased, the sky had cleared and a late afternoon sun sparkled on the water below. Susan had peeked into the room and noticed that Jesse was up. She joined her on the balcony.

"Did you catch a nap?" Susan asked.

"Yes, thank you!"

"Have you chosen a scene name to work under yet?" Susan asked when they were seated in the back of the Bentley with Dennis at the wheel.

"I thought Wilhelmina Willoughby might be suit me."

"Love it!" said Susan.

They arrived at Bartlett's department store in Woodbridge twenty minutes later. Susan instructed Dennis to proceed to the shoe department and start picking out boots, pumps and booties for Jesse to try on. "Size 6?" Susan asked Jesse, who nodded. Then Susan took Jesse up to the top floor studio of Pamela Bartlett, who was cutting a pattern for one of her dressmakers to assemble. Jesse was immediately struck by the beauty and elegance of Pamela, who looked as though she had been born to wear and design exquisite clothes.

"Who have we here?" Pamela asked, a smile lighting her face.

"This is Jesse. She's a discovery of Hugo's," said Susan. "She's going to be working at The Venus Club on staff."

"Charming!"

"She needs some outfits right away and we were hoping you had some samples in her size."

"What are you, about a 0?" Pamela asked, walking around Jesse.

"Something like that," said Jesse.

Pamela quickly took measurements and wrote them down. Then she disappeared into another room for a few minutes. She returned with three short dresses that she handed to Jessie.

"Try these on," she said.

Pamela and Susan watched Jesse don a shiny black PVC apron dress, a cherry red leather halter dress and a white latex sheath. Each outfit fit like a second skin and put Jesse's well proportioned little curves on display to perfection. But the latex felt suffocating to Jesse and she begged to be excused from wearing it. Susan sympathized. "I can't wear latex either," she confided. Pamela went back in the stock room and came out with a white leather zip front mini dress with an open collar that became Jesse as well as the latex had done.

"Are these mine to keep?" Jesse asked, with wonder, for these were garments that would have cost hundreds of dollars per piece.

"Of course," said Susan. "Anthony told me to give you a great shopping trip," she handed Pamela a credit card. Pamela looked at it, looked at Jesse and handed the card back to Susan.

"She's such a little beauty. Really just the girl I'm looking for to model our new ultra-petite line," said Pamela, brushing a tendril of pale blonde hair from Jesse's brow and examining her flawless complexion. "Would you like to be in an ad campaign?" she asked Jesse, who nodded and murmured, "Yes, please!"

"Take good care of the outfits. I'll send Pascal Robbins over to the club tomorrow morning and he'll photograph you in them. And you can keep them for your modeling fee. Is that agreeable to you?"

Susan's midsection had fluttered at the mention of Pascal Robbins, for she had shared an interesting hour with him several months before.

"Have you been photographed by a professional photographer before?" Susan asked Jesse as they went down to the shoe department.

"No, never."

"You're lucky to start with Pascal then. He'll give you all sorts of modeling tips and by the time Carola photographs you, you'll be letter perfect at posing. You've seen her magazines, I'm sure. She's legendary for her glamour photography."

"I want to learn about bondage and strict corseting," Jesse said helpfully.

"Very proper. I can see why Hugo suggested you for the Venus Club."

"It isn't a strict club, though, is it?"

"It's no Roissy. More like a kinky sorority house/local players' club. Anthony wanted to create a spanking club that the girls would enjoy. He's always been a player and he's always patronized pro subs, but he was never in a club that was to his taste. By the way, Hugo introduced me to Anthony when I was a freshman in college, and we've been together ever since."

"I dream of having a dominant boyfriend," Jesse said.

"You're about to have dozens of them," Susan assured her. "I'll immortalize your affairs as The Adventures of Wilhelmina Willoughby."

"I can't wait!" cried Jesse.

Dennis had secured the assistance of the one girl who worked in fine shoes, knowing that she was the newest employee of the shoe salon, the least experienced, the shyest and wrote the most meagre sales. "Today you'll make some good commissions," Dennis told that young lady. And indeed, a half hour later, the hitherto unsuccessful shoe sales lady, was adding Jesse's name and size to her nearly empty blue book, and noting that she had sold her a six-pair assortment of fetish pumps, stiletto booties, thigh high boots and white go-go boots.

After a brief visit to the hosiery and lingerie

departments for some basics, Susan and Dennis drove back to Random Point and delivered Jesse to Hugo Sands' Antiques shop in the village. "Just go in," said Susan to Jesse. "He knows you're coming. We'll be across the street at the bookshop coffee bar waiting for you."

As soon as she entered the empty shop, Jesse was aware of the ticking of dozens of clocks. Hugo emerged from behind a counter, smiling and surrendering to her ecstatic hug. "So, you made it," he said, holding her from him and looking at her. "I'm so proud of you for making such a good impression on my friends."

"I have? Already?" she cried, amazed.

"Well, no one has called to complain so far," he observed.

"As a matter of fact, I have made a good impression," she informed him joyously. "I already have a modeling gig booked for tomorrow!"

"How came this to happen?"

"A beautiful girl named Pamela has given me three fetish outfits to wear, but first, a person named Pascal is going to photograph me in them, for ads."

"Excellent! You'll meet Pamela's husband, Ambrose Bartlett, tomorrow and he'll give you a great session."

"He's married to a beauty like Pamela and he still does sessions?" Jesse marveled.

"He has a lot of playing to get out of his system. He uses the Venus Club to de-stress and feed his endless fetishism for feminine beauty and vulnerability."

"Oh Hugo, I'm in heaven," said Jesse, drinking him in with her wide, amused blue eyes. "Everyone's spoiling me so much, I feel like Sarah Crewe on the morning she wakes up in her garret with a fire in the grate, a down comforter on her bed, tea and muffins on the table and a fur lined dressing gown to put on."

"You've seen the Shirley Temple Little Princess?"

"I was a sickly child and watched old movies on TCM

all day. I think that may be why adults always like me," Jesse said.

Both of them were silent for a moment, considering each other.

"I think you need a spanking," Hugo said at last.

He took her back to his offices behind the shop and found a straight-backed chair. "But first," he said, "do you want to smoke a joint?"

"Yes!" she cried. "Thank you!" During their extensive correspondence, a shared proclivity for cannabis had been resoundingly established, and in fact the legality of said substance in the commonwealth had been an added inducement to quickly vacate her residency in Texas and move East.

While they were smoking, Jesse roamed around the offices of The New Rod Quarterly, looked at the framed covers mounted on the walls in gallery style, wandered into the galley and out back into the vast storage rooms.

He let her poke around as she gave him a full report of everything she'd done and everyone she'd met so far, including her adventure with Dru. Hugo called her a little slut, which she giggled at, and pulled her across his knee while seated on an old steamer trunk. He didn't pull her leggings down, but merely dusted them off in the most casual way. When he noticed how much she seemed to like being across his lap, he smacked her harder. She squirmed and wriggled and ground against his thigh. He smacked her harder and called her naughty but put her from his lap before she'd had enough. She wanted more and smiled at him in a sort of goofy, love struck daze. He took her on his lap right side up, telling her, "Tomorrow is a huge party. Dozens of people will want to play with you. You don't want to be all burnt out from a hard spanking today. We'll play for real some other day."

Jesse was content to keep hugging him, lost in a

sensual love dream come true. She looked up at him and murmured, "Aren't we going to have sex?"

Now he stood her up and shook his head, "You're incorrigible. Didn't you just have sex with Dru three hours ago?"

"Yes, but I've been fantasizing about you for months," she reproached him, taking one of his large hands between her small ones and bringing it to her lips while holding his gaze. He stood up and relit the joint, took a hit and looked at her.

"Of course, I'm flattered, my little sweetheart," he began, "but you'll talk about it and it'll get back to my wife and she won't take it well."

"You have a hard on. I could feel it just now. And I won't tell anyone."

"Yes, you will. Girls always do."

"Come on, just a little quickie. Hard and fast, from behind, like in your stories. I could get up on that trunk on all fours and be just about your waist high in a second," she suggested. "Look," she showed him the elastic waist band of her black leggings, "they pull right down."

And it might have happened in the next instant, had they not both heard the front doorbell tinkle.

"Tomorrow at the party," he promised. "When you're in one of your killer new outfits, in one of the cool playrooms." Hugo was positive the mad chaos of a giant party at the club would prevent this from actually happening and congratulated himself on his newly found discretion.

Laura Sands had come in and they met her in the big first room of the shop. Jesse saw at a glance why Hugo hadn't jumped at the chance to take full advantage of her infatuation with him. Laura was a preppie princess in pegged jeans, a plaid shirt and oatmeal wool cardigan knotted around her slim waist. Laura stopped short at the sight of Jesse as well.

"Oh my," remarked Hugo's wife, "you are something special, aren't you!" She shook Jesse's tiny hand and smiled at her with the joy of a fetish photographer regarding a perfect new model who had never been shot before. "Hugo, we can put her on the cover of the January issue," Laura suggested. "We could do a New Year's Eve motif."

"I'd love to," Hugo said, "but with the party tomorrow, she's bound to get marked. We might have to put it off for a few weeks."

"You do not have to get marked," Laura told Jesse sternly. "You can stop them."

"Laura, be yourself," Hugo said, "this will be her first big spanking party and she's the new girl and look at her. Plus, she's submissive."

"We'll work on that," said Laura.

"Honey, would you take her across to the bookshop and introduce her to Marguerite and Sloan? She could probably use some coffee and a snack too."

While they were walking across the cobbled street Laura asked Jesse how she was finding Random Point so far.

"Well, I'm pretty sure I'm asleep and dreaming," Jesse grinned. "But I'm still trying to figure out why everyone is going to so much trouble and expense over me. I haven't been objectified once yet. I didn't even have to personally thank my new patron."

"It's not going to be like that," Laura assured her. "Never feel compelled to dispense sexual favors to clients, I don't care how masterful they seem. Only do things like that if and when you want to."

"So, it's straight spanking and no sex?"

"It's whatever you want it to be, but you are in control

of that. For example, a total asshole top named Victor will be at the party tomorrow, he'll flip when he sees you and try to book you right away. He'll expect a blow job. But you can refuse. Don't be intimidated. He's a submissive half the time anyway and some day, when you're in the mood, you'll thrash him instead. The point is, you do what you want and only what you want in a dungeon or playroom. Use the club first and foremost for your own orgasms."

"I feel like I'm in that book Island, by Aldous Huxley," said Jesse, "because everything here seems Utopian to me."

"I love the metaphor. You're going to fit in unbelievably well," said Laura.

Marguerite was not in the shop, but they found Sloan behind the coffee bar, as it was relatively empty, Laura and Jesse took seats before him and they were able to hold a lively conversation while he regaled them with tea and petit fours. Jesse couldn't take her eyes off Sloan, whom she now recognized from several of the photo sets she had seen in Hugo's magazine.

"Jesse's going to be on our next cover," said Laura.

"Who are you shooting her with?" Sloan asked, smiling at Jesse.

"Oh, Hugo, I think," said Laura, turning to Jesse and asking, "Don't you think that would be the way to begin?"

"Oh, yes!" Jesse cried. "But someday, I mean, if I do well and there's an opportunity, I would love to ...to pose with you," she told Sloan, her heart pounding with a love at first sight sort of crush.

"How nice you are!" he replied.

While they were drinking tea, Jesse told them about her visit to Woodbridge and the gifts Pamela had given her and the shoes and boots Dennis had helped her to shop for. Sloan told Jesse he had dated Pamela before his marriage and assured her that Pamela would always dress her to perfection, for she loved a beautiful model.

When Laura dropped Jesse off at the Venus Club, she met two early party arrivals from Boston, Amanda Sands and Colby Hodge. Dru was there as well and just before Cassandra entered, with the predominance of blond hair in the room, Jesse couldn't help but blurting out, "Children of the damned?" This endeared her to Amanda instantly and the three nineteen-year-olds merrily spirited their new companion over to Michael Flagg's tavern for dinner.

Meanwhile, Cassandra, well pleased with her new housemate, betook herself to her sister's new home, where she and Carol were going to lay out a plan for the following day as Carol's husband Rusty cooked them dinner. Carol hadn't realized that her new life's companion could and would cook, whenever encouraged to do so. He was more than content to fuss and bustle around the gleaming kitchen while the sisters made lists of errands to run and items to purchase before the Halloween party. Anthony had engaged a company to arrive at nine am the following morning with a truckload of items to decorate the house with.

"Do you think I should awaken the child and invite her to practice yoga with me every morning?" Cassandra asked, as they sampled Rusty's excellent pasta primavera.

"Couldn't hurt," said Carol. "I'll take her to join the gym today too."

"I have to hand it to Hugo," said Cassandra. "He really picked someone I know I'll enjoy. She seems like no trouble at all. And I was missing my own baby girl. This one I can keep for a while."

"I know, and she's so little and cute, you can easily top her."

"You can easily top her. I'd rather hug her."

Chapter Twenty-Four

The Return of Victor

That night, Dru Baxter quite naturally shared Jesse Pomander's single bed in the pretty little downstairs room she had been given, clasping her in his arms all night. The next morning, he left her around eight to seek out Cassandra and offer any assistance he could with the party preparations. He found Cassandra in the kitchen brewing coffee. Outside the sound of a large truck pulling up brought them both to the front porch. It was the crew of decorators from Boston who would strew the house with Halloween monsters and atmospheric trappings.

After a quick shower in her own bathroom, with its elegant faucets and delightful appointments, Jesse got into her skinny jeans and a white shirt, walking shoes and a soft gray wool blazer and ran upstairs to the kitchen. Cassandra was seated at the big table with an extremely good looking thirty something man in a brown tweed suit with several expensive looking cameras on the table in front of him.

Cassandra introduced Jesse to Pascal Robbins, who had been sent by Pamela Bartlett to photograph her in her three new outfits. Jesse asked for coffee with milk and sugar and was invited to help herself to a roll and a serving of creamy scrambled eggs from a pot on the range. Jesse buttered her roll, ate her delicious eggs with joy and sipped the good coffee, all the while staring at Pascal with wide eyes.

"We'll walk out to the summer house in the woods to shoot," he told Jesse. "But you'll have to change there-you won't be able to walk that far in heels."

He had brought a wheeled canvas wagon for her to carefully place her shoes and outfits in.

The white marble gazebo was about a quarter mile into the woods from Cassandra's back door. The morning was slightly overcast, providing perfect light for shooting. Pascal had the fondest possible memory of this summer house, as it was within its open walls he had closed the deal, against all odds, with Amanda Sands the previous year.

"Maybe you'd like to model for me - without costumes someday," he suggested.

"Sure!" the former hotel clerk agreed with alacrity. She was instantly attracted to this handsome older man who seemed so confident yet so unaggressive. He was used to being around beautiful girls and never made an advance until they knew him well enough to like him.

Jesse pulled her wagon full of wardrobe over to the marble seat that went around the whole circular gazebo and began to exchange her casual clothes for the white leather dress and go-go boots. When she was dressed, Pascal scrutinized her barely made up face and simply advised touching up her dark red lipstick, which she did using the mirror in her phone. She'd added nothing to her eyes but mascara.

"Have you ever posed before?" he asked, carrying the wagon out of the set and picking up a camera.

"Not professionally," she said.

"Okay, just follow my instructions and we'll see how you do. I can teach you a lot today."

Pascal found Jesse to be the quickest study he'd ever shot, with a natural instinct for her own best angles and numerous expressions and attitudes.

"Pamela will be very pleased," Pascal said, as they were walking back to the house. "She used to model for me a few years back. I published a whole book of her."

"I want a copy!" Jesse cried enthusiastically.

"I'll send you one."

"Do you have any advice for me?" Jesse asked.

"Yes! Don't get more ink!"

Jesse looked down at the small tattoo of Celtic design decorating her left arm.

"I won't," she agreed.

The house was full of decorators when they returned and a catering truck had arrived from Woodbridge to begin prepping the foods for the party in the large kitchen on the lower floor. As platters and bowls were completed, they were taken in the elevator up to the main kitchen and dining room.

Jesse returned her outfits to her room and looked for Cassandra, who was about to practice yoga in the back garden with her daughter Amanda. They invited Jesse to join them and she quickly changed into leggings and a t shirt and happily did so. This was the perfect way to unwind from her shoot, which she knew had gone excellently.

After this and a second shower, Jesse and Amanda took bikes from the garage and peddled into the village to have lunch at the Bone and Feather Inn. Amanda was already Jesse's close friend, for they had partied together the previous night and seemed to have hundreds of interests in common. In reality, Jesse had never been friends with quite so smart and accomplished a girl as Amanda, but she herself was bright and this was evident to everyone at once. Hugo had taken an interest in her for a reason beyond her beauty. She was rare and special and only needed education and polish to finish her.

"Is it okay with you that I have a huge crush on Hugo?" Jesse asked Amanda over their Caesar salads.

"Every girl in the scene does," said Amanda. "I love

that."

"What do you think of Pascal Robbins? Has he shot you?" Jesse asked.

"He's shot me four times, twice for clothing ads, twice for his own portfolio. Did you like him?"

"Yes! But, he's not in the scene, right?"

"Right. His wife is though. She's an actress, so she taught him everything he needed to know to fake it."

"I've never been around so many attractive older men," confided Jesse. "Have you ever had sex with an older man?"

"I've had sex with Pascal Robbins. Once," Amanda admitted. "But don't say anything. I took pity on him because he wanted me passionately and seemed so sad when I turned him down. It was a spontaneous act of charity. We did it in the summer house, where he shot you today."

"Wow. Really? Does Colby know everything you do?"

"Not everything. I'm cagey. Not that I couldn't deflect any criticism fairly easily. He is not saintly either, I'm sure of that. Even so, he's my one and only here," Amanda touched her heart. "Sometimes we're naughty with others together."

"You've done a lot for a 19-year-old," Jesse said admiringly. "Have you been with other older men?"

"Yes, two in their late 20's, and the oldest has to be at least forty, Mr. Bartlett, who owns the department store, Pamela's husband."

"I keep hearing about him!"

"You'll be playing with him before three days are out," Amanda predicted, "and he'll go gaga for you, he loves a tiny waist. He'll bring you clothes. He gives us all beautiful clothes. I just had sex with him once. We had one bad session that he paid me for by letting me shoot a whole video in his store after hours."

"What kind of video?"

"Spanking. I have a little side gig of a spanking clips store going. It's kind of a part hobby, part economics class project I'm running, with Hugo's help, of course. Anyway, the first time Mr. Bartlett spanked me, it wasn't nice. But he made amends by paying me a huge amount of allowance the second time and giving me a nice scene besides. It included sodomy, hence the big payoff. I used the money to go to Europe with Colby last summer."

"Did Colby know about that?"

"He did, but couldn't really fault me. He's an economics major."

"Do you top him?"

"Only emotionally. That is, he lets me boss him around, but sexually and regarding our scene, he's dominant."

"That's so cool. You said you play with others sometimes, as a couple?"

"We have twice. Hugo has an apartment in Back Bay that I have the key to. Colby and I play house there maybe once a week. Once we invited Dru and Pamela to join us. Dru has been Pamela's boy toy for about a year. Colby and Dru strapped us while we were blindfolded, side by side. But they didn't stop there. We kept our blindfolds on but I can say for sure, I had sex with Dru that night and Colby with Pamela. Another time, Mr. Newton let us use his play room in the mansion to do a spanking and enema scene with Pamela. She wanted to experience that. I played the nurse and Colby was the doctor. It was exquisitely kinky. We all loved it."

"Dru spent the night with me," Jesse revealed.

"That's great! He's so nice, I just completely like him."

At that moment, a shadow fell across the table for a gentleman had entered the dining room and walking past the window chanced to recognize Amanda and paused to address her. He was suited, slightly graying, tall, slim, in his late 40's and not unattractive, though world weary and detached. He spoke with a slight British accent, as though he'd come from a different part of Europe but had been educated in England.

"Excuse me, but aren't you Carola's niece?" he asked Amanda.

"Yes," Amanda replied, puzzled, as she didn't recognize the man. "Have we met?"

"I saw you for a moment at her club in Boston about a month ago. But I couldn't get an introduction. Victor Kesselring," he said, extending his hand. Amanda shook it weakly, feeling her face begin to flush. Victor noticed the instantaneous blush suffuse Amanda's beautiful face and realized Carola must have told her all about him. "May I join you ladies for a moment?" he asked.

"Sure," said Amanda, all the words of warning about this old school master echoing in her brain.

"Obviously, I'm in Random Point for the party tonight. I'm staying here at the Inn," he said, then turned to Jesse. "And who are you?"

"Wilhelmina Willoughby," Jesse promptly responded, with a grin, shaking his hand. So, this was the terrible Victor she'd already heard about. He didn't look that scary. As his gaze took her in from head to toe, she could see he was pleased.

"Are you going to be at the party?" he asked.

"I've just been hired to work at the club as a staff submissive," she replied.

"Lovely," he said.

"Would you excuse me a minute?" Jesse asked, rising from the table. She wanted to comb her hair and retouch her lipstick. Amanda looked after her glumly, knowing what was coming and dreading the inevitable conversation.

"Will you be playing at the party, Amanda?" Victor asked.

"I don't know," she replied, "that depends on my

mood."

"I'd love to play with you, if you were in the mood," he said.

"I heard you play hard and mean. I don't dig that," Amanda said, looking straight into his gray eyes. "But maybe I could be persuaded to top you, if you knelt in front of me and placed a cane in my hand."

Victor blinked and stared at her.

"How old are you?" he asked her.

"Nineteen. How old are you?"

"Forty-nine."

"Haven't learned much in 30 years of playing, have you?" she asked.

"What do you mean?"

"Oh, here's my new little buddy," said Amanda, at Jesse's return, her heart pounding violently at her unaccustomed rudeness, yet knowing that she spoke correctly to this reviled repeat offender.

Victor gave Jesse a bemused half smile as they departed.

Chapter Twenty-Five

Jesse's First Session

Every gentleman who regularly plays in a B&D club, has a favorite dungeon. Ambrose had selected the exam suite at the Venus Club to play in so consistently, that Hope and Cassandra had begun to regard the room as Mr. Bartlett's own.

He always enjoyed beginning by sitting behind the large, beautiful teak desk, with the young lady opposite, and encouraging her to disclose, as to an analyst, her most neurotic tendencies.

He was conducting such an interview with Jesse that afternoon. And just as Amanda had predicted, he had brought Jesse a glamourous outfit, of ivory silk satin capri pajamas and matching slippers. While she changed into the outfit behind a quilted brown leather screen, Ambrose read aloud to her from an imaginary clinical file, saying, "Considering how many things you're into, I'll give you just one order to obey over the next hour."

"Yes?" she asked, emerging and sliding into the leather chair opposite him.

"Don't orgasm until I give you leave."

"Oh!"

"Don't you think you can do that one little thing?"

"Yes!" she declared. Though inwardly, she had her doubts. He was terrifically good looking and meticulously suited, even more elegant than Hugo had been. He was Don Draper from Mad Men. If he drew her across that expensively trousered lap, and held her close to him, in just the way she liked and wanted, and moreover, drew her arm back to her waist pinned it there, she might climax instantly. But he didn't have to know that, she grinned to herself.

"Tell me, Wilhelmina Willoughby," said Ambrose, "are you a role play kind of girl or do you just enjoy the sensation of discipline while you go to some special sub place in your head?"

"I'm not very good at role play," Jesse replied, "it seems silly and I giggle."

"You'll have to get good at it if you want to make movies," Ambrose advised.

"I can learn," Jesse agreed.

"For now, tell me candidly, what don't you like about your behavior?"

Jesse leaned back in the chair and pondered for a moment, then replied, "Well, I'm lazy, undisciplined, self-indulgent, vain, insecure and a little OCD."

"How are you lazy?"

"I procrastinate and vital deadlines pass."

"Does that account for the two-year instead of four-year degree?"

"Yes," she said, casting her eyes down.

"You partied instead of studied," he declared.

"Yes."

"That's inexcusable. Did you learn anything at community college?"

"I did learn a lot about websites."

"That might come in handy here. Cassandra and Hope are weak in that area. I want you to explore that with them no later than tomorrow."

"I will!"

"Now how are you undisciplined?"

"I eat lots of candy."

Ambrose shook his head with disapproval. "Smoke?"

"Just weed."

"No wonder you eat so much candy. You should have a

therapeutic purge."

"Really?" she sat up with merry interest.

"But not right now. It's Halloween, caterers are here, there will be a mountain of terrible treats to tempt you all day and into the night. You'll be only too glad to undergo a restorative cleanse this time next week."

"I won't be able to think about anything else," she admitted.

"Oh yes, I do see here that you fetish clinical fantasies? You even wrote the words 'deeply fetish enema fantasies' and specified that you want to be dressed in white for them."

"Yes! And I've never been subjected to one," she declared.

"Should we get your mistress to wriggle into one of her perfect nurse's uniforms and prep you?" Ambrose asked.

"Oh, I'd love that! Carola is maddeningly beautiful. I want to learn from her and make her proud of me."

"Very wise, she has distinction."

"She's so hot," said Jesse dreamily. Ambrose enjoyed looking at her and listening to her first impressions of his world, his friends and his women.

"You're so cute," she said unselfconsciously. "I can't believe my first session is with a cute man."

"What did they tell you about me?" he asked.

"That you're always really hard the first time."

"Oh, don't worry about that. I'm only that way with tall girls. Now, what liberties will you allow?"

"What did you have in mind?" Jesse asked.

"Sex."

"Oh yes, with a condom."

"Of course."

"Oh, definitely, with you," she declared, looking so genuinely delighted that he had to smile back at her.

Ambrose led her to a long, wide, leather couch and pulled her across his lap.

"This isn't for discipline," he told her, stroking her small, jutting bottom through the silk satin pajama bottoms, "this is foreplay." Then he commenced spanking her soundly, first over the silk and then with her pants pulled down to expose the pinkness of her flawless bottom. She squirmed and ground against his lap. He spanked her again, holding her tightly against him. She turned up to try to look at him, putting her right arm back to her waist. He saw she wanted him to pin her wrist to her waist and immediately did. She caught her breath. The spanking lasted for fifteen minutes, with pauses for probing. She was having the best time of her short but eventful sex life over Ambrose Bartlett's lap. He seemed to know all the right buttons to press or release and she was melting with excitement.

"Do you want to be my pet?" he asked, placing her before him and unhurriedly unbuttoning her pajama top and pulling it open to expose her perfect bosom, peach shaped and cherry tipped.

"Yes."

When he had fully undressed her, he placed her on the spanking bench on all fours and got behind her. He had discovered some minutes before, that no lubricant would be necessary. Jesse watched them in the long, broad framed mirror opposite them, when, Ambrose, also divested of garments, a slim, muscular man, took her by the waist and quickly gained full possession of her body with the ease of a porn star. This greatly endeared him to Jesse. She turned and moved one of his hands from her waist down to press against her lower abdomen and he realized that this, like the wrist pinned to her waist, was her trigger gesture. He slowed down his pumping and pressed his hand more firmly under her stomach, which elicited certain faint murmurs of contentment. Jesse thought, this is what older men have going for them, they can pick up on a signal!

Chapter Twenty-Six

Strategic Meeting in the Lounge

As soon as her session with Ambrose was over, Jesse was summoned to the lounge. She only stopped to change from the silk pajamas into a pair of pegged jeans, black turtleneck and black booties. Cassandra was curled up in a leather club chair, Carola was pouring herself a glass of white wine at the bar, Hope was admiring her reflection, in her new black velvet gown, in a large mirror and Hugo Sands was on his feet. Jesse went and sat on a leather pouf beside Cassandra.

Hugo said, "I've invited a party of four high powered lesbians from Boston to the party tonight and they've booked a group session with you all from ten to eleven. The group is composed of two tops and two bottoms. Carola and Cassandra will top the bottoms while Hope and Jesse sub to the tops. Now, I know we have all resisted the notion of taking money from women for playing, but on a case-by-case basis, these ladies can not only afford it, but are looking forward to enjoying the decadence of being paying customers. This is the kind of new clientele you should all want. I know you practically turned out that pretty Naomi when she tried to pay for a session, and that was fine, but next time a straight lady shows up looking for a spanking from a man, recruit Dru Baxter, Freddie Johanson or Dieter Brandt. All of them are more than capable and would probably enjoy the side gig once in a while."

"What are these ladies paying for all this decadence, just for curiosity's sake," said Carola casually.

"A grand apiece for tonight and a grand apiece to join the club. You'll each take home a thousand tonight and the other four grand will go into the club coffers."

Jesse was dazzled by these figures and thrilled to learn that the nineteen dollars and change in her jeans would be soon supplemented with a thousand dollars, out of which she was required to pay no rent.

"Oh, Jesse, Victor will be attempting to play with you as soon as he arrives. Put him off. He'll leave cane strokes on you and wear you out. You need to be unmarked and fresh. Don't play with anyone before that session."

"Got it," Jesse replied.

"Come to think of it," mused Hugo, "it might be a good idea to put him off indefinitely. You can't model for anyone if you're marked and everyone wants to shoot you now."

"Copy that!" said Jesse, delighted she wasn't going to be marked that night. She'd been spanked hard enough to have marks once and she hadn't liked the look of her skin turned black, blue, yellow and purple.

When the meeting broke up, Carola accompanied Jesse down to her room to decide what she was going to wear for the party and the session. Jesse confided to her mistress how pleasant her time with Ambrose Bartlett had been and mentioned the proposed clinical event. Carola said that sounded good to her. "And if it goes well, we can do a movie version of it someday," Carola said.

"What should I expect from this Victor? He came onto Amanda at the Inn today and she completely shut him down."

"And well she should have! She's not available for sessions."

"Except with Mr. Bartlett?"

"She did play with Ambrose, didn't she? But he's in a different class from Victor. He's one of us. And he's good people. Whereas Victor is a pain in the butt. But you can endure him once in a while. He goes back a long way with Hugo."

"Do I have to service him?"

"You do not. Never do that unless it's for your own amusement."

"Like with Mr. Bartlett, right?"

"Right. Not that I haven't enabled Victor in the past, feeding him submissive girls and tempting them with big tips to cater to him. But he's up against it in Random Point.

Carola decided there was enough time before the party to take Jesse to the gym, enroll her and work out. Cassandra gladly gave Jesse permission to go and equipped her with some of Amanda's work-out clothes, delighted that her sister was taking such a nurturing interest in her new housemate. Dark clouds were massing overhead as they drove into the village and stopped at Polyxena's Health Club and Spa, across the road from Michael Flagg's tavern. The Dutch immigrant's partner, Dieter Brandt, was at the front desk and set up Jesse's membership, which was charged to the club.

"Your name was mentioned today," Carola told him provocatively. The trainer and masseur looked at her with interest. He was a well-muscled, fair-haired man in his middle forties, very trim and clean cut, pleasant featured and by orientation, submissive to dominant women.

"In a good way, I hope?" he replied, in his Dutch accent.

"Only that you might be drafted as a top one of these days, when a woman comes into the club looking for a spanking from a man."

"Does that ever happen?" he asked in surprise.

"It did once, but my sister just found her a boyfriend instead. She doesn't know how to take money from people yet." Dieter chuckled. He was the former submissive of his partner, Polyxena Guzman. But that part of their relationship had ended some time since and now they were merely business partners and friends.

"It would be a great honor to serve any lady client in any way she desired," said he, "so you can count on me."

"I knew that. Now, looking at this young lady, what do you think we should start with here?"

"Weight training today, cardio next time. Take her through your own routine," he advised, intimately familiar with Carola's highly disciplined and scientific work out. "You obey your mistress," he told Jesse, "and just like her, you'll keep the same waist size for twenty years."

"I will!" Jesse promised. And off they went to sweat.

Chapter Twenty-Seven

The Greeters at the Door

"I'll introduce you to everyone and tell you all about them," Susan told Jesse confidingly as they walked a little into the wood behind the house to share a joint. "But how are you doing so far?" Susan asked, as they paused to stare down at the glistening rocks at the bottom of the clear running brook.

"Great, but I'm confused about this Victor ballbuster everyone keeps warning me about."

"You don't have to play with him," Susan said. "Don't even worry about it. We've confounded Victor before."

"I'm already supposed to stall him until after that big session at ten."

"Leave it to me," Susan promised her. "Once my sister, Marguerite and I rescued an adorable submissive from Victor and he couldn't do jack about it."

"But I don't want to disappoint anyone. I feel like I need to start earning my keep soon," said Jesse.

Susan protested, "Don't feel that way. Anthony thought the house needed another staff member and Hugo suggested you for a reason. You belong here with us, anyone can see that."

At seven p.m. the guests began arriving. Susan Ross and Jesse, dressed alike in black leather cat suits and boots, stood ready to greet them. Putting Jesse in an inaccessible outfit was an inspiration of Carola's, in the interest of keeping the new submissive unmarked and unmolested until the important session with the high-powered lesbians from Boston.

The first couple to arrive was Plastridge and Diana Currie. He was big, tall and expensively dressed. She was to him, a fairy, in a peach and blood orange layered chiffon gown that floated around her small hips.

"This is my best friend, Diana and P.C.," Susan told Jesse, and then presented Wilhelmina Willoughby to them.

"A new girl, in residence?" Diana was thrilled. "How do you feel about bondage, young lady?"

"I love it so much!" cried Jesse. Plastridge looked at the tiny blonde and then at his small wife.

"Would you like to play with us?" he asked.

"You can have the loft to yourselves," Susan suggested. "Wilhelmina will be free to join you at eleven."

Diana and her big man continued into the house and the next couple arrived, Pascal Robbins and his wife, Phoebe. Pascal had been hired by Hugo to photograph guests for the next few hours. He was on his way down to the lower level where Carola had transported her photo studio from the Brookline club. A green screen had already been set up. The photos of the guests who wished to appear in the magazine would be published in the next issue of the New Rod Quarterly.

When Pascal and Phoebe were out of earshot, Susan confided to Jesse, "Anthony had an affair with her last year."

"Weren't you upset? She so beautiful."

"I got what was going on. She's been in his plays and she's in the scene too. She couldn't help falling in love with him. Artists are passionate. They tend to hook up. I haven't been all that good myself. Pascal is pretty hot. You could say that I consoled him." Jesse remembered what Amanda had told her about the photographer and reflected that Pascal Robbins was uncannily clever at extracting mercy sex from young blondes.

Three of Amanda's classmates from Harvard now arrived: Ronnie, Thalia and Gigi. When they had gone to put their outer wear in the cloakroom, Susan explained that the young black man was one of Amanda's Harvard boyfriends, a film major who, according to Susan, was also the boy toy of Diana when they were in Europe together the previous summer.

"What's the story on that cute girl Gigi?" Jesse asked.

"Oh, she was Dru Baxter's high school girlfriend," said Susan. Jesse's stomach did a flip.

"The girl with the dirty blonde hair in the Pretty Baby dress, Thalia, practically broke Hugo and Laura up."

"Whaaaa?" cried Jesse.

"She's a junior at B.U who came to Random Point to shoot with Hugo and got him to fuck her."

"I tried to do that. He wouldn't go for it," Jesse admitted. Susan laughed.

"That's so cute, he's trying to be faithful. Here comes some more people."

Now William and Damaris arrived, he sharply suited and she in a luxurious ball gown of her own design.

"William is the architect who remodeled this house.

Now Carmen arrived, dressed to tend bar. Jesse remembered meeting her at Michael's tavern the previous night and they greeted each other warmly. When Carmen had gone towards the lounge, Susan said, "She will sub for you with Victor later. She has a high pain tolerance and will try not to cry. That will amuse him."

"I didn't realize she worked here too."

"Michael spares her one day a week. She's a player. She's normally shy, but she loves the kind of attention she gets in a dungeon."

"She's beautiful. I love her pixie cut."

Next to arrive was Sloan Taylor and his curvy wife Paula. He wore a gray sharkskin suit and she shimmered in a silver lame halter gown.

"He's so cute," Jesse breathed as they passed into the house; Susan replied. "She a counselor at Braemar Prep. Hope's husband teaches there."

A tall blond boy and a lithe dark girl appeared next, both clad for a 1950's prom. After exchanging a warm hug with the boy, Susan introduced them as Carl Adam and Naomi. When they had passed into the house, Susan said, "That's the girl who came here looking for a session with a male top about a month or so ago. He's a classmate of mine from Vassar. Now he's doing research work at MIT. Oh, here comes some more Bostonians."

A smart new couple appeared at the door, in their late twenties, he in a suit, she in a black satin cocktail dress, a tall, slender brunette. Susan introduced them as Cameron and Brooke. Cameron looked at Jesse with academic interest. As soon as they had passed into the house, Susan said, "He's a sex researcher. He pays for interviews and has lots of freelance work to give out transcribing interviews. He'll be getting in touch with you soon."

"Is she a model?" Jesse asked of beautiful Brooke.

"She used to work in a B&D club with Hope, when they lived in Hollywood. David was teaching at Hollywood High, and Brooke was in his senior English class. She and Cameron just started dating."

Husky Freddie Johanson and willowy Alison Albrecht arrived next. Susan said, "Meet your co-workers."

"Me?" Freddie laughed.

"Yes, your name was mentioned today as a go-to top if ever another lady walks in looking for a session with a boy," Susan explained, adding, "Alison has been moonlighting here now and then." Jesse gravely shook both their hands. Susan added, "She's a lot more perverse than she looks." Alison was attired in a prep school uniform, of blazer, pleated skirt, tasseled knee socks and brogues. "You're so smart to wear shoes like that," Susan commented to Alison, who grinned. "You're the only girl whose feet won't hurt five hours from now."

Now a dazzling blonde in a cream brocade evening gown arrived on the arm of an impossibly handsome young man in a faultless suit. Jesse recognized the goddess as the co-owner of the gym she'd joined that day. Susan introduced the gentleman as Raphael Price.

Polyxena looked Jesse up and down with appreciation. "I like when little submissives dress dominantly. It confuses everyone," she said.

"You look marvelous," Raphael complimented Jesse, taking her little hand to his lips for a moment. They too moved on into the house.

"What a beautiful man," Jesse breathed softly.

"He's nice too," Susan said. "Oh, look who's here now!" For, Victor had arrived.

"Wilhelmina, take Victor's coat and hang it in the cloak room," said Susan, and Jesse hastened to obey.

"I want to book her for a session," said Victor, displeased that Susan Ross appeared to have the care of the new girl in her power that night. He hadn't forgotten the Aurora kidnapping either.

"She's engaged all evening," Susan replied.

"Oh, how can that be, it's early," he snapped.

"Word travels fast," Susan said, unruffled.

"Where's the mistress of the house?"

"Not sure. But Carmen is available for a session right now. She's the blonde with the shape behind the bar."

Jesse didn't meet Victor's eyes as she returned to her post. He proceeded huffily into the house.

"He looked pissed," said Jesse to Susan.

Susan shrugged, "He hasn't figured out yet, this is the Venus Club, not the penis club."

Chapter Twenty-Eight

Halloween Monster

Now a large group composed of people Jesse had already met arrived together, Michael Flagg and his wife Marguerite Alexander, Hugo, Laura and the two patrons of the house, Anthony Newton and Ambrose Bartlett, along with his wife, Pamela. And right behind them, entered Colby Hodge, Dru, Carola's new husband, Rusty and Hope's husband, David Lawrence. Susan took Jesse by the hand and they followed the large group of new arrivals into the lounge, where Anthony immediately migrated to the piano and settled there.

Susan looked around her before releasing Jesse's hand, saw Victor sitting at the bar talking to Carmen, and relaxed.

During the hour she had spent at the door with Jesse, Susan had decided to take the younger girl up as a friend. She needed a best friend in Random Point, especially since she and Anthony were to spend the entire season in the village. Pamela had Amanda as her protégé and theirs had developed into a beautiful relationship. Susan saw that Jesse had a temperament perfectly compatible with her own, modest, humorous and highly sexual. She would turn Jesse into a graphic novel character by photographing her posed in dozens of outfits, in scores of positions, juxtaposed with males and females, all over the club and the woods and the shore. They would spend a great deal of time together and Jesse would become a frequent visitor at the house, swimming in their pool, playing tennis on their court and very likely having an affair with their handsome resident pool man, gardener and caretaker, Jaime, as all the pretty, younger girls eventually did. But for now, Susan was only concerned with shielding the newest submissive in the club from a potentially unpleasant encounter with the worst player any of them had ever known.

Jesse looked about her, dazzled by all the beautiful people circulating around the large, well-furnished room, feeling the last edible Susan had fed her starting to kick in and warmed by the affection all the people she had met were lavishing upon her. Then tall, dashing Amanda Sands appeared beside her, strikingly clad in a black PVC mini dress and thigh high boots.

"Come with me," said Amanda, pulling Jesse by the hand and taking her back to her own room. "We're going to put on a little show and you need to get into something more accessible." Amanda's closet was filled with small sized outfits and the Harvard girl quickly extracted a perfect little pale, silky shift to put Jesse in with matching sheer panties, a cream silk garter belt and nude seamed stockings. Dennis was texted in the kitchen, where he was helping Josette plate desserts, to run down to Jesse's room and fetch a pair of light colored high heeled pumps to complete her outfit. Then the girls rejoined the others in the lounge, where Marguerite, gorgeously clad in an apricot Jacquard frock coat and vest, satin breeches, and white ruffled shirt, silk stockings and 18th century style be-jeweled high vamp shoes, her long light red hair pulled back in a black velvet bow, was arranging a bench to bend lithe Naomi over.

In her light chiffon prom gown, the red-haired Naomi looked delightful beside the now similarly positioned Jesse. Amanda stood behind and to one side of Jesse and Marguerite did the same with Naomi as the two spankees had their skirts raised and their sheer panty clad bottoms revealed to the entire room. Anthony, at the piano, had a perfect view of this shapely quartet. Amanda took up a stiff leather strap and Marguerite wielded a small, red paddle. Marguerite had performed in this manner times without number at scene parties, but this was the first time in her life that Amanda Sands had played the top in public, and with another young lady. The whole room was mesmerized.

Amanda instinctively paused before beginning, to arrange the hem of Jesse's skirt and run her hand over the satiny curves of Jesse's small, jutting bottom. At the same time, Amanda allowed her gaze to rest on beautiful Marguerite, an artist with an implement of correction as well as with her pen, now in her late 30's and magnificent, still in possession of a classic hourglass figure, and now serenely happy with her condition in the world. Amanda had read her luxuriously decadent erotica since age fourteen, and had formed many of her notions of the B&D universe from Marguerite's books. Now, to be in the middle of a stunning scene party, center stage, so to speak, with Marguerite, and on equal footing, as an elegant top, with a charming submissive to control, was electrifying. She looked out at the crowd and saw Colby watching them with unconcealed pride and not a little prurient interest, for he had never seen Amanda spank a girl or anyone else. She winked at him and grinned. Few people guessed the extent of Amanda Sands' narcissism, for she never outwardly acknowledged the effect her beauty had on people. She'd been raised by a modest yoga teacher and a dreamy empath who taught her finer things. But Amanda had in fact, long been aware of and grateful for the power her beauty gave her. And in this sublime moment of luxurious public decadence, with the most beautiful small girl in the world at her command, and all eyes upon her, Amanda reveled in being a spanking princess, taking command at nineteen. It was glorious.

After Marguerite and Amanda had let their captives go, each rosy bottomed, Anthony caught Susan's eye. She signed to him that she was hungry and he rose from the piano to join her. "Let's get something, we haven't had a bite since lunch," she said. They proceeded out of the lounge into the hall that was lined with Susan and Laura's framed, color illustrations from their various graphic novels. This hallway led to the dining room, where a buffet was laid. But some rather unpleasant cries of pain, carrying all the way from the furthest playroom, stopped them both and they stood still, looking at each other.

"That doesn't sound good," Anthony said.

"That's gotta be Victor tormenting Carmen," Susan told him, and they began to walk down the hall that led past the school room to the short hall that skirted the terra cotta salon and turned at the hall that led to the exam room and Cape Cod, where the cries were emanating from, now punctuated with a scream of "Mercy!" At which point, the accompanying sound of cane swishes striking flesh also ceased. Anthony pulled Susan into the exam room and closed the door.

"What do you think?" he asked her. He knew exactly who Victor was and felt alarmed for Carmen, whom they all loved.

"She said mercy and he stopped. Maybe they're done," Susan replied. For they were both well aware of scene protocol regarding interfering with another person's session. That kind of thing just wasn't done, unless there seemed to be a very good reason. They heard a door open and the sound of male footsteps going down the hall.

Susan and Anthony found Carmen, completely naked, sitting on a bondage bench and undoing an ankle strap from a spreader bar. Her face was streaked with tears and she turned to show them her cane marks.

"He flogged my feet!" Carmen protested, lifting her shapely legs and showing them the red soles of her pretty feet. She was a lovely natural blonde of medium height, in her middle twenties, with a short, feathery pixie cut, a gym sculpted torso and the strong legs of a runner. Carmen was good natured, modest, smart, hard-working and beloved. She had been Michael Flagg's bartender for years and had recently begun moonlighting at the Venus Club. It allowed the shy girl to express her secret flamboyance in ways that aroused her. The brief attentions her devastatingly handsome boss had paid her were a thing of the past, now that he was married to Marguerite. The club provided an outlet for her frustrations. She had yet to meet the perfect man, or woman, to be her chosen partner, but she was open to all possibilities. However, tonight had not been fun.

"And he whipped my pussy, after I asked him not to!" she continued, allowing Susan to help her re-don her black pants, vest and white shirt and comfortable bartending shoes. Anthony shook his head with disapproval.

"This can't happen here anymore," he said firmly. "This isn't why I made this club."

"We'll go and talk to Hugo. He's the one to confront Victor," said Susan.

"You're getting an extra bonus for tonight," Anthony promised her. She grinned at him.

"I'm okay," she said. "I just would never play with him again."

Hugo took Victor into the library and even poured him a whiskey before dropping the boom.

"Victor, we go back a long way, so I'll make this as painless as possible. The subs here, they aren't for you. They're mostly models who can't be marked. Like that new girl. She has five gigs lined up next week."

"That's disappointing," said Victor.

"But that's incidental. The main point is that our girls

aren't into playing how you want to play."

"If they're submissive, they should be playing the way their tops want, not the way they want," Victor pointed out.

"You don't understand. Your style of playing isn't the right fit for this club. If you want to visit now and then for a session with a top, that's fine, but that's gotta be it."

"Hugo, when did you get so pussy whipped?"

"I like pussies, I don't like dicks," Hugo replied, unruffled.

Victor got his coat from the cloakroom and was leaving in a huff, when he came upon Susan in the hallway heading back to the lounge.

"So once again, you cock block me," he accused bitterly.

"You did it to yourself, yet again," she returned contemptuously.

Impulsively, he reached out and grabbed her by her tiny wrist, and started to pull her into the Rose sitting room, saying, "You need to get something to remember me by!"

"This is a revolting development," thought Susan, as she was dragged over to a brocade sofa. But before Victor could pull her over his lap, Anthony, who had been just a side hallway behind them when Victor had accosted Susan, followed them into the room and casually said, "Susan! I've been looking for you." Anthony turned to Victor, who had instantly let Susan's wrist go. "Do you mind if I reclaim my wife?"

Victor murmured, "Of course," and walked out of the room.

Susan threw her arms around Anthony's waist and looked up at him.

"You saved me from a monster!"

Chapter Twenty-Nine

The Josette-Dennis Situation

"Never mind that jerk, something's going on with Josette," said Anthony, taking her by the hand and leading her towards the back of the house. "I just went out to get a breath of air and I saw her sitting on the back porch crying!"

"Why? What happened?" Susan asked.

"She wouldn't tell me," Anthony replied. "Go and find out what happened."

"Okay, right away," Susan promised and dashed down the hall to the bedroom occupied by Amanda when she visited, which let out on the long, screened in back porch. There she saw little Josette, still in her black pants and neat chef's tunic, curled up on a bench seat and wiping her eyes with a crumpled handkerchief.

"Oh, baby, what's the matter?" Susan asked, sitting beside her. "Did someone hurt you?"

"No," Josette gave a little sob.

"Please tell me what's troubling you, maybe I can help."

Josette drew a long sigh. "I love Dennis!" she confided. "I love him so much it hurts. And he barely knows I'm alive."

"Why do you think that? How do you know he doesn't love you right back?" Susan demanded. "Who could not love you, pretty girl?"

"No, he doesn't. He took that beautiful girl to buy shoes. I could see he was entranced by her."

"He only took her because we told him to."

"You told him to because you knew how much it would

turn him on."

"Well, I guess that's true. He's the natural go-to guy when a shoe shopping errand presents itself," Susan admitted, "but if we'd know how you felt, we wouldn't have sent him with Jesse."

"But that's just part of it. Now he's enraptured with all the mistresses in the house and in their glamourous boots and heels. I haven't seen him in an hour. He's following them around!"

"Oh dear. Josette, may I ask you, have you not played with Dennis yet?"

"No. Not at all."

"Really?"

"I want to very badly," Josette said. "But I don't even think he's into spanking."

Susan weighed her next words carefully before uttering them, knowing her objective was to advance the relationship between Josette and Dennis as much as possible, without revealing any sensitive information about that young man. Once in the past, she had indiscreetly mentioned his sexual submissiveness to a young lady he was interested in and he had been indignant enough to turn Susan under his arm, and spank her extremely hard. This unpleasant encounter had initiated a period of coolness between man and mistress that lasted quite some time, though each had concealed the event from Anthony. Going back even further, in the very beginning of her relationship with Anthony, while she was in art school in Boston, Susan had actually tutored Dennis in the art of corporal punishment, teaching him how to spank her correctly and in recognition of his aptness as a student, allowing him, on a number of occasions, to enjoy all of her favors.

"Oh, he's into spanking," Susan said at last. "He probably hasn't thought of it in your case because you're such a well behaved, agreeable and industrious young lady. Not to mention an employee under his supervision. You will have to make it very clear to him that it's perfectly okay with you if he ever wants to spank you."

"He'd have to notice me first!" Josette protested.

"But he does notice you. Don't you two hang out together after work sometimes?" Susan asked.

"We do. We binge watch English gangster movies and edgy TV series. And we go to Central Park and the museums on our days off. But he never makes a move to touch me! He treats me like a little sister or friend."

Susan pulled out a joint and lit it, then passed it to Josette, who accepted it gratefully. Susan looked at Josette, who looked adorable as always, with her shiny dark bob framing her heart shaped face, with skin like a rosy peach. Susan looked at Josette's tiny black shoes with the round toes and her cuffed white ankle socks.

"After we smoke this entire joint, we're going into Cassandra's bedroom and we're going to exchange outfits. You're my size, down to the shoes," said Susan.

Josette looked at Susan's glove tight black leather cat suit and 5-inch heeled boots, which endowed her small mistress with a powerful kind of glamour. "Anthony will love this," Susan added, chuckling.

Getting high with her mistress/friend, and donning the transformative fetish apparel, all but erased Josette's despair. Her big brown eyes began to sparkle. Susan helped Josette get used to the boots, walking her around and around Cassandra's suite until Josette seemed comfortable. The cat suit fit Josette to perfection, clinging provocatively to her small but shapely bosom, petite but plump bottom and well-rounded thighs. Her waist was charming and her boots took her from 5'2" to 5'7". The Louise Brooks bob was a match for the sophisticated costume and Susan insisted upon dark red lipstick to complete the metamorphosis. Up until that moment,

Josette's notion of the perfect party outfit was a dainty dress with a poufy skirt, but as she gazed at her sleek reflection, she suddenly understood what an impact fine club wear could make.

Susan knew that most of the younger guests had at this point, staked out the schoolroom to play in, taking turns at being teacher. She brought Josette into the room while Colby was taking his turn as teacher and in that capacity, administering a brisk caning to Naomi, the statistical analyst from Boston. Seated at the desks, watching the performance, were Colby and Amanda, Carl-Adam Johanson and Thalia, the Boston University junior.

"Excuse me for interrupting," said Susan to Colby, who had paused in his caning at their entry. Susan pulled Josette behind her by the hand. "But I was told to bring Josette here for a caning. She hasn't been bad, but she wants to try it. Right?" Susan turned to Josette, who was gazing at tall, blond, handsome, smartly suited Colby Hodge with fascination.

"Yes!" she nodded. Though she was hoping to receive her first caning from Dennis, who was English. But Colby looked very stern and dominant at that moment and Josette's heart jumped with excitement.

"You've brought her to the right place!" Amanda said, motioning to Josette to take the desk beside her. "We'll take good care of Josette." Josette eagerly accepted the seat.

"I suggest a warm up spanking first," said Carl-Adam helpfully. He was putting this suggestion into action as Susan slipped out of the room, to find Dennis and tell him about how remarkably different Josette looked in boots and leather and how interested all the boys had suddenly become in her. She even brought Dennis to the door of the schoolroom, so he could look in and see Josette moving about in her outfit. Dennis looked at Susan questioningly.

"You exchanged outfits with Josette?"

"Yes. I always wondered how I'd look dressed as a chef," said Susan, smoothing down Josette's gray tunic over her slim torso.

A few hours later, as he was driving them back to the cliff house, Josette sat in the front seat beside him and he kept turning to look at her streamlined profile in the cat suit.

Chapter Thirty

Wet Sunday Afternoon

The morning after the party, everyone was talking about Wilhelmina Willoughby's fresh beauty and charm, Amanda Sands' stepping into the spotlight as a delicious new top and Josette's debut as a fetish princess, who had played with four different men. Back in their home on the cliff, Susan brought Anthony's coffee and buttered roll to the dining room herself and sat with him as they reviewed the events of the night. They had received a full report of how pleasantly Jesse had acquitted herself with the high-powered dykes from Boston and became the cosseted pet of Diana and P.C. within moments of beginning their bondage session. That was no surprise. The big surprise was Josette, who never seemed to stop blushing the entire night, after her transformation.

"I told them both to sleep late," Susan told Anthony.

"Did your strategy work?" he asked.

"It sure worked on the rest of the boys," Susan replied. "We need to give her a nice fetish wardrobe for Christmas, don't you think? It suits her."

"I'd be surprised if Carola didn't invite her to pose for her soon," Anthony said.

"But your question is fair," Susan mused. "Does he really not know she exists? Or is he just playing it cool, biding his time?"

"I can only guess," said Anthony. "He's not one to babble about his personal feelings."

"I know, he's English."

"I've hinted a couple of times he should spank her."

"Well, he hasn't so far. And she's dying for it."

"Let's give her an extra day a week off while we're here in Random Point and she can come over to the club and play with clients or do videos. You know what I'm talking about, work off some of that energy that isn't getting used."

"It would glamorize her more in Dennis' eyes," Susan predicted.

"I wonder though," said Anthony.

"What?"

"Is he really so submissive he couldn't fall in love with a submissive girl?"

"No! He's just a fetishist. I think he can easily adapt to topping a young, innocent girl who adores him," Susan declared.

Jesse and Dru awoke early, had their coffee in the downstairs kitchen and then began cleaning up the house. He told her he would have to return to Boston that afternoon and asked if she would write and let him know when he should come back to see her. "Won't you come back to see me as soon as you can?" she asked, for they had connected fully and completely every time they went to bed together. He promised he would, warmed to the core by her ardor.

Presently Cassandra found them and brought them up to her kitchen, where there was no end of delicious pastries left over from the party, to which she added a dish of creamy scrambled eggs and a bowl of fresh fruit. Amanda and Colby drifted in to join them and the youthful quartet took their plates out to the back-porch veranda to watch the rain fall as they ate.

"I just remembered," said Jesse, "Mr. Bartlett wants me to help Cassandra with computer work. I aced website construction at college."

"I could help with that too," said Dru. "I'm learning

computer graphics right now."

"Could you show me around her system before you leave today?" Jesse asked.

"I would love to!" Dru said.

Amanda said, "I wonder how Hugo knew you'd fit in so well."

"I've been writing to him constantly," Jesse disclosed. "The magazine was such a revelation to me. I smothered him in hero worship."

"Jesse, after you've settled in a little bit, come visit us in Boston," Amanda said. "You can stay at Hugo's apartment in Back Bay and we'll show you sights and take you out with us."

Jesse felt serenely happy. Had writing perfect letters truly been the magical key to obtaining this extraordinarily appropriate new life?

That afternoon, while Dru and Jesse were seated respectively at Hope and Cassandra's computers, they received an unexpected visit from Anthony Newton, who wanted to talk about the club. Cassandra was summoned, along with Hope.

"They're going to spiff up the website," said Cassandra.

"That's lovely," said Anthony, "but after what happened with Victor last night, I've had some thoughts about the club."

Cassandra and Hope exchanged looks but didn't speak.

"Yes," he continued, "I was thinking that maybe except for word of mouth among our scene friends, you should downplay the sessions angle and advertise the club as a private shooting space with models available, slash play space for couples. And really emphasize the exclusivity and expensiveness of using the facilities. Also, references are a must."

"I agree," said Cassandra.

"Me too," said Hope, who was perfectly happy to enjoy

more layers of protection.

"I'll continue to cover the operating expenses of the house, the accounting and so forth," said Anthony. "I love how you're managing everything, Cassandra. And you were right to take Carola in. She's brought the femdom spirit into the house that the club needed for balance. And her interesting new marriage has lightened her general mood and made her fun to be around."

"I can finally stand her," admitted Cassandra.

"Why didn't you like her?" Jesse couldn't help asking.

"Her perfectionism and image polishing used to get on my nerves. But I can see now, she was stressed out about making her nut for that club in Boston. She is an artist at what she does. In comparison, I'm a poser here," said Cassandra.

"You were in Hugo's first magazine," Anthony pointed out. "So, you're not a poser. You're an original. And you're more about what we're into," he motioned to Susan and himself, "than Carola ever was."

"That's right," said Hope to Cassandra, "you shouldn't doubt yourself. I've seen you play, you give and take a great spanking. And that's what this club is about."

"None of you should ever do anything you don't want to do here," said Anthony. "There are other clubs around that cater to extremes. This club will be famous for its beauty and refinement, not for how hard the girls can be thrashed."

"Dare I hope we've all seen the last of Victor for a while?" asked Cassandra. "He was looking at me in way that seemed to say, if I can't have your daughter, I think I'll try you out. But I managed to slip out of his eye all night."

"You wish you've seen the last of Victor," said Carola from the doorway. She had just come from the gym and was dressed in autumn wools and walking shoes. "He's residing at Polyxena and Raphael's house for the next two weeks while they stay at his villa on Lake Geneva."

Jesse soon discovered there were two delightful paths into the heart of Random Point from the house, one was via tree lined lanes, the other followed the brook that ran behind the club all the way into town. That brisk, overcast November morning, Cassandra had offered Jesse a bike, but Jesse decided to walk along the brook instead, on her way to Hugo's shop. She was dressed in black leggings, a white cowl neck sweater and gray tweed car coat with little walking booties. It had been a lovely, unrushed morning, drinking Cassandra's perfect coffee and staring endlessly at the exquisite art lining the hallways of the club. The Ray Caesars intrigued her the most but framed illustrations and panels from Susan and Laura's graphic novels were the most erotic, with all the handsome tops spanking pretty girls. Dru had gone back to Boston but she was soon to become an official spanking model and might even have the fascinating Sloan Taylor as her first modeling partner. She was going to Hugo's to discuss the scheduling right now. The brook was very beautiful and Random Point was a dream. The colors of autumn, the scent of the woods, even the cloudy skies, gave her so much joy she almost sobbed. For just a few weeks before, she'd shared an apartment overlooking an urban alley with four other kids and stood behind a counter all day at a budget hotel, checking in guests.

When she reached Hugo's antiques shop, he was engaged with some customers and told her to go across the street to the bookshop, find Sloan and agree upon a time when he was free to shoot that week. "Yay!" Jesse thought, hurrying over to the bookshop. She had barely spoken to Sloan at the party, but since he forcibly reminded her of Keanu Reeves, her fantasy brain had been preoccupied with him since first sight. Now she found him just finishing ringing up a sale at the back counter of the atmospheric shop. He looked up and smiled at her, at once recognizing the new beauty of Random Point. She stammered out that Hugo had sent her over to schedule a shoot for them, if he was up for it.

"Really?" Sloan looked amused.

"He didn't mention it to you?"

"No!"

"I hope you have time," she said shyly.

"Of course! Tomorrow is my day off."

"Great, he wanted to do this right away. Can you come by the club at ten am? It will be a piano lesson, shot in the lounge. I'm going to wear a black velvet dress with a frothy crinoline underneath and look very spoiled. Hugo asks that you wear a gray suit and quiet tie."

"Got it," Sloan said.

"You've done two photo shoots for Hugo, haven't you?"

"How did you know?"

"I have a complete collection of the magazines, or as many as I could find. I saw you in them."

"Oh, a true devotee!" said Sloan appreciatively.

"The truest," Jesse agreed.

"So, you know the routine, all the poses, the varying stages of undress, etc.?"

"Yes, I would expect the set will conclude with a caning," she said knowledgeably.

"Have you been caned?"

"Yes. I had a spanking boyfriend in high school and we tried everything."

"That's great. You're so tiny though."

"I'm sturdier than I look," Jesse promised.

"Say mercy if you have to. Or if I'm spanking you, too hard you can squeeze my leg."

"Oh, I'd never do that!"

"Oh! You like to test your limits?"

"I don't know. But I think I have a pretty good tolerance

for spanking!"

After their pleasant interview, Jesse browsed on the upper level of the gallery that contained the bookstore's copious collection of erotica. She made several illustrated purchases, for her little bank account was suddenly full, after modeling for Pascal, doing several sessions and paying nothing for room or board. She took her magazines down to the coffee bar and took a stool at the counter, behind which, Marguerite Flagg, nee Alexander, was serving that day. Ever since Hope had departed, she and Sloan had found it difficult to fill the place to their satisfaction and had arrived at a temporary solution, of splitting the coffee bar duties between them.

"Go and sit with Josette," said Marguerite, nodding to the Newtons' little chef, sitting all alone in a red leather booth and toying with a cappuccino. "I'll bring you whatever you want."

"Thank you! Black tea with lemon and a chocolate chip cookie, please."

Jesse approached the booth.

"Hi, Marguerite said I should join you. Do you mind?"

"Oh, no! Please do. I remember you from the party," said Josette, her heart jumping as she recalled how Dennis had spent an hour with this small Venus helping her buy shoes.

"I remember you too. You made those delicious petit fours that I ate too many of. What's it like working for them? Susan was so nice to me on Halloween."

"It's lovely. They spoil me rotten. I should cook for them just for the room and board. I never had it so good. Plus, they are just fun to be around."

"Does he top you?"

"Oh no. I mean, we did play once, when the club first opened. He gave me a scene. A perfect scene. And he gave me a tiny little cute welcome spanking the day I started working for them, but otherwise, nothing at all like that. It just won't happen. He's a newlywed."

The two new friends began discussing their experiences in the scene in detail. Jesse had more experiences than Josette, who had practically none.

"Mr. Newton wanted me to check out the New York clubs, but I was too intimidated," Josette confided. "This morning he said I should pop over to the Venus Club once a week and see if anyone wants to spank me."

"Yes!" Jesse cried. "Come back with me now and hang out for a while."

"Well, it is my day off," Josette said.

"I'll text Mr. Bartlett that you'll be there this afternoon. He always likes to be the first to play with a new girl, I'm told," said Jesse.

"Wait! I'm not dressed or anything," said Josette, regarding her nubby oatmeal cardigan, brown pegged cords, walking shoes and camel toggle coat. A matching tam set off her straight, shiny black bob prettily.

"Oh, that club is crammed with wardrobe," said Jesse. "Carola has her whole costume and lingerie collection downstairs next to the photo studio."

Just then, Jesse chanced to look up at the counter and saw Marguerite trying to catch her eye, and when she had done so, the leggy redhead placed one finger on her lips and inclined her head to the direction of the booth beside the ones in which the girls sat. It was too tall to see over, but Jesse excused herself for a moment to go up to the counter and exchange a word with Marguerite.

"Victor is sitting in the next booth," murmured Marguerite as she handed Jesse a slice of pink and green frosted cake.

"Ooooh, what's this?" Jesse breathed appreciatively.

"Princess cake. With marzipan."

"Mmmm, thanks!"

As she walked back to the booth, she caught Victor

smiling at her.

It wasn't until the girls were walking along the secluded brook path back to the club that Josette began to dilate on the only subject that really interested her at all these days, Dennis. Oh, she had enjoyed the pretty boys she had been spanked by at the party. Ronnie, the handsome black sophomore from Harvard, had had the best technique; Carl Adam Johanson and Colby Hodge, the two blond jocks, were beyond exciting, with their big, firm, muscle corded laps and Dru Baxter was equally charming. But none of them had an English accent. It was Dennis she dreamed about all day. Jesse became so engaged listening to this tale of apparently unrequited love, that she forgot to warn Josette that the session from hell had been listening to their earnest confessions of inexperience in the scene.

When they reached the house, Jesse took Josette downstairs to her room and they continued to exchange secrets. Jesse began to build Josette's confidence, telling Josette that she was beautiful and praising her skills lavishly. She convinced Josette that Dennis' naturally shy and deferential personality was preventing him from moving in on her as rapidly as another man might. Then they discussed whether Josette should follow Anthony Newton's suggestion of visiting the Club for a session now and then. The notion excited Josette's imagination, but in her heart, she didn't want to be handled by anyone but Dennis.

Cassandra was going out in her car to do a few errands and Josette asked to be dropped off at the package store to buy some wine for the house. While she was inspecting the inventory, she was accosted by Victor in an aisle.

"Oh, hello," he said, "didn't I see you at the party?"

"Yes," she replied, looking up at him, "I kind of popped out at the end. I was in the kitchen most of the time."

"You're the little chef, aren't you?"

"Yes, I'm Mr. Newton's cook," she replied, scrutinizing his face while trying to decide why he was talking to her and if the attention made her happy or anxious. He had the craggy face of a fifty-year-old, a sort of European accent and a world-weary expression, but was not unattractive.

"Should I take your advice on wine?"

"Gee, I don't know," she replied. But when she got a clerk's attention, she ordered six cases of various whites and reds from a list she'd been making and handed over the delivery address and a credit card she had been authorized to use for all household purchases.

"Can I drop you somewhere? I'd love to chat with you awhile," he said affably. She hesitated, having been about to call Dennis to pick her up. She decided to stick with that plan and sent Dennis a text, politely declining the offer and making her way to the door. He followed her outside and detained her to continue their conversation. "Would I be correct in assuming you're a submissive?" he plunged in, taking full advantage of this unique opportunity to occupy her full attention. Her youth, beauty and fresh innocence piqued his excitement and the urge to possess her grew even stronger.

"Is it that obvious?" she asked, looking up at the darkening sky. It would rain again before the hour was out. A sharp breeze was blowing up the street and she did up the toggles on her car coat.

"I'd absolutely love to play with you," he said.

"Me?"

"Yes, why not? I'm a top, you're a bottom. I'm experienced, you're inexperienced. Why don't you come home with me for a while? The house where I'm staying has a great playroom."

"Oh no, I couldn't. I'm waiting for my ride home now." She looked at her phone. Dennis had just texted her back that he'd be with her in ten minutes.

"Why kind of things are you into?" he asked.

"Oh, just spanking really," she confessed.

"Just spanking? No bondage?"

"I don't know. I never tried it."

"What about sexual service?"

"No, I don't think so," she replied firmly, frowning at the ground. Josette thought, "For Dennis maybe, but not for some elderly stranger."

"Come over and visit me next time you're bored," he said, handing her a card with his name and phone number.

"I don't think so. I don't even know you," she protested.

"Are you in the scene or aren't you? I'm a player and a friend of Hugo Sands. What more do you need to know?"

"Maybe a lot."

"Don't you want to start racking up some experiences? How can you tell what you like or don't like until you try different things with different people?"

"I am interested in having experiences," she admitted.

"Don't you want to test your limits?"

"No, should I?"

"Of course, how else do you know how to define your scene persona?"

"I don't think I have a persona. I'm just a girl."

"I tasted some of your confections at the party," he changed the subject abruptly; "You're a brilliant pastry chef." This caused her to flush with pleasure and she reassessed his face.

"Thank you. Then only let me bake for them once a week," she admitted. "They don't want me to make them fat. It's very frustrating. Pastry was my specialty at the Culinary Institute."

At that moment, Dennis drove up in the Bentley.

Josette bid Victor a hasty farewell and jumped into the front seat.

"Who was that you were talking to?" Dennis asked.

"His name is Victor, he was at the party. He's been trying to get me to come to his house and play with him," she replied, in an ordinary tone, as though she were giving a weather report. Dennis looked at her.

"Play with you how?"

"You know, top me."

"If that's the same Victor I've been hearing about for years, I'd stay well away from him!" Dennis said emphatically.

"Really? He's notorious?"

"Highly."

"In what way?"

"I remember a few years back, Susan and Laura rescued a submissive from him."

"Why did she need rescuing?"

"I'm not sure. But I think he was being mean to her."

"Wow."

"Ask Susan about Victor. They're arch enemies. In fact, he acted like a real dick at the party, beat the hell out of Carmen."

"Oh!"

"You weren't seriously thinking about going with him to his house, were you?" Dennis asked.

"Oh no! I was trying to get rid of him the whole time we were talking."

"Oh, good!"

Lightning and thunder announced the commencement of the afternoon rain as they drove up the hill to the house. A conversation he had had with Anthony that morning came back to Dennis then. He'd been laying out a suit and accessories for his employer when Anthony startled him out of a reverie by demanding to know if Dennis ever planned to close the deal with Josette. When Dennis asked what he meant, Anthony elaborated, "Can't you see the small one is in love with you?" When Dennis shook his head in disbelief, Anthony insisted, "I wouldn't kid you about something like that. How do you feel about her?"

"About Josette?" Dennis fumbled for words. "I adore her, of course."

"Who wouldn't? She's adorable even without the cooking. But you can't ignore the cooking either. That girl's a jewel without price. Don't you agree?"

"100%!" Dennis returned.

"I think what I'm asking is, are you into her? Would you like her to be yours?"

"Of course I would. But I'm not good enough for her. As you said, jewel without price."

"Nonsense, Dennis. You too are one of those," Anthony assured him. "I've always appreciated your modesty. It's what makes you so likable. But in this one particular case, with Josette, it's permissible to go slightly out of character. You needn't be deferential with her. Instead, take charge of her. And at the first opportunity, give her a good spanking. That's what she's into, that's what she wants, what she dreams about."

Dennis glanced sidelong at Josette's pretty little profile. Did he really dare lay hands on her? It was easy to imagine her exquisitely smooth, petite, well rounded little body, completely nude and curled up beside him in his bed every night. She was so tiny. Even smaller than Susan. He'd spanked Susan a number of times back in her college days, when she thought nothing of using him as a service top. She had made it clear that the power exchange was all about orgasms and not real in any other sense and he had enjoyed every instant of serving her simple needs. This had happened over eight years before, when they were both extremely young and at the height of sexual curiosity and it had happened casually and without drama. Dennis was certain Mr. Newton knew all about it, he knew everything about his women. Therefore, Dennis felt a measure of confidence as he considered Josette's current needs. Very well, Dennis thought to himself, a new chapter opens. And if Mr. Newton was correct, as he usually was, and Josette truly loved him, it was likely to be a long chapter and one in which he must adopt a new role for himself in the household, or reinforce the existing one in a whole new way.

Chapter Thirty-One

Dennis and Josette's First Scene

It was sunny and unseasonably warm for that Sunday's Farmer's Market and the sky was a dark, brilliant blue. All around the trees were gold and red and the air was perfumed from the open apple barrels and potpourri bins. Dennis had dropped Josette off with a small hand truck and drove off to execute a few errands. She had dressed herself for maximum accessibility, should any opportunity for erotic adventure present itself, in a short gray wool pleated skirt, argyle knee socks that hugged her shapely calves, tasseled brogues, a white shirt and cropped cardigan.

When Dennis returned to fetch her and load up the car, he found her sitting at the coffee bar opposite Victor, apparently engaged in an easy conversation. Upon entering Josette's line of vision, Dennis gave a small nod of his head and she acknowledged him with a start and jumped to her feet. Making a hasty farewell to Victor, Josette pulled the handle of the hand truck, which so far only held a few bags of oranges and pears, and made her way through a small cluster of shoppers to Dennis, who stood waiting for her at one of the cider stands.

"Was that Victor again?" he said at once, while he took the hand truck from her and they fell into step together and headed away from the coffee bar and into the heart of the market.

"Yes."

"Didn't I say to stay clear of him?" Dennis demanded, in a tone she'd not heard him use before.

"Did you?"

"I'm sure I did."

"He appeared when I was getting coffee and it would have been rude not to sit with him for a minute," Josette explained.

"Was he trying to get you to come play with him again?"

"He offered to pay me a thousand dollars to come and cook him dinner. Oh, let's get a pumpkin, I'll make you a better pumpkin pie than you've ever had before," she said, directing Dennis to pick up a small sized pumpkin.

"What's this you're saying now? He's trying to get you to come and cook for him?"

"Just once. On my day off."

"I hope you didn't agree."

"I said I'd think about it," she lied. For she had declined the offer immediately.

"Josette! How could you consider such a thing? You work for Mr. Newton. You can't just go and cook for someone else."

"It would be on my day off. I never signed a contract that I'd cook exclusively for Mr. Newton," Josette pointed out. Dennis frowned and shook his head with grave disapproval.

"How can you be so ungrateful, after how they've spoiled you?" he said.

"Why ungrateful? Why should Mr. Newton care what I do on my day off?"

"I don't say he would actually care. Nevertheless, is an unwritten rule that one doesn't poach someone else's cook."

"Where, in a P.G. Wodehouse novel?"

Dennis stared at her. "You've read Wodehouse?"

"Susan has been giving me her favorite books to read."

"Considering how Susan feels about Victor, you should make it your business to cut him."

"Would you care, personally, if I did something with Victor?"

"I'll show you how much as soon as we get home," Dennis promised.

"What do you mean by that?" she asked, lifting a bunch of pink carnations to her nose.

"Buy those," he advised, "I like the color."

Dennis' quarters above the garage were spacious, well-furnished and altogether pleasant, with the afternoon sunlight slanting in through the blinds. He brought Josette up here as soon as they had stowed the market goods in the pantry. Both their hearts were pounding as he locked the door.

"I overheard them talking about you going to do sessions at the club perhaps, on your day off," Dennis began.

"Oh, really?" she smiled slightly and looked around the room. She saw a sturdy straight backed wooden chair pulled away from the desk.

"I don't like the idea," he said.

"You've thought about it?" she asked.

"Don't you realize you'll be handled and maybe even manhandled by mostly middle-aged men there?" he demanded.

"I hadn't given it much thought," she admitted.

"Victor is pushing fifty."

"Oh, yes, I'm sure that's true," she agreed.

"In any case, you're not a silly B&D girl, you're a professional chef. The very idea of your working in a club is a step sideways."

"I don't think it was ever about anything but collecting some experiences," Josette felt she must point out.

"Well, you needn't go work in a club for experiences. I can give you an experience right now."

"I consent," she said, dropping her gaze to her little

shoes.

He took her by the hand and led her to the chair, sat down and took her across his lap. The pleated wool skirt and bare knees, the socks and shiny shoes, gave him joy. She felt his arm across her waist and his hand smoothing down her skirt over her curvy little bottom. "How hard?" he wondered, knowing it was crucial he get this first encounter right. How many times had he heard Susan complain, "Spanking guys spank too hard!"

He started over her skirt, as they did in the best videos. And by the way she began to move and the cute little sounds she was making, he knew he had found the right stroke and even the perfect tempo.

Dennis paused to slowly fold back her pleated skirt to reveal white and pale pink frilled rumba panties. "Oh, how delicious," he said admiringly. "Is this the type of lingerie you normally fancy?" Josette's outer wear was utilitarian most days. "Or were you expecting someone to undress you today?"

"Maybe hoping," she said over her right shoulder.

"Get up for a moment," he said, "I want you to see how naughty you look, young lady," he said, arranging a triple frame wardrobe mirror opposite them to Josette's right before taking her by the hand, back over his knee. "I hope you appreciate that I'm taking the trouble to give you that same dungeon effect you would have gotten if you'd gone to the Venus Club to play. All the rooms have mirrors."

"Thank you," she said softly, beguiling him with her shyness. She did turn her head to look at the spectacle of herself across the knee of man she loved, for the first time and was thrilled to the core. She thought, "Look how cute I am! OMG, he's so handsome. I'm dying!" And the bliss of it all did well up for a moment in a mini pre-orgasmic rush, a spasm in the center of her stomach that meant a sexy man was taking control. She used to get it when she read mainstream novels that had spanking scenes. Or when the teacher she had a crush on frowned.

"I don't want you to work at any club," Dennis said, spanking her. "Or go to anyone's house to cook for them." The way she moved across his lap, rubbed against his thighs, flirted her bottom at him, aroused his interest in spanking for the first time in years. This is what spanking did to some girls. It's what it had done to Susan. This was ever so much better than if she'd just passively and stoically submitted, then it would have been impossible to read the signals correctly. She was carnation pink when he pulled the frilled panties down to her thighs. He was thrilled that she wore no perfume, for the scent of a wildly excited twenty-two-year-old beauty was infinitely more intoxicating. "Did you hear me, Josette?"

"Yes!"

"Then promise you'll behave yourself like the modest girl I know you are," he warned, before delivering a dozen resounding smacks, each of which caused her to kick her adorable feet, which he loved.

"I do!" she cried. He let her up. She quickly drew her panties back up.

"I want to ask you something," he said, helping her put her clothes entirely back to rights with the deftness of a valet.

"Yes, anything,'" she replied.

"Answer me in complete honesty," he said.

"I will."

"How do you feel about me?"

Josette threw her arms around his neck. He picked her up and carried her into the bedroom.

The following morning, Dennis and Anthony were in Bartlett's doing some early Christmas shopping when Dennis paused before the jewelry department.

"Come in here for a minute and give me some advice?"

Dennis asked his boss, who followed him in surprise. When they got to the counters with rings, Dennis paused. "Will you help me pick out an engagement ring?" he asked.

"I'll even pay for it!" Anthony replied, hardly able to contain his delight.

Chapter Thirty-Two

Jesse and Josette's
Moderately Unpleasant Adventure

Victor was frustrated and faintly amused by the denials and evasions the most attractive new female players in Random Point were meeting his advances with. He'd never encountered so much resistance before, but instead of infuriating him, it intrigued the seasoned master, to whom it never occurred to abandon his pursuit of the three graces, Amanda Sands, Wilhelmina Willoughby and the bite sized Chef Josette. He realized he was least likely to get Hugo's daughter to ever submit to him; for the leggy blonde was too well off to need allowance, too flush with boyfriends and admirers to need a playmate and appeared to be more dominant than submissive. To be sure, he did not dislike the notion of letting her top him and had an idea that he could eventually set something up with Amanda and her stunning aunt Carola to that effect. Meanwhile, he was constantly on the lookout for the new tag team of Wilhelmina and Josette. After eavesdropping on their intimate conversation at the coffee bar, Victor thought he had grasped their main area of vulnerability, their inexperience, a state that seemed to embarrass them both. They both wanted to learn more about the scene to which they had committed. He planned to convince them that he could supply special knowledge.

In spite of his rough, careless style of playing with submissive girls, Victor still had some good friends in Random Point, at least among those ladies he'd now and then subbed to. Polyxena, who remembered him fondly as one of her best customers in Amsterdam, had welcomed him as a guest in Raphael's house and invited him to use her playroom in their absence. Marguerite, who had also topped him a number of times, met him for lunch and flirted with him so provocatively, that he invited her to come back to the house and cane him. And Carola, ever the enabler of tops, very quickly arranged for Marion Craig to come out from Boston as soon as her work schedule would allow, to submit to the harsh master she'd been fantasizing about for so long. That session also took place at Raphael and Polyxena's house, after which, Marion went to The Venus Club and tried to give Cassandra all her session money to let her stay overnight in the loft. Cassandra didn't take the money, but gladly let Marion recover from her caning and the sodomy Victor had subjected her to. Marion had not disliked Victor's rough style but later confided to Hope that he didn't aim correctly or strike carefully, but every which way, like an angry child breaking his toys.

"His arrogance turned me on. It was classic," Marion told Hope when she got to the Venus Club to spend the night. "But his technique was rubbish. He actually left a couple of welts on my thighs."

Victor had enjoyed the afternoon with the hot attorney, but she wasn't a tender twenty-two, like Wilhelmina Willoughby, a fairy child with ice blonde hair and knowing blue eyes. Victor kept homing back to Marguerite's bookshop, where he knew Wilhelmina would soon return.

The next Tuesday afternoon, everything fell into place for Victor's most ambitious dream to come true. It was a mild, mellow day and he was sitting on the sunny patio connected to the coffee shop, in earshot of the brook, leafing through a magazine, when he glimpsed into the shop and saw Jesse and Josette standing at the counter, giving Sloan their order. Then they made their way out to the patio. Victor happened to be seated at one of the wooden tables for four and instantly rose and motioned them over. The girls looked at each other uncertainly. Then Jesse shrugged and led the way to Victor's table.

"Join me, ladies," he said affably and they took seats next to each other opposite him. Josette looked at him wide eyed. Jesse smiled her crooked smile that was impossible to make out. "What have you both been up to this fine day?" he asked. He was absolutely unused to making small talk with submissives. Most of the time, he entered a dungeon when they were already naked, on their knees, eyes averted, awaiting commands and forbidden to speak unless to reply to questions.

"Josette just got engaged," Jesse announced, taking Josette's tiny hand and displaying the small diamond ring Dennis had placed on her finger the previous day. Josette blushed and pulled back her hand.

"But marriage is so boring," Victor observed. "Isn't it the end of fun?"

"Have you been married a long time?" Jesse asked.

"It seems like a very long time," he replied, for his wife of ten years was a high-powered Hollywood agent and even the thought of her exhausted him. "But, as you're soon to be out of circulation," he said to Josette, "more reason than ever to play now."

"Josette played a lot at the party the other night," Jesse said.

"Is that true?" Victor asked.

Josette nodded, the color once more rushing to her face.

"Don't you girls want to ever try anything more adventurous than spanking?" he asked.

"I want to try everything," confided Jesse. "Except under water bondage."

While Victor was considering how best to pilot the conversation to his advantage, Jesse thought back to the previous afternoon, in the blue salon, where Carola was demonstrating hogties to Jesse, using Hope as a model, and the subject of Victor arose.

"It doesn't feel right, 86-ing Victor after all these years," Carola said, using one long piece of rope to complete the entire classic hogtie, with Hope on her stomach, with her knees bent and ankles joined to her bound wrists.

"He isn't entirely forbidden to the club," Hope pointed out, turning her head towards them. "He can still sub here."

"Isn't that really harsh? How can he not feel unmanned by that?" Carola wondered.

"Give me a break," cried Hope. "He's as harsh as it gets with us!"

"I know," Carol agreed, smacking Hope's sheer, panty clad bottom. "See?" Carol said to Jesse, "when you've got them in this hog tie, you can spank them a bit too."

"He's been getting away with murder for years because mistresses like you happily feed him girls like me, trusting a hundred-dollar tip will make everything okay." said Hope. "Name a single girl you know who ever liked his stupid scene?"

"Oh, the odd masochist," Carol replied. "He gave Marion the scene she thought she wanted. Maybe that was good. Now she knows all about it."

"He's old school," said Hope, "he plays to satisfy himself. And because he's always gotten what he wants from an unending stream of well-trained submissives, he's never questioned it."

"Is it fair to change the rules after all these years of him getting exactly what he wants for the price he's never balked at?" Carola wondered.

"New club, new rules," said Hope firmly.

The conversation had gotten Jesse wondering about The Story of O. It had been her favorite book, until she found Marguerite Alexander's stories. Pauline Réage had written a book that her lover would like. But the girls in Roissy were merely beautiful sex robots, expressionless, emotionless, there to be used, available in every orifice, to any man who wore the ring of Roissy. It had been a hot story. But Jesse did not wish to be available to any man. She only wished to be handled and used and penetrated in every orifice by cute men who were also smart and kind and knew what they were doing.

"Then we shouldn't even call you girls submissive," Carola observed.

"Correct," Hope said. "We're role players. Our actual souls are not for rent."

"Wow," said Carola, "you really didn't enjoy that last session with Victor."

"Say you're sorry," demanded Hope.

"I'm sorry," said Carola.

"Kiss my bottom," said Hope. Carola placed a small kiss on the cheek she'd just smacked through the sheer nylon.

"Then I forgive you," Hope replied.

Jesse came back to the moment and looking intently into Victor's eyes, said bluntly, "We heard about how you play from Carmen. It's why you've been restricted to sub sessions at the Club."

Victor sighed in resignation, seeing he had no leverage in this argument. He looked defeated and it gave Josette a pang, for she was highly compassionate. She whispered something in Jesse's ear. Jesse looked at her in surprise. Josette whispered something else and sat back.

"Tell him your idea," Jesse prompted Josette.

"How much if we come visit you at your house?" Josette asked.

"Whatever the going rate is," he replied, becoming instantly electrified.

"We'll take half -- if you pledge to play with us like a

gentleman," Jesse said.

Then Josette pulled a small tissue wrapped package from her bag and handed it across the table to Victor. "It's a THC-infused bouchon. I baked it myself. Eat it now and we'll be over to see you in ninety minutes," Josette said.

"And if that doesn't turn you nice, you're beyond redemption," Jesse declared, for she had tried one of Josette's cannabis cupcakes and found them divine.

As they crossed the street to Hugo's shop, Josette asked Jesse to help her conceal their upcoming adventure from Dennis, if possible. Jesse said she didn't think that would be possible, since they were doing this to power wash Victor's public image and if it succeeded, the event would inevitably be discussed in Dennis' hearing.

"Don't worry. We'll say it was our idea of a kinky little bachelorette party. If he doesn't think that's super cute, give him the ring back."

They found the shop empty and Hugo in his office. He had been writing up a report on the party for the magazine and welcomed them to sit in the wooden swivel chairs opposite his desk. Jesse immediately disclosed her plan of rescuing Victor's reputation in the eyes of the Venus Club, by conferring a visit upon him and holding him to a high standard of behavior once there. Josette produced one of her magnificent tissue wrapped confections and presented it to Hugo. "We gave him one of these to eat, to put him in a good mood," she said.

"It'll get him fucked up," Jesse explained. Hugo grinned.

"You girls may actually be onto something," he commented, unwrapping and sampling the heavenly confection. "Oh my god," he said, "That's good. But why go to all this trouble for Victor? I thought everyone was more or less glad to get rid of him."

"My mistress has a soft spot for him," said Jesse; "she

was pleading his cause yesterday. If I can get him reinstated, she'll be proud of me."

"You want to please Carola, do you?" Hugo was amused.

"Yes, I worship her," Jesse replied.

"Are you sure you want to go out there unchaperoned?"

"We will trust in the bouchon to tame the beast," said Jesse gravely.

"I don't understand you girls. Everyone complains about Victor and when we finally get rid of him, you're making a date. And you, young lady," Hugo said to Josette sternly, "why are you a part of this reckless antic?"

"I'm supporting my friend," Josette explained.

"My mistress thinks that bad sessions can be useful," Jesse explained, "a sort of education."

"Your mistress Carola, I take it, not Cassandra," Hugo observed.

"Of course," Jesse agreed. Hugo munched thoughtfully, looking at them.

"What should we wear?" Jesse asked, "To soften him up."

"Something accessible. Go in Carola's wardrobe, she has lots of double sets of cute short dresses for her videos. Zip mini dresses and thigh high boots, no pantyhose. Black lace lingerie underneath."

"Okay, we'll go back to the club and change," Jesse said, rising.

"I hope you don't actually expect Victor to understand what it means to play like a gentleman. By the way, what does that mean?" Hugo asked.

"Basic spanking, possibly caning, possibly toys, possibly sex, on a case-by-case basis," said Jesse, as though she'd gone over this litany many times as her repertoire.

"What about nipple clamps?" Hugo asked. "He'll want to use those on you. He's used to being able to do that to submissives in houses."

Josette was shaking her head vigorously, her little hands going protectively to her bosom.

"I'd be up for trying them," said Jesse thoughtfully.

"Well, be very clear about which one of you he can put the clamps on and the toys in, understand?" Hugo said.

"We will," Jesse agreed.

"He'll want a blow job."

"We won't do that," Jesse answered for both of them. She would have gone so far to please Mr. Bartlett, for she had enjoyed every moment of being with him, but he was Ambrose Bartlett.

As they were walking out, Hugo finished the last crumbs of bouchon and said, "Tell me again why you're doing this?"

"He keeps stalking us," Jesse explained. "He's inflamed. We'll never get rid of him. He'll wind up kidnapping us. It's best just to get it over with."

"And what about your mistress?" Hugo asked Josette. "She won't be happy to think of Victor getting his hands on you."

Josette looked pained at this.

"You can still back out and let this little slut go over there alone," Hugo advised Josette. "Because Dennis will also be displeased when he hears about this, which he naturally will."

"It'll be okay," Jesse quickly said; "It's her bachelorette party."

The girls found perfect matching black PVC mini dresses and thigh high boots without looking more than five minutes through Carola's vast wardrobe room. Then they checked the time, saw they still had half an hour before they needed to leave, and found Hope to confide their plan to and receive advice and moral support from. Like Hugo, Hope was conflicted about the girls' bestowing this gift of their submission on the unworthy object in question, merely to uphold tradition and not hurt the feelings of a pompous, unpleasant top, mainly out of respect for his patronage to Carola's club throughout the years as well as being one of Hugo's collector clients. In the end, she mainly approved of the gesture, for it was kind. But it also begged the question, why did these insensitive tops truly merit so much consideration?

When the girls drove out to Raphael Price's splendid compound, they found that the bouchon had done its job, which was to render Victor relaxed and even smiling. At least until they were all in Polyxena's well-equipped play room in the guest house behind the main house. Then he became serious, demanding and not disposed to chat. But he seemed to grasp that that afternoon's activities would amount to a more restrained version of his usual scene.

He was mollified by the obvious care with which the girls had dressed and the respectful attitude they were displaying. When he had them unzip and step out of the tiny dresses, he admired their pert, petite figures, set off to creamy perfection by black lace push up bras and sheer backed string bikinis. When he bade them kneel and bend over the spanking bench, side by side, neither balked when he pushed their smooth thighs apart. He spanked them with his hand, hard and fast. Then with a leather paddle. Then with a small maple paddle. Each of them cried out with each stroke, casting him beseeching looks over their shoulders. He merely stood them up, unhooked their bras and took them in turn, over his lap for more hard hand spanking. Josette cried almost the whole time, Jesse not at all.

He'd decided to switch to flogging and once again, positioned them kneeling, side by side, now each fully nude, their boots off and little pink soled feet upturned. Then he noticed that the girls were holding hands as they waited for the lashes to fall, and got a new idea. His eyes darted around the walls of the dungeon, where various implements of correction and restraint were neatly hung in related clusters. He considered the strap-ons he saw on display and their accompanying phalluses, thought of ordering Wilhelmina to get one down, don it and penetrate Josette while he whipped her, but these pieces belonged to the medium sized mistress Polyxena, who was used to dominating male submissives; he doubted any of the harnesses could be tightened to snugly gird Wilhelmina's tiny hips, nor did it seem quite appropriate to expect the equally small Josette to accommodate any of the large, male taming dildoes he could see. Then he spotted a shelf of butt plugs of varying sizes and got a better idea.

Moving the girls to the long, wide bondage bed in the middle of the room, he told Josette to lie on her back and let him leather cuff her wrists together above her head. She naturally clamped her smooth, white thighs together and flinched when he briefly stroked her small black Venus mound with his fingertips, then pushed her thighs apart.

"Get on top of her, Wilhelmina," Victor ordered Jesse. Jesse looked uncertainly at Josette, who gave a tiny nod. "Now take this well and your job is done," he said, shaking out the many lashed flogger. Jesse climbed on top of Josette and slowly lowered her torso down. Victor pushed her down and the girls' small, round bosoms were crushed together. Jesse buried her face against Josette's throat and under her sleek black bob, breathing in her friend's scent −marzipan. "Are you okay with this?" Jesse whispered in Josette's ear.

"Yes," Josette whispered, wanting to giggle, because this part was weird and fun.

The next sound Jesse heard was indistinct, but she realized it had something to do with lube, because the next sensation she received was of a few drops of a liquid being drizzled between her cheeks. An instant later she received the rude shock of a six-inch butt plug being carelessly inserted halfway into her bottom. She cried out and he pulled it back out an inch. "Ow!" she said, with emphasis, looking back at him reproachfully.

"You'll get used to it," he said and pushed her face back down against Josette's neck. Then he pushed it back in another inch. "Don't let it slip out," he warned, and commenced the flogging. It wasn't a light whipping, but he aimed more carefully with this, his implement of choice, than with the traditional corporal punishment tools, and each stroke found its target at the center of each cheek, rather than her thighs or the small of her back. As Jesse had assured Hugo, she didn't mind a hard punishment and each time the whip came down, it drove her own blonde public mound against Josette's. In a half minute, she got used to the butt plug and it ceased to hurt, but felt deeply exciting instead. She could almost forget the unpleasant Victor and just feel the sensations of penetration, flagellation and control wash through her. In minutes, her clitoris was electrified and burst into a deliciously naughty orgasm, whose spasms did indeed eject the plug. Victor stopped flogging her, tossed away the plug and ordered them to keep grinding, but to turn their faces towards him. His hand did the rest and in a moment, Jesse felt his liquid benediction fall upon her bottom.

The girls were dressed and ready to depart. Then Victor being Victor, handed them exactly half of what he would have paid to see them at the club, just as Jesse had suggested. But Josette, who had been brought up in a one-bedroom apartment in lower Manhattan by her single bartending mom, knew the value of money and Victor's lack of generosity upset her. Josette pulled Jesse to her and whispered in her ear.

Jesse nodded and looking at Victor said, "Josette just reminded me, we'd offered to take half if you behaved like a gentleman. But you turned this into a porno and hurt me with the plug. Plus, I'm too marked to shoot for a week. We didn't spoil the scene by raising objections, and then there was the bouchon."

Now relaxed and in a pretty good mood, Victor laughed and handed them the other five hundred dollars.

It was Jesse's first so-so experience as a professional and she reflected that it could have been worse. For her own part, Josette marveled that tops could so radically differ in style. Victor didn't even seem to aim before striking. It was the difference between being treated as a playmate and as an object. Now she was glad she hadn't gone into Club Paddles and let a total stranger spank her. They might have been just as careless as Victor but without any allowance. And now she had to tell Dennis what had happened. This made her heart contract uncomfortably.

Meanwhile, the most beautiful part of the afternoon was that Josette and Jesse had shared a kinky, scary, extreme BDSM experience that would remain a shared, rarified memory for the rest of their lives. Indeed, a friendship had just begun that would flourish over decades, growing stronger and deeper every year. While this was probably her first and last paid session, Josette felt delighted that in one afternoon she'd learned more about the scene than years of reading books and watching videos had taught her. For example, she'd discovered, that just grinding against another girl's muff, she could come! That particular aspect of the afternoon was not likely to be repeated. Jesse and Josette might well have developed an intense girl crush on each other, were there no handy boys in the picture to attend to their needs, but this was far from the case. Jesse was already fairly swimming in male admirers and Josette was newly engaged and only a few days into her physical love affair with Dennis. But the girlish companionship the newest residents of Random Point had begun to enjoy, burnished their first autumn in New England with gold.

From now on, they'd spend part of almost every day together, exploring the village, walking in the woods, shopping in Woodbridge, or watching spellbound, as Carola demonstrated numberless ways of turning their fellow fetishists on. Josette's kitchen duties felt relatively light. Her employers required no breakfast beyond rolls and coffee, though she soon discovered they both adored her biscuits and could happily eat them for breakfast every day. They loved her salad-sandwiches and soups for lunch. They had guests for dinner several times a week. The lightness of these requirements allowed for Josette to combine visits with Jesse with her morning shopping or they would meet midafternoon at Marguerite's bookstore and then depart into the woods or walk over to Damaris and Pamela's dress shop, or have afternoon tea at the Ball and Feather. The girl from Texas and the girl from lower Manhattan were awash in unspoiled, natural beauty for the first time in their lives, each and every day, and this was a balm to their senses.

"Are we being rewarded for being good girls?" Josette wondered to Jesse one day in the woods.

"For being bad ones," Jesse corrected her.

Chapter Thirty-Three

Accommodations Will Be Made

Dusk was falling and it had grown distinctly chilly as Josette got home and entered the mansion through the kitchen door. She found Dennis pacing and he grabbed her into his arms the moment she entered. Then he held her away from him, startled at the sight of her in the shiny black mini dress and 4" heeled black thigh high boots.

"I've been wondering where you got to, wow, what are you dressed for?" he asked, turning her around to look at her from every attractive angle. "You look fantastic!"

Josette felt cheered by the look of admiration in his eyes.

"I did something I'm pretty sure you'll disapprove of," she blurted out, blushing.

"That doesn't surprise me, in that outfit."

"But, maybe if you can think of it in terms of a very small bachelorette party, you'll forgive me," she explained.

"I could forgive you anything if you'd wear those boots often," he said, sweeping her up in his arms and carrying her from the house to his apartment, including up the stairs. She marveled at and complimented his strength, not knowing that Dennis had been sharing Anthony's personal trainer at the gym for years.

Once they were in Dennis' quarters, Josette told him the whole story of the afternoon's adventure. She was surprised that the account made him smile rather than frown.

"Oh Josette," he said, kissing the palm of her tiny hand, "I'm not here to approve or disapprove of anything you decide to do. I have too much respect for how hard you work and how dear you are."

Dennis spoke from the heart, for her suddenly belonging to him, felt like awakening from a years' long emotional slumber. For the entire duration of his employment with Anthony and Susan, he'd been something between an insider and an outsider. Beautiful scene girls and women, who came and went in his employer's house, year after year, looked upon him kindly, let him amuse himself by helping them with their shoes and their corset strings. But it had been many years since Susan had had need of his intimate services. And somehow, he had never found a girlfriend. With his large salary and a plentiful supply of dominatrixes in New York, he had been at liberty to satisfy his perverse urges on a biweekly basis with professional mistresses. Since he tipped generously, actual sex was often involved and he was not frustrated. But the last few days, he had experienced the exquisite sensation of a beautiful young girl, to whom he was fiercely attracted, wrapped in his arms, from midnight to dawn, the scent of marzipan emanating from her hair. This was bliss, it was everything.

"Josette," Dennis said, "there's something I must tell you before we get married, in case it changes anything between us."

"What is it?" she asked, with trepidation.

"It's about my orientation."

"You mean being submissive?" she asked.

"Well, yes, but how did you know?" he asked. "Did Susan tell you?"

"No. I figured it out when Mr. Newton told you to take me shoe shopping."

"Really? That was enough?"

"Dude, I was brought up in Alphabet City and I've been watching fetish porn since I was eleven. How could I not know that a foot guy was submissive?"

"So, you're okay with that?" Dennis asked.

"I'm great with it. It means you'll never try to bully me or take advantage of my submissiveness. And it makes you more sensitive to my needs. You have tons of finesse going for you. You have style. And you're super sweet. That guy we visited today, he had zero finesse. The only good idea he had was tying Jesse on top of me, which was very hot."

Dennis hugged her against him, electrified by how sexy she looked and felt in the skintight PVC with those splendid boots on her tiny feet. She broke away from him to stroll across the room to a triple mirror at one end. She was not accustomed to seeing herself in this style of costume and it turned her into a different young lady, possessed of glamor and power. Her black bob and creamy white skin set the outfit off to perfection. Her legs looked especially provocative in the thigh high boots.

"Listen," she told him, "we both get paid well. You probably go to mistresses in New York. Continue to do that. Get your domination from them. Meanwhile, I'll wear all those sexy shoes we bought that day in New York, when we go out and hang out, and let you pamper my feet as much as you like, whenever you like. I never wore hot outfits before because I was too busy working, had no one to wear them for and couldn't afford them. I like looking hot! We can totally make this work. We understand each other."

Chapter Thirty-Four

Cassandra Ponders

Hope and Cassandra were walking along the brook in the woods behind the house one raw November morning, with a gray sky above threatening imminent rain and talking about the marvel that was Jesse Pomander.

"She's been getting up even before me, starting the coffee and answering the first round of queries," said Cassandra.

Hope replied, "That amazes me, since she's been staying out at Michael's until closing most nights. Kids her age usually sleep until noon if they can."

"Hugo texted me this morning to send her over to him as soon as we spare her, he's going to start giving her writing assignments for the magazine."

"Oh, she'll love that!" Hope said.

"She's made herself so useful, I have practically nothing to do," Cassandra said.

"You'll have to do more sessions," Hope observed.

Cassandra laughed but said, "I'll probably take on more transcribing work from Cameron. Speaking of whom, he came onto me yesterday."

"Cameron did? Really? What happened?" Hope stopped short.

"Well, we finally did my interview yesterday and after we were done he asked if I would consider having sex with him."

"What did you say?"

"I told him to stop teasing me and then the phone rang and when I was done with my call, he'd gone."

"Wow, I'm beginning to think our Cameron is a sort of spanking Casanova," chuckled Hope.

"Why so? Did he come onto you too?"

"Yes, we did it on my birthday. He's fucking Brooke, he fucked Naomi, I'm sure Carola said they had sex before she left Brookline and now he wants you too?" Hope asked. "We should take him out in the woods and switch him like we did to Dru that time. Just for being such a slut."

After a few minutes of companionable silence, Cassandra confided, "I wonder if I'm ready to start looking for a man of my own."

"A boyfriend?" Hope asked.

"A something," Cassandra replied. "I can't keep sleeping with other women's men."

"Is that what you've been doing, Mistress?" Hope smiled.

"It seems so. Anthony, Michael, Ambrose...they're all lovely, but they belong to other ladies, as does Cameron, if I decide to give in to him too," said Cassandra, carefully omitting Hope's husband, David, from the list of her amatory admirers.

"My mistress is surely entitled to a man of her own," Hope agreed. "Have you done a reading about this yet?"

"Oh no, I haven't touched the cards since before Amanda was born," Cassandra said. "I knew Hugo wouldn't have wanted me to infect her with superstition. And truthfully, I lost interest in all of that around the same time. My tendency towards magical thinking tarnished my relationship with Hugo. He never respected me because of it. I couldn't raise a child with someone who thought I was an idiot. But as soon as I left him, I realized, I had been one."

"I just don't understand why you didn't even give Hugo a chance to raise his own daughter," Hope said.

"I didn't think he wanted to be a family man and a

baby would have forced that on him. And I didn't know if it would be wholesome for a spanking fetishist to raise a child. Amanda wound up being into spanking anyway, ironically, but at least she didn't have to feel conflicted about her own father. Don't you think he would have indulged her too much? She's so much in his image."

"Yes," Hope agreed, "He would have spoiled and confused her. But, do you still love Hugo? Does it bother you he's with Laura?"

"I do love him, but I respect her too and they're practically newlyweds."

"So, we just have to work on getting you someone of your own," Hope declared.

Cassandra agreed, "I think it's time."

Meanwhile, Hope decided to solve the happy problem of Cassandra not having enough to do, by booking her mistress into as many sessions as she could possibly intrigue. Cassandra paused to look in surprise at Hope across the office one morning, as she heard Hope describe the roster of talent on hand that day and evening at The Venus Club. "Today we have beautiful, petite, blonde, 22 year old Wilhelmina Willoughby, the scene's newest debutante and budding spanking model, who takes a great spanking and loves bondage; tomboy Carmen, another blonde, mid-twenties, stunning body, pixie face, a switch who can take a hard spanking and hard bondage; Mistress Carola, who needs no introduction, Me, Hope Lawrence, I'm sure you've seen my movies; and Cassandra, is also a beautiful switch who takes a great spanking, and incredible bondage. Who would I recommend for tickling? Wait, have we played before? Is this Mickey?" Hope listened, smiling as Cassandra watched her. "Oh, Mickey I'd definitely recommend Cassandra for your first visit to us. She has no objection to playing fully nude and she has a heavenly figure. Great,

I'll put you in the book with Cassandra for four pm."

"Tickling? Me?" Cassandra said when Hope looked up.

"Have you ever done a tickling session, Mistress?"

"No."

"Are you ticklish?"

"Yes, horribly so, especially my feet."

"Perfect. That was a client I used to see years ago in L.A., cute Korean man. He just wants to tie you nude, on your tummy, so he can tie your ankles together and tickle your feet and the rest of you too. Tickling sessions are hard. The clients usually want to spend an hour and they want you to giggle and squirm the whole time. Are you up for it?"

"Wouldn't he have more fun with the little one?" Cassandra asked doubtfully.

"Oh, he'll get around to her and Carmen and whoever else happens to visit when he's in town.

"You should have told him I'm in my forties," Cassandra remonstrated with Hope, who simply grinned at her.

Cassandra who generally lived up to her name, could see Hope's plan, to distract her from being loverless by foisting as many sessions on her as possible. Rather than try to fight her best friend's strategy, Cassandra took herself the next afternoon, to Bartlett's to replenish her bra and panty drawer.

Ambrose Bartlett happened to be in his office, and as he periodically scanned the bank of cameras on the wall next to his desk to keep his eye on every department in the store, he noticed the mistress of the Venus Club in Lingerie. Leaving his desk, he took two flights of stairs down to the foundations department and surprised Cassandra at the panty counter at the back of the large department.

"How nice to see you," he said, genuinely pleased to show off his beautiful store to this lady who charmed him so. Cassandra smiled back at him, suddenly aware of how attractive he was and remembering how competently he had run their little sex scene on Hope's birthday, letting Hope go and keeping her behind in the salon to serve his needs. He was smooth and adept, he had game. The color rushed to her face as she realized that she was about to do something quite out of character.

"I was going to buy some string bikinis, if you have some," Cassandra said.

"Of course, we do," he grinned, inclining his head at the salesgirl behind the counter, "Bring out the nicest string bikinis we have in a small," he told her. When she'd disappeared into the stockroom room to hunt down their most expensive French panties, Ambrose glanced around the salon to think of what would go best with new panties.

"Can I come upstairs to your office and try them on for you?" Cassandra surprised him by saying.

He looked at her quizzically, but replied with alacrity, "Please do!"

When the girl brought out a dozen styles, in various luxurious fabrics, Ambrose told Cassandra to bring them all and they immediately departed fine lingerie and took the elevator up to the fourth floor.

"What are you up to, young lady?" he asked, in the elevator.

"Just remembered Hope's birthday and how much fun that was," Cassandra confided, no longer blushing, but with her heart pounding.

"I'm so glad you liked that," he said. "And thank you for coming to see me today."

When they got into Ambrose Bartlett's office, he locked the door and took her back into his private lounge and locked that door.

"I really am going to start working on finding a

boyfriend soon," Cassandra promised, unselfconsciously unbuttoning her shirt and unzipping her jeans before dropping them on the floor.

"Don't work too hard," Ambrose said, "I like this version of you."

A few days later, Cassandra went to Hugo in his shop to ask his advice. She found him winding his dozens of clocks.

"I think I do need a man of my own," she explained, "But how best to proceed? Do you still run personal ads?"

Hugo looked at her thoughtfully. Then he said, "I wouldn't go in that direction, if I were you. Keep it organic. Someone will pop up. You've only been back in town six months."

"I know, but, you're the networking guy," Cassandra pointed out.

"But think about it, honey, you weren't even in the scene when I met you, I got you into it."

"You didn't have to try too hard though," she reminded him.

"I know, you were naturally disposed to learn a new angle on sex. But it wasn't innate."

"Oh, I don't know," Cassandra smiled, "I used to read bodice rippers in high school."

"Let me put it this way, you're running a club and you're inundated with the scene 24/7. You can afford to broaden your field."

"I see your point," she agreed and went home to the club.

The next morning, she was just up and dressed and about to make her way to the kitchen, where coffee was already brewing, when she looked out her bedroom window and noticed a god standing in her back garden at the opening of the path into the woods. She only had a moment to take him in before he disappeared into the path by the brook, but it was enough time to notice his towering height, thick thighs in jeans, broad shoulders and trim waist girded by a faded leather bomber jacket; and glimpse his striking face, severe yet pleasant, weather beaten, yet youthful. Then Cassandra remembered a conversation she'd had with William Random, the previous afternoon at the gym, while they were taking turns doing sets on the vertical leg press.

Cassandra reminded William of the pyramid playhouse house he had constructed for her twenty years before, behind her headshop in the village. She asked him if he could build her another one, behind the Venus Club, for intense bondage sessions and the occasional mummification. William had assured her that she might have one by Christmas and said he'd send over his man in the next few days to take measurements. This fierce creature in her woods now must be that man.

Cassandra got her coffee and found Jesse already at her computer station in the office, in a violet velvet robe and slippers.

"Darling, did you notice a man in our back yard just now?" Cassandra asked.

"Oh, yes, I let him in the side gate. His name is Wally Pell. He said he's here about a pyramid. I told him you'd be up soon and he said he'd walk in the woods for a bit."

"Did you offer him coffee?"

"Yes, Mistress. He declined but said maybe later."

"I only got a fleeting impression, but wasn't he kind of cute?" Cassandra asked idly, sipping the coffee.

"If mountains are cute, he's adorable!" Jesse agreed.

"He looked past his first youth though, didn't he?" Cassandra asked. "I mean, he didn't seem younger than me, for example, did he?"

"Mistress, you look thirty-two. He's pushing fifty,"

Jesse replied.

"That's what I thought," Cassandra grinned. "Perfect!"

She pulled a tweed coat on over her sweater and jeans and went out the back door to find Wally Pell. He was just reemerging from the woods into the back yard when she met him.

"Hello, I'm Cassandra," she said, smiling.

"Wally," he said, smiling back at her. "William sent me to measure for the pyramid. Do you know exactly where you want it to go?" he asked, with a trace of a Boston accent.

Cassandra led him to the furthest corner on the west side of the yard, in sight of the corner playroom called Cape Cod. "Is this close enough to run electricity to it?" she asked.

"Oh, sure thing," he concurred. "Do you need a bathroom in it too?"

"Is that possible? With a commode, sink and shower?"

"Yes, of course," he said. "I can also put in windows all around with automatic shudders," he added.

"I'd also like a smooth walkway put in from the house, something that won't catch a 5-inch stiletto heel. Can you give me a nice path like that?"

"Absolutely!" he assured her, smiling as he envisioned Cassandra in stiletto heels.

"Wonderful!" she cried. This would be like adding an extra bedroom to the property, for any guests who wanted to sleep on a big, leather bondage bench. "But before you proceed, I'd better go over the costs with your boss," she said. "The last time William built me a pyramid, it was more modest." And she explained about her head/psychic shop and how she'd used the small wooden pyramid for card readings.

"I wish you'd read my cards for me," said Wally.

"Really, you're interested in arcana?"

"Who isn't?" he replied guilelessly. Then he asked

suddenly, "Was that your daughter who let me in?"

"No, Jesse's my friend, she lives here with me. I do have a daughter though, she's at college."

"Well, you'll have a great pyramid," he assured her, noticing she didn't mention a husband and that she wore no wedding band. "I'll line it with cedar like we did in the loft."

"Oh, were you in on the remodel of this place?" Cassandra asked as he made some notes in a small tablet.

"I oversaw the whole thing," he said. "It was the first house I worked on when I became William's project manager two years ago. It took months. I hope everything is working fine."

"Everything is flawless. I compliment your work! Please, come back to the house and drink coffee with me."

When Wally was looming in her kitchen, with a coffee mug in his big hand, looking around at his handy work, she began to question him about himself.

"I owned a gym in Woodbridge for almost twenty years," he disclosed.

"I remember William being so excited when that gym opened," she said.

"You lived here then?"

"I did. You had martial arts classes, right?"

"I had everything, at one point or another, but it was a thankless business. Lots of stress, not much cash. And a few years ago, when the Dutch Treat took over the Random Point gym and upgraded it to Beverly Hills standards, the few ladies I had fled from my jockish and undoubtedly squalid gym. So, I decided to change direction. I sold my gym and went to work for William."

"Do you know how much my pyramid will really cost?" Cassandra asked.

"I don't know if he's giving you a discount."

"Well, we are old friends, if he was building it for a stranger, how much would he charge?"

"I can't give you a quote yet. I have to talk to him first."

"Get quotes for both with and without the plumbing and electricity."

"Copy that," Wally agreed. "So, you lived in Random Point long ago, but just moved back?" he asked. She nodded. "What do you do?" he asked candidly. She stared at him blankly for an instant, wondering what to say.

"I work from home," she said at last.

"Well, you have a great home to work from," he said cheerfully.

"Would you like to see the final version of the house you remodeled?" she asked.

"Yes! The last thing I did here was fit up one of the parlors as a classroom with a consignment of vintage desks I hunted down at a swap meet in Vermont."

Noting this, Cassandra took him to the school room first, where Susan's illusion mural of the Edwardian street scene instantly caught his attention.

"That was painted by the sister-in-law of the man who bought this house," said Cassandra. "My patron," she explained.

"Are you an artist as well?" Wally asked.

"No, this is a B&D club. I'm its mistress."

"B&D?" he echoed, puzzled.

"Bondage and Discipline," she elucidated.

"What?"

"Why else would we need a school room?"

Cassandra took him down several corridors to the exam room and showed it to him. Then she showed him Cape Cod, with the rustic whipping post.

"You're not in the scene, are you?" she asked.

"I don't think so," he said, with wonder, reevaluating the slender brunette before him.

"But you know what I'm talking about, right?" she asked, taking him to the elevator and downstairs, to Carola's world, with all of Carola's imported dungeon furniture and trappings.

"Vaguely," he admitted.

"So, you've known William Random for twenty years, but don't know he's been a model in spanking magazines?"

"Really? No, I mean, he's been my climbing buddy for years, but we've never discussed anything like that," said Wally.

"You know Hugo Sands?"

"The owner of the antiques shop, of course."

"He's also been publishing a spanking magazine with personal ads for decades."

"Really?"

"So, you're totally vanilla?" Cassandra asked.

"I guess so," Wally shrugged. She grinned at him.

"Well, don't tell anyone what I told you. I'm keeping a low profile in the village with my club."

"What happens at this club?" he came to perch on a bar stool when they came to a stop in the sprawling lounge.

"Well, a couple of things. First, my sister Carola and Hugo Sands use the premises to shoot photosets and videos. Secondly, I, my sister, Carola, the girl you met, Jessie and Hope Lawrence, who used to run the bookstore coffee shop, all do spanking and bondage sessions here with exclusive clients. And thirdly, scene couples come here to play in the playrooms and sometimes overnight with us in the loft. When the pyramid is finished, that will be another weekender destination for players."

"I get the picture. That's neat. I never would have guessed that from looking at you," said Wally.

"Tell me what you would have guessed," Cassandra said.

"I will, but first tell me something else. Are you currently married?"

"I'm recently divorced. Hugo Sands is my daughter's

father, but I raised her in San Francisco. I only came back here six months ago after the gentleman I was with for many years there hooked up with another lady. I sold my head shop there and came back here, where I was happy twenty years ago."

"So, you're unattached at the moment?" Wally asked.

"I am completely unattached. What about you?"

"Well, first, thank you for asking. I am also completely unattached."

They smiled at each other. "But can I ask you a direct question?" he asked.

"I love direct people, they save everyone time and confusion. Gather all the facts you crave," she encouraged him.

"Great, because I could easily get confused about what you've told me. So, where do you actually fit into all of this, Cassandra? When you say you're the mistress, for example, what exactly does that mean?"

"You're correct in being confused. In most cases, you wouldn't have to ask. When you meet my sister Carola, for instance, you'll see immediately what it means to be a mistress in a B&D club. You already seem to sense the title confers a dominant authority and that doesn't quite match me. No, don't deny it, but it's okay, you're right. I'm not that kind of mistress. But I am the mistress of this club in the sense that I run it. My own personal preference, I don't mind in the slightest sharing with you, is for sexually dominant men who are a little kinky, but I also like and admire regular vanilla men who are hot and sensitive, especially if they're handy with tools and lumber."

"Sweet!" he rejoiced.

They agreed he was to come back and start the job as soon as possible and Wally went back to Random Construction to get the estimate from William, who was at work in his studio, on the new theatre building he had been commissioned to design for Braemar Prep.

"She wants a graded path, electricity, plumbing and windows," Wally said.

"Okay, great. We'll build her a little showplace."

"She wants an estimate before we start."

"Oh, forget that. I want to give the pyramid to the club. I may send a bill for the labor to the guy who bought her the house. He won't mind. Didn't you like her?"

"She was adorable. Can I drag this job out?"

William grinned. "Did she tell you about the Club?"

"She did. I had no idea. I need some sort of crash course on – what did she say – the Scene?"

"I never mentioned it because I figured if you were in it, we'd have met at some event. And people in it tend to keep a low profile because it's no one's business, unless they're already in it."

"Well, how do you get in it?" Wally asked affably.

"You don't have to be in the scene to date Cassandra," William pointed out helpfully.

"She said something like that, but I suddenly find myself fascinated by all of this female mischief going on in little Random Point."

"Well, drag the job out as long as you like, hang around her, you'll find it time well spent.

Chapter Thirty-Five

Priscilla Dashwood

While it was written in the stars that Wally Pell would be Cassandra's sweetheart, neither suspected that a vigorous rival for her attentions and affection was emerging to obstruct Wally's progress. This was Felix Pildash, the gentleman who had taken a lease on the lighthouse after Polyxena moved in with Raphael Price a few months before.

Little was known about Felix, and yet, much was evident. His affluence was obvious, for the lighthouse was an expensive rental. He was also one of Hugo's long-time subscribers and thus a welcome new member guest of the Venus Club. He seemed to identify as a submissive switch, initially interested only in sessioning with dominants. He was a tall, broad shouldered, curly haired Englishman, perhaps forty-five years old, soft spoken, inclined to smile and tease, courteous and relaxed. No one really knew what he did. Ever since the club had opened in the summer, Felix had visited every three weeks and always on a Friday afternoon.

The first mistress Felix had seen was Carola, who had spanked, tied, teased and finally caned him. He was enchanted by her beauty, style and strict, elegant mode of conducting a scene. She was sharp and formal and discouraged casual conversation while playing. She aimed accurately and stung without devastating.

Next, the Brit had engaged the Dutch domina Polyxena Guzman, who visited The Venus Club to do the occasional session that interested her, her schedule of supervising at her own gym permitting. Since Polyxena had nothing to prove, she always admitted to attractive men, that she was a switch. In this case, Felix eagerly welcomed the opportunity to top her in the first half hour of their session, reddening her stunning bottom with a hand spanking, and then letting her top him for the second half. Again, Felix was completely delighted with the experience and begged Polyxena to let him take her to dinner afterwards. He took her to her favorite inn and she signed him up for a gym membership. He was beginning to quickly penetrate the inner circle of the Random Point scene and everyone who met him, immediately liked him.

Felix's third excursion to the club rewarded him with a session with Marguerite, who, like Polyxena, condescended to perform the occasional top session with interesting visitors to the village. It was an all-caning session and it left Felix in raptures. Unlike Polyxena, Marguerite did not speak of her submissive side, but gave the Englishman a classically disciplinary experience that left him gasping and a little bit welted. Marguerite's Amazonian magnificence beguiled Felix and her style as a caning mistress seduced him into a state of complete surrender. Because she had her husband Michael Flagg's attentions to look forward to later, Marguerite made no use of Felix's surrender, but did find caning his smooth, plump bottom a pleasure.

Next, Felix played with the lead switch of the house, the ravishing Hope. As with Polyxena, he spanked Hope first, and went submissive to her afterwards, easily switching personas. As a spankee, Hope's beauty and affability overwhelmed him; as a spanker, she was equally charming at pretending to be strict. Again, Felix left the Venus Club tingling with awakened senses and a renewed appreciation for feminine power.

It was only on the fifth visit to the Venus Club that Felix noticed the mistress, Cassandra, who walked in beauty through her own domain. He asked if she was available to play and she offered to fulfill any fantasy he might suggest that was compatible with her inclinations. She had heard from all the others how agreeable Felix was to play with, how meticulously clean, how polite and upbeat, and as a player, how adept. But she sensed that he clearly preferred to go submissive, and therefore, did not mention her versatility as a switch.

Felix said he had always dreamed of being hypnotized into submission, and into a subservient female persona, such as a naughty or lazy scullery maid in a Weimar republic bordello.

Cassandra laughed and said, "Oh darling, you don't have to be hypnotized. When I tell you: you are my little Heidi, that's who you will be. But we must take you down to wardrobe first and get you properly focused." Felix obeyed Cassandra without argument, following her down to Carola's massive wardrobe room, where they found a vintage housemaid's uniform with a white apron and cap already set aside. Cassandra dressed a dress form with the outfit, while Felix watched. Then she had Felix carry the dress form into Carola's largest dungeon on the lower level, fitted out with a whipping post, caning bench and bondage bed. She had him set the dress form, now clad in the dainty maid's outfit, in a wall niche opposite the bench, where anyone bent over the bench, might focus on it. The idea was for Felix to be able to imagine himself a petite girl, inhabiting the evocative costume, while behind him, Cassandra might belabor his bared, out thrust bottom, to his heart's content, which she thoroughly did.

As she predicted, Felix leapt into the fantasy with both feet, slipping into a kind of imaginary paradise of perfect discipline, while the reality of the strokes being administered by Cassandra physically electrified him. She had read his needs as perfectly as any top ever had. What he wanted was what every sub wanted, to be the focus of his top's undivided, intuitive attention. Moreover, she had the gift of communicating love through discipline.

Instead of waiting three weeks before returning to the Venus Club, Felix was back the next Friday afternoon, having booked another session with Cassandra, and requesting, in a text, that the dress form be draped in an 18th Century bodice this time and the session take place in the elegant dark blue salon with the burgundy furniture. This time, Felix wanted to imagine the outrageously pretty little flirt Dolly from Barnaby Rudge, receiving the spanking she deserved but never got in Dickens' novel. Cassandra had never read that book but there was a complete set of Dickens in the club library and she read it in the intervening week before the session, hugely entertained.

This session also pleased Felix mightily and therefore, no one was surprised when he was back again the following Friday, also to see Cassandra, with a new outfit request and a new character to inhabit. But before the third playroom encounter occurred, Cassandra's new fanboy invited her to an intimate dinner, in the lighthouse, which he proposed to cook for her himself. She accepted with alacrity for she had a small proposal to put to him, which she knew would delight her new admirer.

Respectful of her vegetarianism, her host was putting the finishing touches on a white wine fettuccini dish, with a lovely aroma, as she browsed around his sitting room and studied his bookshelves.

"Wow," she cried, "you have a complete set of Priscilla Dashwood bodice rippers?"

"Have you read her?" he asked, turning the flame under his sauce very low before approaching Cassandra with excitement.

"Yes! My daughter Amanda discovered them when she was in junior high and turned me onto them. We read most of these. We always thought –" Cassandra began, but instantly realizing that what she was going to say – that she and Amanda suspected that the author of the books was really a man, based on the number of references to bosoms – might ruin her host's pleasure in the books, she finished with, "– that the author was into it, since pretty much every book had a corporal punishment scene."

"The author is into it," Felix said.

"Oh, you know her?" Cassandra asked.

"I am her."

After Felix's excellent dinner, they sat at the planked wooden table, sipping their wine and sharing a joint while Cassandra told him of an idea she had to enhance his fantasy life.

"I assume you're not now nor have ever been a regularly practicing cross dresser?" she asked.

"That's absolutely true," he readily agreed, "though you'd think I would be, considering how much I mentally experience my fictional females' sex lives. Oh, I've thought of it, but I don't have the physicality to carry it off without looking or feeling ridiculous. I'm just too thick."

"And it's not really you," Cassandra added. "But, that doesn't mean you can't own a cool fetish garment that unisexually transports you, the minute you put it on, into a different persona."

"What did you have in mind, Mistress?" he asked, with amusement. Everything about Cassandra charmed and amused him.

"Well, I'm going into Boston tomorrow to have lunch with Amanda. You could join us, I know she'd love to meet you, and then we could visit a wonderful leather shop I know and get you a black leather vest."

"You mean a Leatherman style vest?" he asked.

"Exactly, something that you can wear right next to your skin and will wrap you tightly, like a corset would one of your heroines. Leather feels so good and smells so good, you'll may even want to sleep in it sometimes."

"I like your idea," he said. "But about your daughter – are you going to tell her you met me at the club?" Felix asked, vibrating with pleasure at the piquancy of this idea.

"Of course. We have no secrets and she's in the scene. I'm sure she'll let you spank her at some future party, just off the enjoyment your books gave her."

"I imagine she's beautiful?"

"So beautiful. But she's a Harvard girl with a smart, hunky boyfriend, so don't get infatuated, that won't go anywhere," said Cassandra, not unkindly, but firmly. "However, she'll be thrilled to be your loyal friend."

All of this was most agreeable to Felix, who had spent his whole lifetime up until that point, sublimating his submissive and what he imagined to be classically feminine impulses, into his historical novels, with their ravishingly beautiful heroines and the rude (but aristocratic) suitors who ravished them first and courted them later. He had made quite a good income from these paperbacks over the last twenty years and was able to travel widely and lavishly, maintain several residences and live a modestly luxurious lifestyle. But it was only in the last ten or so years he'd begun to judiciously hunt for and play with famous tops the world over. He was neither very critical or very demanding. He craved beauty and charm in the practitioner and a certain amount of skillful control with a cane. As long as those elements were present, he was satisfied. The tops who had disappointed or turned him off, were the ones who decided to treat him as a slave or a very small child. He was, rather, a sensualist who longed to sexually submit, while in the female persona, to enthusiastic discipline, administered firmly but with affection. He wanted to please, not serve; he wanted to love and be loved. Gentle, interested, fully engaged Cassandra seemed to be the first mistress he had ever met, who completely "got" him and he couldn't believe his good fortune.

On the next Friday night, Felix announced to Cassandra that he was no longer in a submissive mood. However, he booked his session with her rather than Jesse or Hope and requested that she wear a skirt and sweater. When she asked what he had in mind, he countered with a question of his own.

"Did you say you and Amanda both liked my books because of the spanking scenes?"

"Yes!" Cassandra laughed. "They were as good as any story in Hugo's magazine."

"Does that mean you yourself like spanking?"

"Of course I like spanking. This is my club!"

"I mean, you like getting spanked too?"

"Very much," she replied.

"Well, today I'd like to spank you," he said.

"Really? Great!"

This went well. Felix was a good spanker with a big, friendly hand and wide, muscular lap. He held her close to him and complimented the beauty of her bottom effusively. He spanked, stroked, chatted, spanked, squeezed and chatted, spanked, caressed and finally putting her upright, asked permission to kiss her. She let him. He asked if he could touch her. She said yes. He squeezed her firm, peach shaped bosom through her cashmere polo sweater. He asked if they could lock the door. She locked the door. He asked her to undress for him. She shed her clothes and revealed her taut, smooth, yoga pampered body, letting her long brown hair fall about her shoulders. He said he practiced safe sex and asked if he could take her then. She reached out and touched the front of his casual trousers and felt a ramrod erection under the twill. She said yes and they fell into each other's arms.

The following day, Cassandra and Felix drove into

Boston together, went shopping in the Combat Zone for the leather vest, and joined Amanda for lunch in a Back-Bay gastro pub. Duly stunned by Amanda's beauty and confident vivacity, their new admirer sat back and allowed the university girl and fledgling player, to steer the conversation. Amanda wanted to talk about Felix's books, who his favorite authors were and his current project, the novel he would be working on throughout the following year, in Random Point. After lunch, the trio split up, Felix taking himself off to a friend's townhouse, where he would spend the night and Amanda and Cassandra repairing to Hugo's apartment on Boylston Street.

As soon as they got into Cassandra's car Amanda disclosed a surprising development to her mother.

"Isn't he a nice man?" Cassandra asked gaily. "He has such a strange and fascinating sexuality too."

"He's adorable, but how could things get this far without you telling me?"

"What do you mean by this far?" Cassandra asked, pulling into a parking space near their building.

"Mother, he's going to ask you to marry him!"

"Why do you think so?"

"He practically told me as much while you were in the loo."

"Oh, he's just being silly," Cassandra grinned. Then she remembered something more interesting than even a marriage proposal from a famous author. "But something big did happen this week I wanted to tell you about. It might even be life changing."

They went up to Hugo's apartment and into the master bedroom, where Cassandra began unpacking her overnight bag. Amanda slatted the Venetian blinds to let in the pale, late afternoon sun, then perched on a mahogany chest of drawers to chat with her mother.

"Did I text you the other morning about a heroic figure showing up in my back yard then disappearing into the mist before my eyes?"

"No."

"I must have gotten distracted. But it happened exactly like that. Even having barely glimpsed this fellow, I got a definite sense that he was meant for me."

"For your exclusive use?"

"Possibly, yes."

"And did he ever reemerge out of the mist?"

"He did. He's building me a pyramid behind the house, for sessions. His name is Walter Pells. He works with William Random."

"And he's handsome?"

"Plain, but monumental. He must be 6'5". An Olympian."

"Mother, you're flushing."

Cassandra grinned. "Wally Pells," she repeated. Amanda grinned back at her.

"In the scene?"

"Not at all," Cassandra said. "Hugo thinks I shouldn't try for a scene guy anyway. He says I get plenty of scene at the club."

"He is wise. But what of Priscilla Dashwood?" Amanda asked.

"I like Felix. We even had sex the other day."

"How was it?"

"Oh, lovely. What else did he tell you when you were alone just now? Did he tried to make a play for you?"

"Me?" Amanda laughed.

"I thought it would be fun for you to meet, but we can't let him have too much of you," Cassandra said. "he'll fall in love and things will get awkward fast."

"It's you he's falling in love with," Amanda corrected.

"That was before you came into the picture. He's probably already imagining playing with us together, us both topping him, or him watching me top you. Hugo warned me about this when I first opened the club, that whenever you were around it, spanking men would make fantastic assumptions about us."

"Now that you mention it," Amanda said, "there was a fellow at the party who tried to objectify us both."

"Who?"

"I think his name was Freddie. Cute man but he pissed me off asking me if you spanked me."

"Freddie Johansson. He's very nice, a regular. In fact, his girlfriend Alison does sessions now and then. They both work at Braemar. What did you say?"

"I told him not to be impertinent and to go stand in the corner."

Cassandra beamed, "You never disappoint me." She stretched out on the luxurious counterpane that covered the big bed.

"Speaking of the only person who did spank me as a child," Amanda began, "did you know Sensei is in Boston this week?"

"Yes," said Cassandra, "are you going to show him around Harvard?"

"Yes, Colby and I are having dinner with him tomorrow night."

"When he told me he'd be out, I invited him to come visit me in Random Point and see how I'm living," Cassandra disclosed.

"I'm glad. He feels so guilty about what happened."

"I know. That's why I want him to see just how good I have it now, what a favor he did me," Cassandra admitted. "He's a great guy."

"Sensei was the best stepfather ever," Amanda said, "and I will always honor him. But I love that Hugo is my actual father and that he is enjoying my being in his world. I'll have to not gush about him too much to Sensei. I don't want to hurt his feelings."

Cassandra spent the afternoon strolling through Back

Bay window shopping, and then met Amanda and Colby for dinner in Cambridge and a moonlight walk around the frosty campus. The next morning, she awoke around eight, brewed her coffee, practiced yoga for a half hour, took a bath and dressed in black jeans, boots, and a soft woolen shirt for the drive back to the Cape with Felix, who was to come pick her up at eleven. After a light breakfast of a buttered roll and tea, she read the headlines on Hugo's computer while she waited for her ride.

When Felix hadn't arrived by 11:20, she texted him with a question mark. He texted back, not immediately, but three minutes later, "Sorry, little slow getting going today."

Cassandra looked at her phone with a sensation of disquiet. She texted back, "Are you coming now?"

Several minutes passed. Then he texted, "I think I may go get a quick haircut."

Cassandra was confounded. What the hell was he up to?

"Okay," she texted back. Remembering where Hugo kept his weed, she filled a pipe and smoked it, ruminating about her new admirer's bad manners. Was he trying to make her mad enough to thrash him, without the benefit of a scheduled session? More objectification! This was unacceptable.

She put on her coat, put her phone in its outer pocket and her credit cards in an inner pocket and went out into Back Bay. She'd seen an interesting shop on the next block she wanted to revisit.

She stood in front of the shop and looked at the ensemble that had caught her eye the previous day. It was a long puffer coat, of a delicate green gold hue, trimmed luxuriantly with a golden faux fur shawl collar and elegantly frogged in the style of a 19th C Mongolian princess or Russian aristocrat. It had a matching hat, also fringed with tawny fur. Cassandra could picture herself in this stunning garment, in the woods behind her house, strolling with Wally Pell on a misty, frosty morning. On many frosty winter mornings. Her nut-brown hair would look marvelous against the fur collar and Pell would find her irresistible. Then he would take her in his big, Sterling Haydn arms. And because she was now living rent free, with her utilities paid and allowance coming into her bank account constantly, she didn't think twice about going into the shop and leaving eighteen hundred dollars to carry away the coat and caplet.

Back in Hugo's apartment, Cassandra hung her tweed coat in the closet, resolving to have Amanda bring it to her when she came out to Random Point the following week. For now she fancied she might have to travel home light.

When she glanced at her phone she saw that Felix had texted her while she was shopping, "Just ran into an old friend from college and might catch a quick bite with him. Is it okay if we leave by two?"

It was now 12:30 p.m.

Cassandra immediately texted back, "Never mind, I'll catch the train home."

Then she calmly placed her overnight bag in the closet and loaded up her purse with what she needed for the trip back on the train. She didn't actually think she'd have to take the train, and of course, Felix began frantically texting her that he'd be over to get her as soon as he could. Cassandra didn't reply to any of his new texts, but reloaded Hugo's pipe and sat in his front window seat, overlooking Boylston Street, and smoked until Felix's arrival twenty-eight minutes later. He was looking flushed and contrite, and began mumbling feeble apologies. Cassandra placed the insouciant hat on her head and began to wrap herself up in the luxury coat, looking into a full-length mirror as she zipped then toggled it closed.

She didn't speak to him until they were in his car and driving out of Boston.

"Is there something bothering you, Felix?"

"Why? What do you mean?" he glanced at her, nervously.

She shrugged, "You were two hours late picking me up. I'll admit, I barely know you, but this surprised me."

"I'm sorry, I guess I felt hurt." he admitted.

"About what, Felix?"

"You never came by my hotel yesterday."

Cassandra digested this, realizing that she had never come to see how he looked in the leather vest or inquired how he liked having it on, whether it had created the anticipated magic. And how much more magical the entire acquisition would have been, with her hands-on christening of it. Not that he had any right to expect that sort of follow-up without officially inviting her to visit him at his hotel with her paddles and straps. But had she actually violated any rules of scene etiquette by simply asking him to lunch with her and Amanda in Boston?

She knew what Carola would do with a cranky submissive behaving like this, but then again, that was the old Carola, who wasn't yet comfortably situated and still relied on booking as many sessions as possible to make her monthly nut. She would have made him pull over, taken him into the woods, and thrashed him with a switch or his own belt. That would have truly made Felix her slave. She didn't want a slave. One ended by being enslaved by their slave. And since she didn't want to make him crave her even more violently than he currently did, she would certainly not reward his tantrum with a genuine punishment session.

"We never talked about me visiting the hotel," Cassandra said. "And I thought I had mentioned I was spending the evening with my daughter and her boyfriend."

"I guess I should have figured that out," he admitted.

"I think I moved way too fast, inviting you to come to

Boston with me," Cassandra said. "And right after having sex like that," she added. "You went from client to playmate to friend overnight. So, I'm not blaming you for having certain expectations. I'm new to mistressing, so please forgive my fumbling."

"Nothing to forgive. I apologize for keeping you waiting. That was very rude," he said earnestly.

Neither of them spoke for a few minutes, then Cassandra said, "Amanda thinks you're in love with me."

"Yes, I told her that."

"Love me as a friend," Cassandra advised.

"Really? Just as a friend?" he sounded distressed at this.

"I can be a very good friend," she assured him.

"But, you let me make love to you."

"I did. I'm like that sometimes."

"It went well, didn't it?"

"Very well."

"But, you wouldn't consider being my lady?"

"Today, my affections are otherwise engaged," she said, thinking of Wally Pell.

"Oh!" he sighed, crushed.

"I'm sorry."

Neither of them spoke for many minutes, each lost in their own thoughts. Then Cassandra said, "Let's pull off here and drink some hot cider," as a familiar country store and café loomed into view.

A few minutes later, they were sitting in a rustic booth with mugs of hot cider and hot pretzels before them.

"So how did you spend the rest of your day yesterday?" Cassandra asked Felix, who still looked crestfallen.

"Oh, I saw a friend from college perform in As You Like It and she joined me for dinner afterwards," he replied, perking up at the recollection of his very pleasant evening in Boston.

"Did you! And what happened after dinner with this gifted former classmate?" Cassandra asked, correctly reading the smile that now touched his lips.

"We had sex," he admitted.

"Wow," exclaimed Cassandra. "What a little slut you are."

"That's true," he grinned.

"Kinky sex?"

"Well, I spanked her," he replied, adding, "I've been spanking her since we were at university. She was one of my girlfriends at Cambridge."

"Felix, you obviously had a great night. I order you to book a session with Carola for the caning you deserve for pouting for three hours today."

"Why Carola?" he asked, "Why not you?"

"Because it doesn't suit me to."

"Well, I do adore Carola, so I will obey," he pleasantly agreed.

"It was incorrect of me to suggest the trip, the silly vest gambit. I had no business trying to reprogram your sexual psyche. Combining that with meeting my daughter, it was a makeshift mess of stuff that didn't belong together. I shouldn't try to be a creative mistress. I don't have the follow through."

"Don't sell yourself short, darling," said Felix; "I wore the vest over a plaid shirt and black jeans to see the play and go to dinner. My friend loved it. She started rubbing up against me as soon as we were back at my hotel, inhaling the leather. I kept it on while we were having sex. She insisted. She has an actual leather fetish. And then, after she left – she has a husband– I tried the vest on just against my skin, and it immediately woke me up again. So, I did have a marvelously erotic night and some of it was due to the silly vest. Thank you, my most creative mistress."

Chapter Thirty-Six

The Long-Awaited School Room Scene

One chill and foggy weekday afternoon in early November, Josette was in the kitchen of the Venus Club, with Cassandra, Hope and Jesse, giving the staff a lesson in preparing paneer masala. Suddenly they all heard the sound of a large truck pulling up out front and unloading bulky equipment.

"That must be the pyramid crew," Hope observed, going to the kitchen window to look out at the driveway between the main house and the guest loft, where a small grading machine was already trundling towards the back yard. When Hope turned to look at Cassandra, she couldn't help but notice that her mistress was blushing.

"Maybe Wally Pell would like to try the dish when it's done," Hope suggested, for she had already been fully apprised of Cassandra's infatuation with the construction site supervisor.

"The sauce should simmer for four or five hours," said Josette.

"Invite him to dinner when his shift is over," Hope prompted Cassandra, who was already on her feet and reaching for a silver thermos to fill with coffee for Wally.

When she had left the room, Jesse looked at Hope and asked, "Is Mistress in love?"

"I think she is," Hope replied, mesmerized at how quickly Josette could mince an onion. "Maybe I'll have David stop in after he's done with drama club, and sample this exquisite fare."

"Oh, please do!" cried Jesse, "Do you think he would

look over a story I've been working on for Hugo's magazine, if he has the time?"

"Of course!" Hope guaranteed.

Cassandra stood watching and waiting on the end of the back porch closest to the new work site and only went to meet Wally after she saw him give initial instructions to his small crew.

"I brought you some coffee," she said, handing him the thermos. He smiled down at her.

"Thank you," he said, "how are you today?"

"I came out to invite you to come have a bite with us after your shift," she explained. "Mr. Newton's chef is here teaching us how to cook Indian food. Do you like paneer masala?"

"I love Indian food!" he said enthusiastically. "Thank you so much!"

He walked back with her to the porch and leaned against the railing to drink his coffee.

She confided, "I'm seeing my ex tomorrow for the first time in eight months. He's visiting with my daughter in Boston today and tomorrow he's coming here."

"I guess you're on pretty good terms?"

"Yes. That is, he knows I was okay with the breakup, but I know he still feels guilty about it. I want him to see that I'm actually way better off now than I was when we were together."

"How could anyone break up with you?" Wally wondered, gazing at her with admiration.

"Thank you for saying that. I have to be careful though, not to seem as though I'm showing off," she continued musing, disclosing the secrets of her soul as though she'd known Wally for decades instead of a week. "He's not materialistic. If he thinks I've fallen under the spell of all these rich possessions," she gestured towards the woods, "he'll feel responsible for my surrendering to decadence and it will distress him."

"Ladies don't usually talk about their exes so kindly," Wally observed.

"I have only good feelings about Danny. He helped me raise Amanda so beautifully. You'll see that when you meet her. He's just a very calm and wholesome influence, no trouble at all, like a cat."

"Alley cat," Wally observed with a grin.

"I love all cats."

"Do you have one?"

"Not at the moment."

"I'm fostering some kittens. Would you like them? I really need to place them. I'm not home enough to keep them company."

Cassandra beamed.

The delicious curry was duly consumed by Cassandra, Hope, Jesse, Wally and David just as dusk fell, after which, Wally brought in wood and built a fire in the library hearth for the girls before taking his departure. Cassandra walked him to the door and said she supposed he got tired early, being in construction. He protested that he didn't want to wear out his welcome.

"You couldn't," she assured him. "In fact, I was going to ask you to build a second fire for me, in my bedroom." And that was the last anyone else in the house saw of Cassandra or Wally that night.

Meanwhile, Hope disappeared back to the kitchen to clean up, while David read Jesse's piece for Hugo's magazine on her tablet. Jesse sat on the hearth rug patiently waiting for David's opinion. In ten minutes, he looked up at her with approval.

"Very good writing, young lady," he said. "You're talented."

"What grade would I get if I was in your class?"

"A-"

"Why minus?" she asked with disappointment.

"You haven't punctuated your dialog correctly."

"Oh!"

"Get me a down a novel," he said, gesturing at the shelves lining the walls. "Anyone will do," he added. Jesse went to a shelf at random and picked out Six Tales from the Jazz Age by F. Scott Fitzgerald.

"Have you read it?" he asked.

"No, should I?"

"I should say so, he includes spanking references."

"Who else does that? I mean, besides Heinlein," Jesse asked.

"Let me think. Aldous Huxley, James M. Cain, Sinclair Lewis, Ian Fleming, and I'm pretty sure PG Wodehouse was one of us."

"Let me make a note of those," Jesse said, taking her tablet from him and quickly adding the authors to her reading list. As for Wodehouse, she spied a thick Jeeves omnibus on the shelf and decided to take that to bed that night.

"In any case, open up a page of Fitzgerald at random," instructed David; "and carefully observe where the quotes, commas, periods, etc. are placed. There will be a test."

"A test?"

"Of course."

"When?"

"In approximately ten minutes. Meet me in the school room while I tell Hope what's going on," said David.

David found Hope stacking the dish washer and explained that he had to give Jesse a short lesson in punctuation but it wouldn't take more than fifteen minutes. Hope gave him a thumbs up of approval and told him about a cache of new birch rods Wally had conjured up for them to Carola's specifications.

"She's never tried the birch," Hope said.

"What's her tolerance?" David asked.

"Pretty high for a tiny girl."

David met Jesse in the school room, where she was still studying the hardcover copy of Fitzgerald stories with painful concentration.

"Okay, Jesse, put the book down and go to the black board. Bring me your tablet with the story first."

Jesse obeyed David, opening the tablet to her text.

"Now, I'm going to read you one of your sentences aloud and you're going to write it out on the black board with perfect punctuation. Do you understand?"

"Or what will happen?"

"Need you honestly ask?"

"So, if I punctuate the sentence perfectly, nothing will happen?"

"Who said that?"

"Oh, okay," Jesse smiled. For she was sure she could punctuate one of her sentences perfectly now, but was loath to forfeit a possible punishment from David Lawrence.

Therefore, when David read aloud several of her own sentences, she wrote out and punctuated them correctly.

"But you're still getting a birching, for not using your grammar checker before letting anyone see your work," said David.

"A birching?" Jesse's blue eyes widened. David looked at her seriously as he discovered the birches in a bench. They were made of thin, light, smooth, supple twigs, neatly trimmed at one end, and bound together at the other with a crude but comfortable leather handle.

At first, he sat on a straight-backed wooden chair with a wide seat and beckoned her to him, taking her over his knee. Jesse was clad in a wool polo sweater and a plaid, pleated skirt, with nubby tights and stack heeled booties. On Carola's insistence, Jesse was to dress like a mid-twentieth century coed or pinup girl whenever possible and Jesse aspired to the same aesthetic. When Hugo had first told her of the position as a house submissive, Jesse had envisioned nude floor scrubbing while crawling around with sex toys inside her. Instead, she found herself a member of an exclusive sorority, studying literature and playing with mostly dreamy tops. And David Lawrence was the most devastating of all, an actual English teacher, and handsome. Jesse was beside herself with excitement and barely realized he was spanking her hard, over her frilly panties.

Once she was warmed up to the point of kicking her little legs and squirming to get off his lap, he picked her up under his arm and brought her into the cloakroom that flanked the school room, where there was a leather spanking bench placed before several mirrors, and this he bent her over. He let her feel the whippy birch over her panties, but soon pulled them down and off, to fully expose her small, jutting, pink and white bottom.

"Slow and hard?" he asked, giving her a sample that made her catch her breath. "Or light and fast?" he asked; and a flurry of light birch strokes followed.

She turned her beautiful little head to look at him and murmured. "Hard and fast!"

"Really?" he asked, rubbing and squeezing her firm bottom for the first time. She parted her slim thighs and still bent over, quite deliberately darted her little hand to brush across the front of his tweed trousers, in just the area where she expected his erection to be. He caught her hand by the wrist.

"What the hell are you doing, Jesse?" he demanded, turning to look in the mirror, which she'd turned back to face, seeing her small, naughty face looking up at his.

"Nothing."

"What are you thinking?"

"Touch my pussy and find out," she suggested.

"I'll spank your pussy!" he threatened, but only birched her, hard and fast. This fully occupied her attention for several minutes, as her gasps proved. He kept on thrashing her as he pondered whether to satisfy his newest pupil. He looked at his watch. They'd been playing for no more than ten minutes. As if reading his mind, Jesse cried, "It'll only take a minute!"

"You think I carry condoms with me, you little slut?" he demanded, pausing to contemplate her pink striped skin.

"There's a whole box of them in the crayon cabinet," Jesse helpfully suggested, popping up, "shall I bring one?"

"And what about Hope?"

"She won't mind. She knows I'm crushing on you like crazy. I make her talk about you all the time to me. Ask her. Oh, please, Mr. Lawrence! I just have to get fucked by my favorite English teacher. It will make me so much smarter!"

"All right, but just this once," he said, and she was back in a flash with the necessaries. "This is your party, and it's going to be a short one, so tell me exactly how you like it," David said to Jesse, unzipping his trousers.

"Oh please, from behind so I can look in the mirror and watch both our faces!" she cried, bending over again for him.

Jesse had made an accurate prediction, the completion of the seduction did not take long, for David, already worked up from birching the pocket Venus, thrilling to the feel of her tight, creamy, twenty-two-year-old pussy and the image of her beautiful face before him, reacting to his thrusts, was intensely aroused. Young girls fiercely crushing on him was a way of life with David, but they were always his students and therefore, inaccessible. With a knowledgeable professional submissive who was also sexually experienced, the equation was balanced and he didn't feel creepy. In his fifteen years of teaching, he had only given in twice to longing girl students who had practically begged him to spank them; it was an excellent record, considering the onslaughts of stalking he had endured over the years.

Jesse took P.G. Wodehouse to bed with her while Hope and David got in his car and drove back to their cottage.

"Lovely dinner, wasn't it?" Hope asked on the way home.

"I loved it!" David agreed.

"How did Jesse like her birching?"

"You were right, she has a great tolerance."

"Did you fuck her?" Hope asked casually.

"Why would you think that?" he asked, glancing at her. She was smiling.

"Because I know Jesse and I know you. There's no way you could resist her."

When David didn't reply, Hope went on, "It was bound to happen. You pick me up every night. Some nights, I'm with a client and Jesse entertains you. Or you entertain her. In any case, she's been hanging out with you for three weeks, of course she's in love with you. And when a girl like Jesse falls in love, she has to close the deal."

David sighed, "You're smart."

"It's okay," Hope said. David looked at her, relieved at her amusement. Then she added, "I fucked Cameron."

"Brooke's boyfriend?" David was startled, piqued, jealous and amused all at once. "How did that happen?"

"It was on my birthday. Remember, we were doing half price quickie sessions at the club that day? He was one of them."

"I didn't realize you were so attracted to him," David said, realizing he could only react to this news as pleasantly as Hope had to his admission of infidelity.

"I wasn't, but he's clever enough to have gotten around me with flattery. You know I'm a sucker for that sort of thing. He told me Hope Spencer Lawrence needs something sensational to write in her diary the day she turned thirty."

"Fair enough," he said, adding, "As long as we're telling the truth tonight, on my own initiative, I also seduced your boss."

"What?" Now Hope was genuinely surprised. "You fucked Cassandra? When, how and indeed, why?" she cried.

"The first time, right after you started working there. I went over to give her a spanking for turning you out. You were out of town and I booked a session with her. I was half kidding, of course, but it was fun to have a good, old fashioned reason to spank a lady and you know Cassandra, she's such a good sport and so charming, I couldn't help fucking her."

"You said the first time?"

"The second time was when you went to Boston for your birthday. When you said you were staying over-night I figured, why not go and see Cassandra again. And I spent the night with her."

Hope laughed, "In that case, I'll see you and raise you one more extra marital hook-up from that very night."

"You fucked someone in Boston when you stayed at Hugo's apartment?"

"Amanda's boyfriend, Colby Hodge. Amanda had to study that night. He brought me the key to the apartment. He's nineteen and spanker and I'm me. It couldn't have been otherwise."

David and Hope looked at each other and laughed.

"Two for two," he said.

"Two for two," she agreed.

Chapter Thirty-Seven

Phoebe and Pascal

Something happened on the evening of Jesse's first photoshoot with Sloan Taylor that upset Pascal Robbins' equilibrium. He wasn't in the best mood. He disliked evening shoots; no one had maximum energy, including himself. And this one was going to be both difficult to light and shoot, as the set was the third-floor gallery of Marguerite and Sloan's bookshop, and the narrow spiral staircase leading to it. The gallery was also accessible by a second, normal staircase behind the wall, but customers who were able to, used the picturesque one. Naturally, Hugo had stipulated that Jesse be photographed walking up and down the curving staircase, in a tight skirt, heels and sweater, and this portion of the shoot alone would take an hour. Then they would move up to the gallery, where the action would take place, with another lighting challenge. Pascal had no concerns about his models, he'd shot them both before and Sloan was able to assist Pascal in prepping the areas, but the shoot didn't actually commence until all the customers left, a little after six.

It was a cold, drizzly evening and Pascal craved an Irish coffee to get himself going. He asked Sloan if there was anywhere close he could get one. Sloan assured the photographer that his request would be seen to at once and quickly repaired to the flat he kept above the store for a bottle of whiskey, asking Marguerite, to get one more pot of coffee started before she closed up the bar for the night. In less than eight minutes, Pascal had been handed a thick ceramic mug of Irish coffee, which he sipped at with contentment as he gazed out the gallery window at the rain splashed village street below, the windows of Hugo's Antiques across the street going dark as Hugo dimmed the lights for the evening. Then the image that would upset him for the rest of the night, caught his eye.

His pretty wife Phoebe, in knee boots and a trench coat, a small beret perched atop her auburn head, just opening an umbrella, was hurrying across the cobbled street to Hugo's shop. As soon as she reached the windows, she lifted her head, looked down the narrow street, smiled and waved at someone. In a moment, she was joined on the sidewalk by a tall, husky, jolly man, also in a trench coat and carrying an umbrella. Just as they reached each other, Phoebe's umbrella went up and blocked the view of their upper bodies entirely from Pascal's sight. It was so dark, despite the soft light of the old street lamps, that he couldn't make out the disposition of the four legs, but it seemed to him that they moved closer together. He was sure they had hugged and kissed when they met, as all theatre people did, but he wanted to see what that looked like. He knew this fellow to be Baldwin Rosemead, Phoebe's co-star in the revival that Anthony Newton had staged of Kiss Me Kate in the area not long ago. The tenor had also obtained a role in Newton's upcoming new production, along with Phoebe. Rehearsals for that were set to commence in the early spring, so the two performers had every reason to greet each other with warmth and enthusiasm. But Pascal was disturbed. For they walked off, possibly arm in arm and disappeared into the foggy night. And he had an excruciating three shoot before him.

Pascal had done spanking shoots before and rarely enjoyed them. Too many changes of position, expression and rearrangements of apparel were necessary; and even when the model was stripped down to the bare, a whole range of shots had to demonstrate the changes in coloration from the start to the end of the spanking. Nor did these shoots pay particularly well. He got a straight $500 per shoot, with the option to take as many glamour shots of the model as he wanted for his own portfolio, which was what made the mediocre fee more attractive. Hugo and Carola always provided him with exquisite models who had no problem with nudity. But this evening, he resolved to save the glamour shoot with Jesse for another time and place.

The shoot finally wrapped at nine-thirty. Hugo and Pascal spent another fifteen minutes taking down the lights and wrapping cords. Hugo helped the photographer load this gear into the back of Pascal's SUV, paid him in cash for the shoot and said good night. Hugo still did most of his own shoots, but when he found a new cover girl like Jesse, he felt justified in paying a professional for a more perfect end result.

Pascal drove directly home to the little 1950's cottage he and Phoebe were renting for the season on a tree shaded back lane of Woodbridge, five miles down the road from Random Point. He parked on the driveway beside Phoebe's Mini Cooper, which he touched the hood of before going in. In spite of the chill in the air and rain pounding down, the car was still warm, as though it had just been parked a few minutes before.

"So, she just got home," he thought. He went into the house. A few soft lights were on in the sitting room, a stick of incense burning, Bitch's Brew was spinning on a turntable that had come with the quaintly furnished house and Pascal saw a light on in the master bath. He opened the door and saw Phoebe in a bubble bath, her hair pinned up and a bath brush in her hand.

"Hi!" she said gaily, "How was the shoot?"

The sunken bathtub was rimmed by a colorfully tiled ledge, wide enough to sit on. Pascal said, "This reminds me of that scene in that video you've watched a hundred times, where the fellow pulls the girl out of a bubble bath and spanks her with a bath brush."

"The Spanking Neighbors? Do I remind you of Star Chandler?"

"How did you spend your evening?" he said, deftly snatching the bath brush out of her hand, looking at it, pacing.

"Oh, I ran into Wynn in the village and we had dinner," she replied, without hesitation.

"What did you do after dinner?"

"Nothing. Came home."

"Dinner took three hours?"

"Where do you get three hours from, Pascal?" Phoebe stood up abruptly and had wrapped a large blue bath sheet around her petite, curvy body before he could frame a reply. He watched her as she sat on the edge of the tub and dried her tiny feet before inserting them into dainty slippers.

"Your car is still warm and it's forty degrees out. You just pulled in."

"Oh, don't be silly, I've been here some time," she corrected him mildly, letting down her hair in the mirror and running a brush through its silky strands.

"I don't think I've ever seen you take a bath at night."

"What a bizarre statement," she said. "How could you even know that? We're not joined at the hip."

"I know your habits, you never take a bath at night, unless we're in a hotel."

"What are you getting at?" she demanded.

"Where did you go for dinner?"

"Where else? The Ball and Feather."

"That's convenient. There are rooms upstairs."

"Pascal, are you implying that Wynn and I rented a room to have sex?"

"How else? He's married too, I recall."

"How about we had dinner and sat and talked over a bottle of wine, as friends will?" she cried.

"That's your story, huh?"

"Why not?"

"But is it the truth?"

"Isn't it plausible?" she asked satirically, going past him and down the hall to their bedroom.

"What's that supposed to mean?" he demanded, following her, without relinquishing the bath brush.

She was already concealed behind a painted screen, donning a handsome velvet dressing gown, in which she emerged a second later. He supposed it came from being in the theatre, that Phoebe was able to dress and undress so quickly. He never had a chance to grab her dripping body and turn her under his arm at the edge of the tub. Now she seemed to be admitting that he ought to have.

"I'm just teasing you," she assured him. "Why would I commit adultery with a teddy bear when I have a panther at home?" For she had caught sight of him in her vanity mirror and he was pacing again, with the bath brush. "Why are you so jealous tonight?"

"Because I saw you from the window, meeting Wynn and your body language told a different story than the one you just tried to sell me."

"Really? You were able to pull yourself away from the new twenty-two-year-old eye candy long enough to look out a window?"

"You're talking about the new model?"

"You can't seem to get enough of her."

"Ridiculous. I did one fashion shoot with her for Pamela and tonight was for Hugo. I have no interest in her whatever, besides that she's a good model."

"And a blonde. You love blondes."

Pascal was startled, wondering if Phoebe knew about his recent adventure with Susan Newton or his enchantment with Amanda Sands. Girls always talked about such things with their girlfriends and they all went to the same gym, frequented Michael's tavern and shopped at Bartlett's.

"Don't try to make this about me. You've been up to no good tonight with that big ham."

"Prove it,' she challenged carelessly.

"Oh, I'll prove it," he said, grabbing her by the wrist and pulling her across his lap on the vanity chair. He had tossed the bath brush aside and merely spanked her with his hand, rather hard. "Tell me the truth," he demanded, pausing before pulling up her robe to bare her beautiful bottom.

"If I tell you the truth, will you not spank me anymore?" she bargained, for one of Pascal's spankings went a long way.

"No."

"Then why should I tell you the truth?"

Pascal didn't bother to reply but continued smacking her vigorously, with his own characteristic rhythm, until she was squirming to escape his rapidly descending palm.

"Okay!" she cried, "I was hoping you'd see me and Wynn walk by. I wanted to give you something to think about during the shoot. Instead of the twenty-two-year-old."

"Weak!" he declared and went on paddling her.

"It's true. I want to be on your mind. I want you to be jealous of me!" she insisted. He let her up, shaking his head in resignation.

"You're such a good actress, I'll really never know," he concluded, stretching his hand towards her to take her back on his lap, right way up.

Chapter Thirty-Eight

Old Friend, New Player

The next afternoon at one pm, Danny Yu drove up to the Venus Club in his rental car, got out and slowly walked up to the front door, looking up and down pleasant, wooded Pine Tar Road. The look of the lane brought a smile to his handsome features. He was a lithe, compact, Asian American, in jeans, boots, a sweater and warm jacket. His age was indeterminate, his face unlined and his step light, but he might have been as old as fifty. He carried a big bunch of white roses.

He was admitted into the house by Jesse, who accepted the roses and led him immediately back to the lounge, where he was met by Cassandra, who kissed and hugged him warmly at once. After Jesse left with the roses, Danny paused to take Cassandra in, for he'd never seen her dressed so, in a clinging cream knit sweater dress, sheer hose and lacing 5" heeled cream booties, her long, soft brown hair down and parted on the side, with a jeweled butterfly holding it back behind one ear, golden bracelets on her wrists, drops in her ears and a heavy gold circlet around her throat. Her lips were plum red.

She told Danny their lunch would be prepared by a little female chef who normally cooked for her patron, but as it was her afternoon off, Cassandra had, with permission, hired her to prep a dazzling vegan repast for her guest of honor. Also joining them at lunch would be her sister Carola, whom Danny had met on only a few occasions over the years, Hope, the assistant manager of the club, Jesse, the newest staff member, and a visiting bondage model from California, Juni Park.

While Josette prepared the luncheon, with Jesse and Hope assisting, Cassandra showed Danny around the entire club, both floors, and took him into the loft as well. She told him they could walk in the woods after lunch and have a long, private talk. Meanwhile, Danny was fascinated by all the specialized bondage furniture and equipment, especially on the lower level of the club, comprised of the accoutrements from Carola's Brookline dungeon. The St. Andrews Wheel amazed him. Danny asked no questions, but with a quiet smile of approval, encouraged Cassandra to tell him everything she wished him to know about the beautiful and costly fittings of the club, which was also her home. They ended up in her master suite, and she showed him how the shutters opened up and revealed her back garden and how a door opened up to the back porch, so that she could walk straight into the garden from her bedroom.

"Oh, before I forget," Danny said, bringing an envelope out of an inner jacket pocket and handing it to her.

"What's this?" she asked.

"I've sold the house and yoga studio in San Francisco. We're moving to rural Oregon. That's your share of the profits."

"Really?"

"Of course! We paid for the house together and built the business together. Did you think I wouldn't get your payout in your hands as soon as I could?"

"I never even thought about it," Cassandra smiled, opening the envelope. "Wow!" she cried. "A million five?"

"What did you think houses were going for in San Francisco these days?"

"I'm overwhelmed. I had no idea."

"That should make a considerable dent in whatever you paid for this place," Danny observed.

"Oh, I didn't pay anything for it. Didn't Amanda fill you

in on any of this?"

"She only said you were doing great and I'd have to see how great for myself because I wouldn't believe it. I knew you'd moved back here with what you realized from selling your psychic shop, and were starting a B&D club and were going to call on some of your old Random Point connections to help you get started."

"I did. And they got me started."

"I'll say."

They went into the dining room and Danny was introduced around to all the beautifully dressed young ladies, including Cassandra's stunning sister Carola, who wanted to look at her sister's ex disapprovingly, but couldn't quite pull it off, he was simply too nice a man. Danny gave them all his attention in turn, but his gaze lingered on the delicious little Korean American doll, Juni Park, a round faced beauty of infinite charm, twenty-one years old, five feet tall, with size five shoes and every sort of naughtiness sparkling in her large brown eyes.

The last guest to arrive was Hugo Sands, who immediately and without reserve, vigorously shook Danny's hand.

"Come by the shop later," Hugo said. "And tell me as many stories as you can remember about what Amanda was like when she was small."

Lunch was a great success. The food was delightful, the girls full of fun and Danny Yu drank it all in with pleasure. None of this was expected but all of it gave him joy.

After the repast, Hugo departed, Cassandra changed from her high heeled booties into walking boots, and she and Danny started down the wooded path that ran by the brook behind her house. It was a chilly, overcast early November day, but they were warmed by the food and Cassandra was in her luxurious new Mongolian coat and hat, her hands in a pair of new cashmere gloves. They strolled through the woods, arm in arm.

Finally, he broke the companionable silence with a chuckle.

"What?" she demanded.

"So, you went from a humble, modest shop keeper and yoga practicing mom, to being a dominatrix out of a James Bond movie, surrounded by glamorous, dangerous women, living mortgage free in a mini mansion. I only have one question, who did you have to fuck?"

"I didn't have to fuck anyone, but I wound up fucking everyone. Or rather, they wound up fucking me. It was crazy, Danny. The second I got back to the village, one man after another starting coming onto me, and I made it with all of them. And most of them paid me for it too. And it hasn't stopped either. I have boys half my age trying to interest me. I don't know why. But it feels good!"

"I know why," Danny said. "You're sexy as hell. Especially dressed the way you are today."

"Thank you, Danny. You were key in helping me keep my figure all these years," she said.

"Oh, Sandy, I'm ecstatic to see you like this, morphed into an exotic but powerful butterfly. But tell me something, how much of that stuff back at the house is really you?"

"What do you mean?"

"I mean, have you been a fetishist all along? And if so, why didn't you tell me?"

"You never asked me."

"But, why did you never bring it up as foreplay?"

"I just assumed if you were interested in something, you'd let me know," Cassandra said simply.

"What I'm getting at is, to what extent are you into all of this?"

"Well, you know Amanda's father publishes a spanking magazine and that I did modeling for it when I was with him. I'm sure I told you that."

"You did mention it, in passing," Danny admitted.

"Correct. But after all, you and I had a lovely sex life, didn't we? I always thought so," Cassandra assured him. "You were the perfect size and shape for anal sex."

"I know, but now that I think about it, how could you not be bored?" he asked.

"Honestly, Danny, I almost forgot about the scene entirely, until Amanda went to college and discovered herself to Hugo. He came out to see me a few weeks later. I mentioned to you I'd met him for dinner. I didn't tell you that we played for the first time in almost twenty years. It brought it all back, how much I liked playing, how much I missed it."

"And by playing you mean...?"

"Oh, well, he spanked me," Cassandra admitted. "For not telling him about Amanda."

"And that's when you decided to do what you're doing now?"

"Oh no. Not at all. First, Mr. Newton, my patron to be, sent me a Venus Club ring. At that point, The Venus Club was just a local group of scene ladies and girls who were going to party together. Then, pretty much the next day after I got the ring, you told me you wanted a divorce. I decided to interpret the ring to mean that I was to return to its sender in Random Point."

"So that's why you took it all so calmly," Danny reflected. "I marveled at your self-control at the time."

"You can feel good, Danny. You enabled me to free myself from a toilsome shopkeeper's life after twenty-five years. And I've been luxuriating in that freedom since I got set up in this place. Now let me do something for you."

"For me? What do you mean?"

"I mean I'm not the only fetishist walking along this path at the moment," she said, leading him into the marble summer house that came up along the way and sitting down with him on the circular bench that ran around its perimeter.

"What do you mean?" he asked, pulling her over to sit on his lap as she always used to do. "Warm me up," he said, locking his arms around her waist and burying his face in her golden faux fur collar.

"Danny, I saw what engaged your interest at the house, it was the extreme bondage furniture on the lower level. And I saw who engaged your attention at the table, the exquisite Korean bondage model who is visiting us."

"Yes, Juni Park," Danny agreed.

"I saw you looking at her tiny feet."

"You never did miss anything."

"Please allow me to kick back for the generous settlement you brought me, a perfect bondage session for you with Juni Park. In fact, you haven't checked into a hotel yet, have you?"

"No, I was going to the Ball and Feather Inn for the night."

"Please, be my guest instead. You can have the loft. It's very comfortable."

"You think she'd be interested?" Danny asked.

"Of course, she's here to work. And I saw her flirting with you. I'll set it all up for you when we get back, shall I?"

"Thank you," Danny grinned, kissing her on the cheek. "You're not like anyone else."

"This is my new calling, fantasy fulfillment," she told him merrily, "and this is an easy one! I'm just intrigued you were able to keep a heavy bondage fetish a secret from me for all these years. How did you indulge?"

"There's a particular club in Chinatown where I've gone to play for my entire adult life," Danny confided. "I'll miss it when we move to Oregon."

"Wow, great, so you've practiced, you know what you're doing," she said with interest. They got up to start back to the house.

"Sandy, did you know that Amanda turned out to be kinky too?"

"Of course, she's been producing spanking clips since freshman year. I no longer give her an allowance, she makes her own money. When did you find out?"

"Oh, years ago. She was in tenth grade. I came home in the afternoon to get something and heard her playing spanking with her boyfriend in her room. And it went on for a long time, way too long to be a one off. I've been wondering ever since if it was all my fault."

"What do you mean?" Cassandra laughed.

"I did spank her, two or three times, when she was about three. She was in a phase for a couple of weeks when she deliberately naughty to get attention. Then it vanished and it never happened again. But ever since I realized she was into it, I've wondered if it was my fault," Danny said.

"That's ironic. I keep Amanda entirely away from her real father's influence until she's eighteen, specifically to avoid any deviancy from confusing her childhood, and pure vanilla Sensei turns her into a pervert anyway."

"So, you agree it was my fault!" Danny cried.

"I'm afraid so," she agreed. "Because the real reason I kept Amanda away from Hugo was that I was afraid he'd spoil her to death, allow her beauty to go to her head – I knew she'd be beautiful – and never exert the slightest discipline. You gave her a backbone, Danny. You were the best possible role model. Hugo is the perfect father for her now, but you were solid for her entire childhood. And you see how great she's doing. Don't think of her being a fetishist as a flaw, but rather as an asset. That's how she regards it."

The rest of Danny's sojourn in Random Point was even more pleasant and surprising. In the late afternoon, he visited Hugo's shop and they talked long and intimately as they wandered through the aisles and Hugo showed Danny objects of interest. Then they enjoyed tea and sandwiches at a small café on the same block, and parted new friends.

Dusk had fallen by the time Danny got back to Cassandra's house on Pine Tar Road. She installed him in the loft and told him he was scheduled to play with Juni Park at eight. He availed himself of the spa, steam room and sauna, bathed and rested until the appointed hour, when he met the diminutive bondage model in the lower floor playroom equipped with the revolving St. Andrew's Cross and biggest leather bondage bed Danny had ever seen.

Juni Park was awaiting him, nude beneath a champagne silk robe with matching slippers. There was rope and everything else he needed and there was Juni, her lustrous eyes sparkling with fun, though her outer demeanor could not have been more submissive. Carola was timing their session, but after an hour, they were neither of them ready to stop playing.

"Mistress, I want to continue with Danny off the clock," Juni told Carola at the door of the dungeon. "I like him so much, I'm going to spend the night with him."

Carola looked at her little protégé quizzically. "Really?"

"He just gets me," Juni disclosed. "Will you tell Mistress Cassandra?"

"With pleasure, little Venus," said Carola, amused, and allowed Juni to close the door.

The next morning, while Juni slept in, Danny appeared in the kitchen to request snacks to bring her in the loft, where he had set the coffee to brew. Cassandra made up a tray of fruit, bread and cheese.

"You look extremely well rested," said Cassandra, handing him a cup of coffee, flavored to his taste.

"Oh Sandy," Danny sighed, "what a girl she is."

"She blew up Carola's phone with texts while you were sleeping about how you're the best bondager she ever met and how much she wishes you could work together. I highly doubt you'll be allowed to leave Random Point without making your first bondage video."

"I wish," Danny grinned.

"Why not?"

"Me? I'm no actor."

"You've done a hundred yoga videos."

"And what if someone recognized me?"

"The only one who would be a bondager. You know how hard you have to look to find quality material."

"I never looked at much material. I was always more eager to be hands-on."

"My sister will be over in an hour or so to try to persuade you."

"Are you serious?"

"Carola's never shot a super cute Asian couple doing bondage before."

"I don't think my new wife –"

"Don't tell her."

"I can't lie."

"Lie by omission."

"But if she were to find out..."

"Say it was on your bucket list. She has a sense of humor, I assume?"

"You don't remember Megan very well, do you? She's earnest and intensely correct."

"Well, mull it over," Cassandra suggested.

In the end, Danny decided to shoot not only with Carola and Juni, but to also do a photo shoot with Juni for Hugo's New Rod Quarterly, for Hugo had similarly, never featured an Asian man spanking an Asian girl in his magazine, and Juni Park was made to wear a school uniform. Thus, with two shoots logged in, one an hour length bondage video for Carola, model money in his pocket, and just one perfect photo of Juni on his phone (along with all of her contact info), Danny Yu departed two days later, for the West Coast, his memorable visit to Random Point suddenly presenting his interesting life with a significant change of course.

Chapter Thirty-Nine

Winter Reconfiguration

As the month advanced, plans were made for a Thanksgiving feast at Anthony and Susan's house. This was to be Amanda's first Thanksgiving with both Hugo and Cassandra. And all of her new Random Point friends were invited.

Josette was to be aided in the preparations by Dennis, Jesse and Dru. In addition to her excitement about the coming dinner event, for which the entire responsibility was hers alone, Josette was also agog about her upcoming nuptials, which were to take place the first week in December, followed by a lavish two-week honeymoon in England and Italy, unwritten by Anthony. First, Josette was to meet Dennis' family in London, then the newlyweds were to spend the remainder of their holiday sampling culinary wonders in Rome, Milan, Venice and Florence.

The pyramid was beginning to rise in the far corner of the back garden and Wally had added to the daily delights and responsibilities of the Venus Club a pair of kittens he'd been fostering. Jesse eagerly volunteered to attend to their needs and immediately seduced them into sleeping with her every night downstairs. Within days of moving to the club, the cats were running in the woods to play. Stopping into the house to check on them once a day became part of Wally's routine, but he was careful not to knock on the back door unless he saw Cassandra's face smiling at him from one of the windows. She often brought him coffee or a thermos of hot soup and they spent fifteen minutes chatting. She asked him what he did on his days off. He told her he worked out, walked on the beach, ate out, watched film noirs and when the weather was nice, took his boat out. She offered to keep him company during his next day off.

The next morning, Cassandra awoke with the pleasant sensation of being in possession of a splendid new lover. But a jarring note assailed her peace of mind when she sat down at the computer in her office and opened an email that arrived with the heading: "You Treacherous Hypocrite". Cassandra quickly read the body copy that followed, with a confused mind and pounding heart.

The letter read:

"I knew you were being phony when you pretended to take it so well that Danny was leaving you for me. You had everyone fooled. No one could be nicer, more civilized than Cassandra. But all along you were planning a magnificent revenge, the very destruction of a good man's soul. You were legendary for your purity. More like a high priestess of perversity. Well, feel satisfied. The love of my life is dead to me now.
    The Only Briefly Second Mrs. Yu,
    Megan"

"Danny, what the hell is going on?" Cassandra cried a moment later, as she got her ex-husband on the phone.
    "Sandy?"
    "I just got a crazy email from Megan. How did she find out about the video?"
    "I told her."
    "Oh no! Why?"
    "Because..." he hesitated.
    "Yes, because why?"
    "Because I wanted her to leave me."
    "What's this you're saying now?"

"I'm in love with Juni Park."

"Oh!"

"Juni says she loves me too," said Danny. "I know it makes no sense, she's so young and I'm so old."

"You're not that old."

"I know I'm too old for Juni, but she doesn't care. She wants to be with me. It was her idea, not mine. As soon as I told her Megan had left me, Juni asked me to come to L.A. and live with her. She said I can get all sorts of work as a rigger and we could do lots of shoots together."

"You never really did love Megan, did you, Danny?" Cassandra asked.

"She loved me though, and the intensity of her fever for me made me think I loved her too," Danny admitted.

"So, you essentially knew, when you told her about playing bondage out here, that she'd freak out?"

"Of course, I knew. I could have kept it all a secret from her forever, but I suddenly realized, I didn't want to move to Oregon and open another yoga studio with Megan. I wanted to keep tying Juni up and having her melt submissively against me in bed at night."

"Wow Danny. To think I never knew," Cassandra sighed. "But how am I supposed to cope with this monumental guilt trip Megan has laid on me?"

"By remembering that she moved in on your man, without the slightest regret?" suggested Danny coolly.

"She was opportunistic," Cassandra agreed.

"What did she write to you?"

"That I destroyed your soul."

"She believes all kinky sex is anti-feminist," Danny disclosed.

"And you've been able to hide your kinkiness so well," Cassandra observed.

"But she's wrong," Danny insisted.

"Should I respond to the email?"

"No. Block her."

"Really?"

"I'll put enough cash in her bank account to allow her to get resettled. We've only been married a few months, so she has no actual claim on the bulk of my assets. But I'll be as generous as I can," he said.

"Well, where are you going now? Right to L.A.?"

"Yes, Juni is renting a house in Laurel Canyon and I'm going to move in there with her and help her with her monthly nut."

"Come back for Thanksgiving with Juni," said Cassandra. "We'll put you up. And we can all be together with Amanda."

"I would love that," Danny said, adding, "You're the best enabler a rogue partner ever had."

Chapter Forty

The Last Singleton in Random Point

At Josette's request, she was married to Dennis, on the first day of December, at the Venus Club. A Justice of the Peace was engaged and the ceremony was conducted in the lounge, so that Anthony could play the Wedding March for them. Josette's cute bartender mom was present and radiant with joy at acquiring such a refined and well-paid son in law to remove the burden of repaying Josette's student loans from her daughter and herself.

The bride had a bespoke white leather mini dress from Damaris, set off with thigh high boots, which Dennis laced for her. All of their scene friends in the village were gathered at the Venus Club to partake of the reception. Plus one.

Felix Pildash noticed this one, a curvy English rose, in a smoky blue cocktail dress, with a long blonde bob, parted on one side, framing a mischievous face. He slid onto the stool beside her and said, "Hello, I'm Felix."

"Belinda," said the girl, looking up from her champagne flute with a ready smile. "I'm the groom's sister."

"I knew you were English," he said, noting her accent. "I am too."

"You're the romance novelist, aren't you?" she guessed, "Marguerite was telling me you live here now. I've read a number of your books!"

"Did you like them?"

"Oh, I thought they were lovely!" Belinda replied enthusiastically. "And so well written."

"How nice you are," Felix said. "How do you know

Marguerite?"

"I'm her little girl's nanny."

"How did you get into that line of work?"

"Well, my brother did so well in service with Mr. Newton, that instead of going to University, I went to nanny school. Then Dennis got me my position with the Flaggs."

"But, you're not in the scene, are you?"

"What scene?"

"The spanking scene."

"The what?" she laughed.

"You can't live with Marguerite and not know about the scene."

"No?" she smiled, "Why not?"

"Don't you live with Marguerite and Michael?"

"Yes."

"And you never hear them playing?"

"Playing?"

"Playing spanking."

"I have read her books, so I do know what you're talking about, come to think of it. But Michael owns the house next door to this one, and they often spend the night there while I stay at her house with Felina. That may be why I never hear them playing."

"So, you have no interest in that kind of erotica?" Felix pressed the matter, since she was still smiling pleasantly and didn't seem uncomfortable.

"I didn't say that," Belinda grinned. She allowed Carmen, behind the bar, to refill her champagne glass.

"I'm confused," Felix admitted.

"I'm lonely." Belinda confided. "I feel left out. Nobody plays with me."

"Do you want to play?"

"Yes!"

"Have you ever told anyone that you wanted to play with them?"

"Of course not. I don't get asked to play at parties. I'm always taking care of baby."

"May I ask if you're seeing anyone?"

"I'm seeing everyone," she replied matter-of-factly.

"Are you being naughty?"

"Not at the moment, but in five minutes, who knows?"

"Explain what you meant by that statement."

"You know my boss owns a tavern, right?"

"Yes, I've been there many times." Felix replied.

"Me too, on my nights off. I have my pick of townies, tourists, students on holiday. Michael always gives me a heads up if someone seems shady. He's a former detective and notices everything."

"All of this is very interesting," said Felix. "You seem like quite a handful."

"You look strong."

"And you look sexy as hell. Greek statues would envy your shape. Who's taking care of baby now?"

"Oh, the Randoms' nanny has both little girls tonight. We're best friends."

"Suppose someone did ask you to play, what role do you see yourself playing?"

"What are my choices?"

"You can give or receive, top or bottom, dominate or submit, order or comply. Which would suit you?"

"Which do you think would suit me?"

"If you're asking, you must be submissive," Felix decided.

"Writers understand the human heart!" she declared passionately.

"Is that you or the champagne?" Felix asked.

"I have a lot of time to read," Belinda confided. "And mistress owns a bookstore. You are a literary man," she told him with conviction.

"I am that, darling."

"And a literary woman, too!" she chuckled,

remembering Felix's penname.

"Are you being cheeky?"

"Do people play in other ways besides spanking?" she asked suddenly.

"Shall I show you around the club so you can see?" he asked.

"This is a club?"

"Yes, for players only."

Felix led Belinda through the house to Cape Cod, the furthest and most rustic playroom, which was decorated with a shoreline mural, had two windows on the woods and was dominated by a wooden whipping post and large, leather bondage bed. An armoire and chest of drawers contained toys, harnesses, clips, clamps, cuffs, rope, massaging wands, and numerous corporal punishment implements in leather and wood.

"Now this reminds me of that scene in *Lady Rowena's Dilemma*," mused Belinda, looking up at the whipping post and referencing one of Felix' eighteenth century bodice rippers. "When Lady Rowena must witness her favorite maid being cruelly punished by her recently deceased mamma's wicked second husband, now Lady Rowena's stepfather."

"Oh my god, you really have read my books?" he grinned.

"Of course, there is precedent for male authors writing in the female first person," Belinda went on speculatively, while circling the whipping post and putting paid to the flute of champagne she had brought along. "Samuel Richardson adored writing as a girl. And even Dickens dabbled in it, with Esther Somerson of *Bleak House*."

Felix goggled at her. "I told you, I have a lot of time to read," she explained.

He said, "You asked whether there were other ways to play besides spanking. I can lock the door behind us and demonstrate a few, if you'll let me."

"What do you propose doing to me?" she asked.

"If I tell you everything, that will spoil the surprises," he pointed out.

"Do I get a safe word?"

"Mercy is the gold standard."

"Do I have to remove any articles of clothing?" she asked helpfully.

"Yes, all of them," he replied, sitting on a heavy, straight backed wooden chair to watch her disrobe.

"All?" she asked.

"It will just make it easier," he explained.

"Make what easier?"

"Teasing you after you're tied up," he explained. "Here, I'll help you get started," he cried, springing up, going behind her, and unzipping her halter dress, then nimbly regaining his seat. Belinda looked at him and let the dress slip to the floor. She stepped out of it and away from the pool of blue satin. "Oh my god, you're stunning," he breathed, taking her in. A glove tight blue brocade waist cinch with garters held up her nylon stockings, nipped her waist and completely exposed her saucy, bosom to his view. She turned to let him ogle her creamy, voluptuous bottom for a moment, before facing front again.

"Come on, young lady," he said, and taking her by her soft, bare upper arm, led her to the whipping post and turned her so that her back was against it. "You didn't tell me you were cinched. You can keep that splendid corset on, everything delicious is exposed by it, in any case."

She let him cuff her slim wrists and fasten them above her head to a brass ring. Her ankles he spread about two feet apart and fastened with cuffs to a leg spreader bar. A thrill went through her when he pulled the blue satin G-string aside to expose her fair curled pubic mound. "Oh, how sweet," he breathed, "You actually have a muff!" He dropped to his knees for a moment and placed one kiss upon it, before rising again. "I'll return to the darling, I promise," he said.

He teased her with feathery touches, tickles and caresses, lavishing adoration on her breasts, worshipping her calves and thighs, his lips ravishing her throat, ears and upper arms. She writhed and squirmed against the post for eighteen minutes, by the slim grandfather clock that stood in one corner of the room, before crying, "Mercy! No more teasing. Fuck me now, Felicia Dashwood!"

Felix released her from the cuffs and spreader bar and sat her on the huge, carved wooden chair, then pulled up a stool before her to gently release her from her shoes.

"Thank you!" she breathed, allowing him to take each stockinged foot between his hands and rub away the fatigue of being on three-inch heels for five hours.

"Now I understand why the concubines all insisted on their foot massages in Raise the Red Lantern!" Belinda exclaimed.

"Wait," he said, "it gets better. Get up and I'll get you out of the corset." He turned her facing away from him, slightly loosened the laces going down her back, then turned her back to face him and unhooked the seven small hooks going down the front of the garment, which then fell away from her Venus form.

"Oh, that feels so good!" she cried.

"So I was told once by a mistress who allowed me to release her from her cinch," Felix confided. "Well, now that you're completely unencumbered, we can address that marvelous suggestion you made."

"Yes, let's address it very hard!" Belinda agreed, looking at the long, broad bondage bed, walking to it, sitting on it, lying on it, rolling back and forth in sheer pleasure at being out of the corset and off the high heels. Felix kept looking at her as he undressed and thinking she might be the best and most enduring gift Random Point could bestow upon him. He pictured her waking up beside him at the Lighthouse and smiled.

The End

About the Author

Born in the Bronx in 1953, Eve graduated from Vassar College in 1975. She began working as an in-house editor for Academy Press, a major San Fernando Valley adult magazine publisher, in 1979 and remained with the company for seven years, freelancing articles and fiction to esoteric fetish publications on the side, until 1986, when she was discovered by Nu-West, a producer of spanking videos.

Eve started publishing her Shadow Lane fiction series that year and also met her future husband, Tony Elka, through a personal ad in a Nu-West magazine. Eve then began performing in spanking videos, which reinforced her credibility as an authentic female voice in a hitherto male-dominated industry. Eve and Tony formed Shadow Lane, their eponymous production company, and with the help of a third partner, graphic designer Butch Simms, published a series of refined and artistic spanking magazines in the 1990's through the early 2000's, including their flagship publication, Stand Corrected.

The late Barney Rossett, legendary publisher of Grove Press and a pioneer of first amendment rights, was the first to publish Eve's collected magazine stories as full-length novels, under the Blue Moon imprint.

Between 1987 and 2019, Shadow Lane produced 240 high quality spanking videos, written and directed by Eve, and designed to appeal to female enthusiasts as well as males. Eve lost Tony in 2020, after a beautiful and fruitful 34-year relationship that included expanding the social spanking community through personal ads, publications and gala national parties.

Eve is currently working on a new fiction series. She resides in Las Vegas. Eve enjoys hearing from readers and is happy to answer any questions related to the scene. She may be emailed at:

eve_howard@icloud.com

www.shadowlanestore.com

Reader Reviews about
the Shadow Lane Series

"I've become addicted to the 'Random Point' series so much that I can't wait until the next chapter. I've ordered the first two Shadow Lane volumes and have re-read them over and over. I never tire of them. Eve is the only person I know who can make an enema sexy."

"I discovered Shadow Lane about a month ago. Prior to that time I thought I could write excellent spanking erotica. Then I ordered, 'The Problem with Laura.' This is just a note to commend Eve Howard's spectacular talent and to say thanks for an incredible erotic experience."

"I have just completed 'Return to Random Point' and decided that I had to write about how much I enjoyed it. I have not been so aroused since reading my first discipline novel many years ago, about a girl raised in England and 'coming of age' as I believe they put it. More recently I have enjoyed reading Grant Andrews' My Darling Dominatrix and Ann Rice's 'Beauty' series. It seems that women, though, have the right touch when it comes to writing about this subject. Eve, especially, knows how to touch that erotic nerve and bring it to a pure, raw sensuality until one feels that he/she is near bursting with lust."

"I, for one, have always loved (and by loved I mean devoured... breathlessly) Eve Howard's novelettes. To read them... especially when I was just 'coming out'... was to feel completely validated. I truly identified with each and every heroine; the feisty, sassy ones, the shy, demure ultra 'subby' ones... the young ones, and the more mature.

I loved the gentle yet firm "taken in hand" nature of the romantic variety of spanking discipline that Eve always incorporated into the stories. I loved that the plots were not complicated... but, feasible nonetheless. I loved the depictions of sexual escapades after many of the spanking interludes. I appreciated that the girls were cherished and adored by the affably rogue-ish gents... that the submitting was willing and desired... that it was consensual.

I like the settings... having grown up in New England and living here almost my whole life. I LOVED the idea of the bookstore (which I always find sexy). Then and now. I could cite many passages too, but I fear I've rambled enough. Eve was/is always my favorite spanking author."